5,00

Keeping Faith

Books by Jodi Picoult

Songs of the Humpback Whale

Harvesting the Heart

Picture Perfect

Mercy

The Pact

Keeping Faith

Plain Truth

Salem Falls

Perfect Match

Second Glance

My Sister's Keeper

Vanishing Acts

The Tenth Circle

Nineteen Minutes

Change of Heart

Handle with Care

JODI PICOULT

Keeping Faith

This edition first published in Australia and New Zealand by Allen & Unwin in 2009
First published in Australia in 1999
First published in the United States in 1999 by William Morrow and Compnay Inc., New York

Copyright © Jodi Picoult 1999

All rights reserved. No part of this book may be reproduced or transmitted in any form or by any means, electronic or mechanical, including photocopying, recording or by any information storage and retrieval system, without prior permission in writing from the publisher. The Australian *Copyright Act* 1968 (the Act) allows a maximum of one chapter or 10 per cent of this book, whichever is the greater, to be photocopied by any educational institution for its educational purposes provided that the educational institution (or body that administers it) has given a remuneration notice to Copyright Agency Limited (CAL) under the Act.

Allen & Unwin
83 Alexander Street
Crows Nest NSW 2065
Australia
Phone: (61 2) 8425 0100
Fax: (61 2) 9906 2218
Email: info@allenandunwin.com
Web: www.allenandunwin.com

Cataloguing-in-Publication details are available from the National Library of Australia
www.librariesaustralia.nla.gov.au

ISBN 978 1 74175 800 9

Printed in Australia by McPherson's Printing Group

10 9 8 7 6 5 4 3 2 1

FOR LAURA GROSS—

Ten years ago you believed in me so strongly that you managed to convince the publishing world I was worth the risk, too. Here's to another forty or fifty years of business, and friendship. *Now* do you see why I couldn't dedicate this to Padre Pio?

ACKNOWLEDGMENTS

While researching this book, I was for the first time shooed out of someone's office. It quickly became clear to me that simply bringing up the concept of God for conversation was likely to raise people's hackles. Add to that my plot, and it became an all-out war. So, for their open-mindedness in considering my ideas along with their strong religious convictions, I'd like to thank the following people: Rabbi Lina Zerbarini, Herman F. Holbrook, Father Ronald Saunders, Father Andrew F. Kline. Kudos also to my physicians-on-call, Dr James Umlas and Dr Spencer Greene. Thanks to Nancy Veresan, and to Kim Keating—who has moved beyond legal expert to become a valued contributor to my books. I only hope she's ready for the next one. And to the various psychiatric professionals who made my characters and my court case come to life, a heartfelt thanks: Dr Tia Horner, Dr Burl Daviss, Dr Doug Fagen. My appreciation to Sarah Gross for her prompt responses to e-mail questions. Thanks to Jane Picoult and Laura Gross for their insightful first-reader comments; to Beccy Goodhart for her painstaking editing and for helping me deliver my masterpiece before she delivered her own; to Camille McDuffie, who I know will jump through hoops to make people read this book. And finally, my gratitude to Kyle, Jake, and Samantha van Leer . . . and their dad, Tim—for getting through all those baths and bedtime stories without me, so that I'd have time to write.

prologue

August 10, 1999

UNDER NORMAL CIRCUMSTANCES, Faith and I should not be home when my mother calls and invites us to come see her brand-new coffin.

'Mariah,' my mother says, clearly surprised when I pick up the phone. 'What are you doing there?'

'The grocery store was closed.' I sigh. 'The sprinklers in the produce section had a flood. And the dry cleaner had a death in the family.'

I do not like surprises. I live by lists. In fact, I often imagine my life like a September loose-leaf binder—neatly slotted and tabbed, with everything still in place. All this I attribute to a degree in architecture and my fervent intent to not turn into my mother as I grow older. To this end, every day of the week has a routine. Mondays I work on the frames of the tiny dollhouses I build. Tuesdays I build the furnishings. Wednesdays are for errands, Thursdays for housecleaning, and Fridays for tending to emergencies that crop up during the week. Today, a Wednesday, I usually pick up Colin's shirts, go to the bank, and do the food shopping. It leaves just enough time to drive home, unload the groceries, and get to Faith's one o'clock ballet class. But today, due to circumstances beyond my control, I have entirely too much time on my hands.

'Well,' my mother says, in that way of hers. 'It seems you're fated to come for a visit.'

Faith suddenly bounces in front of me. 'Is it Grandma? Did she get it?'

'Get what?' It is ten o'clock, and already I have a headache.

'Tell her yes,' my mother says on the other end of the phone line.

I glance around the house. The carpet needs to be vacuumed, but then what will I do on Thursday? A heavy August rain throbs against the windows. Faith spreads her soft, warm hand over my knee. 'Okay,' I tell my mother. 'We'll be right over.'

My mother lives two and a half miles away, in an old stone house that everyone in New Canaan calls the Gingerbread Cape. Faith sees her nearly every day; stays with her after school on days I am working. We could walk, if not for the weather. As it is, Faith and I have just gotten into the car when I remember my purse, sitting on the kitchen counter.

'Hang on,' I tell her, getting out and cringing between raindrops, as if I might melt.

The phone is ringing by the time I get inside. I grab the receiver. 'Hello?'

'Oh, you're home,' Colin says. At the sound of my husband's voice, my heart jumps. Colin is the sales manager for a small company that manufactures LED exit signs, and he's been in Washington, D.C., for two days, training a new rep. He is calling me because it is like that with us—tied as tight as the lacing on a high-top boot, we cannot stand being apart.

'Are you at the airport?'

'Yeah. Stuck at Dulles.' I curl the telephone cord around my arm, reading between the round vowels of his words for all the other things he is too embarrassed to say in a public venue: *I love you. I miss you. You're mine.* In the background a disembodied voice announces the arrival of a United flight. 'Hasn't Faith got swimming today?'

'Ballet at one o'clock.' I wait a moment, then add softly, 'When will you be home?'

'As soon as I can.' I close my eyes, thinking that there is nothing like an embrace after an absence, nothing like fitting my face into the curve of his shoulder and filling my lungs with the scent of him.

He hangs up without saying good-bye, which makes me smile. That's Colin, in a nutshell: already rushing to come back home to me.

It stops raining on the way to my mother's. As we pass the long soccer field that edges the town, vehicles begin pulling onto the road's narrow shoulder. A perfect, arched rainbow graces the lush grass of the playing field. I keep driving. 'You'd think they'd never seen one before,' I say, accelerating.

Faith rolls down her window and stretches out her hand. Then she waggles her fingers in front of me. 'Mommy!' she yells. 'I touched it!'

Out of habit I look down. Her fingers are spread and streaked with red and blue and lime green. For a moment, my breath catches. And then I remember her sitting on the floor of the living room just an hour before, her fists full of Magic Markers.

My mother's living room is dominated by an unappealing Naugahyde sectional couch the color of skin. I tried to talk her into leather, a nice wing chair or two, but she laughed. 'Leather,' she said, 'is for *goyim* with *Mayflower* names.' After that, I gave up. In the first place, I have a leather couch myself. In the second, I married a *goy* with a *Mayflower* name. At least she hasn't coated the Naugahyde with a protective plastic wrap, the way my grandmother Fanny did when I was little.

But today, walking into the living room, I do not even notice the couch. 'Wow, Grandma,' whispers Faith, clearly awed. 'Is someone in it?' She falls to her knees, knocking at the highly polished mahogany rectangle.

If things had gone according to plan, I'd probably be choosing cantaloupes at that moment, holding them to my nose for softness and sweetness, or paying Mr Li thirteen dollars and forty cents, and receiving in return seven Brooks Brothers shirts, so starched that they lay like the torsos of fallen men in the back of the station wagon. 'Mother,' I say, 'why do you have a casket in your living room?'

'It's not a casket, Mariah. See the glass on the top? It's a coffin table.'

'A coffin table.'

My mother sets her coffee mug on the clear plate of glass to prove her point. 'See?'

'You have a coffin in your living room.' I am unable to get past that one sticking point.

She sits on the couch and props her sandaled feet on the glass top. 'Well, I know that, honey. I picked it out.'

I cradle my head in my hands. 'You just went to Dr Feldman for your checkup. You know what he said: If you take your blood pressure medication religiously, there's no reason to believe you won't outlive us all.'

She shrugs. 'This is one less thing for you to do, when the time comes.'

'Oh, for God's sake. Is this about the new assisted-living community Colin mentioned? Because I swear, he only thought you'd—'

'Sweetie, calm down. I don't plan to kick the bucket anytime soon; I just needed a table in here. I liked the color of the wood. And I saw a piece on *Twenty/Twenty* about a man in Kentucky who was making these.'

Faith stretches out on her back beside the coffin. 'You could sleep in it, Grandma,' she suggests. 'You could be like Dracula.'

'You've got to admit, the craftsmanship is to die for,' my mother says.

In more ways than one. The mahogany is exquisite, a smooth, glossy sea. The joints and bevels are neat and defined, the hinges bright as a beacon.

'It was a real bargain,' my mother adds.

'Please don't tell me you got a used one.'

My mother sniffs and looks at Faith. 'Your mommy needs to loosen up.' For years now, my mother has been telling me this in one form or another. But I cannot forget that the last time I loosened up, I nearly came apart.

My mother gets down on the floor with Faith, and together they yank at the brass pallbearer's handles. Their blond heads—Mom's dyed, my daughter's fairy-white—are bent so close I can't tell where one ends and the other begins. Their horseplay manages to jerk the coffin a few inches toward them. I stare at the flattened hollow left in its wake in the carpet, then try as best I can to fix it with the edge of my shoe.

Colin and I are luckier than most. We married young, but we've stayed married—in spite of some fairly intense bumps in the road.

But there's a chemistry involved, too. When Colin is looking at me, I know he's not seeing me with ten pounds left behind from pregnancy or the fine strands of gray in my hair. He pictures my skin creamy and tight, my hair hanging down my back, my body a college student's. He remembers me at my best, because—as he says every now and then—I'm the best thing he can remember.

When we go out to dinner occasionally with his colleagues—the ones who have collected trophy wives—I realize how fortunate I am to have someone like Colin. He puts his hand on the small of my back, which is not as tanned or slender as those on some of the younger models. He proudly introduces me. 'This is my wife,' he says, and I smile. It is all I've ever wanted to be.

'Mommy.'

It has started to rain again; the road is swimming in front of me, and I've never been a very confident driver. 'Ssh. I have to concentrate.'

'But, Mommy,' she presses. 'This is really, really important.'

'What is really, really important is getting to your ballet lesson without getting us killed.'

For one blessed moment it is quiet. Then Faith begins kicking the back of my seat. 'But I don't have my leotard,' she whines.

I swerve onto the side of the road and turn to look at her. 'You don't?'

'No. I didn't know we were going there straight from Grandma's.'

I feel my neck redden. We are all of two miles from the dance studio. 'For God's sake, Faith. Why didn't you say something before?'

Her eyes fill with tears. 'I didn't know we were on our way to ballet until now.'

I slam my hand against the steering wheel. I don't know if I am angry at Faith, at the weather, at my mother, or at the damned sprinklers in the grocery store, all of which have managed to screw up my day. 'We go to ballet every single Tuesday after lunch!'

I pull onto the road and make a U-turn, ignoring the prick of guilt that tells me I'm being too hard on her, that she's only seven. Faith begins to shriek through her tears. 'I don't want to go home! I want to go to ballet!'

'We're not going home,' I say through clenched teeth. 'We're just going to pick up your leotard, and then we'll go to ballet.' We'll be twenty minutes late. I envision the eyes of the other mothers, watching me hustle Faith through the doors in the middle of a class that has already started. Mothers who've managed to get their children to class on time in the middle of this flash flood, mothers who do not have to work hard to make it look so easy.

We live in a century-old farmhouse, which is bordered on one side by a forest and on the other side by a meticulous stone wall. Our seven acres are mostly woods, tucked behind the house; we're close enough to the road that at night the headlights of passing cars sweep over the beds like lighthouse beacons. The farmhouse itself is full of opposites that still attract: a sagging porch backed by brand-new Pella windows, a claw-foot tub with a Shower Massage, Colin and me. The driveway dips, rising at the end near the road and again near the house. As we turn down it, Faith gasps in delight. 'Daddy's home! I want to see him.'

So do I, but then I always do. No doubt he's taken an earlier flight and come home for lunch before returning to the office. I think about the other mothers already in the parking lot of the ballet studio, and then of seeing Colin, and suddenly being twenty minutes late seems entirely worthwhile. 'We'll say hi to Daddy. Then you get your leotard, and we've got to go.'

Faith bursts through the door like a marathon runner at the ribbon finish. 'Daddy!' she calls, but there is no one in the kitchen or the family room, nothing but Colin's briefcase neatly centered on the table to prove that he is here. I can hear water running through the old pipes. 'He's taking a shower,' I say, and Faith immediately heads upstairs.

'Hang on!' I shout after her, certain that the last thing Colin wants is to be surprised by Faith if he's strolling around the bedroom naked. I rush behind her, managing to get to the closed door of the master bedroom before Faith can turn the knob. 'Let me go in first.'

Colin stands beside the bed, wrapping a towel around his hips. When he sees me in the doorway, he freezes. 'Hi.' I smile, going into his arms. 'Isn't this a nice surprise?'

With my head tucked up beneath his chin and his hands loosely clasped around my waist, I nod to Faith. 'Come on in. Daddy's dressed.'

'Daddy!' she cries, barreling straight for Colin at groin level, something that we've laughed about often and that has him moving into a protective crouch, even as he holds me.

'Hi, cupcake,' he says, but he keeps looking over Faith's head, as if expecting to find another child waiting in the wings. Steam rolls from the seam of the closed bathroom door.

'We could put on a video for her,' I whisper, leaning close to Colin. 'That is, assuming you're looking for someone to wash your back.'

But instead of answering, Colin awkwardly untangles Faith's arms from his waist. 'Honey, maybe you should—'

'Should what?'

We all turn toward the voice coming from the bathroom.

The door swings open to reveal a damp, dripping woman, half wrapped in a towel, a woman who assumed that Colin's words were meant for her. 'Oh, my God,' she says, reddening, retreating and slamming the door.

I am aware of Faith running from the bedroom, of Colin going after her, of the water in the shower being turned off. My knees give out, and suddenly I am sitting on the bed, on the wedding-ring quilt Colin bought me in Lancaster, Pennsylvania, after the Mennonite woman who crafted it told him that the symbol of a perfect marriage was an endless circle.

I bury my face in my hands and think, *Oh, God. It is happening again.*

Book I

THE OLD TESTAMENT

one

Millions of spiritual creatures walk the earth
Unseen, both when we wake and when we sleep.

—John Milton, *Paradise Lost*

THERE ARE CERTAIN THINGS I do not talk about.

Like when I was thirteen, and I had to take my dog and have her put to sleep. Or the time in high school that I got all dressed up for the prom and sat by the window, waiting for a boy who never came. Or the way I felt when I first met Colin.

Well, I talk a little about that, but I don't admit that from the beginning I knew we were not meant to be together. Colin was a college football star; I'd been hired by his coach to tutor him to pass French. He kissed me—shy, plain, scholarly—on a dare from his teammates, and even muddled by embarrassment, it left me feeling gilded.

It is perfectly clear to me why I fell in love with Colin. But I have never understood what made him fall for me.

He told me that when he was with me, he became someone different—a person he liked better than the easygoing jock, the good ol' fraternity boy. He told me that I made him feel admired for what he was instead of what he'd done. I argued that I wasn't a match for him, not tall or stunning or sophisticated enough. And when he disagreed, I made myself believe him.

I don't talk about what happened five years later, when I was proved right.

I don't talk about the way he could not look me in the eye while he was arranging to have me locked away.

Opening my eyes is a Herculean effort. Swollen and grainy, they seem resolved to stay sealed shut, preferring not to risk the sight of something else that might turn the world on end. But there is a hand on my arm, and for all I know it might be Colin, so I manage to slit them enough that the light, sharp as a splinter, comes into view. 'Mariah,' my mother soothes, smoothing my hair back from my forehead. 'You feeling better?'

'No.' I am not feeling anything. Whatever Dr Johansen prescribed over the phone makes it seem as if there's a foam cushion three inches thick around me, a barrier that moves with me and flexes and manages to keep the worst away.

'Well, it's time to get moving,' my mother says, matter-of-fact. She leans forward and tries to haul me from the bed.

'I don't want to take a shower.' I try to curl into a ball.

'Neither do I.' My mother grunts. The last time she'd come into the room, it was to drag me into the bathroom and under a cold spray of water. 'You're going to sit up, damn it, if it sends me to an early grave.'

That makes me think of her coffin table, and of the ballet lesson Faith and I never did manage to get to three days ago. I pull away from her grasp and cover my face, fresh tears running like wax. 'What is the matter with me?'

'Absolutely nothing, in spite of what that cretin wants you to believe.' My mother puts her hands on my burning cheeks. 'This is not your fault, Mariah. This isn't something you could have stopped before it happened. Colin isn't worth the ground he walks on.' She spits on the carpet, to prove it. 'Now sit up so that I can bring Faith in here.'

That gets my attention. 'She can't see me like this.'

'So, change.'

'It's not that easy—'

'Yes, it is,' my mother insists. 'It's not just *you* this time, Mariah. You want to fall apart? Fine, then—do it after you've seen Faith. You know I'm right, or you wouldn't have called me to come over here and take care of her three days ago.' Staring at me, she softens her voice. 'She's got an idiot for a father, and she's got you. You make what you want of that.'

For a second I let hope sneak through the cracks in my armor. 'Did she ask for me?'

My mother hesitates. 'No . . . but that's neither here nor there.'

As she goes to get Faith, I adjust the pillows behind my back and wipe my face with a corner of the comforter. My daughter enters the room, propelled by my mother's hand. She stops two feet from the bed. 'Hi,' I say, bright as any actress.

For a moment I just delight in seeing her—the crooked part of her hair, the space where her front tooth used to be, the chipped pink Tinkerbell polish on her fingernails. She folds her arms and sets her colt's legs and mulishly presses her beautiful bow of a mouth into a flat line.

'Want to sit down?' I pat the mattress beside me.

She doesn't answer; she barely even breathes. With a sharp pain I realize that I know exactly what she's doing, because I've done it myself: You convince yourself that if you keep perfectly still, if you don't make any sudden moves, neither will anyone else. 'Faith . . .' I reach out my hand, but she turns and walks out of the room.

Part of me wants to follow her, but a larger part of me can't muster the courage. 'She's still not talking. Why?'

'You're her mother. *You* find out.'

But I can't. If I have learned anything, it is my own limits. I turn onto my side and close my eyes, hoping that my mother will get the hint that I just want her to go away.

'You'll see,' she says quietly, laying her hand on top of my head. 'Faith is going to get you through this.'

I make her think I am asleep. I do not let on when I hear her sigh. Or when I watch, through narrowed eyes, as she removes from my nightstand an X-acto knife, a nail file, and a pair of embroidery scissors.

• • •

Years ago when I found Colin in bed with another woman, I waited three nights and then tried to kill myself. Colin found me and got me to the hospital. The ER doctors told him they had been able to save me, but that isn't true. Somehow that night, I got lost. I became another person, one I do not like to hear about, one I would certainly not recognize. I could not eat, I could not speak, I could not command enough energy to throw the covers off my body and get out of bed. My mind was frozen on a single thought: If Colin didn't want me anymore, why should I?

When Colin told me that he was having me committed to Greenhaven, he cried. He apologized. Still, he never held my hand, never asked me what I wanted, never stared into my eyes. He said I needed to be hospitalized so that I would not be left alone.

Contrary to what he thought, I wasn't alone. I was several weeks pregnant with Faith. I knew about her, knew she existed before the tests came back and the doctors altered the course of treatment to meet the needs of a pregnant, suicidal woman. I never told anyone there about the pregnancy, just let them figure it out themselves—and it took me years to admit that was because I was hoping to miscarry. I had convinced myself that it was Faith, a small ball of cells inside me, who made Colin turn to another woman.

Yet when my own mother says that Faith is going to keep me from getting so deeply depressed that I can't claw my way out, she may not be far off the mark. After all, Faith has done it before. Somehow, during those months at Greenhaven, being pregnant became an asset instead of a liability. People who would not listen to what I had to say when I was first committed stopped to remark on my swelling belly, my glowing cheeks. Colin found out about the baby and came back to me. I named her Faith, a real *goyishe* name according to my mother, because I so badly needed something to believe in.

I am sitting with my hand on the bridge of the phone. Any minute now, I tell myself, Colin is going to call and tell me it was a run of dementia. He will beg not to be held responsible for this small bit of insanity. If *I* do not understand something like that, who will?

But the phone does not ring, and sometime after two in the morning I hear a noise outside. It is Colin, I think. He's come.

I run to the bathroom and try to untangle my hair, my arms stiff and aching from disuse. I swallow a capful of mouthwash. Then I rush into the hall with my heart pounding.

It's dark. There's no one moving about; nothing. I creep down the staircase and peer out the sidelight that frames the front door. Carefully I ease the door open—it creaks—and step onto the old farmer's porch.

The noise that I thought was my husband coming home to me is a pair of raccoons, thieving around the trash can. 'Go!' I hiss at them, waving my hands. Colin used to snare them in a Hav-A-Heart trap, a rectangular cage with a levered door that didn't cause harm to the animal. He'd hear one screaming after being shut in and would carry it off to the woods behind the house. Then he'd walk back, the cage empty and neat, with no sign of the raccoon's having been there. 'Abracadabra,' he'd say. 'Now you see it, now you don't.'

I retreat inside, but instead of heading upstairs I see the moon reflecting off the polished dining-room table. In the center of the oval is a miniature replica of this farmhouse. I made it; it is what I do for a living. I build dream houses—not out of concrete and drywall and I-beams, but with spindles no bigger than a toothpick, squares of satin that fit in the palm of my hand, mortar based with Elmer's glue. Although some people ask for an exact replica of their house, I have also created antebellum mansions, Arabian mosques, marble palaces.

I built my first dollhouse seven years ago at Greenhaven, out of popsicle craft sticks and construction paper, when other patients were making God's-eyes and origami. Even in that first attempt there was a spot for every bit of furniture, a room to suit each personality. Since then I have built nearly fifty others. I became famous after Hillary Rodham Clinton asked me to make the White House for Chelsea's sixteenth birthday—complete with an Oval Room, china in the display cabinets, and a hand-sewn United States flag in the Executive Office. Customers have asked, but I do not make dolls to go with the houses. A piano, however tiny, is still a piano. But a doll with a beautifully painted face and finely turned limbs is always, at its heart, made of wood.

I pull out a chair and sit down, gently touching my fingers to the sloping roof of the miniature farmhouse, the pillars that hold up its porch, the small silk begonias in its terra-cotta planters. Inside it is a cherry table like the one this dollhouse sits upon. And on that miniature cherry dining-room table is an even smaller replica of this dollhouse.

With the flick of a fingertip I shut the front door of the dollhouse. I brush my thumb along the stamp-sized windows, sliding them down. I secure the shutters with their infinitesimal latches; I shelter the begonias beneath the Lilliputian porch swing. I close up the house tightly, as if it might need to stand through a storm.

Colin phones four days after leaving. 'This wasn't the way it was supposed to happen.'

Presumably, by this he means that Faith and I weren't supposed to interrupt. Presumably, we had forced his hand. But of course I do not say so.

'It's not going to work with us, Mariah. You know that.'

I hang up the phone while he is still talking, and pull the covers over my head.

Five days after Colin has left, Faith is still not speaking. She moves around the house like a silent cat, playing with toys and picking out videos and all the time watching me suspiciously.

My mother is the one who manages to plumb through the muteness to figure out that Faith wants oatmeal for breakfast, or that she can't reach the Playmobil village on the top shelf, or that she needs a drink of water before going to bed. I wonder if they have a secret language. I don't understand her; she refuses to communicate, and all in all it reminds me of Colin.

'You have to do something,' my mother repeats. 'She's your daughter.'

Biologically, yes. But Faith and I have little in common. In fact, she might as well have skipped a generation and come straight from her grandmother, so close are those two. They have the same grounding in whimsy, the same rubber resilience, which is why it is so strange to see Faith moping around. 'What am I supposed to do?'

My mother shakes her head. 'Play a game with her. Go for a walk. At the very least, you could tell her you love her.'

I turn to my mother, wishing it were that simple. I've loved Faith since she was born, but not the way you'd think. She was a relief. After first wanting to miscarry and then months on Prozac, I'd been certain she'd appear with three eyes or a harelip. But the easy, normal birth gave way to the reality of a baby I could not make happy, as if my punishment for thinking the worst of her were to be disconnected before we ever had a chance to bond. Faith was colicky; she kept me up all night and nursed with such a vengeance my belly cramped at each feeding. Sleep-deprived and unsettled, I would lay her on the bed at times, stare at her wise, round face and think, *What on earth do I do with you?*

I figured that motherhood would be something that descended naturally, the same way my milk came in—a little painful, a little awe-inspiring, but part of me now for better or for worse. I waited patiently. So what if I didn't know how to use a rectal thermometer on my child? So what if I tried to swaddle her and the blanket never tucked tight? Any day now, I told myself, I am going to wake up and know what I am doing.

It was sometime after Faith's third birthday that I stopped hoping. For whatever reason, being a mother will never come easily to me. I watch women with multiple children effortlessly settle everyone in place in their vans, while I have to check Faith's safety belt three times, just to make sure it's really snapped tight. I hear mothers lean down to speak to their children, and I try to memorize the things they say.

The thought of trying to get to the bottom of Faith's stubborn silence makes my stomach flip. What if I can't do it? What kind of mother does that make me? 'I'm not ready,' I hedge.

'For God's sake, Mariah, get over yourself. Get dressed, brush your hair, act like a normal woman, and before you know it, you won't be acting anymore.' My mother shakes her head. 'Colin told you you were a shrinking violet for ten years, and you were stupid enough to believe him. What does he know from nervous breakdowns?'

She sets a cup of coffee in front of me; I know that she considers it a triumph to have me sitting at the kitchen table, instead of holed up in bed. When I was committed, she was living in Scottsdale, Arizona—where she'd moved after my father died. She flew in after my suicide attempt and went home when she felt assured that the danger was over. Of course, she hadn't counted on Colin's having me institutionalized. When she discovered what he had done, she sold the condo, returned here, and spent four months overturning the legal writ so that I could be released of my own volition. She never believed Colin was right to have me sent to Greenhaven, and she's never forgiven him. As for me, well, I don't know. Sometimes, like my mother, I think that he shouldn't have been deciding how *I* felt, no matter how unresponsive I was at the time. And sometimes I remember that Greenhaven was the one place I felt comfortable, because there nobody was expected to be perfect.

'Colin,' my mother says succinctly, 'is a schmuck. Thank God Faith takes after you.' She pats my shoulder. 'Do you remember the time you came home in fifth grade, with a B-minus on your math test? And you cried like you thought we were going to put you on the rack—but we couldn't have cared less? You did your best; that's what was important. You tried. Which is more than I can say for you today.' She looks through the open doorway, to the living-room floor, where Faith is coloring with crayons. 'Don't you know by now that raising a child is always a work in progress?'

Faith picks up the orange crayon and scribbles violently over the construction paper. I remember how last year, when she was learning letters, she'd scrawl a long stream of consonants and ask me what she'd spelled. 'Frzwwlkg,' I'd say, and to my surprise I made her laugh.

'So go already.' My mother pushes me toward the living room.

The first thing I do is trip over the box of crayons. 'I'm sorry.' I gather fistfuls in my hands, set them back in the holiday Oreo tin we use to store them. When I'm finished, I rock back on my heels, to find Faith staring coldly at me.

'I'm sorry,' I say again, but I am not speaking of the crayons.

When Faith doesn't respond, I look down at the paper she's been drawing on. A bat and a witch, dancing beside a fire. 'Wow—this is really neat.' Inspiration strikes; I pick up the drawing and hold it close. 'Can I keep it? Hang it downstairs in my workshop?'

Faith tips her head, reaches for the picture, and rips it down the middle. Then she runs up the stairs and slams her bedroom door.

My mother comes in, wiping her hands on a dish towel. 'That went well,' I say dryly.

She shrugs. 'You can't change the world overnight.'

Reaching for one half of Faith's artwork, I run my fingers over the waxy resistance of the witch. 'I think she was drawing me.'

My mother tosses the dish towel at me; it lands unexpectedly cool against my neck. 'You think too much,' she says.

That night while I am brushing my teeth I catch sight of myself in the mirror. I am not unattractive, or so I learned at Greenhaven. Orderlies and nurses and psychiatrists look through you when you are disheveled and complaining; on the other hand, a pretty face gets noticed, and spoken to, and answered. At Greenhaven I cut my hair short, into honey-colored waves; I wore makeup to play up the green of my eyes. I spent more time on my appearance during those few months than I ever had in my life.

Sighing, I lean toward the mirror and wipe a spot of toothpaste from the corner of my mouth. When Colin and I moved into this farmhouse, we replaced this bathroom mirror.

The old one had been cracked at the corner—bad luck, I said. The new mirror, we didn't know where to hang. At five-foot-four, eye level for me was not eye level for Colin. A foot taller and lanky, he laughed when I'd first held up the mirror. 'Rye,' he said, 'I can barely see my chest.'

So instead we put the mirror where Colin could see it. I would stand on tiptoe to see the whole of my face. I never quite measured up.

In the middle of the night I feel the blankets rustle. A drift of air, a soft solidness pressed against me. Rolling over, I wrap my arms around Faith.

'This is what it would be like,' I whisper to myself, and I let my throat swell up before I can even finish my thought. Her arms come around me like a vine. Her hair, tucked beneath my chin, smells of childhood.

My mother used to tell me that when push comes to shove, you always know who to turn to. That being a family isn't a social construct, but an instinct.

The flannel of our nightgowns hooks and catches. I rub Faith's back in silence, afraid to say anything that might ruin this good fortune, and I wait for her breathing to level before I let myself fall asleep. This one thing, this I can do.

The town where we live, New Canaan, is large enough to have its own mountain, small enough to hold rumors in the nooks and crannies of the weathered clapboard storefronts. It is a town of farms and open land, of simple people rubbing shoulders with professionals from Hanover and New London who want their money to go a little bit further in real estate. We have a gas station, an old playground, and a bluegrass band. We also have one attorney, J. Evers Standish, whose shingle I've passed a million times driving up and down Route 4.

Six days after Colin has left, I answer the front door to find a sheriff's deputy on the porch, asking me if I am indeed Mrs Mariah White. My first thought is for Colin—has he been in a car accident? The sheriff reaches into his pocket and pulls out an envelope. 'I'm sorry, ma'am,' he says, and he is gone before I can ask him what he's brought me.

The first concrete act of divorce is called a libel. It's a little piece of paper that, held in your hand, has the power to change your whole life. I will not know until months later that New Hampshire is the only state that still calls it a libel, instead of a complaint or a petition, as if part of the process, however amicable, involves a slight to one's character. Attached to the note is the piece of paper that says a divorce is being served against me.

Thirty minutes later I am sitting in the waiting room of J. Evers Standish's office, Faith curled in the corner with a battered Brio train set. I would not have brought her, but my mother has been gone all morning—off, she said, to get us both a surprise. A door behind the receptionist opens, and a tall, polished brunette walks out, hand extended. 'I'm Joan Standish.'

My jaw drops open. 'You are?' For years, in passing the building, I've pictured J. Evers Standish as an older man with muttonchops.

The attorney laughs. 'The last time I checked, I was.' She glances at Faith, absorbed in creating a tunnel for the train. 'Nan,' she asks her receptionist, 'could you keep an eye on Mrs White's daughter?' And as if I am pulled by a thread, I follow the lawyer into her office.

The funny thing is, I'm not upset. Not nearly as upset as I was the afternoon Colin left. Something about this libel seems completely over the top, like a joke with the punch line forthcoming. Something Colin and I will laugh about when the lights are out and we're holding each other a few months from now.

Joan Standish explains the libel to me. She asks me if I want to see a therapist or hear about referral programs. She asks what happened. She talks about divorce decrees and financial affidavits and custody, while I let the room whirl around me. It seems impossible that a wedding can take a year to plan but a divorce is final in six weeks—as if all the time in between, the feelings have been dwindling to the point where they can be scattered with one angry breath.

'Do you think Colin will want joint custody of your daughter?'

I stare at the attorney. 'I don't know.' I cannot imagine Colin living without Faith. But then again I cannot imagine myself living without Colin.

Joan Standish narrows her eyes and sits down on her desk, across from me. 'If you don't mind my saying so, Mrs White,' she begins, 'you seem a little . . . removed from all this. It's a very common reaction, you know, to just deny what's been legally set into motion, and therefore to just let the whole thing steamroll over you. But I can assure you that your husband has, in fact, started the judicial wheels turning to dissolve your marriage.'

I open my mouth, then snap it shut again.

'What?' she asks. 'If I'm going to represent you, you'll have to confide in me.'

I look into my lap. 'It's just that . . . well. We went through this, sort of, once before. What happens to all . . . this . . . if he decides to come back?'

The attorney leans forward, her elbows resting on her knees. 'Mrs White, you truly see no difference between then and now? Did he hurt you last time?' I nod. 'Did he promise you he'd change? Did he come back to you?' She smiles gently. 'Did he sue for divorce last time?'

'No,' I murmur.

'The difference between then and now,' Joan Standish says, 'is that this time he's done you a favor.'

Our seats for the circus are in the very first row. 'Ma,' I ask, 'how did you get tickets this close?'

My mother shrugs. 'I slept with the ringmaster,' she whispers, and then laughs at her own joke. Her surprise from yesterday involved a trip to the Concord TicketMaster, to get us all seats at the Ringling Brothers Circus, playing in Boston. She reasoned that Faith needed something that might get her excited enough to chatter again. And once she heard about the libel, she said that I should consider the trip to Boston a celebration.

My mother hails a man selling Sno-Cones and buys one

for Faith. The clowns are working the stands. I see some that I recognize—could they be the same after all these years? One with a white head and a blue smile leans over the low divider in front of us. He points to his suspenders, polka-dotted, then to Faith's spotted shirt, and claps his hands. When Faith blushes, he mutely mouths the word 'Hello.' Faith's eyes go wide, then she answers him, just as silently.

The clown reaches into his back pocket and pulls out a greasepaint crayon. He cups Faith's chin in one hand, and with the other draws a wide, splitting smile over her lips. He colors musical notes on her throat and winks.

He hops away from the divider, ready to entertain some other child, and then turns back at the last minute. Before I can manage to duck away, he reaches for my face. His hand is cool on my cheek as he paints a tear beneath my left eye, dark blue and swollen with sorrow.

Although it is not something I remember, when I was little I tried to join the circus.

My parents took me to the Boston Garden every year when Ringling Brothers came to town, and to say I loved it would be an understatement. In the weeks leading up to the show I'd wake in the middle of the night, my chest tight with flips and my eyes blind with sequins, my sheets smelling of tigers and ponies and bears. When I was actually at the circus, I'd school my eyes not to blink, aware that it would be gone as quickly as the cotton candy that melted away to nothing in the heat of my mouth.

The year I was seven I was mesmerized by the Elephant Girl. The daughter of the ringmaster, glittering and sure, she stepped on the trunk of an enormous elephant and shimmied up it, the way I sometimes walked up the playground slide. She sat with her thighs clamped around the thick, bristly neck of the elephant and stared at me the whole time she circled the center ring. *Don't you wish,* she said silently, *that you were like me?*

That year, like all the other years, my mother made me get up ten minutes before the intermission, so that we could beat the bathroom lines. She towed me to the ladies' room, both of us crowding into the tiny stall, and she loomed like a djinn with her arms crossed over me as I squatted to pee. When I was done, she said, 'Now wait till I'm finished.'

My mother tells me that I had never crossed the street without reaching for her hand, never reached toward a hot stove; even as an infant, I'd never put small objects in my mouth. But that day, while she was in the toilet, I ducked beneath the door of the stall and disappeared.

I do not remember this. I also do not remember how I made my way past the green-coated security guards, out the door, and into the huge lot where the circus had set up its trailers. Of course, I do not remember how the ringmaster himself announced my name in hopes of finding me, how the murmurs of a lost little girl ran like fire, how my parents spent the show searching the halls. I can't recall the chalky face of the circus hand who found me, who pronounced it a wonder that I hadn't been trampled or gored. And I can't imagine what my parents thought, to discover me nestled between the lethal tusks of a sleeping elephant, my hair matted with straw and spit, his trunk curled over my shoulders like the arm of an old love.

I don't know why I'm telling you this, except to make you see that maybe, like eye color and bone structure, miracles are passed down through the bloodlines.

The Elephant Girl has grown up. Of course, I cannot be sure they are one and the same, but here is a woman in a spangly costume with the same red-gold hair and wise eyes as the girl I remember. She leads a baby elephant around the center ring and tosses it a purple ball; she bows grandly to the audience and lets the elephant wave over her shoulder. Then from the side curtains comes a child, a little girl so like the one in my past that I wonder if time stands completely still beneath a big top. But then I watch the Elephant Woman help the girl ride the baby elephant around the ring, and I see that they are mother and daughter.

A look passes between them, one that makes me glance at Faith. Her eyes are so bright I can see the Elephant Girl's sequins reflected in them. Suddenly the clown who was here before is leaning over the divider, motioning wildly to Faith, who nods and falls over the railing into his arms. She waves back at us, her face mobile as she marches off to be part of the pre-intermission extravaganza. My mother scoots into Faith's seat. 'Did you see that? Oh, I knew we should have brought the camera.'

And then in a buffet of light and booming voice, the circus performers and animals parade around the trio of rings. I look around, trying to find Faith. 'Over there!' my mother calls. 'Yoo-hoo! Faith!' She points past the ringmaster and the caged tigers to my daughter, who is riding in front of the Elephant Lady on a tremendous tusked beast.

I wonder if other mothers feel a tug at their insides, watching their children grow up into the people they themselves wanted so badly to be. The searchlights wing over the crowd, and in spite of the cheers and the fanfare I can still hear my mother surreptitiously unwrapping a Brach's butterscotch candy in the belly of her purse.

A trained dog, spooked by something, leaps out of the arms of a clown in a hoopskirt. The dog streaks between the ringmaster's legs, over the satin train of a trapeze artist, and just in front of Faith's elephant, causing it to trumpet and rear up on its legs.

If I live to be a hundred, I will never forget how long it took to watch Faith tumble to the sawdust, how panic swelled into my eardrums and blocked out all other sound, how the clown who'd befriended her rushed over, only to bump against the juggler and knock the spinning knives out of his hands, so that the three bright blades fell and sliced across my daughter's back.

Faith lies unconscious on her belly in a hospital bed at Mass General, so small she barely takes up half the length of the mattress. An IV drips into her arm to ward off infection, the doctor says, although he is confident because the lacerations were not deep. Still, they were deep enough to require twenty stitches. My jaw is so tight from being clenched that a shudder runs down my spine, and my mother must know how close I am to falling apart, because she has a quiet word with a nurse, touches Faith's hair, and pulls me out of the room.

We don't speak until we reach a small supply closet, which my mother appropriates for our use. Pushing me against the wall of sheets and towels, she forces me to look her in the eye. 'Mariah, Faith is all right. Faith is going to be just fine.'

Just like that, I dissolve. 'It's my fault,' I sob. 'I couldn't stop it.' I do not say what I'm sure my mother is thinking, too—that I am not crying just for the knives that scored Faith, but for retreating into depression after Colin left, maybe even for choosing Colin as a husband in the first place.

'If it's anyone's fault, it's mine—I bought the tickets.' She hugs me hard. 'This isn't some kind of punishment. It's not like an eye for an eye, Mariah. You're going to get through this. Both of you.' Then she holds me at arm's length. 'Did I ever tell you about the time I almost killed you? We went skiing, and you were all of about seven, and you slipped off the chairlift when I was adjusting my poles. You were dangling there, twenty feet above the ground, while I grabbed onto the sleeve of your little coat. All because I wasn't paying attention.'

'It's not the same. That was an accident.'

'So was this,' my mother insists.

We walk out of the supply closet and into Faith's room again. Words the psychiatrists had used at Greenhaven to describe me circle in my head: *compulsive and idealistic, rejection-sensitive, poor self-confidence, a tendency to over-compensate and to catastrophize*. 'She should have gotten someone else as a mother. Someone who was good at this sort of thing.'

My mother laughs. 'She got you for a reason, honey. You wait and see.' Announcing that she's off to get us coffee, she heads for the door. 'Just because other parents roll with the punches doesn't mean it's right. The ones who are most nervous about screwing up, Mariah, are the same ones who care enough to want things to be perfect.'

The door shuts behind her with a sigh. I sit down on Faith's bed and trace the edge of her blanket. *If I can't have Colin*, I think, *please let me have her*.

I don't realize I've spoken aloud until my mother comes

in with the coffee. 'Who are you talking to?' I flush, embarrassed to be caught bargaining with a higher power. It is not as if I believe in God. When I was a child, my family wasn't very religious; as an adult, all I have is a healthy dose of skepticism—and, apparently, the urge to beg in spite of this when I really, really need help. 'No one. Just Faith.'

My mother presses the coffee into my hand. The cup is so hot it burns my palm, and even after I set it on the nightstand my skin still smarts. At that moment, Faith blinks up at me. 'Mommy,' she croaks, and my heart turns over: Her first word in weeks is all mine.

two

'Sure, lots of people believe in God. Lots of people used to believe the world was flat, too.'

—Ian Fletcher
in *The New York Times*, June 14, 1998

August 17, 1999

IAN FLETCHER IS STANDING in the middle of hell. He paces around the new backdrop of the set, running his hand over the gas pipes that will produce flame, and the jagged peaks of rock. He scrapes off a bit with his thumb, thinking that brimstone isn't all it's cracked up to be. 'It's too damn yellow. Looks like some New Age druid circle.'

His set decorator glances at the associate producer. 'I think, Mr Fletcher, that the fire-and-brimstone thing was smell-related.'

'Smell?' Ian scowls. 'What's that supposed to mean?'

'It's sulfur, sir. You know, you burn it, and it stinks.'

Ian glares at the set decorator. 'Tell me,' he says softly, threateningly, 'what's the point of a smell-related special effect in a visual medium like television?'

The man quails. 'I don't know, Mr Fletcher, but you—'

'But I what?'

'You wanted fire and brimstone, Ian.' The voice comes from the tangle of cameras and microphones just off to the left. 'Don't blame the fellow for your own mistakes.'

At the sound of the executive producer's voice, Ian sighs

and runs a hand through his thick, black hair. 'You know, James, the only thing that makes me think there might be a higher power after all is the way you always manage to drop in at the absolute worst moment.'

'That's not God, Ian, that's Murphy's Law.' James Wilton steps into the circle of sulfur and glances around. 'Of course, if you rediscover religion, that would be one way to boost ratings.' He hands Ian a fax with the latest Nielsen numbers.

'Shoot,' Ian mutters. 'I told you CBS wasn't the way to go. We ought to reopen negotiations with HBO.'

'HBO isn't going to come within ten feet of you if you keep ranking in the bottom third.' James breaks off a piece of sulfur and holds it to his nose. 'So this is brimstone, eh? Guess I always kind of pictured it as a big black fireplace.'

Ian absentmindedly glances at the new set. 'Yeah, well. We'll design a new one.'

'Oh?' James says dryly. 'Should we pay for it with the huge bonus from your pending Nike endorsement? Or with the incoming grant from the Christian Coalition?'

Ian narrows his eyes. 'You don't have to be so cynical. You know that six months ago, when we did the specials, we got an incredible Nielsen share for the time slot.'

James walks from the set, leaving Ian to follow. 'They were specials. Maybe that was the appeal. Maybe a weekly show loses its novelty.' He turns to Ian, his face grave. 'I love what you do, Ian. But network executives have notoriously short attention spans. And *I've* got to bring them a winner.' Taking the fax from Ian's hand, James crumples it into a ball. 'I know it goes against your nature . . . but now would be a good time to start praying.'

Although he'd been asked by countless journalists, Ian Fletcher refused to isolate the incidents in his life that made him stop believing in God. In fact, not only did he admit to being born a nonbeliever, he made a living out of trying to convince the world that everyone was born a nonbeliever and that faith was something one was subtly schooled to accept—like cow's milk, or potty training—because it was socially acceptable. Religion, he argued, made a wonderful panacea.

Ian's offhand comparison of devout Catholics to toddlers who believed that a Band-Aid itself cures the wound was hotly debated in the op-ed pages of *The New York Times*, in *Newsweek*, and on *Meet the Press*. He asked why Jews were the Chosen People yet continued to be targeted for persecution. He asked why Catholics were the only ones who ever saw the Virgin Mary in fountains and morning mists. He asked how there could be a God when innocent children got raped and maimed and killed. The more outspoken he became, the more people wanted to listen. In 1997 his book, *God Who?*, spent twenty weeks at number one on *The New York Times* nonfiction bestseller list. He became a guest at Steven Spielberg's home and was invited to sit in on White House round-table discussions and focus groups concerning a variety of cultural issues. That July a *People* magazine featuring Ian Fletcher on the cover sold out in twenty-four hours. A speech in Central Park drew more than a hundred thousand spectators. And in September 1998, Ian Fletcher met with TV executives and became the world's first teleatheist.

He formed a company—Pagan Productions—borrowed cues from the Reverends Billy Graham and Jerry Falwell, and then put on a show. Huge TV screens behind him played images of mass destruction—bombs, land mines, civil wars—while Ian's stirring, unmistakable Southern drawl challenged the concept of a supreme, loving being who would allow things to come this far. He developed a large following and cultivated a reputation as Spokesman of the Millennium Generation—those cynical Americans who had neither the time nor the inclination to trust in God for their future. He was opinionated, brash, and bullheaded, which won him the appeal of the eighteen-to-twenty-four-year-old sector. He was highly educated—a Ph.D. in theology from Harvard—which made the baby boomers take note. But clearly Ian Fletcher's greatest attribute—the one that endeared him to women of all ages and made him a natural for the small screen—was the fact that he was handsome as sin.

Two hours later Ian bursts into the office of his executive producer. 'I've got it!' he crows, oblivious to the way that

James is motioning to him to be quiet, as he's on the phone. 'It's perfect. It's going to make you one very rich man.'

At that, James turns toward Ian. 'I'll get back to you,' he says into the receiver and hangs up. 'Okay, you've got my attention. What's the grand plan?'

Ian's vivid blue eyes are shining, and his hands are busy diagramming and punctuating his enthusiasm. He looks exactly like the kind of angry, spirited orator who drew James to him in the first place, as the voice of a spiritually lost country. 'What do you do if you're a Bible Belt televangelist and your ratings take a dive?'

James considers this. 'You sleep with your secretary, or extort money.'

Ian rolls his eyes. 'Wrong. You take your show on the road.'

'Like in a Winnebago?'

'Why not?' Ian says. 'Think about it, James. Preachers at the turn of the last century built congregations with grassroots revival meetings. They pitched a tent in the middle of nowhere and made miracles happen.'

James narrows his eyes. 'I can't quite imagine you in a tent, Ian. Your idea of "roughing it" is settling for The Four Seasons instead of The Plaza.'

Ian shrugs. 'Desperate times call for desperate measures. We're going to go slumming with the masses, my friend. We'll hold the world's first antirevival.'

'If viewers don't tune in to you at home, Ian, why should they tune into you in Fuck-all, Kansas?'

'Don't y'all get it? That's the whole catch. Instead of making cripples throw down their crutches and having blind people see, I'm going to uncover hoaxes. I'm going to rip apart all these so-called miracles. You know—go to Lourdes with scientists and prove that the statue's not crying tears, it's condensation. Or find the medical reason why a guy who's in a coma for nineteen years suddenly wakes up good as new.' He leans forward, grinning from ear to ear. 'People believe in God because they don't have any other explanation for things that happen. I can change that.'

Slowly, James smiles. 'You know,' he admits, 'this actually isn't a bad idea.'

Ian reaches for the newspaper on the corner of James's desk. He tosses one section to his producer and then takes his own and spreads the pages wide, like the wings of a great bird. 'Call your secretary and have her run on out to the newsstand. We need the *Globe*, the *Post*, the *L.A. Times*,' Ian orders. '*Someone* saw Jesus' face on his pizza at dinner last night. Now we've just got to find him.'

August 30, 1999

COLIN WHITE SITS in his business suit on a bench at the playground, watching mothers and nannies chase toddlers beneath the jungle gym. His egg-salad sandwich remains in its plastic wrapper, untouched. Without even taking a bite, he balls it up and stuffs it back into the brown paper bag from the deli.

That little girl, the one on the monkey bars, looks something like Faith. Same curl to her hair, even if it's a shade too dark. She keeps making it to the third rung, then slipping free and falling to the ground. Colin remembers Faith doing the same thing: practicing and practicing until she could make it across. He wants to move closer, but he knows better. In this day and age it will only make him look like a pedophile, not a man who simply misses his child.

He runs his hands through his hair. What the *hell* was he thinking? The answer was, he hadn't been thinking at all when he'd brought Jessica back to his house that afternoon. A ballet class is not a sure thing; he should have known that Faith and Mariah might come home unexpectedly. In the three weeks that have passed, he can still remember every nuance of the looks on Faith's and Mariah's faces when Jessica walked out of the bathroom. He can still remember how Faith stared right through him when he finally caught up to her in her bedroom, as if she was old enough to know that the excuses he was making were transparent.

He had hurt Mariah, too, but then again, living with a

woman who refused to accept that there was any problem with their marriage would take its toll on a saint. Every time he tried to force Mariah to face facts, he left shaking, afraid that he'd come home and find her trying to kill herself. Initially he'd gone out with Jessica just to have someone to confide in.

And now he loves her.

Colin closes his eyes. It's one hell of a mess.

The little girl on the monkey bars finishes swinging over the last rung and lands a few feet away from Colin, kicking up a cloud of dust. 'Oh,' she says, grinning up at him. 'Sorry.'

'No problem.'

'Can you tie my shoe?'

He smiles. One thing he has learned about young children: To them, adults are interchangeable. Anyone of similar fatherlike age might be asked to take care of these things. He bends down over the laces of her sneaker, realizing at close range that this girl is younger than Faith, heavier, unmistakably different.

The girl climbs the short ladder on one end of the monkey bars. 'You watch me,' she calls out, artlessly proud. 'This time I'm going to get it right.'

Colin finds himself holding his breath as the child swings out with her left arm, then her right, reaching for the metal rungs and curling her knuckles over them, even though it is an unlikely stretch, even though it is sure to leave her aching. He continues to watch, until he sees her safely across to the other side.

For seven, she knows a lot of things. She knows that monarch caterpillars live in the folds of milkweed leaves, that tights are never as tight as leggings, that 'We'll see' always means 'No.' She has learned enough of the world to realize that it is a place of grown-ups, and that the only way to leave her mark is to speak at the ends of their sentences and act so much like them that they sit up and take notice. She knows that the minute she falls asleep, her teddy bear's sewed-shut eyes snap open. She knows that truth can cause a sharp pain behind your eyes and that love sometimes feels like a fist around your throat.

She also knows, although everyone is careful to keep it from her, that they are all still talking. Faith has been home from the hospital for three days now, although she isn't comfortable wearing a shirt yet. Every time she does, she feels the cuts open up and bleed, and she worries that in the winter she will either freeze to death or else leak bone dry.

During the day Grandma comes over and plays spit and go fish, and she doesn't care at all that Faith is wearing only her shorts. Her mother sits on the couch and stares at Faith's back when she thinks no one is looking, as if Faith couldn't feel the weight of her eyes anyway. When Grandma leaves after dinner, sometimes there are conversations with big, fat, white spaces, so that it seems like whole hours pass between the sentences Faith and her mother speak.

Tonight Faith is picking at the peas on her dinner plate when the doorbell rings. Grandma raises her eyebrows, and her mother shrugs. They are like that, can speak without saying a thing, because they know each other so well. With Faith and her mom, though, it's a different type of quiet, one brought on by not knowing each other at all. Faith watches her mother go to the front door, and as soon as she's out of sight, Faith takes a forkful of peas and hides them under her thigh.

'Oh!' Her mother's voice is full of air and light. 'You're just in time for dinner.'

'I can't stay,' Faith hears her father answer. She stiffens, feels the peas pop beneath her leg. She has seen her father once since That Day. He came to the hospital with a big stuffed teddy bear that was the ugliest one she'd ever seen, and the whole time he held her hand and talked to her she was picturing that lady that came out of the bathroom as if she lived there. She does not know why the woman was taking a shower in the middle of the afternoon, or why that made her mother cry. She knows only that the whole event had a color about it, like the scribbles of a crayon gone crazy off the page—the same blue-black she sometimes imagined when she was lying in bed and could hear, through the walls, her parents fighting.

Her father walks into the kitchen and kisses her on the

forehead. 'Hey, cookie!' He pretends not to look at her back the same way her mother does. 'How's my pumpkin pie?' Faith stares at him, and she wonders why he calls her only by the names of food.

'For God's sake, Mariah!' Her grandma gets to her feet. 'How could you let him in?'

'For Faith—I had to.'

Grandma snorts. 'For Faith. Right.' She comes closer to Faith's father, and for a moment Faith wonders if Grandma is going to sock him one right then and there. But she only pokes him in the side with her finger. 'Good-bye, Colin. You're not needed.'

'Lay off, Millie, will you?'

Her mother reappears with a plate. 'Here,' she sings. 'No trouble at all.'

'Mariah, I can't stay. I told you that.'

'It's only dinner—'

'I have other plans.'

'You could cancel them. It would be nice for Fai—'

'Jessica's waiting in the car,' her father says tightly. 'All right?'

Faith scurries away from her father's voice, taking shelter beneath her grandmother's arm. Her mother wilts into a chair, the plate clattering so that peas spill across the table like polka dots. Her father's jaw is working funny, no words coming out. Finally he says, 'I just wanted to see my daughter. I'm sorry.' Then he touches Faith's shoulder and walks out.

'God, Ma! Did you have to say that?'

'Yes! Since you wouldn't!'

'I don't need your help.' Faith's mother presses her hands to her head. 'Just leave.'

Faith begins to panic. She did not want her father there either, but that was only because she knew that it would all come down to a scene like this. Once in school her teacher had filled a bowl with water and sprinkled pepper on top. Then she dripped dishwashing soap down the side, and the pepper went flying away. For some reason, when Faith thinks of her mother and father, that always comes to mind, too.

'Faith,' her grandmother says, 'maybe you should sleep at my house tonight.'

Her mother shakes her head. 'No way. She's staying here.'

'Wonderful!'

Faith tries to figure out what is so wonderful about it. She wants to go to her grandmother's. Her mother will just mope around and stick a video in the VCR for her. At her grandma's, she gets to sleep in the guest room, with the beastly black sewing machine in the corner and the box of buttons and the small bowl of sugar cubes on the nightstand.

But then her grandmother is saying good-bye and her mother is muttering about reverse psychology and it is just the two of them, with all the dishes on the table. For a long time Faith watches her mother. She sits with her head in her hands, so still that Faith thinks she's fallen asleep. Unsure of what to say or do, Faith pokes her. 'Want to play a game?'

When her mother looks up, Faith thinks that she has never in her life seen anything so sad. Except maybe the tortoise at the San Diego Zoo two summers ago, which had lifted its great head and stared right at Faith, willing her to help him go back to where he once had been.

Her mother's voice is thin and creaky. 'I can't.' She walks out of the room, leaving Faith behind to wonder, once again, what magic words might keep her mother close by.

Mariah has always believed there ought to be a network for the lovelorn, patterned after Alcoholics Anonymous, devoted to helping those who are crippled by broken hearts. *Surely there are enough of us*, she thinks, people who would benefit from a buddy system for the moments when you catch your sweetheart with his arm around another woman, or when he calls but does not want to speak to you, or when you see in his eyes that he has already started to forget you. She imagines having the name of a Good Samaritan who will talk on the phone like a seventh-grade girlfriend, draw you a dartboard with his face on it, take the ache away.

But instead she stares at the small business card with her psychiatrist's beeper number. She is not supposed to call unless it is an emergency, which in her case would probably mean the profound desire to cut open her wrists or hang herself from the closet rack. She wants to talk to someone, but she does not know whom. Her mother is her closest friend, but she's just sent Millie away. Other women she knows have husbands who work with Colin; they are couples who are probably going out to dinner with him and Jessica. She feels something bitter rise in the back of her throat. It does not seem right that this woman should get her husband, her friends, and her old life.

There is much Mariah has to do. She ought to check on Faith, give her her antibiotics, change the dressing on her stitches before she goes to bed. She ought to call her mother and apologize. At the very least she ought to clean up the dinner table.

Instead she finds herself staring at the bed. All night she imagines that she is falling into dips and runnels of the mattress, as if Colin and Jessica have literally left their marks. She tugs the comforter off and makes herself a nest on the floor. She piles the sheets on top and lies down, picturing Colin's face the way she once did in her narrow bed in a college dormitory. She stays perfectly still, oblivious to the tears that come without warning, a geyser, a hot spring with the power to heal.

Her mother is crying, Faith knows, hard enough that she can't catch her breath. It's a quiet sound, but all the same as hard to block out with a pillow as her parents' fights used to be. It makes her feel like crying, too. Faith thinks about calling her grandmother but remembers that her grandmother takes the phone off the hook at 7:00 P.M. to foil telemarketers. So she curls up on top of her bed, shirtless, holding the old bear that smells like Johnson's Baby Shampoo.

She stays that way for a long time, and then dreams about a person wearing a long white nightgown who is sitting across from her. Immediately—she's been warned of strangers—she shrinks away.

'Faith,' the person says. 'You don't have to be afraid.'

Long dark hair, sad dark eyes. 'Do I know you?'

'Do you want to?'

'I don't know.' Faith wants so badly to touch the night-gown of this stranger. She's never seen anything like it. It seems so soft you might fall into it and never find your way out. 'Are you a friend of my mom's?'

'I'm your guard.'

She thinks about that for a moment, puzzling out whether or not a person you've never seen before can slip unannounced into your life.

'Who are you talking to?' Suddenly Faith's mother stands in the doorway, her eyes red and swollen and her hands holding a tube of Bacitracin.

Startled, Faith glances around the room, but the stranger—and the dream—is gone. 'Nobody,' she says, then turns around so that her mother can tend to her stitches.

Two nights later Mariah wakes up with a start. She walks barefoot down the hall, aware before she even gets there that Faith is missing.

'Faith?' she whispers. 'Faith!' She rips the comforter from the empty bed and checks in the closet. She peeks her head inside the bathroom and then clatters down the stairs to check in the playroom and the kitchen. By now her head is throbbing and her palms are damp. 'Faith,' she yells, 'where are you?'

Mariah thinks of the stories she's read in the news, of children who've been abducted from their own houses in the dead of the night. She imagines a hundred different terrors that exist just beyond the edge of the driveway. Then she sees a flash of silver through the window.

Outside in the yard Faith is gingerly crawling across the pressure-treated beam that forms the top of the swing set, ten feet above the ground. She's done it before, catlike, and terrified Mariah, who was certain she'd fall. 'Do you mind telling me what you're doing out here in the middle of the night?' Mariah says softly, so as not to startle her.

Faith glances down, not at all surprised to be discovered. 'My guard told me to come.'

Of all the things Mariah expected to hear, that is not one of them. 'Your *what?*'

'My guard.'

'What guard?'

'My friend.' Faith grins, giddy with the truth of it. 'She's my friend.'

Mariah tries to remember the faces of Faith's little playmates. But none have come to visit since Colin left, their families adhering to the New England tradition of keeping one's nose out of a neighbor's bad business, lest it be contagious. 'Does she live around here?'

'I don't know,' Faith says. 'Ask her.'

Mariah suddenly feels her chest pinch. Since Greenhaven she has pictured her mind as a series of glass dominoes, capable of being felled by a puff of breath in the right direction. She wonders if dissociation from reality is genetically based, like hair color or a tendency to gain weight. 'Is . . . is your friend here now?'

Faith snorts. 'What do you think?'

A trick question. 'Yes?'

Faith laughs and sits up, straddling the beam and swinging her feet. 'Come down before you get hurt,' Mariah scolds.

'I won't get hurt. My guard told me.'

'Bully for her,' Mariah mutters, climbing onto one of the swings so that she can grab for her daughter. As she comes closer, she can hear Faith singsonging under her breath to the tune of 'Pop Goes the Weasel': '"But the fruit o-of the tree . . . which is in the mid-dle of the garden . . ."'

'Inside,' Mariah says with authority. 'Now.'

It is not until her daughter is tucked into bed that Mariah realizes, for the first time since the circus accident, Faith's back has healed enough for her to be wearing a nightgown.

Except for the fact that Dr Keller's Barbie is bald, Faith likes playing with the toys. There are Koosh mitts and a dollhouse and crayons shaped like ducks and pigs and stars. The Barbie, though, gives her the creeps. It has little pimply holes where its hair ought to be, and it looks all wrong. It reminds Faith of the time she dropped a Baby Go Potty doll and its chest cracked off to reveal a pump and batteries, instead of the storybook heart she'd imagined there.

Mostly, though, Faith likes coming to see Dr Keller. She thought that maybe she'd have to get shots or even that test where they stick the really long Q-tip down your throat, but Dr Keller only watches her play and sometimes asks her questions. Then she goes off into the room where Faith's mother is waiting, and Faith gets to play even longer all by herself.

Today Dr Keller is sitting on a chair, writing in her notebook. Faith picks up a puppet, one with a queen's crown, and then lets it slide off her hand. She digs her hands into the tub full of crayons and lets the colors fall through her fingers. Then she walks across the room and stares down at the bald Barbie. She grabs it and carries it over to the dollhouse.

It's not a fancy dollhouse, not like the ones her mom makes, but that's not such a bad thing. Whenever Faith gets too close to one of her mother's dollhouses, she gets yelled at, and if she manages to take out a tiny chair or finger a miniature braided rug, she always thinks she's going to break it if she even *breathes* the wrong way. This plastic dollhouse of Dr Keller's is clearly for kids, clearly for someone to play with. Not just for show.

Ken and another Barbie, this one with hair, are crammed into the tiny bathroom of the dollhouse. Ken is facedown in the toilet. Faith picks him up and walks him to the bedroom. She mashes him against the Barbie with hair, holding her tight. Then she takes the bald Barbie and props her against the bedroom wall to watch.

Dr Keller scoots her chair closer to the dollhouse. 'There are lots of people in that room.'

Faith looks up. 'It's a father and a mother and another mother.'

'Two mothers?'

'Yeah. This one'—she touches the doll in Ken's arms—'does all the kissing.'

'How about the other one?'

Faith gently strokes the bald head of the second Barbie. 'That one does all the crying.'

'You're what?'

Jessica's face falls, and immediately Colin knows he has made another mistake. 'I thought you'd be happy,' she says, and then bursts into tears.

For the life of him, Colin doesn't know what to do. He is certain that Jessica is expecting him to do or say something appropriate, but all he can think of is the moment years ago, when the doctors at Greenhaven told him that Mariah had tested positive for pregnancy. After a moment he puts his arms around Jessica. 'I'm sorry. I *am* happy.'

Jessica lifts her face. 'You are?' Her voice shakes.

Colin nods. 'Cross my heart.'

She turns in his embrace and twines herself around him like a jungle vine. 'I knew you'd say that. I knew you'd see this as a second chance.'

For what? he thinks, and then realizes she is speaking of a family. He smiles at her, past the sudden constriction of his throat. Jessica's eyes are shining as she takes his hand and places it on the flat plane of her belly. 'I wonder who it'll look like,' she says softly.

Colin tries to picture the face of the child they might have created. He closes his eyes, but all he can see is Faith.

Mariah straightens with a groan, having finished tying Faith's sneakers into double knots. It is Thursday, the day for vacuuming and returning library books and buying fresh corn at the farmstand and, these days, for Faith's appointment with Dr Keller. 'Okay. Let's go.'

'Mommy,' Faith says, 'you have to do hers, too.'

Sighing, Mariah squats again and pretends to tie the shoes of Faith's imaginary friend. 'Mommy . . . she's got *buckles*.'

After a moment Mariah stands. 'Are we ready now?' She cuts in front of her daughter, grabs her purse, and opens the front door. Once Faith is outside, Mariah remains for a moment, so that her guard has a chance to walk out the door, too.

A smile wreathes Faith's face, and she slides her hand into Mariah's on the way to the car. 'She says *thank you*.'

Mariah never would have chosen Dr Keller as her own psychiatrist. For one thing, she is so organized that Mariah always finds herself checking to see if she's left something back in the car—her keys, her pocketbook, her confidence. And Dr Keller is beautiful, too—young, with hair the rich color of a fox's back and legs that she always remembers to cross. Mariah learned years ago that she did not want to talk to someone like that. Dr Johansen was just her speed—short, tired-looking, human enough that Mariah did not mind revealing her failures. But Dr Johansen had been the one to suggest that Faith see someone to help her understand the divorce. Mariah wanted Faith to see Dr Johansen, but he didn't treat children. He recommended Dr Keller, and even called the office to help Mariah get a fast appointment.

Mariah does not want to admit, even to herself, that she is at the root of Faith's hallucinations. After all, the doctors at Greenhaven said they couldn't be sure that the baby inside her would not be damaged by Prozac. And they couldn't say *how*.

Mariah forces her gaze to Dr Keller's. 'I'm worried about this imaginary friend.'

'Don't be. It's perfectly normal. Healthy, even.'

Mariah raises her brows. 'It's healthy and normal to talk to someone who isn't there?'

'Absolutely. Faith's created someone to give her emotional support twenty-four hours a day.' Dr Keller pulls out a sheet of drawing paper from Faith's file. 'She calls this friend her guard, which only reinforces the behavior—she has someone to protect her now, so this never happens again.'

Mariah takes the paper and smiles at the simple drawing of a little blond girl. It's Faith—she can tell by the purple dress with the yellow flowers, which Faith would wear every single day if given the opportunity. She's drawn her hair in braids that look like sunny snakes, and she's holding the hand of another person. 'That's her friend,' Dr Keller says.

Mariah stares at the figure. 'Looks like Casper the Friendly Ghost.'

'She may very well be. If Faith's conjuring up a mental

vision of this person, it's probably something she's seen somewhere else.'

'Casper with hair,' Mariah amends, her finger tracing the floating white body and the brown helmet around the face. 'Some guard.'

'What's important is that it's working for Faith.'

Mariah takes a deep breath and jumps off the cliff. 'How do you know it is?' she asks quietly. 'How do you know this friend isn't someone she's hearing in her head?'

Dr Keller pauses for a moment. Mariah wonders how much she knows about her own hospitalization, how much Dr Johansen has revealed. 'In the first place, I wouldn't classify it as a hallucination. That would suggest that your daughter is having psychotic episodes, and you haven't indicated any changes in behavior that would lead me to believe that.'

'What sorts of changes?' Mariah says, although she knows very well what they are.

'Dramatic ones. Trouble sleeping. Staring spells. Aggression. Changes in eating habits. If she's walking around at three in the morning and saying that her friend told her to go climb onto the roof of the house.'

Mariah thinks about Faith crawling across the top of the swing set in the middle of the night. 'No,' Mariah lies, 'there's nothing like that.'

Dr Keller shrugs. 'Then don't worry about it.'

'How about when she wants her friend to get into bed with her? Or eat at the table?'

'Go along with it. Don't make it a big deal, and eventually Faith will feel secure enough to just let it go.'

Let her guard down, Mariah thinks, and almost smiles.

'I'll talk to her about this friend again, Mrs White. But really, I've seen a hundred of these cases. Ninety-nine of those children turned out absolutely fine.'

Mariah nods, but she is wondering what happened to the other *one*.

Colin smiles at the VP of Operations for the chain of nursing homes. 'This'll just take a minute,' he says, and he casually leaves the office to rummage in the trunk of his car. Hard to sell the merits of a damn exit sign when it shoots sparks the minute he plugs it in. Luckily, Colin has a spare in the trunk; he can blame the other on faulty wiring at the plant in Taiwan.

The sample is buried in a box. Gritting his teeth, Colin shoves his hand along the side, feeling for a telltale wire, then grasping and extracting what turns out to be a small barrette.

How it got into his sample box, he can't imagine. He remembers the last time he saw Faith wearing it, winking silver against the waterfall of her light hair. She keeps her barrettes and ponytail scrunchies in an old cigar box that Colin's own grandfather once gave him.

Forgetting the nursing home VP, forgetting the exit sign that now dangles from the box like a broken droid, Colin runs the pad of his thumb over the edge of the barrette.

He has been to the obstetrician with Jessica. He has heard the new baby's heartbeat. But it is very hard to pretend that he is thrilled about this unborn child, when he has made such a mess of things with the one he's already got.

He has tried to call her, and once he even watched her at the school playground from a distance, but he backs away before making contact. The fact of the matter is, he does not know what to say. Every time he thinks he has the apology right, he remembers how Faith stared at him when he came to visit her in the hospital after the circus accident—silent and judgmental, as if even in her limited range of experience she knew he did not measure up. Being a father, Colin knows, is no AT&T commercial, no simple feat of tossing a ball across a green yard or braiding a length of hair. It is knowing all the words to *Goodnight Moon*. It is waking a split second in the middle of the night before you hear her fall out of bed. It is watching her twirl in a tutu and having one's mind leap over the years to wonder how it will be to dance at her wedding.

It is maintaining the illusion of having the upper hand, although you've been powerless since the first moment she smiled at you from the rook's nest of your cradled arm.

He thinks about Faith so much these days that he cannot imagine how she ever slipped from his mind long enough to let him make the monumental mistake of sleeping with Jessica in his own home.

Colin sighs deeply. He loves Jessica, and she's right—it is time to reinvent himself. So he makes a silent promise: to be a better father this time around, to make sure that Faith reaps the benefits of the new leaf he is going to turn over. He tells himself that as soon as he straightens out his life, he'll come back for Faith. He'll make it up to her.

'Mr White,' the nursing-home executive says impatiently from the doorway. 'Can we get on with this?'

Colin turns around, shoves the barrette into his pocket. He picks up the new sample and smoothly launches into a diatribe on its energy and monetary savings, wondering all the while how someone who makes a living by helping people safely escape cannot for the life of him see the way out.

September 6, 1999

MILLIE EPSTEIN PICKS UP her Diet Coke and settles next to her daughter on the living-room couch. 'Well, consider it a blessing. She could have dreamed up a British soldier with a big furry hat as a guard, and then complained that he wouldn't fit in the backseat of the car.'

Mariah rolls her own can of soda across the plane of her forehead. 'She's supposed to start school next week. What if the other kids tease her?'

'Is that what you're worried about? Really, Mariah. She's seven. By next week she won't even remember this.'

Mariah skims her lip along the sharp edge of the soda can. '*I* did,' she says quietly.

Her mother comes up swinging. 'There was nothing wrong with you. Colin made you believe you were *meshugge* when you were only a little bit under the weather.'

'It was a clinical depression, Ma.'

'Which is not the same as thinking an alien is beaming radio messages into your brain.'

Mariah turns in her seat. 'I never said I was schizophrenic.'

'Honey.' Millie touches her daughter's shoulder. 'You had an imaginary friend when you were about five, too. A boy named Wolf, who you said slept at the foot of your bed and told you vegetables were to be avoided at all costs.'

'Is that supposed to make me feel better?' Mariah's head is beginning to pound. Picking up the remote, she turns on her mother's TV. There is nothing on but soap operas, which she can't abide, an infomercial, and a Martha Stewart program. She flips through the lesser-used channels of the satellite dish and settles on a syndicated sitcom.

'No, go back.' Millie grabs the remote. 'I like listening to his accent.'

Mariah frowns at an installment of Ian Fletcher's anti-evangelical show, watching him strut around like a jaded cock of the walk. Accent, hah. He probably picked it up from a voice coach. She has never understood the mass philosophical appeal of this man, but then again she has never been interested enough in religion to want to entertain its alternative. 'I think the reason people watch him is because they believe that if he keeps mouthing off, God's going to hurl a lightning bolt down during a live broadcast and let the world watch him fry.'

'That's very Old Testament of you.' Millie pushes the mute button. 'Maybe you remember more of Hebrew school than I thought.'

Mariah blinks. 'I went to Hebrew school?'

'For a day. Your father and I thought we'd try to do the conventional thing by you. Some of your friends went to Sunday school, so . . .' She laughs. 'You came home and said you'd rather take ballet.'

It does not surprise Mariah. When she was a child her religious affiliation was purely social, the kind of Jew whose family attended temple only on High Holy Days, and then just to see what everyone else was wearing. Mariah can remember seeing Santa in the mall and wishing she could crawl into his lap. She can remember how on Christmas Day, when the rest of the world was celebrating, her family would go to the Chinese restaurant for dinner and then out to a movie, where they were the only people in the theater.

It surprised no one when Mariah married an Episcopalian.

Mariah cannot recall ballet class, but she realizes that although she can still configure her feet in the basic five positions, she would be hard-pressed to recite all Ten Commandments. 'I didn't know—'

'Oh!' Millie exclaims. 'This is his big tour! The one he's taking across America! Tuesday he was in New Paltz.'

Mariah laughs. 'New Paltz has a big atheist population!'

'Just the opposite. He was there because some church claimed to have a statue oozing blood. Turned out to be a limestone deposit or something.'

A line of type flashes at the bottom of the screen: HOULTON, MAINE, LIVE! The camera pans, catching T-shirts emblazoned with THE LIMB OF LIFE: THE JESUS TREE. Then it narrows on a close-up of Ian Fletcher, framed in the doorway of an RV. 'Gorgeous man.' Millie sighs. 'Look at that smile.'

Mariah doesn't glance up from the *TV Guide* she's skimming. 'Well, of course,' she says. 'He's probably having the time of his life.'

Ian has never been so miserable in his life. He is hot and sweaty, has a killer headache, and is quickly coming to hate Maine, if not the entirety of New England. Worse still, he can't look forward to a respite when the broadcast is finished. His producer refused to book him a decent hotel, saying that a guy who wants to go on a grassroots tour ought to be willing to let his Italian loafers touch the ground. So—for appearance's sake—Ian's production crew gets to stay at the Houlton Holiday Inn, while Ian camps out in a glorified tin can.

He's not about to reveal that accommodations are vitally important to a man who cannot sleep at night, but only prowls about, exhausted. His insomnia is no one's business but his own. Still, Ian can't even begin to describe the anticipation he feels at the prospect of bringing down this whole little Christ show. Whatever hoax he picks next to unravel will damn well be situated near a Ritz-Carlton.

At a signal from James he steps out of the godforsaken Winnebago, several reporters closing around him. He pushes through them and steps onto an empty milk crate that someone has left behind. 'As y'all may know,' Ian says, gesturing to the small and devoted knot of people gathered in front of the McKinneys' sprawling apple tree, 'there's been some question in recent days whether Houlton, Maine, is indeed the site of a religious miracle. According to William and Bootsie McKinney, the morning of August twentieth, following a severe thunderstorm, Jesus appeared to them in a split branch of this Macintosh tree.'

Ian turns toward it. Actually, the way the rings of the tree have grown and the delicate lines of dried sap do sort of resemble a long-chinned, dark-eyed visage. Like conventional pictures of Jesus, if one believes in that sort of thing. Ian deliberately smacks his open palm over the image, covering it. 'Is there a face here? Maybe. But if the McKinneys were not pious Catholics who attended mass regularly, would they have seen Jesus? Or might they have said it looks like Orville Redenbacher, or Great-uncle Samuel?' He waits for the suggestion to sink in before adding, 'Is a religious miracle truly inexplicable and divine? Or is it a coincidental meeting of what's been programmed in one's mind with what one wants to see?'

At the quick gasp of one of the nuns, the Houlton parish priest steps forward. 'Now, Mr Fletcher,' Father Reynolds says. 'There are documented cases of religious miracles that have even been approved by the Holy See.'

'Like that sighting of the Virgin Mary in a Mexican subway puddle a few years back?'

'I don't believe that has reached the approval stage yet.'

Ian snorts. 'C'mon, Father—if you were the Virgin Mary and you wanted to choose a place to appear, would you pick the oil sheen on a subway platform? Can't you accept the possibility that this may not be what it seems?'

The priest taps his finger against his chin. 'I can,' he says slowly. 'Can you?'

At the titter that runs through the crowd, Ian realizes he's lost his momentum. Goddamn live TV. 'Ladies and gen'lemen, I'd like to introduce Dr Irwin Nagel, of Princeton University's Forrestal Campus. Doctor?'

'Wood,' the professor says, 'is made up of several types of xylem cells, including vessels, which conduct materials and strengthen the stem of the tree. The so-called picture inside here is only a natural process of the xylem. As the tree gets older, the innermost layers stop conducting food and get clogged with resin, gum, and tannin, which harden and darken. The face that the McKinneys have seen is actually just a conglomeration of deposits in the tree's heartwood.'

Ian nods as his producer comes to stand beside him. 'What do you think?'

'I don't know if they're buying it,' James whispers. 'I liked your subway thing, though.'

Dr Nagel suddenly lifts up a large, dangerous-looking pair of hedge trimmers. 'Now, I've got the McKinneys' permission for this,' he says, as he randomly selects a branch and hacks it off. The pale sapwood seems to blush, and then within moments the demarcations of the tree's rings are clearly visible. 'Well, there. It kind of looks like Mickey Mouse.'

Ian steps forward. 'The professor means that the apparition of the face of Christ is, literally, a fluke of nature. That it happened is not extraordinary for a tree of this size and age.' On impulse Ian takes a black marker from his pocket and draws a shape on the exposed insides of the tree. 'Roddy,' he calls to a familiar reporter, 'what is this?'

The man squints. 'That's the moon.'

Ian points to Father Reynolds. 'A bowl.'

'A semicircle,' says Professor Nagel.

Ian sets the cap on his marker with an audible click. 'Perception is a very powerful thing. I say this isn't the face of Jesus. That's my opinion. It may or may not be true, and I can't prove it, and you have the right to doubt what I say. But by the same token, when Bill McKinney and Father Reynolds say, 'Yes, this is the face of Jesus,' well, that's just an opinion, too—and one that can't be proved. It doesn't matter if the pope agrees with them, or the President, or the majority of the whole damned world. It's certainly what they see. But it may or may not be a fact. And if you *don't* believe me, how *can* you believe them?'

'You know, half the time I don't even understand what he's saying, and I still think he's terrific,' Millie announces. 'Look at that priest. He's practically purple.'

Mariah laughs. 'Can we turn this off, Ma? Or is Jerry Springer coming on next?'

'Very funny. He's a poet, Mariah. Just you listen to him.'

'He's using someone else's script,' Mariah says, as Ian Fletcher lifts up a Bible and begins to read with heavy sarcasm.

'"But the fruit of the tree which is in the middle of the garden, God hath said Ye shall not eat of it; neither shall ye touch it, lest ye die."' Faith comes into the room and slips onto the couch. 'I know that poem.'

The funny thing is, the biblical verse seems familiar to Mariah, too, although she can't understand why. It has been years since Mariah has studied a Bible, and as far as she knows, Faith's never even *seen* one. She and Colin had put off their daughter's religious instruction indefinitely, since neither of them could consider it without feeling like a hypocrite.

'"And the serpent said to the woman . . ."'

Faith mutters something beneath her breath. Assuming the worst, Mariah crosses her arms. 'What was that, young lady?'

'"Ye shall not surely die."'

As the words leave Faith's mouth, Ian Fletcher repeats them on TV, and then plucks an apple from the McKinneys' tree to take a large, provocative bite. That's when Mariah recalls where she's heard Fletcher's verses before—just days ago, when Faith was playing on the swing set in the middle of the night, humming them softly. Just days ago, when Faith—who has never been to church or temple in her young life, who has never attended Sunday or Hebrew school—was singing from the Book of Genesis as if it were any other jump-rope rhyme.

The men and women who work at Pagan Productions in L.A. keep a healthy distance from Ian Fletcher, frightened by his bursts of temper, his ability to turn their own words back on themselves, and their instinct for self-preservation—in the event Mr Fletcher is wrong about God, they don't want to be cast into the lake of fire along with him on Judgment Day. They are paid well to respect their employer's privacy and to firmly deny requests for interviews. It is for this reason that no one outside Pagan Productions knows that Ian leaves every Tuesday morning, and that no one has any idea of where he goes.

Of course, people who work for Ian hypothesize like mad: He has a standing appointment with a mistress. He attends a witches' coven. He calls the pope, who is, unbeknownst to his followers, a silent partner in Pagan Productions. Several times, on dares, the bravest employees have tried to follow Ian when he disappears in his black Jeep. He manages to lose all of them by winding around the Los Angeles Freeway. One swears that he tracked Ian all the way to LAX, but nobody believes him. After all, where can you fly round-trip in time to be back for a tape-editing session that same night?

On the Tuesday morning of the week that Ian kicks off his grasssroots antirevival at the Jesus Tree, a black stretch limousine pulls up alongside the Winnebago. Ian is discussing with James and several associate producers the reactions his recent comments have received in the press. 'I've got to go,' Ian says, relieved to see the car approach. He's had to juggle time and make concessions, since this week he is leaving from Maine rather than L.A.

'You've got to go?' James asks. 'Where?'

Ian shrugs. 'Places. Sorry, I thought I mentioned I'd be cutting out early today.'

'You didn't.'

'Well, I'll be back tonight. We can finish up then.' He grabs his briefcase and his leather jacket and slams out the door.

Exactly two and one half hours later he crosses the threshold of a small brick building. He navigates the hallways with the confidence of someone who has been there before. Some of the people he passes nod as he makes his way to the recreation center, equipped with oak tables and televisions and chintz couches. Ian heads for a table in the far corner occupied by a man. Although it is warm in the room, Michael wears a crewneck sweater with a button-down oxford shirt.

His hands flutter over a pack of cards, which he turns over one at a time. 'Queen of diamonds,' he murmurs. 'Six of spades.'

Ian slips into the chair beside him. 'Hey there,' he says softly.

'King of hearts. Two of spades. Seven of hearts.'

'How have you been, Michael?' Ian scoots closer.

The man's shoulders rock from side to side. 'Six of clubs!' he says firmly.

Ian sighs, nods. 'Six of clubs, buddy.' He moves back a distance. He watches the cards flip in succession: red, black, red, black. Michael turns over an ace. 'Oh, no,' he says. 'Ace—'

'In the hole,' Ian finishes.

For the first time, Michael makes fleeting eye contact with Ian. 'Ace in the hole,' he echoes, then goes back to counting cards.

Ian sits quietly until exactly one hour has passed since his arrival—not because Michael has acknowledged his presence but because he knows that Michael *would* notice an absence even a few minutes shy of the routine. 'See you in a week, buddy,' Ian murmurs.

'Queen of clubs. Eight of hearts.'

'All right, then,' Ian says, swallowing hard. He walks out of the building and begins the journey back to Maine.

Something Faith has recently discovered is that if you squinch up your eyes really tight and rub them hard with the balls of your thumbs, you see things: little stars and greeny-blue circles that she imagines are her irises, as if there's some kind of mirror on the insides of her eyelids that makes this vision possible. She pulls at the edges of her lids and sees a flurry of red, the color she thinks that anger must be. She has been doing it a lot, although yesterday, when school started, it didn't work that well. Willie Mercer said that only babies would carry a Little Mermaid lunchbox, and when she whispered to her guard, trying to ignore him, Willie laughed and said she was Looney Tunes. So she closed her eyes to shut him out, and one thing led to another, and before she knew it the school nurse was calling home to say that Faith wouldn't stop rubbing her eyes; it must be conjunctivitis.

'Do your eyes hurt, Faith?' Dr Keller asks now.

'No, everyone just thinks they do.'

'Yes. Your mom told me about school yesterday.'

Faith blinks, squinting into the fluorescent lamps. 'I wasn't sick.'

'No.'

'I just like doing it. I see things.' She tips up her chin. 'Try it,' she challenges.

To her surprise, Dr Keller actually takes off her glasses and rubs her eyes the way Faith has been doing. 'I can see something white. It looks like the moon.'

'It's the inside of your eye.'

'Is it?' Dr Keller puts her glasses back on. 'Do you know this for sure?'

'Well, no,' Faith admits. 'But don't you think maybe your eyes are still looking around even when the lids are down?'

'I don't see why not. Do you see your friend when your eyes are closed like that?'

Faith doesn't like talking about her guard. But then again, Dr Keller took off her glasses and rubbed her eyes, something Faith never imagined she would do. 'Sometimes,' Faith says in the tiniest voice she can manage.

Dr Keller looks at her carefully, which hardly anyone else ever bothers to do. Usually when Faith talks, her mother just says 'Uh-huh' and 'Really?' but she's actually thinking of a gazillion other things while Faith is trying to tell her something. And Mrs Grenaldi, her teacher, doesn't look anyone in the eye. She stares just over the top of the kids' heads, as if they all have bugs crawling through the parts of their hair.

'Have you had your friend a long time?'

'Which friend?' Faith asks, although she knows she can't fool Dr Keller.

The psychiatrist leans forward. 'Do you have other friends, Faith?'

'Sure. I play with Elsa and Sarah and with Gary, when my mother makes me, but Gary wipes his snot on my clothes when he thinks I'm not looking.'

'I mean other friends like your guard.'

'No.' Faith considers. 'I don't know anyone else like her.'

'Is she here with us now?'

Faith glances around, uncomfortable. 'No.'

'Does your guard talk to you?'

'Yes.'

'Does she ever say scary things to you?'

Faith shakes her head. 'She makes me feel better.'

'Does she touch you?'

'Sometimes.' Faith closes her eyes and jams her thumbs into them. 'She shakes me at night to wake me up. And she hugs me a lot.'

'That sounds nice,' Dr Keller says. 'I bet you like that.'

Embarrassed, Faith nods. 'She says she loves me best.'

'Then she's only *your* friend? Not anyone else's?'

'Oh, no,' Faith says. 'She has other friends. She just doesn't see them so much right now. It's like how I used to go over to Brianna's house all the time, but now she goes to a different school so I don't get to play with her a lot.'

'Does your guard tell you about her other friends?'

Faith repeats several names. 'She played with them a long time ago, not anymore.'

Dr Keller has become very quiet. This is strange; usually she asks Faith questions, questions, questions until Faith is ready to cover her ears. Faith watches the doctor's hands, which are shaking just a little bit, like the way her mother's did when she was taking pills.

'Faith,' Dr Keller says finally, 'does it . . . do you like—' She takes a deep breath and continues. 'Did you ever pray to have a friend like this?'

Faith wrinkles her nose. 'What's praying?'

From the light in her eyes Mariah knows that Dr Keller is on the verge of a breakthrough. Or maybe it has already happened; it is difficult to tell, since Faith is playing so nicely on the other side of the observation window. Dr Keller sits down at her desk and gestures for Mariah to do the same. 'Faith mentioned some names to me today: Herman Joseph, from Steinfeld. Elizabeth, from Schonau. Juliana Falconieri.' Dr Keller glances up.

Mariah shrugs. 'I don't think we know any Hermans. And is Schonau close to here?'

'No, Mrs White,' Dr Keller says softly. 'It's not.'

Mariah laughs nervously. 'Well, maybe she's making those names up. I mean, if she managed to create an imaginary friend . . . ?' She lets her voice trail off, and she feels her palms begin to sweat, although she does not know why she's nervous.

Dr Keller rubs her temples. 'Those are very complicated names for a seven-year-old to spontaneously invent. And they aren't fabricated. They are, or were, people who existed.'

More confused, Mariah nods. 'Maybe it's something they're learning in class. Last year Faith was an expert on the rain forest.'

'Does she attend parochial school?'

'Oh, no. We're not Catholic.' Mariah smiles hesitantly. 'Why?'

Dr Keller sits on the edge of the desk, across from Mariah. 'Before I married and became a psychiatrist, I was Mary Margaret O'Sullivan from Evanston, Illinois. I received communion every Sunday and had a big party for my confirmation and went to parochial school until I was accepted at Yale. In my school, I *did* learn about Herman Joseph. And Elizabeth, and Juliana. They're Catholic saints, Mrs White.'

Mariah is speechless. 'Well,' she says, because she does not know what is expected.

Dr Keller begins pacing. 'I don't think we've been hearing Faith just right. Her *guard* . . . the words . . . they sound alike.'

'What do you mean?'

'Your daughter,' Dr Keller says flatly. 'I think she's seeing God.'

three

The mind is its own place, and in itself
Can make a heaven of hell, a hell of heaven.

—John Milton, *Paradise Lost*

September 20, 1999

AT GREENHAVEN THERE WAS a woman who believed that the Virgin Mary lived in the shell of her ear. 'All the better,' she told us, 'to whisper prophecies.' From time to time she invited the nurses and the doctors and the other patients to look. When it was my turn, I got so close that for the slightest moment I noticed a pulsing in some inner pink membrane. 'Did you see her?' she demanded, and I nodded, not certain which of us this made seem more insane.

Faith has been out of school as much as she's in, and I haven't worked on one of my dollhouses in two weeks. We spend more time at the hospital than in our home. We know now, thanks to an MRI and a CT scan and a battery of blood work, that Faith does not have a brain tumor or a thyroid problem. Dr Keller has asked her colleagues about Faith's behavior, too. 'On the one hand,' she said to me, 'almost all adult psychotic hallucinations have to do with religion, the government, or the devil. On the other hand, Faith is functioning in a totally normal way, with no other psychotic behavior.' She wanted to put Faith on Risperdal, an antipsychotic drug. If the imaginary friend went away, that would be that. And if she didn't, well, I would cross that bridge if and when we came to it.

Faith can't be talking to God; I know this. But in the next breath I wonder, *Why not?* Things have happened before without precedent. And a good mother would stick up for her child, no matter how bizarre the story. But then again, if I start saying that Faith is seeing God, that she isn't crazy—well, everyone will think that *I* am. Again.

To give Faith the Risperdal I have to mash the pill in a mortar and pestle and mix it with chocolate pudding to mask the taste. Dr Keller says that antipsychotics work fast; that unlike with Prozac and Zoloft, we don't have to wait eight weeks to see if it's taken hold. In the meantime, we just have to wait and see.

Faith is sleeping now, curled on her side beneath her Little Mermaid comforter. She looks like any other child. She must know I'm here, because she stretches and rolls over and opens her eyes. They are glazed and distant with the Risperdal. She has always favored Colin in features, but with a start I realize that right now she looks like me.

For a moment I think back to the months I spent at Greenhaven—watching the door close behind me and lock, feeling the prick of the sedative in my arm, and wondering why Colin and an ER psychiatrist and even a judge were speaking for me, when I had so much I wanted to say.

I honestly don't know what would be worse to find out in this case: that Faith is mentally ill or that she isn't.

'Sleep,' Faith parrots. 'S-L-E-E-P.'

'Excellent.' Second grade has brought spelling words our way. '*Keep*.'

'K-E-E-P.'

I place the list on top of the kitchen table. 'You got them all right. Maybe *you* ought to be the teacher.'

'I could be,' she says confidently. 'My guard says everyone has things to teach people.'

Just like that, I freeze. It has been two days since Faith's mentioned her imaginary playmate, and I was beginning to believe the antipsychotic medicine deserved the credit. 'Oh?'

I wonder if I can reach Dr Keller by pager. If she'll discontinue the drug just on the strength of my own observations. 'Your friend is still hanging around?'

Faith's eyes narrow, and I realize that she hasn't been talking about her guard for a very important reason: She knows that it's gotten her into trouble. 'How come you want to know?'

I think about the answer Dr Keller would offer: *Because I want to help you.* And then I think about the answer my mother would give: *Because if she's important to you, I want to get to know her.* But to my surprise, the words that come from my mouth are entirely my own. 'Because I love you.'

It seems to shock Faith as much as it's shocked me. 'Oh . . . okay.'

I reach for her hands. 'Faith, there's something I want to tell you.' Her eyes grow round, expectant. 'A long time ago, before you were born, I was very upset about something. Instead of telling people how I felt, I started acting different. Crazy. I did something that scared a lot of people, and because of it I was sent somewhere I really didn't want to be.'

'You mean, like . . . jail?'

'Kind of. It doesn't matter now. But I wanted you to know that it's okay to be sad. I understand. You don't need to act different to get me to see that you're upset.'

Faith's chin trembles. 'I'm not upset. I'm not acting different.'

'Well, you didn't always have this guard of yours.'

The tears that have been building in her eyes spill over. 'You think I made her up, don't you? Just like Dr Keller and the kids at school and Mrs Grenaldi. You think I'm just doing this to get noticed.' Suddenly she draws in a sharp breath. 'And now I'm going to have to go to that jail place for it?'

'No,' I insist, hugging her close. 'You're not going anywhere. And I'm not saying you made her up, Faith, I'm not. It's just that I was so sad once that my mind made me believe something that wasn't true—that's all I'm saying.'

Faith's face digs into my shoulder as she shakes her head. 'She's real. She *is*.'

I close my eyes, rub my thumb against the bridge of my

nose to ward off the headache. Well, Rome wasn't built in a day. I stand up and gather an empty platter, left over from the afternoon's treat of cookies. I am halfway to the kitchen when Faith tugs on the bottom of my shirt. 'She wants to tell you something.'

'Oh?'

'She knows about Priscilla. And she forgives you.'

The plate I am holding drops to the floor.

When I was eight years old, I wanted a pet so badly that I began to collect small creatures—frogs and box turtles and, once, a red squirrel—and secretly bring them into the house. It was the turtle crawling over the kitchen counter that finally turned the tide. Rather than risk salmonella poisoning, my mother came home one day with a kitten, mine for the promise that I'd leave other creatures outdoors.

I named the kitten Priscilla, because she had been a princess in my favorite library book that week. I slept with her on my pillow, her tail curled over my brow like a beaver hat. I fed her the milk from my cereal bowls. I dressed her in doll clothes and bonnets and cotton socks.

One day I decided I wanted to give her a bath. My mother explained to me that cats hate to get wet and that they'd lick themselves clean rather than go anywhere near water to wash. But then again, she'd said Priscilla wouldn't like being swaddled and walked in a toy baby carriage, and she'd been wrong about that. So on a sunny afternoon when I was playing in the backyard, I filled up a bucket with water and called for the cat. I waited until my mother was out of sight and then dunked Priscilla into the water.

She fought me. She scratched and twisted and still I managed to hold her in the water, convinced I knew best. I scrubbed her fur using a bar of Ivory that I'd stolen from my parents' bathroom. I was very careful to wash all the trouble spots my mother always reminded me about. I was so careful, in fact, that I forgot to let her up to breathe.

I told my mother that Priscilla must have fallen into the bucket, and because I was crying so hard, she believed me. But for years I could feel the bones shifting beneath the slack fur. Sometimes, there is a tiny weight in my palm that I curl my hand around as I sleep.

I never got another cat. And I never told a soul.

'Mariah,' my mother stares at me blankly. 'Why are you telling me *now*?'

I glance toward my mother's guest bedroom, where Faith has gone to play with a tin of buttons. 'Did you know?'

'Did I know what?'

'About Priscilla? That I drowned her?'

My mother rolls her eyes. 'Well, of course not. Not until five minutes ago.'

'Did Daddy?' My mind is doing calculations—Faith was only two when my father died; how much could she remember from back then?

My mother lays a hand on my arm. 'Mariah, are you feeling okay?'

'No, Ma, I'm not. I'm trying to figure out how my daughter knows a secret about me that I never in my life shared with anybody. I'm trying to figure out if I'm having a setback or if Faith's going crazy, or if—' I break off, ashamed at what I am about to admit.

'What?'

I look at my mother and then down the hallway, where the sound of Faith's voice lingers. It is not something I can just say, the way other mothers brag about their child's ability to solve math problems or do the backstroke. It offers up an agenda. It draws a line, and forces the person I am speaking with to toe up. 'Or if Faith's telling the truth,' I whisper.

'Oh, for God's sake!' my mother exclaims, scowling. 'You *are* having a setback.'

'Why? Why is it so hard to accept that Faith might be talking to God?'

'Ask Moses' mother.'

Just then, something strikes me. 'You don't believe her! Your own granddaughter!'

My mother peers down the hall to make sure Faith is still occupied. 'Could you lower your voice?' she hisses. 'I didn't say that I don't believe Faith. I'm just reserving judgment.'

'You believed in *me*. Even when I tried to kill myself, when Colin and a judge and the entire staff at Greenhaven said I had to be committed, you stuck up for me.'

'That was one thing. That was an isolated incident, and I was going against Colin's word.' She throws up her hands. 'People are still being killed in the name of religion, Mariah.'

'So if she was seeing Abraham Lincoln, or Cleopatra, that would make a difference? God's not a four-letter word, Ma.'

'Still,' my mother says. 'It might as well be.'

September 23, 1999

IN THE MAIL that afternoon I get the electric bill, the phone bill, and divorced.

The envelope looks official, stamped with the address of the Grafton County Courthouse and thick with a sheaf of papers. I slit it open with my thumb and get a paper cut. Just like that, in six weeks, my marriage is over. I think of traditions I've heard from other parts of the world—Native Americans leaving a man's shoes outside a tepee; Arabs saying 'I divorce you' three times—and suddenly they don't seem as silly. I try to imagine Colin and his attorney, standing in front of the judge at a meeting I did not even know about. I wonder if I am supposed to keep this paper in my safe-deposit box, nestled beside my marriage license and my passport, but it is hard to imagine so many years fitting into such a tiny space.

Suddenly my heart feels too big for my chest. For years I've done what Colin wanted me to do. I acted like women I'd once watched from a distance: wearing boiled-wool jackets and Lilly Pulitzer prints, inviting his colleagues' children to tea parties, draping garland over the mantel at Christmas. I turned into a shell he could be proud of. I was his *wife*, and if I'm not that any longer, I don't really know what to be.

I try to envision Colin in his college football uniform. I try to see him grasping my hand at our wedding. I try, but I can't succeed—the pictures are too fuzzy or too distant to do the memory justice. Maybe this is how it works with failures of the heart. Maybe you edit your history, so that the stories you tell yourself become legend, so that accidents never happened. But then again, all I will have to do is look at Faith and know that I am only fooling myself.

I toss the mail onto the kitchen table like a gauntlet. The worst thing about endings is knowing that just ahead is the daunting task of starting over.

'God help me,' I say, burying my face in my hands, and I let myself cry.

'Mommy,' Faith yells, racing into the kitchen, 'there's a book about me!' She dances around me as I chop carrots for supper. 'Can we get it? Can we?'

I look down, because I have not seen her this animated in a while. The Risperdal initially made her groggy and slow. It is only in the past day or so that her body seems to have overcome these side effects. 'I don't know. Where did you hear about it?'

'From my guard,' she answers, and I feel that familiar twist of my insides. Faith pulls the stool beneath the dry-erase memo board and with great concentration scrawls *I. I. Swerbeh*. 'That's the guy who wrote it. Please?'

I look at the carrots, splayed like pickup sticks on the butcher block. At the chicken, naked and blushing with paprika, waiting on top of the oven. The library in town is only a ten-minute ride. 'Okay. Go get your library card.'

Faith is so excited that I feel a pang of guilt, since I am planning to use this as proof that her mind is playing tricks. When there is no *I. I. Swerbeh*, maybe she'll believe there is no guard.

Sure enough, there is no record of this author on either the library's computerized card catalog or the dusty old shelved one. 'I don't know, Faith. This doesn't look promising.'

'At school, the librarian says that because our town's little, we sometimes have to borrow books from other libraries at other schools. And we can if we fill out a piece of paper. So maybe we just have to ask the librarian here.'

Humor her, I think. Holding Faith's hand, I approach the children's librarian. 'We're looking for a book by an I. I. Swerbeh.'

'A children's book?'

Faith nods. 'It's about me.'

The librarian smiles. 'Well, I guess you've checked the catalogs. It's not an author I'm familiar with . . .' She stops, tapping her chin. 'How old are you?'

'I'm going to be eight in ten and a half months.'

The librarian squats down to Faith's level. 'How did you find out about this book?'

Faith's eyes dart toward me. 'Someone showed me the name. Wrote it down.'

'Ah.' The librarian takes a piece of paper from her desk. 'I used to teach first grade. It's developmentally normal at that age for children to reverse letters.' She writes the author's name backward. 'There you go. Makes a little more sense.'

Faith squints at the word, sounds it out. 'What's a HEBREWS?'

'I think the book you're looking for is right over here,' the librarian says, plucking a Bible off the reference shelf. She opens up to the Book of Hebrews, Chapter 11, and winks.

'It is!' Faith crows, spotting the letters of her name. 'It is about me!'

I stare at the page. Forty verses, all about what has already been accomplished by faith.

Faith begins to read, limping over the words. '"Now faith is the sub . . . sub . . ."'

'Substance.'

'"The substance of things hoped for,"' she repeats. '"The evidence of things not seen."' As she continues, I close my eyes and try to come up with a valid explanation. Faith might have seen this before, might have noticed her name sandwiched between other unfamiliar words. But we don't even own a Bible.

I have always envied people who believe strongly in religion, people who could face a tragedy by praying and know that it would be all right. As unscientific as it seems, well, it would be nice to lay the responsibilities and pain on someone else's larger shoulders.

If you had asked me a month ago whether or not I believed in God, I would have said yes. If you had asked me whether I'd like my child to grow up with that same belief, I would have said yes. I just wasn't willing to teach it to her.

I *hadn't* taught it to her.

'Tell your God,' I whisper. 'Tell her that I believe.'

As far as I know, before this all happened Faith had asked me only once about God. She was five, and had just learned the Pledge of Allegiance in school. '"Under God,"' she recited to me, and then in the next breath, 'What's God?' I floundered for a moment, trying to find a way to explain without dragging religious differences, or for that matter, Jesus into it.

'Well,' I said, thinking of words that she'd know, 'God is kind of like the biggest angel of all. He's way up in the sky, living in a place called heaven. And His job is to watch over us, and make sure we're all doing okay.'

Faith mulled this over for a moment. 'He's like a big baby-sitter.'

I relaxed. 'Exactly.'

'But you said He,' Faith pointed out. 'All of my baby-sitters are girls.'

As hard as it is to hear Dr Keller saying Faith is having psychotic hallucinations of God, it is harder to consider the alternative. Things like this do not happen to little girls, I tell myself during a sleepless night, until I realize I have no right to make that judgment. Maybe this is a seven-year-old stage, like looking for monsters under the bed or falling for Hanson. The next morning I leave Faith with my mother and drive to Dartmouth College's Baker Library. There I ask a librarian some questions about children's perceptions of God and then walk through the dark maze of bookshelves until I find the book she's recommended. I'm expecting Dr Spock, some treatise on child-rearing, but instead she's directed me to Butler's *Lives of the Saints*.

Just for the heck of it, I crack the old book open, figuring I can have a good laugh before I go about finding Dr Spock. But before I know it I've spent the entire day reading about young Bernadette Soubirous from Lourdes, France, who in 1858 spoke to the Virgin Mary several times. About little

Juliana Falconieri, fourteenth century, who saw Christ and let him give her flower garlands. About other child visionaries at Fatima. About all these children, some as young as Faith, some as nonreligious, who were nonetheless singled out.

I begin to scribble notes on the pad I keep in my pocketbook. Of all the visionaries from the thirteenth, fourteenth, and even nineteenth centuries, the ones who saw a lady described a blue-mantled Virgin Mary. The ones who saw a vision in a white gown, with sandals and long dark hair—the ones who called it God—all were referring to a man.

All but Faith.

'So?' I whisper, when I get back to my mother's. 'How was she?'

'Fine,' my mother booms. 'She's not asleep.'

'What I meant is whether she's been . . . you know. Seeing things.'

'Oh, right. God.'

I push past her and walk into the kitchen, where I pull a banana from its brothers and begin to peel the skin. 'Yes. That.'

My mother shrugs. 'It's a stage. You'll see.'

I take a bite of the fruit, which lodges in my throat. 'What if it's not, Ma?' I ask, swallowing hard. 'What if this doesn't go away?'

My mother smiles gently. 'Dr Keller will find some other medicine that works.'

'No, I don't mean that. I mean . . . what if it's real?'

My mother stops wiping down the counter. 'Mariah, what are you saying?'

'It's happened before. There were other kids who saw . . . things. And Catholic priests and the pope or someone authenticated it.'

'Faith isn't Catholic.'

'Well, I know that. I know we've never been religious. But I'm wondering if that's something you're given a choice about.' I take a deep breath. 'I'm just not sure if you and me and a psychiatrist are the people who ought to be judging this.'

'Who should be?' my mother asks, then rolls her eyes. 'Oh, Mariah. You aren't going to take her to a priest.'

'Why not? They're the ones who have experience with apparitions.'

'They'll want proof. A statue crying tears, or some paraplegic getting up and walking.'

'That's not true. Sometimes they just go on the strength of the child's word.'

My mother smirks. 'And when did you become such an expert on *goyim*?'

'This isn't about religion.'

'No? Then what is it about?'

'My daughter,' I say thickly, as tears come to my eyes. 'There's something different about her, Ma. Something that people are going to start whispering about and pointing at. It's not like she has a birthmark I can hide under a turtleneck and pretend it's not there.'

'What good is it going to do to talk to a priest?'

I don't know. I have no idea what I've been hoping for—some sort of exorcism? Some vindication? Suddenly I can clearly remember standing on the corner of the street at a red light years ago, certain that everyone could see the scars hidden beneath my sleeves. That everyone knew I was subtly, irrevocably different from them. I don't want this for my daughter. 'I just want Faith to be normal again,' I say.

My mother looks at me squarely. 'All right. You do what you have to. But maybe you shouldn't start at a church.' Rummaging through her ancient, crammed Rolodex, she extracts a business card. It's yellowed and dog-eared—either much used or too long forgotten. 'This is the name of the rabbi in town. Whether or not you want to admit it, your daughter's Jewish.'

Rabbi Marvin Weissman. 'I didn't know you went to temple.'

'I don't.' She shrugs. 'It just sort of got passed along to me.'

I pocket the card. 'Fine, I'll call him first. Not that he's going to believe me. In all the books I read today, I didn't find a single Jewish person who had a religious vision.'

My mother rubs her thumbnail on the edge of the counter. 'And what does that tell you?'

Although I've passed the temple in New Canaan many times, I have never gone inside. It is dark, musty. Long, thin collages of stained glass flank the walls at measured intervals, and a Hebrew-school bulletin board is gaily decorated with the names of students. Faith shudders closer to me. 'I don't like it here. It's creepy.'

Privately, I agree, but I squeeze her hand. 'It's not creepy. Look at the pretty windows.'

Faith considers the panels and looks at me again. 'It's still creepy.'

Down a hallway, there are approaching footsteps. A man and a woman stride into the entryway, still arguing. 'Is there anything nice you can say?' the woman shouts. 'Or do you just go out of your way to make me look like an idiot?'

'Do I look like I'm trying to get you upset?' the man thunders. 'Do I?' Oblivious to Faith and me, they yank their jackets from hangers in the coatroom. Faith cannot take her eyes off the couple. 'Don't,' I whisper. 'It's not polite to stare.'

But still she watches them, her eyes wide and sad and oddly trancelike. I wonder if she is remembering Colin and me, if the fights we tried to muffle behind a closed bedroom door still managed to carry. The couple walks out the door, their anger palpably linking them, as if they are holding tight to the hands of their only child.

Suddenly Rabbi Weissman appears, wearing an ombré plaid shirt and jeans. He is no older than I am. 'Mrs White. Faith. I'm sorry about being late. I had a previous appointment.' The angry couple. Were they here for some kind of counseling? Was that what other people did when their marriages were falling apart?

When I continue to say nothing, he smiles quizzically. 'Is there something wrong?'

'No.' I shake my head, well and truly caught. 'It's just that I always expect rabbis to have long, gray beards.'

He pats his smooth-shaven cheeks. 'Ah, you've been watching *Fiddler on the Roof* too much. What you see is what you get.' He slips a hard candy into Faith's hand and winks. 'Why don't we all come into the sanctuary?'

Sanctuary. Yes, please.

The main room of the temple has high beams and a fluted ceiling, pews neatly set like teeth and a *bema* covered with a rectangle of blue velvet. The rabbi pulls a small pack of crayons from the pocket of his shirt and gives them to Faith, along with a few sheets of paper. 'I'm going to show your mom something. Would that be okay?'

Faith nods, already pulling out the colors. The rabbi leads me to the back of the room, where we have a clear view of Faith, and also privacy. 'So your daughter is talking to God.'

Put so bluntly, it makes me blush. 'I think so, yes.'

'And the reason you wanted to see me?'

Shouldn't that be evident? 'Well, I used to be Jewish. I mean, I was raised that way.'

'You've converted, then.'

'No. I just sort of lapsed out of it, and then married an Episcopalian.'

'You're still Jewish,' the rabbi says. 'You can be an agnostic Jew, a nonpracticing Jew, but you're still a Jew. It's like being part of a family. You have to screw up pretty badly to get kicked out.'

'My mother says that Faith's Jewish, too. Technically. That's why I'm here.'

'And Faith's talking to God.' It's just the slightest movement, but I incline my head. 'Mrs White,' the rabbi says. 'Big deal.'

'Big deal?'

'Lots of Jews talk to God. Judaism assumes a direct relationship with Him. The issue isn't whether Faith is talking to God . . . but rather if God is talking to *her*.'

I mention the quote from Genesis that Faith sang like a nursery rhyme, the chapter in the Bible. I tell him of my drowned kitten, the story that no one else ever knew. When I'm finished, Rabbi Weissman asks, 'Has God given your daughter any messages? Any suggestions for rooting out the evil in the world?'

'No, she hasn't.'

The rabbi pauses. '*She?*'

'That's what Faith tells me.'

'I'd like to speak to her,' Rabbi Weissman says.

A half hour after I leave the rabbi sitting with Faith in the sanctuary, he joins me in the entryway of the temple. 'Maimonides,' he says, as if we have been in the middle of a conversation, 'tried to explain the "face" of God. It's not a real face, because that would make God no better, really, than a man. It's a presence, a sense that God is aware. Just as God makes us in His own image, we make Him in our image, too—so it makes sense in our own heads. According to the Midrash, there were several incidents when God was revealed in form. At one, the Red Sea crossing, God appeared as a young warrior and hero. At Sinai God appeared as an elderly judge. Why did God look like a judge at Sinai and not at the Red Sea? Because at the Red Sea the people needed a hero. An old man would not have fit.' He turns to me. 'Of course, this is something you're familiar with.'

'No. I've never heard it before.'

'Really?' Rabbi Weissman scrutinizes me. 'I asked Faith if she could draw a picture of the God she sees.' He hands me a sheet of paper, crayoned on one side. I prepare to be unimpressed—after all, I've seen Faith draw this imaginary friend before. But this picture is different. A woman dressed in white sits on a chair, cradling ten babies in her arms, babies that are black, white, red, and yellow. And although the artwork is crude, this mother's face looks something like my own.

'Are you saying she thinks God looks like me?' I ask finally.

Rabbi Weissman shrugs. 'I'm not saying anything. But other people might.'

Dressed as he is in a slick Italian suit, with his neatly combed hair and his crisp manners, Dr Grady De Vries, expert on childhood schizophrenia, does not look like the kind of man who would spend the better part of three hours down on the floor beside Faith, playing with the bald Barbie. And yet I've been sitting at the observation window watching him do just that. After some time he and Dr Keller come through the adjoining door to the psychiatrist's office. 'Mrs White,' Dr Keller says, 'Dr De Vries would like to speak to you.'

He sits down in a chair across from me. 'You want the good news or the bad news?'

'Good.'

'We're taking Faith off the Risperdal. Your daughter is not psychotic. I've studied psychosis in children for over twenty years. I've published books and papers on it and have been an expert witness at trials and—well, you get the idea. Faith is, in all manners but one, a mentally healthy and reasonably content seven-year-old girl.'

'What's the bad news?'

Dr De Vries rubs at his eyes with a thumb and forefinger. 'That Faith *is* hearing something, and talking to someone. There's too much knowledge there, that's age and situationally inappropriate, to chalk it up to a figment of her imagination. But it's not a physical illness, and it doesn't appear to be a mental one either.' He glances at Dr Keller. 'With your permission, I'll ask Dr Keller to present this case next week at a psychiatric symposium, to see if our colleagues might have some answers.'

Through the observation glass I watch Faith launch a Sky Dancer into the air. When it hits the fluorescent lights, she laughs and tries to do it again. 'I don't know . . . I don't want her to be some kind of spectacle.'

'She won't be present, Mrs White. And the case will be presented anonymously.'

'If you do this, will you figure out what the problem is?'

Dr De Vries and Dr Keller exchange a look. 'We hope so, Mrs White,' he says. 'But it may not be something we can fix.'

four

> There lives more faith in honest doubt,
> Believe me, than in half the creeds.
>
> —Alfred, Lord Tennyson

September 27, 1999

WHEN ALLEN MCMANUS is assigned to cover symposiums, he looks upon it as an extra six hours of sleep. From time to time enough highbrow doctors congregate at the Boston Harbor Hotel to warrant sending out a stringer from *The Boston Globe*. No matter that most of the time Allen McManus writes obituaries—he's the one who gets sent. Obviously his editor-in-chief realizes the connection: Most of these godawful conferences are enough to bore a person to death.

Allen slouches in the rear of the auditorium. He's already written down the name of the symposium, which he figures is enough for the two lines of type it deserves. He's ready to cover his face with his hat and take a nap. But then an attractive woman walks up to the podium. That sparks Allen's curiosity. After all, in spite of his profession, he's not dead yet. Most of the speakers at these symposiums are crusty old turds who remind him alternately of his father and the priest from his childhood in Southie who used to rap his knuckles when he didn't quite measure up as altar boy. He sits up, interested in his surroundings for the first time that day.

The woman is slender and fine-boned, her no-nonsense

hair sluiced behind her ears as she settles her notes on the podium. 'Good morning, I'm Dr Mary Keller.' Allen watches her eyes flicker over her notes, hesitate. 'Ladies and gentlemen,' she says, 'given the unorthodox subject I'm about to present, I'm not going to read my prepared paper. Instead I'd like to tell you about two case studies. The first is a current patient, seven years old, whose mother brought her in for treatment. The subject has developed an imaginary friend, one that she refers to as her God. The second case study occurred over thirty years ago.' Dr Keller tells of a child at parochial school, forced to kneel for long stretches as penitance. She talks of a day when this five-year-old felt something stir beside her, something warm and solid, only to turn and see nothing at all.

'The question I place before you today is this,' Dr Keller says. 'If there is no physical component to a delusion, if there is no diagnostic framework in which to fit the behaviors as a generally accepted mental illness, what are we left with as a diagnosis?'

Allen can feel the doctors in the row before him subtly shifting. *Holy cow,* he thinks, guessing where she's headed. *This woman is committing professional suicide.*

'If physical and mental illness is ruled out, is it within the realm of a psychiatrist to authenticate the behavior? To say that, possibly, the delusion is really a vision?' She slowly runs her eyes over the entire disbelieving audience. 'The reason I am asking you this is that I know for a fact that at least one, if not both of these subjects, is telling the truth. I know this because the child kneeling in the chapel, and feeling . . . something indescribable . . . was *me*. And because thirty years later, in my own office with another child as a subject, I have felt it again.'

Allen McManus tears his eyes away from Dr Keller, slips out the back of the auditorium, and places a call to his editor.

At the departure gate Colin watches Jessica check their tickets for the hundredth time. She looks like any other business traveler, with her tailored suit and laptop case—she looks like Colin himself. To see her, no one would know that at the end of this ten-day sales conference in Las Vegas, she plans to get married in a drive-through church and gamble her way through a weeklong honeymoon.

'Are you excited?' she purrs, leaning into him. 'Because I am.'

'I, uh, need to hit the bathroom.' Colin gives her a smile and walks off, ostensibly toward the men's room. He does not know how he feels about getting married in Las Vegas. Performed by a hack justice of the peace, with an Elvis impersonator serenading them and bargain bouquets available for five dollars a pop, it will be considerably different from his wedding to Mariah.

It had been Jessica's idea. They were headed to Vegas anyway for the conference. 'Besides'—she had laughed, rubbing her abdomen—'imagine the stories we can tell him.'

He wonders now if his marriage to Mariah might have lasted, had he married her at the Light of the Moon chapel in Vegas instead of at St Thomas's in Virginia, with more pomp and circumstance than a royal wedding. If he'd been willing to do—what was it called? the hora!—or break a glass beneath his foot, if he hadn't just assumed that his way was the right way, maybe their differences wouldn't have been so pronounced. As it is, Colin blames himself for what happened to his ex-wife. He asked her to bend to his wishes so much that she actually broke.

Instead of entering the men's room, Colin sits down in a narrow phone cubicle and calls his former home. 'Mariah,' he says when she answers.

There is a moment's pause. 'Colin.' Even though he tries not to, he can hear the thread of delight wrapped around her voice. It makes him uncomfortable; it always has. Who in his right mind wants to be someone else's savior?

Colin presses his forehead against the metal wall of the booth and tries to find the words for what he must say. 'How's Faith's back?' he asks instead.

'Much better. She's wearing shirts now.'

'Good.'

In the silence that follows, Colin suddenly remembers how uncomfortable Mariah once was with spaces in conversation. She'd rush into sentences, chatter about nothing, rather than sit through the delay. Yet here she is, closemouthed, as if she is trying to hold in a secret just as much as he is.

'You're okay?' she finally asks.

'Yeah. Headed to Las Vegas for a conference.'

'Oh,' she says softly, flatly, and he knows what she means with that one word: *How is it your life has gone on?* 'I guess you're calling for Faith, then.'

'Is that . . . would it be okay?'

'You're her father, Colin. Of course it's okay.'

There is a shuffle of static, and before Colin can say anything else to Mariah, Faith is on the line. 'Hi, Daddy.'

'Hey, cupcake.' He wraps the metal snake of the phone line around his arm. 'I wanted to tell you I'm going away for a few weeks.'

'You always go away.'

It strikes Colin that she is right. With the amount of travel he does for his job, his memories of Faith—and presumably hers of him—almost always involve good-byes or reunions. 'But I always miss you.'

'I miss you, too.' Faith sniffs and hands the phone back to Mariah.

'Sorry,' she says. 'She's a little unpredictable these days.'

'Well. It's understandable.'

'Sure.'

'She's just a kid.'

'I know. I'm sure she appreciates that you called.'

Colin marvels at how strange they both sound: Mariah's words had once rifled over him like a waves on the beach, continuous patter about dry-cleaning tickets and school conferences and sales at the grocery store that he never really listened to, never noticed, until they stopped and he saw with surprise that he was buried up to his neck in the sand of this marriage. He wonders how you can go in the blink of an eye from speaking words that are as thoughtlessly dropped as pocket change to this, where even the most benign conversation wrings you dry.

'So . . . was that all?' Mariah hesitates just the slightest moment before asking, 'Or did you want to talk to me?'

There are so many things to discuss: the wedding, how Mariah's faring, how odd it seems to be miles apart and still feel as if there is a high, deep wall he is peering around. 'That was all,' Colin says.

September 29, 1999

IAN PAYS THREE PEOPLE just to read the newspapers from around major cities in the United States and Europe. Every morning at eight o'clock these assistants are expected to report to his office with two dubious mystical events. On a morning two weeks into his Grassroots AntiRevival Campaign, they sit in the tight quarters of the Winnebago. 'All right, now.' Ian turns to David, his youngest employee. 'What did you dig up?'

'Two-headed chicken and a seventy-five-year-old who gave birth.'

'Get out,' scoffs Yvonne. 'The record's that Florida woman.'

The story doesn't particularly move Ian either. 'What have you got that's better?'

'Crop circles in Iowa.'

'I don't want to get mixed up with that. Believing in God and believing in aliens are two completely different ruses. Wanda?'

'There's a bizarre source of a light at the bottom of a Montana well.'

'Sounds like radioactive waste. Anything else?'

'Well, as a matter of fact, yes. In Boston there was some excitement at a psychiatric symposium.'

Ian grins. '*There's* an oxymoron.'

'Yeah, I know. It seems some doctor tossed out the idea that if a delusion can't be disproved, it just might be real.'

'That's my kind of shrink. What delusion, exactly?'

'The psychiatrist has a patient—a girl—who she thinks might be seeing God.'

Ian's body begins to hum. 'Is that so? Who's the kid?'

'I don't know. Psychiatrists don't release names at these symposiums. They're just "the subject."' Wanda fishes in her jeans pocket. 'I did get the psychiatrist's name, though,' she says, handing Ian a piece of paper.

'Miz Mary Margaret Keller,' Ian reads. 'She couldn't disprove a delusion, huh? She's probably had the kid studied by fifty people just like her. What she needs is someone like me.'

When there is a knock on the door, Rabbi Weissman looks up from his books. Groaning, he realizes it's ten o'clock. Time for another counseling session with the Rothmans.

For the briefest of moments he considers pretending that he's not there. There is nothing he dislikes more than sitting while the Rothmans sling insults at each other with such vitriolic force that he fears being caught in the crossfire. He understands the role of the rabbi when it comes to helping members of his congregation, but this? Marital therapy? The rabbi shakes his head. More like target practice.

With a sigh, Rabbi Weissman fixes a smile on his face and opens the office door, momentarily stunned by the sight of Eve and Herb Rothman kissing in the hall.

They break away with a flurry of embarrassed apologies. Rabbi Weissman watches with disbelief as the couple pulls the two armchairs closer together before sitting down. Surely this isn't the same man who last week called his wife a scheming cow bent on milking him of his hard-earned money. Surely this isn't the same woman who last week said that the next time her husband came home smelling like a harem she would slice off his *baytsim* in the middle of the night. 'Well,' he says, raising a questioning brow.

Eve's fingers tighten on her husband's. 'I know,' she says shyly. 'Isn't it wonderful?'

'It's better than wonderful,' Herb enthuses. 'It's not that we don't love you, Rabbi, but Evie and I aren't going to be needing your services anymore.'

Rabbi Weissman smiles. 'That's the kind of rejection I like. What brought this about?'

'It was no one thing,' Eve admits. 'I just started feeling differently.'

'Me, too,' Herb says.

If the rabbi recalls correctly, he had to separate the couple like two prizefighters at the last meeting, to keep them from physically assaulting each other. The Rothmans talk for a few more minutes, then wish the rabbi well and leave the office. Rabbi Weissman stares after them, shaking his head. God has truly intervened. Even He would have laid down odds that the Rothman marriage was too far gone to fix.

It certainly wasn't anything that *he* said—he would have clearly remembered a breakthrough in this case. He would have marked it down on a Post-it, left a note to himself on his calendar. But there's no record from last week in the datebook, nothing at all.

There's just the time of their meeting, and recorded beneath it, at 11:00 A.M., the name of little Faith White.

In the middle of the night Faith wakes up and curls her hands into fists. They hurt enough to make her whimper, just like the time Betsy Corcoran had dared her to hold on to the flagpole on the coldest day of last winter and her skin had nearly frozen right to the metal. She rolls over and stuffs her hands beneath her pillow, where the sheets are still cool.

But that doesn't help either. She fidgets a little bit more, wondering if she ought to get up and pee now that she's awake or just sit here and wait for her hands to stop hurting. She doesn't want to go in to her mother yet. Once she'd gotten up in the middle of the night and her foot had felt like the size of a watermelon and all tingly, but her mother had said it was just pins and needles and to go back to bed. Even though there were no pins and needles on the floor, and when Faith had checked, there were none sticking out of the sole of her foot either.

She rolls over again and sees her guard sitting on the edge of the bed. 'My hands hurt,' she whimpers, and lifts them for inspection.

Her guard leans forward to look. 'It will only hurt for a little while.'

That makes Faith feel better. It's like when she's hot and sick sometimes and her mother gives her the little pills that she knows will make her headache disappear. Faith watches her guard lift her left hand first, and then her right, and put a kiss right in the middle of each palm. Her lips are so warm that Faith jumps at first and pulls her hands back. When she looks down, she can see it: her guard's kiss printed on her skin in a red circle. Thinking it is lipstick, Faith tries to rub at it with her thumb, but it does not come off.

Her guard carefully folds Faith's fingers shut, making a fist. Faith giggles; she likes the idea of holding fast to a kiss. 'See how I love you?' her guard says, and Faith smiles all the way back to sleep.

September 30, 1999

IT WOULD BE NICE if Ian could say that his sixth sense for rooting out deception is what leads him directly to Faith White, but it is not true. Like any other master planner, he knows that the best way to stay informed is to keep a finger in every pot. So after Dr Keller flatly refuses a meeting with him, he sets into motion Plan B.

It takes a half hour to find a supply closet in the local hospital and to locate a pair of clean scrubs. Ten minutes to brief Yvonne with the pertinent information and watch her walk through the sliding glass hospital doors, dressed to blend in.

She comes back fifteen minutes later, her face glowing. 'I walked straight up to the scheduling nurse for MRIs and told her that Dr Keller hadn't received the reports back on a seven-year-old patient. So she goes, "Oh, Faith White?" and she looks it up in her computer and says they were sent out a week ago. Faith White,' she repeats. 'Just like that.'

But Ian has moved on. He's already running his finger down the long line of Whites in the phone book. Pulling his cell phone from his pocket, he calls the first name on the list. 'Hello. I'm looking for Faith White's mother? Oh. My apologies.'

He does it twice more, with no success, and then reaches

an answering machine: 'You have reached Colin, Mariah, and Faith. Please leave a message.'

Ian circles the address and looks up at his employees. 'Bingo.'

New Canaan is not an easy town to get around. With the exception of Main Street, which turns into the sturdier and more serviceable Route 4 on both ends, there is not much that stands out. The school, the police station, the hairdresser, the professional building, and the Donut King are the sentries that let you know you're passing through New Canaan. But unless you know your way through the narrow lanes that run between cornfields or up winding paths that cut over Bear Mountain, you do not realize that you're missing the farmhouses and old Capes where the residents of New Canaan actually live.

The members of the Order of the Great Passion mill in and around the Donut King. Tired and irritable from their cross-country trek from Sedona, they seem more driven to find the nearest restroom than a new Messiah—the original goal that brought them to New Canaan. Brother Heywood, their leader, walks across Main Street, looking over the stretch of land that belongs to a registered Holstein farm. New Canaan, he thinks. The land of milk and honey. But truth be told, he has no idea if he's led his flock to the right place. The Messiah might just as well be in New England, New York, New Brunswick. From his pocket he withdraws a set of runes and casts them into the dirt at his feet. He is rubbing one of the carved stones against his thumb when he is nearly suffocated by a blast of grit and dirt.

The Winnebago that comes flying too fast around the corner sends Brother Heywood stumbling back. He gets to his feet and shades his eyes, trying to get the license-plate number—not that he plans to report it, having subscribed to a noninterventionist philosophy some years ago, but old habits die hard. However, his eye is drawn from the blue license plate to the brightly painted fireball emblazoned on the recreational vehicle's rear door.

Brother Heywood stuffs his runes back into his caftan

and from a second pocket quickly extracts a pair of folding binoculars.

IAN FLETCHER, he reads. THE SEARCH FOR TRUTH.

Well, you'd have to be living under a rock to not know the name Ian Fletcher. His face is on a billboard right on the outskirts of Sedona, and his show is syndicated to kingdom come. In a way Heywood's fancied himself like the tele-atheist—willing to buck the system and face public ridicule all in the name of religion. Except that Brother Heywood's expectations for the final outcome are considerably different from Ian Fletcher's.

Still, he knows what Fletcher does for a living, and he's heard about the antievangelical cross-country tour. There's only one reason he can think of that would make Ian Fletcher come to New Canaan, New Hampshire—and it means that the Order hasn't been on a joyride after all. Making sure no one is watching, Brother Heywood lifts the binoculars and mentally maps out the path to a distant white farmhouse, the place where the Winnebago finally comes to a stop.

On Thursday Mariah spends the morning watching the video *Agnes of God*, and so gets a late start food shopping. When she pulls up to the elementary school, ready to pick Faith up for the day, the trunk is full of groceries. The bell rings, and Mariah takes up her usual position, beside a large maple tree at the edge of the first-grade classroom pod, but Faith does not appear. She waits until the last of the children have dribbled out of the school, then walks into the office.

Faith is huddled on the overstuffed purple couch beside the secretary's desk, crying, her leggings torn at the knees and her hair straggling out of its braid and sticking against her damp cheeks. She's stretched out her sleeves and hidden her fists inside them. She wipes her nose on the fabric. 'Mommy, can I not go to school anymore?'

Mariah feels her heart contract. 'You love school,' she says, dropping to her knees, as much to comfort Faith as to block the curious gaze of the school secretary. 'What happened?'

'They make fun of me. They say I'm crazy.'

Crazy. Filled with a righteous fury, Mariah slips an arm around her daughter. 'Why would they say that?'

Faith hunches her shoulders. 'Because they heard me talk to . . . her.'

Mariah closes her eyes and makes a silent appeal—to whom?—to solve this, and fast. She pulls Faith upright and holds her mittened hand, tugging her out of the main office. 'You know what? Maybe you can stay home from school, just for tomorrow. We can do things, you and me, all day.'

Faith turns her face up to her mother's. 'For real?'

Mariah nods. 'I used to take special holidays sometimes with Grandma.' Her jaw tightens as she remembers what her mother had called it: a mental-health day.

They drive through the winding roads of New Canaan, Faith slowly beginning, in bits and pieces, to relay the school day to Mariah. At the turn to their driveway, Mariah rolls down the window and picks up the mail, marking the number of parked cars lining the road. Hikers, or birdwatchers, taking to the field across the road. They get that up here quite often. She continues to drive, and then she sees the crowd that surrounds the house.

There are vans and cars, and for God's sake, a big painted Winnebago.

'Wow,' Faith breathes. 'What's going on?'

'I don't know,' Mariah says tightly. She turns off the ignition and steps from the car into a throng of nearly twenty people. Immediately cameras begin flashing, and questions are hurled at her like javelins. 'Is your daughter in the car?' 'Is God with her?' 'Do you see God, too?'

When Faith's door cracks open, the questions stop. Mariah watches her daughter get out of the car and stand nervously on the slate path that leads up to the house. Lining it are a dozen men and women in caftans, who bow their heads as Faith looks at them. Standing behind, and slightly apart, is a man smoking a thin cigar. The face seems familiar to Mariah. With a start she realizes that she's seen him on TV—Ian Fletcher himself is leaning against her crabapple tree.

Suddenly Mariah knows exactly what is going on. Somehow, some way, people are beginning to hear about Faith.

Feeling sick, she wraps an arm around her daughter's shoulders and steers her up the porch. She pulls Faith into the house with her and locks the door.

'How come they're here?' Faith peeks out the sidelight and is yanked away by her mother before she can be seen.

Mariah rubs her temples. 'Go to your room. Do your homework.'

'I don't have any.'

'Then find some!' Mariah snaps. She walks into the kitchen and picks up the phone, tears already thickening her throat. She needs to call the police, but she dials a different number first. When her mother answers on the second ring, Mariah lets the first sob out. 'Please come,' she says, and she hangs up.

She sits at the kitchen counter, her palms spread on the cool Formica. She counts to ten. She thinks of the milk and the peaches and the broccoli sitting in the trunk of her car, already beginning to rot.

Ian Fletcher is very good at doing his job. He is ruthless, he is driven, he is single-minded. So he fixes his eyes on the little girl, this next subject of his, and watches her get out of the car.

But his attention wanders to the woman beside Faith White. The look of fear on her face, her unconscious grace, the instinctive slip of her arm over her daughter—all draw Ian's eye. She is small and fine-boned, with hair the color of old gold. It is pulled back from her face, which is pale and free of makeup and quite possibly the most naturally lovely thing Ian has seen since climbing the falls in South America. She's not classically beautiful, not perfect, but somehow that only makes her more interesting. Ian shakes his head to clear it. He carouses with models and movie stars—he should not be swayed by a woman with the face of an angel.

An *angel?* The very thought is traitorous, ludicrous. It's the goddamned Winnebago, he decides. Spending the night on a foam cot, instead of a deluxe hotel mattress, is aggravating his insomnia to the point where he can't think straight, to the point where anyone with a pair of X chromosomes becomes attractive.

Ian focuses on Faith White, walking beneath her mother's arm. But then he makes the mistake of glancing up—and meets the gaze of Mariah White. Cool, green, angry. *Let the battle begin*, Ian thinks, unwilling and unable to look away until she firmly shuts the door.

'Name one thing—other than the existence of God—that we take on blind faith,' Ian challenges, his voice rising like a call to arms over the small group of people gathered to listen. News of Ian's presence has by now attracted a number of onlookers, in addition to several members of the press. 'There's nothing! Not a single thing. Not even the sun rising every day. I know it's going to be there, but that's something I can prove scientifically.'

He leans against the railing of a wooden platform hastily erected beside the Winnebago for media moments like these. 'Can I prove God is there? No.'

He watches people from the corner of his eye, whispering to each other, maybe even second-guessing what made them come to see this miraculous Faith White in the first place. 'You know what faith is, what religion is?' He looks pointedly at the scarlet-suited members of the Order of the Great Passion, gathered close with scowls on their faces. 'It's a *cult*. Who gives us religion? Our parents brainwash us when we're four or five and most receptive to fantastical ideas. We're told we have to believe in God, so we do.'

Ian raises a hand in the direction of the White farmhouse. 'And now the word of a little girl who—I might add—is just at the right age to believe in fairies and goblins and the Easter Bunny as well—is enough to convince you?' He levels the crowd with a calculated gaze. 'I ask all y'all again: What else do we believe in with blind faith?'

At the profound silence, Ian grins. 'Well, let me help you out. The last thing you believed in with absolute, unshakable conviction was . . . Santa Claus.' He raises his brows. 'No matter how impossible it seemed, no matter how much evidence to the contrary, when you were a child you wanted to believe, and so you did. And as rude as the comparison sounds, it's not all that different from believing in the existence of God. They both grant a boon based on whether you've been naughty or nice. They both go about their work without being seen. They rely heavily on the assistance of mythical creatures—elves in one case, angels in the other.'

Ian lets his eyes touch on one of the cult members, one local reporter, one mother clutching an infant. 'So how come y'all don't believe in Santa nowadays? Well, because you grew up, and you realized how impossible the whole thing was. Santa Claus went from being a fact to being a real good story, one to pass on to your children. The same way your parents told you about God when you were a kid.' He hesitates for a moment, letting the silence thicken. 'Can't you see that God's a myth, too?'

Millie Epstein slams her car door violently. Mariah's beautiful old farmhouse is flocked by lunatics, from what she can see. At least twenty people are milling around on the long driveway, some even bold enough to trample the grass edging the front porch. These include a handful wearing bizarre red nightgowns, a few curious locals, and two vans with television call letters spangled across their sides, complete with reporters. Millie shoves them all out of her way until she reaches the porch, where she finds the chief of police. 'Thomas,' she says. 'What kind of circus is this?'

The police chief shrugs. 'Just got here myself, Mrs Epstein. From what I can tell, based on the reporters over there, there's one group saying that your granddaughter is Jesus or something. Then there's another guy who's saying that not only is Faith not Jesus, but that Jesus doesn't exist.'

'Can't we get them off Mariah's lawn?'

'I was just about to do that myself,' he admits. 'Course, I can only keep 'em as far back as the road. It's a public venue.'

Millie surveys the group. 'Can we talk to Faith?' a reporter shouts. 'Bring her out!'

'Yeah!'

'Bring out the mother, too!'

The voices crescendo, and, horrified, all Millie can do is

listen. Then she crosses her arms over her chest and stares out at the crowd. 'This is private property; you don't belong here. And you're talking about a child. A *child*. Would you really take the word of a seven-year-old?'

From the front of the crowd comes the sound of someone clapping, slowly, deliberately. 'My congratulations, ma'am,' Ian Fletcher drawls. 'A rational statement, right in the middle of a maelstrom. Imagine that.'

He comes into Millie's line of vision, continuing to walk forward until she can see that it is Ian Fletcher, the one from the TV show, and that as handsome as he is and as mellifluous his voice, she knows that she's made a horrible error in judgment ever to have found him attractive. Millie's tossed the crowd a crumb of doubt, just so that they'll have something to feed on other than her granddaughter. But this man . . . this man scatters doubt in order to have them all eating out of the palm of his hand.

'I suggest you leave,' Millie says tightly. 'My granddaughter is of no interest to you.'

Ian Fletcher flashes a smile. 'Is that a fact? So you don't believe your own granddaughter? I guess you know that a child who says she's talking to God is just that . . . a child who says she's talking to God. No bells, no whistles, not even any miracles. Just a group of fawning cult members who are already three shades shy of reputability. But that's certainly not enough to create a frenzy over, is it now?'

His words are honeyed; they run over Millie and root her to the porch. 'Ma'am, you're a woman after my own heart.'

Millie narrows her eyes and opens her mouth and then, clutching her chest, falls to the ground at Ian's feet.

Mariah throws open the front door and kneels over her mother. 'Ma!' she cries, shaking Millie's slack shoulders. 'Call an ambulance!'

There are a few scattered camera flashes. Ignoring them, Mariah bends over Millie, leaning her ear close to her mother's mouth. But she feels no breath, no telltale stir of her hair. It's her heart, it's her heart, she knows it. She squeezes her mother's hand, certain that if she lets go just the tiniest bit, she will lose her.

Moments later the ambulance roars up the driveway, spraying gravel, getting as close as it can given the mélange of vans and news trucks and the Winnebago. The paramedics race up the porch stairs. One gently pulls Mariah out of the way and the other begins to do CPR.

'Oh, God,' Mariah whispers, her voice tiny. 'Oh, God. God. Oh, my God.'

Oh, guard. Guard. Oh, my guard. From the hiding spot where she has been huddled since sneaking out of the house, Faith's head swings up. And her summons sounds so much like her mother's that for the first time she realizes what she's been saying all along.

Ian watches Mariah White tearfully argue with the paramedics, who refuse to let Faith ride along in the ambulance. The chief of police intercedes, promising to bring her daughter down to the hospital as soon as backup arrives to get everyone off her property. With his hands in his pockets, he watches the ambulance roar out of the driveway.

'Nice work.'

Ian startles at the voice and finds his executive producer holding out a set of car keys. 'Here you go. You'll get network coverage tonight for sure.'

For badgering an old woman into cardiac arrest. 'Well, now,' Ian says. 'Can't ask for much more'n that.'

'So what are you waiting for?'

Ian clutches the keys. 'Right,' he says, falling quickly into James's expectations and looking around for the producer's BMW. He doesn't even bother calling for a cameraman, knowing they'll never be allowed to set foot in the hospital. 'Don't go drag-racing my Winnebago,' he shouts, then speeds off.

In the ER waiting room he watches the fuzzy-reception TV, tuned to kiddie cartoons. There is no sign of Mariah White. Faith arrives ten minutes later in the company of a young policeman. They sit a few rows away, and every now and then she turns in her seat to stare at Ian.

It's downright disconcerting. Ian hasn't got much of a conscience, so his work rarely puts him in a contemplative state of mind. After all, the people he usually upsets the most are the goddamned Southern Baptists, of which he was once one and who, in Ian's mind, are so busy swallowing their daily doses of Jesus that they need to come up choking on their self-righteousness from time to time. Once a woman fainted clear away in the middle of his Central Park speeches, but that isn't at all the same thing. Faith White's grandma—Ian doesn't even know her name—well, what happened happened partly because of something he'd said, something he'd done.

It's a story, he tells himself. *She's no one you know, and it's your story*.

The policeman's beeper goes off. He checks it, then turns to Faith and asks her to stay put. On his way to a bank of phones, the cop stops at the triage nurse's desk and speaks quietly, no doubt asking the woman to watch the kid for a minute.

When Faith turns to stare at him again, Ian closes his eyes. Then he hears her small, thin voice. 'Mister?'

She is suddenly sitting beside him. 'Hello,' he says, after a moment.

'Is my grandma dead?'

'I don't know,' Ian admits. She doesn't respond, and—curious—he glances down at her. Faith huddles against the armrest of the chair, brooding. He doesn't see someone touched by God. He sees a scared little girl.

'So,' he says, uncomfortably trying to ease her mind. 'I bet you like the Spice Girls. I *met* the Spice Girls,' he confides.

Faith blinks at him. 'Are you the reason that my grandma fell down?'

Ian feels his stomach clench. 'I think I am, Faith. And I'm very sorry.'

She turns away. 'I don't like you.'

'You're in good company.' He waits for her to move, or for the policeman to claim her, but before this can happen, Mariah White walks out of the ER, red-eyed and searching. Her eyes find Faith, and the girl jumps out of her seat and into her mother's embrace. Mariah stares coldly at Ian. 'The policeman . . . he was . . .' Ian stumbles over the words, gesturing down the hall.

'You get away from my daughter,' she says stiffly. With her arm around Faith, she disappears back through the swinging doors of the ER.

Ian watches them go and then approaches the triage nurse. 'I assume Mrs White's mother didn't make it.'

The nurse doesn't glance up from her paperwork. 'You assume right.'

The thing about tragedy is that it hits suddenly, with all the power and fury of a hurricane. Mariah holds Faith's hand tightly as they stand beside her own mother's body. The ER cubicle is empty of medical personnel now, and a kind nurse has removed the tubes and needles in Millie's body for the family's private good-bye. It is Mariah's decision to let Faith in. She doesn't want to do it, but she knows it is the only way Faith will believe her when she says that her grandmother is gone.

'Do you know,' Mariah says, her voice thick, 'what it means if Grandma's dead?'

Before Faith can answer, Mariah begins to cry. She sits down on a chair beside Millie's body, her face in her hands. At first she does not pay attention to the screeching sound on the other side of the gurney. By the time she looks up, Faith has managed to drag the other folding chair over. She stands on the seat, her cheek pressed to Millie's chest, her arms awkwardly wrapped around her grandmother's body.

For a moment Mariah feels the hair on the back of her neck stand up, and she touches her palm to it. But her gaze never wavers from Faith—not when Faith lifts herself up on her elbows, not when Faith places her hands on either side of Millie's face and kisses her full on the mouth, not when Millie's arms rise stiff and slow and cling to her granddaughter for dear life.

five

A simple child
That lightly draws its breath,
And feels its life in every limb,
What should it know of death?

—William Wordsworth

September 30, 1999

FOR MANY HOURS after my mother comes back to life, I cannot stop shaking. I sit in the ER while the same doctor who signed her death certificate now gives her a battery of exams and guardedly pronounces her healthy. I tuck my hands beneath my thighs and pretend that it is perfectly normal for a woman who's been pronounced DOA to now walk around the halls of the hospital.

The doctor wants to keep my mother overnight for observation. 'No way,' she insists. 'I'm running, I'm jumping, I'm not even breaking a sweat. I should always be this healthy.'

'Ma, it's probably not such a bad idea. You were in cardiac arrest.'

'You were *dead,*' the physician stresses. 'There were guys in med school who had stories of corpses sitting up in the morgue just as the body bag was being zipped. I always wanted to have a story like that myself.' As my mother and I exchange a look, he clears his throat. 'At any rate, we'll want to do a cardiogram, a CT scan, some other tests, and check your heart medication.'

My mother snorts. 'Make sure I'm not a vegetable, you mean.'

'Make sure you don't have a relapse,' the doctor corrects. 'Let me get a nurse to wheel you up to a patient floor.'

'Thank you very much, I can walk,' my mother says, hopping off the table.

The doctor starts to leave the cubicle, still shaking his head. I hurry across and touch his sleeve, motioning just outside the curtains. 'Is she really all right? Is this some glitch in her nervous system, you know, and an hour from now she'll be comatose?'

The doctor looks at me thoughtfully. 'I can't say,' he admits. 'I've seen flat-line patients in the OR sputter and come around. I've seen people in comas for months wake up and start talking like nothing's happened. I will tell you that your mother was clinically dead, Mrs White. The paramedics said so in their report—hell, I said so in my *own* report. Is this a temporary recovery? I don't know. I've never seen anything like it before.'

'I see,' I say, although I don't.

'Her heart shows virtually no sign of trauma. Of course, we'll want to do further studies, but right now it seems as strong as a teenager's.' He pats my forearm. 'I can't explain it, Mrs White, so I won't even try.'

'Will you just stop already?' My mother shrugs off my supportive arm. 'I'm fine.'

She strides out of the ER, pushing ahead of me and Faith. The triage nurse crosses herself. The paramedic who drove the ambulance, gossiping now with the desk nurse over a danish, drops his Styrofoam cup of coffee onto the floor.

'Excuse me,' my mother says, stopping an intern. 'Which way to the elevators?' The woman points, and my mother looks back at me. 'Well? Are you just going to stand there?'

She marches down the hall, right past Ian Fletcher, who is staring at us with such disbelief that, for the first time in hours, I laugh.

• • •

While the phlebotomists poke and prod my mother, Faith and I sit in the waiting room on the patient floor. She looks pale and tired; purple smudges the size of thumbprints are just beneath her eyes. I don't realize that I've spoken my question aloud until Faith's small face lifts. 'I did what you wished for,' she whispers.

I swallow hard. 'You had nothing to do with Grandma getting better. You understand?'

'You asked her,' Faith murmurs. 'I heard you.'

'I asked *who*?'

'God. You said, "Oh, God. God. Oh, my God."' Faith rubs her nose on the shoulder of her shirt. 'And she heard you. She told me what to do to make you feel better.'

I bow my head and stare at my daughter's sneakers. One is untied, the laces straggling on the linoleum like any other kid's. But my child has been talking to God. My child has apparently just performed a miracle.

I fight the urge to burst into tears. This whole thing has been a prolonged nightmare, and before I know it Colin will shake me and tell me to roll over and go back to sleep. Children are supposed to go to school, play on swing sets, skin their knees. This is the stuff of TV movies, of novels. Not of everyday, ordinary life.

My thumbs absently rub a callus on the inside of Faith's palm. 'What's this?'

Faith hides her hands in her lap. 'From the monkey bars.'

'Not from . . .' How do I say this? 'Not from touching Grandma? It didn't . . . hurt you?'

Faith shakes her head. 'It felt like being on the hill of the roller coaster, going down.' She stares at me, confused. 'Mommy, didn't you want Grandma to be okay?'

I fold her into my arms, wishing I could take her inside me again and protect her from what is certain, now, to come. 'Oh, Faith. Of course I did. *Do*. It just scares me a little that you might have been the one to make it happen.' I stroke her hair, her shoulders.

'It scares me a little, too,' Faith whispers.

• • •

Woman Dies, Comes Back to Life

---

1 October, 1999; New Canaan, NH—Yesterday, at approximately 3:34 P.M., Mildred Epstein passed away. At 4:45 P.M., she sat up and asked what she was doing in the hospital.

Epstein, 56, was visiting her daughter's home in New Canaan when, witnesses say, she clutched her chest and fell to the ground. EMTs on the scene performed CPR for over 20 minutes, but never managed to revive her. She was pronounced dead on arrival at Connecticut Valley Medical Center by Peter Weaver, M.D. 'I've never seen anything like it,' Weaver told reporters last night. 'In spite of the corroborative stories of many witnesses and trained emergency medical personnel, tests prove that Mrs Epstein's heart shows no indication of trauma, much less of having stopped for over an hour.'

Sources indicate that Epstein went into cardiac arrest after verbally sparring with Ian Fletcher, the teleatheist known for denying the existence of God. He was preparing a piece on Epstein's granddaughter, concerning the controversial claim that the child has been communicating with God. Neither Ms Epstein nor Mr Fletcher could be reached for comment.

'You know, this doesn't count,' Ian says, stretching back in his chair. 'When I said fresh seafood, I wasn't talking about tuna casserole.'

'It was this or Donut King.' James grins. 'Crullers or Chicken of the Sea.'

Ian shudders. 'Do you know how much I'd pay for a good cut of Angus beef right now?'

'You could probably pilfer a whole cow from the dairy outfit across the road. There's so damn many I bet no one's been keeping count.' James pats his mouth with a napkin. 'At least you're in a restaurant.'

'That's like saying traveling in a Winnebago is similar to going on safari.'

'No—it's like going on a grassroots revival. Or so you told me several weeks ago.' The producer leans forward. 'C'mon, Ian, you're just picking up steam. The *NBC Nightly News* aired your segment with the grandmother buying the farm, and ran it hourly on the late-night editions.' James lifts his coffee cup. 'I have a good feeling about this one. The kid's the hook—people don't expect her to be making it all up. Which is only going to make it more spectacular when you draw back the curtain.'

Ian smiles faintly. 'Worth suffering accommodations in steerage, at the very least.'

'Look at it this way: if this story puts you back in the game, you'll never have to look at an RV as long as you live.' James reaches for the check, laughs, and pulls out his credit card. 'I actually used to like camping, as a kid. Didn't you ever do that?'

Ian doesn't respond. James's childhood was probably a bit different from his own recollections. 'Oh, that's right. You were never a kid.'

'Nope.' Ian smiles. 'I sprang fully formed from the brow of my executive producer.'

'Really, Ian. I mean, we've known each other—what?—seven years? And all I know about you before you started in radio is that you got a Ph.D. at that inferior school in Boston.'

'That inferior school in Boston had the superior judgment to leave *you* to the likes of Yale,' Ian says. Feeling the prick of unease, he pretends to yawn. 'I'm beat, James. Better head back to the old homestead.'

James cocks a brow. 'You? Sleepy? Like hell.'

For a moment Ian tenses. How could James know about his insomnia? How could he know that the last time Ian remembers getting more than a few hours of rest was several years ago? Has James seen him leave the Winnebago in the night to walk the woods or the plains or the prairie of whatever particular hell he's stuck in?

'You're just feeling cornered,' James deduces, 'and trying to change the topic.' Ian relaxes, safe in his privacy. 'I'm serious, Ian. I'm asking as a friend. What were your parents like? How'd you grow up?'

Overnight, Ian thinks, but he does not say so. He pushes back from the table. 'I've got a powerful hunger for a cruller just now,' he answers, slipping his façade into place with a grin. 'Care to join me?'

October 3, 1999

FORTUNATELY, THE POLICE have forced Ian Fletcher and the members of that weird cult and the fifty or so other gawkers who've turned up all the way off our property. Unfortunately, that doesn't get them far enough away. The road—a public venue—is only a half acre away from the house, so we can see them from the windows. And that means they can see us, too.

I haven't let Faith play outside, although she is restless and whining. They clamor for *me* when I step out for the briefest moment; what would they do to *her*? I even wait until after midnight to sneak outside with the trash, trying to set it out for collection without being barraged by reporters. I steal past the swing set and under the fringe of oak trees.

'Penny for your thoughts.'

I jump up. Behind the glowing tip of match is Ian Fletcher. He lights the cigar and clamps it between his teeth, inhaling.

'I could have you arrested,' I say. 'You're trespassing.'

'I know. But I don't think you will.'

'You're wrong.' I immediately head toward the house, ready to call the police.

'Don't,' he says quietly. 'I saw you moving around inside, getting ready to come on out here, and I just wanted to ask after your mother.' He gestures toward the collection of cars at the edge of the road. 'Without everyone listening.'

'What about her?'

'Is she all right?'

Without taking my eyes off him, I nod. 'No thanks to you.'

Is it my imagination, or does Ian Fletcher actually blush? 'Yeah, I'm sorry. I shouldn't have . . .' He hesitates, then shakes his head.

'Shouldn't have *what*?'

His eyes are bright and burning; they hold me. 'I just shouldn't have. That's all.'

'An apology from Ian Fletcher? I ought to get this on tape.' But the next moment he is gone, and the only sign he's been there at all are the red embers of his cigar at my feet.

October 4, 1999

THE NEXT DAY I go to the hospital, where Dr Weaver plans to test my mother's heart again. To my shock, I find her waiting in the lounge on the patient floor with Ian Fletcher. 'Mariah,' she says, as if we are all getting together for tea. 'This is Mr Fletcher.'

I grip Faith's hand so tightly she yelps. 'We've met. Would you excuse us for a moment?' I pull my mother aside, Faith in tow. 'Do you want to tell me why he's here?'

'Calm down, Mariah. I swear, you're headed for a heart attack yourself. I invited Mr Fletcher—' she pauses, smiles at him and nods, '—so that he can get his story and then get the heck out of our lives. Let him film whatever he wants; I've got nothing to hide.'

I pinch the bridge of my nose. 'What makes you think he's not going to label you as some kind of zombie or vampire and stick around anyway?'

'Because I know.'

'Oh, great. Well, that clears it all up for me.' I tighten my hold on my daughter. 'Faith doesn't want him here either.'

'She's reacting to your vibes, sweetheart.'

'I don't have vibes. There are no such thing as vibes.'

'There's no such thing as God either, right?' My mother smiles innocently.

'All right,' I say. 'This is your dog-and-pony show. If you want Ian Fletcher here, it's your business. But he's not speaking to me or to Faith, and I'm not setting one foot in that examination room unless you make that clear to him.'

Ian Fletcher huddles with his camera crew and executive producer in the corner of the examination room. He promises to limit his investigation to my mother and smugly produces her signed consent form, as well as one from the hospital to film, when I challenge him on it. He orders gurneys moved and lighting arranged and scowls when I move Faith away from the scope of the camera. Me, I stand beside a hospital administrator there to oversee the filming, and we both play watchdog. When Fletcher motions his cameraman to lean in over the doctor's shoulder for a close-up of the medical chart, I interrupt. 'That's confidential.'

'As is this entire procedure, Miz White. Your mama did put her signature on a contract that said we could film with a handheld unit to our satisfaction.'

'I don't care about your satisfaction.'

Ian Fletcher looks at me and smiles slowly. 'Pity,' he says.

I walk away, wondering what had happened to the man who was so solicitous the night before. Is this his television persona, as opposed to his private one?

With my arms crossed, I watch as Ian Fletcher's cameraman zooms in on my mother's cardiogram and stress test. 'Mrs Epstein,' Dr Weaver says finally, 'you have the constitution of an eighteen-year-old. You may even outlive me.' He turns to Ian, clearly tickled by these fifteen minutes of fame. 'You know, I'm a man of science, Mr Fletcher. But there's no scientific explanation, short of a cardiac transplant, to explain the dramatic change between Mrs Epstein's routine blood-pressure checks and stress-test results during her physical a month ago versus today. Not to mention, of course, the phenomenon of . . . resuscitation.'

A slow gratification spreads through me, partly because my mother's health has been validated, partly because it feels good to beat Ian Fletcher. I glance at him in triumph, just in time to see him whisper to the cameraman, who turns his body so that the video camera is no longer focused on my mother but behind her—on Faith.

She's sitting in the corner, coloring on a prescription pad. 'No,' I whisper, and then I spring into action. 'She is not your subject!' I shout, moving between the cameraman and my daughter, filling up his field of vision so that he stumbles back. 'You give me that tape! You give it to me right now!'

I reach for the camera, but the man holds it over his

head. 'Jesus, Mr Fletcher,' he says, appealing for help. 'Get her off me!'

Ian Fletcher steps forward, palms raised. 'Miz White,' he soothes, 'take it easy now.'

I round on him. 'Don't you tell me what to do.' From the corner of my eye, I see the cameraman still recording. 'Make him shut the damn thing off!'

Ian nods slightly, and the cameraman lowers the camera. The tension drains from my body, leaving me rubbery. I move away from Faith, shaking, and look up to find my mother, Ian Fletcher, the hospital administrator, and the doctor all staring at me, speechless. 'No,' I manage, then clear my throat. 'I said *no*.'

After Fletcher leaves, a nurse takes Faith to get a sticker, leaving me alone with my mother as she dresses. 'It's my fault,' she says. 'I thought if I invited Fletcher, we would get rid of him faster.'

'No such luck,' I murmur.

We wait quietly for Faith to return, thoughts running our own circles of guilt. 'Mariah, you know what they say about dying?'

I look at her. 'What?'

'About the bright light and all. The tunnel.' She picks at a cuticle on her thumb, suddenly unable to look at me. 'It's not like that.'

I swallow, my mouth dry as a desert. 'No?'

'I didn't see a light. I didn't see angels. I saw my mother.' She turns to me, her eyes bright. 'Oh, Mariah. Do you know how long it's been? Twenty-seven years since I've seen her. It was a gift, you know, to be able to look at all the things that I've already forgotten—the way her nails were bitten down and the color of the roots that had grown out past the hair dye . . . even the lines on her face. She smiled at me and told me that I couldn't come yet.'

My mother unexpectedly laces her fingers through mine. The older we've grown, the less we've touched. As a child I'd crawled into her lap; as a teenager I shied from her hand when it tried to straighten my collar or fix my hair; as an adult I found even a quick good-bye embrace too maudlin, too full of things we did not yet want to say. 'I always wondered why God was supposed to be a father,' she whispers. 'Fathers always want you to measure up to something. Mothers are the ones who love you unconditionally, don't you think?'

Faith returns with four stickers covering her shirt. It is decided that she'll wait with my mother in the hospital lobby while I move the car from the faraway lot to short-term parking.

I am at the edge of the lot when I hear footsteps. 'I'm always telling you I'm sorry,' Ian Fletcher says, falling in beside me.

'That's because you're always doing reprehensible things,' I answer. 'I want that tape.'

'You know I can't give it to you. But you have my word that I won't use any shots that include Faith.'

'Your *word*,' I snort. 'Like you gave me your word you wouldn't film her in the first place.'

'Look, I shouldn't have filmed her without your permission. I already said that.'

I start walking.

'Hey. Hey!' He grabs my arm as I start to leave. 'Can you just hang on a second?' Releasing me quickly, as if he's been burned, he stuffs his hands into the pockets of his jeans. 'I want to tell you something. I don't believe your claims about your daughter—alleged resurrection included—and I'm still going to prove you wrong. But I respect what you did in there.' He clears his throat. 'You're a good mother.'

My jaw drops. I realize that lately I've been so busy flying by the seat of my pants and protecting Faith, I haven't had time to wonder whether I'm doing it right. This man, this horrible man who's barreled—uninvited—into our life, this man who does not know me from Eve, has imagined me as the person I've always wanted to be—a fiercely loyal lioness, a natural mother.

I don't know whether to laugh or cry. Certainly I know better than most that circumstances can turn you into someone you've never been before. I think of ordinary women who've moved two-ton cars to save pinned toddlers, of mothers who step in front of a bullet heading for their child in a move as easy as breathing. Maybe I'm one of them now. But I'd willingly return to second-guessing myself if it meant that Faith would go back to normal.

'Mr Fletcher?' I wait until he is looking right at me, expecting a thank-you, and then I slap him as hard as I can across the face.

six

He that is not with me is against me.

—Luke 11:23

October 6, 1999

IAN'S GRANDMOTHER HAD BEEN a dyed-in-the-wool Southern belle who wore her religion like a Kevlar vest. 'Thank God I'm a Christian woman,' she'd say, her litany dragged out for show when she found out that her husband had left her for the Jolly Donut waitress, or when she got word that the estate had been sold out beneath her to make way for a J. C. Penney store. And then, when God didn't quite come through for her, she'd sneak out the bottle of bourbon she kept in the tank of the downstairs toilet and take up His slack.

The Southern Baptist miasma in which Ian had been raised was a far piece from Yankee skepticism. Down South, communities were built around their churches. In some places still, religion had Southerners by the throat, and a man's worth was judged by what house of God he frequented. Truth be told, Ian feels considerably more at home with the Yankees, for whom religion is an afterthought, rather than a staple of living. In the North there is room for doubt . . . or so Ian had thought, until he saw the reaction to Millie Epstein's passing and subsequent revival.

He has, through an inside source, managed to review

Millie Epstein's charts. Three distinct medical professionals signed the woman off as dead. And yet Ian himself saw her hale and hearty just days ago.

His ratings are climbing again, which will last about as long as an ice cube in July, unless he manages to add fuel to the fire. Fuel that doesn't seem to be forthcoming from the Millie Epstein angle. He buries his head in his hands and considers his next move. One of the things he's learned is that there are skeletons in everyone's closet, things no one ever wants the world to discover. He, of all people, should know.

Allen McManus has just unwrapped his Twinkie when the personal line on his phone begins to ring. 'Yeah?' he growls, picking up the receiver. He's told his wife not to call him at work. Christ, it's the only place he gets a little peace.

'Do you know about Lazarus?'

The voice is low, disguised. Certainly not his wife's. 'Who the hell is this?'

'Do you know about Lazarus?' the voice repeats. 'Who else had something to gain?'

'Look, buddy, I don't know what—' He hears a sharp click and a dial tone. 'Lazarus. What the fuck.'

It must be a Halloween prank, Halloween being just around the corner and everyone knowing, by virtue of Allen's byline, that he writes the obits. Certainly if some joker is going to bring up the idea of raising the dead, the call will be forwarded to Allen. He has just dismissed it from his mind when a fax begins to come in on the Obituary Department line. With a sigh, he walks over to the machine—probably some celeb whose passing was picked up on the AP wire—and squints at the grainy picture of a woman beneath the banner of *The New Canaan Chronicle*, wherever the hell *that* is.

WOMAN DIES; COMES BACK TO LIFE.

Lazarus.

Allen sits back down. He wishes he could remember what the Bible says, exactly, about Lazarus. Then again, he doesn't know if he's ever really read that story in the Bible. He leans across the aisle toward a colleague. 'Barb, you got a Bible?'

She laughs. 'Yeah, sure, right next to my Wite-Out. Why? You seen God?'

'Forget it,' Allen scowls. *New Canaan Chronicle*. A nothing paper if he's ever seen one. Yet here is this story about a woman who came back to life right in that little pissant town.

New Canaan was where that lady psychiatrist was from, too.

Allen skims the article a second time. Buried in the fourth paragraph—there it is—*Epstein's granddaughter . . . has been communicating with God*.

Well, for Christ's sake. How many other kids in that town would fit Dr Keller's description? Allen considers what this means—a little girl who sees and speaks to God, who suddenly can perform miracles. That's a front page on the New Hampshire section for sure.

Who else had something to gain?

That's what the caller said. Resurrection is certainly in Millie Epstein's best interests . . . unless it wasn't a resurrection at all. Allen glances at the article again. That Ian Fletcher guy is hanging around, which has to mean that he, too, senses something isn't quite right. Who, then, would benefit from a mock miracle? The kid, for one. But kids that age always have managers to promote their business.

In this case, it would probably be her mother.

October 7, 1999

JUST AFTER FIVE in the morning Mariah hears the front door open. She bolts out of bed and tears down the stairs. Grabbing up an umbrella from the stand in the front parlor, she brandishes it like a bat and searches the shadows for an intruder. 'Come on!' she yells, heart pounding. 'You want pictures? You want an exclusive? Show yourself, you bastard!'

But nothing moves, nobody stirs. Cursing, she tosses the umbrella down and through the sidelight catches a glimpse of Faith, barefoot and in her nightgown, pushing a doll stroller across the grass.

Mariah glances at the small entourage at the edge of the road. The cult from Arizona remains blessedly asleep on the far side of the stone wall; the reporters who've waited for an appearance by Faith during the day are conspicuously absent. In fact, the only person watching Faith is Ian Fletcher, haggard and grim, standing in the doorway of the Winnebago.

'Hi, Mommy.' Faith waves. 'Want to play with me?'

Mariah swallows the protest she is about to make. 'Your feet . . . aren't you cold?'

'No, it's nice out.' Faith bends toward the stroller. 'Isn't it?' she coos, and tucks a blanket around her doll.

Except the doll is moving. Its tiny brown fists beat at the morning fog, and below the curly cap of its hair is a wide, circular sore. Faith lifts the baby out of the stroller and cuddles him to her cheek. 'What a good boy.'

It is then that Mariah notices a slight woman hidden behind an ash tree at the edge of the driveway. She has a scarf wrapped around her head, and her eyes never leave the infant, although she makes no move to get him back from Faith.

Faith puts the baby back in her toy stroller and moves him to the doll high chair that she's dragged out to the front lawn, where she pretends to feed him pieces of toy fruit. The baby smiles and kicks his feet against the legs of the high chair. He laughs so loud that a photographer awakens and points a camera at Faith, taking pictures with alarming speed.

Mariah, jolted out of her stupor, steps off the porch and strides toward her daughter. 'Sweetie, I think we have to go in now.'

Faith squints at the sun pushing against the horizon. 'Oh. It was just getting fun.'

Mariah touches her hair. 'I know. Maybe we'll come out later.' As she says this, her gaze roams across the sparse crowd and locks on Ian Fletcher's impassive face. In all this time he has not moved, has done nothing more insidious than observe. Mariah forces her attention back to Faith. 'I think you ought to bring him back to his mother now.'

Faith carefully lifts the baby and presses her lips against the sore on his forehead. She walks to the ash tree and gives the infant to his sobbing mother. The woman clearly wants to say something to Faith, but she cannot catch her breath to do so. Faith touches her lightly on the hand, where her fingers cradle the baby's head. 'Bring him back to play, okay?'

The woman nods and wipes her eyes. Faith slips her hand into her mother's, and Mariah is overwhelmed by the sensation of holding on to someone she does not know at all. How can it be that she grew Faith inside her, and felt her push her way into the world, and gave her a home for seven years, without knowing that this was coming?

She is about to step onto the porch with her daughter when she sees Ian Fletcher brazenly walking up the driveway. He's brought back the plastic doll stroller and the little feeding chair, as well as the small basket of toy fruits and vegetables. Mariah takes the toys from him. 'Excuse us,' she says stiffly.

He falls back, regarding Faith. 'I wish I could.'

After the unexpected appearance of Faith White, Ian returns to the Winnebago. He is even more sure of his suppositions now that he's watched her play like any other seven-year-old kid. Clearly, the ringleader is the mother. The moment she showed up, the kid stopped—the healer came to heel. For whatever reason, Mariah White is the mastermind behind this show.

He's seen charlatans before, men and women gifted at perpetuating a hoax. Usually they're in it for the money, or the fame. And that's the one thing that doesn't quite add up for Ian. There's something about Mariah's eyes that makes him think of a victim, instead of a swindler. As if she'd really rather this whole thing not be happening.

Hell, she's a good actress, is all. Beauty can be a terrific disguise, because of its power of distraction. The purity of her features, even stamped with sleep—those gorgeous legs eating up the yard as she crossed to her daughter—why, that's just a decoy. More smoke and mirrors, like her little girl's miracles. Faith White is no more seeing God and raising the dead than Ian is himself.

October 8, 1999

'THIS,' RABBI WEISSMAN says to Mariah, 'is Rabbi Daniel Solomon.'

The man in the tie-dyed shirt holds out his hand and grins. 'I like to think I have the name of the wise king for a reason.' Mariah does not crack a smile. She reaches behind her, where Faith is burrowing against her hip and peeking at the strangers.

'I'm the spiritual leader of Boulder's Beit Am Hadash Congregation,' Solomon says.

Mariah glances at his shirt, at his long, ponytailed hair. Right, she thinks. If you're a rabbi, I'm the queen of England.

'Beit Am Hadash,' the rabbi explains, 'means "house of a new people." My congregation is part of the Jewish renewal movement. We draw upon Kabbalah, as well as Buddhist, Sufi, and Native American traditions.' He glances at Rabbi Weissman. 'We'd like to know more about Faith.'

'Look,' Mariah says, 'I don't really think I have anything to say to you.' She would not have even let the rabbis inside, except for the fact that to leave them on the porch seemed inhumane. Mariah sends Faith into the playroom so that she can't overhear the conversation. 'The last time I saw you, Rabbi Weissman, I got the distinct impression that you weren't very impressed with Faith. You thought this was an act I was making her perform.'

'Yes, I know,' Rabbi Weissman says. 'And I'm still not convinced. But I took it upon myself to call Rabbi Solomon. You see, Mrs White, after you left the synagogue, the strangest thing happened: A couple that was having marital problems reconciled.'

'What's strange about that?' Mariah says, a familiar twinge in her chest as she lets her mind brush over Colin.

'Believe me,' Weissman says. 'They were irreconcilable, until the day you visited with your daughter.' He spreads his palms. 'I'm not explaining this very well. It was just that after I read the newspaper article about your mother, I was struck by the possibility that, in some people's minds, there might be a connection between this couple's reconciliation and

Faith. It reminded me of something Rabbi Solomon had said at a rabbinic council a couple of years ago. We had posed the question of what God would say to a prophet nowadays. I said that there would have to be a message—you know, that peace is coming to Israel, or that this is the way to defeat the Palestinians—something that your daughter isn't hearing during her conversations with God. However, Rabbi Solomon felt that a divine message wouldn't be about ferreting out evil, but instead about how man is treating man. Divorce, child abuse, alcoholism. Social ills. That's what He'd want fixed.'

Mariah stares at him blankly. Rabbi Solomon clears his throat. 'Mrs White, may I talk to Faith?'

She sizes up the man. 'For a few minutes,' Mariah reluctantly allows. 'As long as you don't upset her.'

They all walk into the playroom. Rabbi Solomon kneels, so that he is at eye level with Faith. 'My name is Daniel. Can I tell you a story?'

Faith creeps around Mariah's hip, nodding shyly. 'The people who come to my temple believe that before there was anything else, there was God. And God was so . . . well . . . *full* that creating the world meant shrinking a little bit to make space for it.'

'God didn't make the world,' Faith says. 'It was a big explosion. I learned in school.'

Rabbi Solomon smiles. 'Ah, I've learned that, too. And I still like to think that maybe God was the one who made that explosion, that God was watching it happen from somewhere far away. Do you think it could have happened like that?'

'I guess.'

'Well, like I was saying. There was God, sucking in to make some room for the world, filling vessels with energy and light and setting them into the new space. But during Creation, the vessels couldn't hold all the energy, and they broke. And all the sparks of light from God in these vessels got scattered around the universe. Pieces of the broken vessels fell, too, and became the bad things in the world—we call that *clipot*. My friends and I believe that our job is to clean up all the *clipot* and get rid of them, and to gather up all the bits of light that are scattered and get it back to God. So maybe when you say a blessing and eat a kosher chicken at Shabbat, the holy sparks in the chicken are released. If you perform a *mitzvah* for someone else—help them out a little—more sparks get released.'

'We don't keep kosher,' Mariah says to Rabbi Solomon. 'We're not traditional Jews.'

He plucks at his T-shirt and grins wryly. 'Neither am I, Mrs White. But Kabbalah—Jewish mysticism—can even explain why a little girl who has never gone to temple or said a prayer might be closer to God than someone else. No one can lift up all those sparks by himself. In fact, the ability to find sparks at all may be buried so deep in you that you stop believing there's a God. Until someone else comes along, with so much light in her that you can't help but see your own, and when you're together that light grows even brighter.' He touches the top of Faith's head. 'God may be talking to Faith because of all the people she's going to reach.'

'You believe?' Mariah breathes, almost afraid to say it aloud. 'You haven't even spoken to her, and you think she's telling the truth?'

'I'm a little more open-minded than Rabbi Weissman. The couple he was counseling . . . well, that all could be a coincidence with your daughter's visit. But then again, it may not be, and Faith may have the answers. If God was going to show up in 1999, I don't think He'd grandstand or preach. I think He'd be just as low-key as your daughter's suggested.'

Faith tugs on the rabbi's sleeve. 'He's a She. God is a girl.'

'A girl,' Solomon repeats carefully.

Mariah crosses her arms. 'Yes, according to Faith, God is a woman. Can Jewish mysticism explain *that?*'

'Actually, Kabbalah is founded on the premise that God is both male *and* female. The female part, the *Shekhinah*, is the presence of God. It's what was broken when all those vessels shattered. If Faith is seeing a woman, it makes perfect sense. The presence of God is exactly what would make her able to heal and to have people congregate around her. What she may be seeing is a reflection of herself.'

Mariah watches Faith scratch her knee, uninterested,

and then asks the question she's been holding tight inside. 'Boulder's a long way away, Rabbi Solomon. Why are you here?'

'I'd like to take Faith to Colorado with me, to learn more about her visions.'

'Absolutely not. My daughter's not a spectacle.'

The rabbi glances toward the windows that look out the front of the house. 'No?'

'I didn't invite them here.' She fists her hands at her sides and looks at Faith. 'I didn't ask for this to happen.'

'For what to happen, Mrs White? God?' He shakes his head. 'The *Shekhinah* doesn't go where she's not wanted. You have to be open to the presence of God before it comes to dwell. Which is maybe why you're having such a hard time with this in the first place.' His eyes are like amber, holding the past preserved. 'What happened to you, Mariah,' he asks softly, 'that makes you fight so hard to not be a Jew?'

She remembers the one time she went to church as a little girl, with a friend, how she was surprised by the fact that Jesus supposedly loved everyone, even people who made mistakes. The Jewish God, you had to make yourself worthy of. Mariah wonders, not for the first time, why a religion that prides itself on being open-minded makes you jump through so many hoops.

She is suddenly overwhelmed by the thought of two rabbis in her house. 'I'm *not* Jewish. I'm not anything.' She looks at Faith. '*We're* not anything. I think you should go.'

Rabbi Solomon holds out his hand. 'Will you think about some of the things I said?'

Mariah shrugs. 'I don't know. I don't look at my daughter and see the presence of God, Rabbi Solomon. I don't look at her and think she's full of divine light. I just see someone who's getting more and more upset with what's going on around her.'

Rabbi Solomon straightens. 'Funny. That's what many Jews said two thousand years ago about Jesus.'

• • •

October 10, 1999

THE LAST THING Father Joseph MacReady does before donning his vestments is exchange his battered cowboy boots for the soft-soled black shoes of a priest. He's anticipating a full house. Early-morning mass on Sunday in New Canaan tends to be packed, most of the Catholic inhabitants of the town preferring to lose a few hours' sleep on the weekend if it means getting the rest of the day to relax in their gardens or on the golf courses in neighboring towns. *Today*, he thinks, *might be the day*. He braces his hands on the scarred table and lifts his gaze to the frieze of the crucifixion. He thinks back to the moment years ago when he was drifting cross-country and suddenly realized that he could have taken his Harley into the Pacific and still gotten nowhere.

Now, even after decades of leading mass, he prays before each one for a sign that he made the right decision, a sign that God is with him. He stares at the crucifix for another second, hoping. But, as for the past twenty-eight years, nothing happens.

Father MacReady closes his eyes for a moment, trying to gather the Holy Spirit before walking into the church to his congregation.

There are eight people there.

Clearly stunned, he steps up and begins to deliver the mass, his mind whirling. There is no single reason he can think of to cause his flock to dwindle from eighty to eight over the course of a single week. He rushes through the Holy Eucharist and the sermon, shocking his altar boy, who is usually fidgeting less than ten minutes into the service. After the final 'Amen,' he hurries to remove the vestments and stand at the rear doors of the church to say good-bye to the faithful few. But by the time he gets there, half are already in the parking lot.

'Marjorie,' he calls to an elderly woman whose husband died the year before. 'Where are you off to this morning in such a hurry?'

'Oh, Father,' she says, dimpling. 'To the Whites' house.'

Well, that only confuses him more. 'You're going to Washington?'

'No, no. The little girl. Faith White. The one who's seeing God. I didn't think it made up for missing mass, myself.'

'What about this little girl?'

'Haven't you read the *Chronicle* this week? People are saying she's got God talking to her. Even had some miracles come to pass. Brought a woman back from the dead, I hear.'

'You know,' Father Joseph says, considering, 'I just might like to tag along.'

Mariah turns the cylinder of cherry on the lathe, watching the ribbons of wood fly like streamers as she touches the rich block with a sculpting tool. It will be the fourth leg of a Queen Anne dining-room table for the current dollhouse. Her eyes wander to her work station, where the intricately carved trio of legs sits beside the oval island of the miniature tabletop.

Today is not the day for making furniture. In fact, she is not supposed to be working at all, at least according to her self-imposed calendar. But these days nothing has gone according to schedule. Yesterday was spent getting her mother discharged from the hospital, after over a week of testing and examination by cardiac experts. Mariah had wanted her mother to stay at the farmhouse, but Millie was having none of it. 'You're five minutes away,' she told Mariah. 'What could go wrong?' Mariah had finally given in, knowing that she could cajole her mother into spending days, at least, at the farmhouse simply by saying that Faith needed company. She'd helped her mother get settled at home again, facing only one awkward moment when they both stopped suddenly at the coffin table. Without any complaint from her mother, she'd dragged it out to the garage, out of sight and out of mind.

Mariah is devoting today to making up for lost time. She pulls a ruler from her breast pocket and examines the leg on the lathe. It is off by two millimeters; she will have to start over. Sighing, she discards the wood and then hears the doorbell ring.

It is an unexpected sound—no one's ventured past the

police block at the end of the driveway lately. Maybe it's the mailman with a package, or the oil-delivery truck.

She opens the front door and finds herself staring at a priest. Her mouth tightens. 'How come the police let you pass?'

'A professional perk,' Father Joseph admits, unruffled. 'When God locks a door, He opens a window. Or at least sets a good Catholic officer at the end of your driveway.'

'Father,' Mariah says wearily, 'I appreciate your coming here. I can even understand why you'd want to. But—'

'Do you? Because I'm not sure *I* do.' He laughs. 'St Elizabeth's was empty this morning. Apparently your daughter is fierce competition.'

'Not intentionally.

'I don't think we're ready for another religious onslaught,' Mariah says. 'There were some rabbis here Friday, talking about Jewish mysticism—'

'You know what they say about mysticism: Starts in mist, ends in schism.'

A grin tugs at Mariah's mouth. 'We're not even Catholic.'

'So I hear. Episcopalian and Jewish, right?'

Mariah leans against the doorjamb. 'Right. So why would you even be interested?'

Joseph shrugs. 'You know, when I was a chaplain in Vietnam, I met the Dalai Lama. There were a bunch of us, and we spent a great deal of time beforehand talking about what we should give him to eat, to drink, what we should call him. 'His Holiness,' that was what someone suggested, although that was also what we called the pope, and let me tell you we fought tooth and nail over that one. But you know what, Mrs White? The Dalai Lama had this . . . this energy around him, the likes of which I'd never felt before. Now, he isn't Catholic, but I won't rule out the possibility that he's a figure of profound spiritual enlightenment.'

A dimple appears in Mariah's cheek. 'Careful, Father. That's probably grounds for excommunication.'

He smiles. 'His Holiness has a lot more on his plate than to follow my transgressions.'

There is something so *secular* about him that Mariah

thinks—under different circumstances—she would ask this stranger to sit down, to share a pot of coffee. 'Father . . .'

'Joseph. Joseph MacReady.' He grins. 'Willing and able, too.'

Mariah laughs out loud. 'I like you.'

'I like you, too, Mrs White.'

'However, now I think you ought to go.' She shakes his hand, well aware that he has not once asked to speak to Faith. 'If I need you, I'll call the church. But no one's really proved that any miracles have occurred.'

'Yes, it's only word of mouth. Then again, Matthew, Mark, Luke, and John were just telling what they saw as well.'

Mariah crosses her arms. 'Do you really believe that God would speak through a child? A technically Jewish child, at that?'

'Far as I've been told, Mrs White, He has before.'

October 11, 1999

'MOVE THAT LEAF a quarter inch to the right,' the producer says, tilting his head toward the shot lined up in the monitor. The lights that the electrician and lighting director have set up make Teresa Civernos squint and instinctively cover little Rafael's eyes with her hand. He bats it away, and for the hundredth time that day she glories in his strength and his coordination. Hugging him close, she touches her lips to the smooth, unbroken skin of his brow.

'We're ready, Ms Civernos.' The voice is as rich as honey, and it belongs to Petra Saganoff, the star reporter for *Hollywood Tonight!*.

In the background, the producer glances up. 'Can you bring the baby up a little closer? Oh, that's perfect.' He makes an okay sign with his hand.

Petra Saganoff waits for a makeup artist to do one last touchup on her face. 'You remember what I'm going to ask you, now?'

Teresa nods and looks nervously at the second camera, fixed on her and the baby. She forces herself to remember that this was her idea, not theirs. She was going to take out a novena to St. Jude in the *Globe*, but realized that there was a way to reach more people. Her cousin Luis worked in L.A. on the Warner Brothers lot, where the *Hollywood Tonight!*'s studio was located. He was dating the girl who did Petra Saganoff's wardrobe. Teresa had told him to ask. And within twenty-four hours of Rafael's being released from Mass General with a clean bill of health, Petra Saganoff was in Teresa's tiny apartment in Southie, prerecording a segment for later broadcast.

'Three,' the cameraman says. 'Two. One . . . and—' He points to Petra.

'Your baby didn't always look this healthy, is that right?'

Teresa feels herself flush. Petra had told her not to flush. She must remember. 'Yes. Just days ago Rafael was a pediatric AIDS patient at Massachusetts General Hospital,' Teresa says. 'He contracted the virus from a blood transfusion at birth. Last week he was pale and listless; he was fighting thrush and PCP and esophagitis. His CD-four cell count was fifteen.' She clutches the baby tighter. 'His doctor said he would die within the month.'

'What happened, Mrs Civernos?'

'I heard about something. Someone, I mean. There is a little girl in New Hampshire who people say is talking to God. My neighbor, she visits shrines and places like that, and she asked if I wanted to go with her. I figured I had nothing to lose.' Teresa smooths the hair over Rafael's head. 'Rafael was running a fever when we got there, so I was walking with him just before dawn when this girl—her name is Faith—came outside. She brought a doll stroller, and she asked if she could play with my son. She walked him and laughed with him and pretended to feed him for about an hour.' Teresa looks up, tears in her eyes. 'She touched him. She kissed him here, where he had an open sore. And then we went back to Boston.

'The doctors—we went in the next day—did not recognize him. Overnight his sores were healed. His infections were gone. His T-cell count was twenty-two thousand.' She beams at Petra. 'They tell me it is all medically impossible. Then they say that Rafael is not an AIDS patient anymore.'

'Are you saying your son was cured of AIDS, Mrs Civernos?'

'*I* think so,' Teresa says. 'God has touched this little girl, this Faith. It's a miracle. There is nothing I can say to make her understand how much I want to thank her.' She nuzzles her cheek against Rafael's head.

The producer motions to the cameraman, who stops filming. Petra taps a cigarette out of a silver holder and confers with her producer, their backs to Teresa. 'Yeah,' he says, laughing at something Petra's said. 'You collect more nuts than a squirrel.'

Teresa overhears. 'This is no joke. This really happened.'

'Sure.' Petra grins. 'And I'm the Virgin Mary.'

'It's true. She brought her own grandmother back to life.' Furious, Teresa gets up and grabs her big leather handbag. She rummages for the directions to New Canaan, the ones she'd carefully plotted out with her neighbor on an intricately folded map of New Hampshire, and throws it at the famous anchorwoman. 'Go ask her yourself,' she says, and, turning on her heel, she escapes to the bathroom with Rafael and locks herself in until she hears Petra Saganoff and her entourage leave.

October 12, 1999

ON THE PLANE, Ian sets his headphones to the channel for the in-flight newsmagazine. With a satisfied sigh he turns his attention to the screen centered over the business-class cabin.

But instead of seeing CNN, Ian finds himself staring at Petra Saganoff, the talent for some entertainment fluff show. 'Oh, for Christ's sake,' he says, flagging down a flight attendant. 'Don't you have anything else?'

She shakes her head. 'I'm sorry, sir. We get whatever tape they give us.'

Scowling, Ian whips off his headphones and tucks them into the seat pocket in front of him. He bends forward for his briefcase, figuring that he can at least run the numbers of his latest Q-rating and see where in the nation he was most recognizable. As he sits up again, he notices the woman that Petra Saganoff is interviewing.

She looks vaguely familiar.

He shuffles through the pile of papers in his hands and—*the baby*. Ian glances at the small screen and watches the child in the woman's arms kick and squirm. He reaches for the earphones he's discarded. ' . . . his sores were healed. His infections were gone . . . ' Ian hears, and suddenly remembers where he has seen the woman before. On the front lawn at the New Canaan farmhouse, watching her son get jostled around in a doll stroller by Faith White.

A muscle jumps in Ian's jaw. Now she's raised the dead *and* cured AIDS?

'God has touched this little girl . . .' he hears the woman say.

'Oh, shit,' Ian murmurs. He should hop on the next return flight. He should mount a campaign, he should double his efforts. He should blow Faith White's ridiculous succession of miraculous cures for the incurable right out of the water.

And he also knows that he won't—that, as planned, he'll continue on to see Michael before returning to New Canaan.

He forces his attention back to the papers in his lap, but envisions a pair of hands turning cards: red, black, red, black. On the screen, the AIDS baby who was limp as a rag two days ago is laughing and animated in his mother's arms.

The question is only in his mind for a moment before it's squelched. And yet Ian can still hear it ringing in his ears, as joyful and resonant as a long note that a choir has stopped singing: *What if, this time, I'm wrong?*

October 13, 1999

WITH THE INTENSE FOCUS of a seven-year-old, Faith packs the canvas tote bag her mother usually takes to the library with the things she needs to run away. These include her teddy bear, a change of underpants, and a box of Ritz crackers she's stolen from the pantry. Also her Wonder Woman Superfriend

Membership Certificate and a glowing plastic ring that she found in the sandbox at the park and has always believed to be a little bit magic. She waits until she hears her mother turn on the shower in the master bath, and then she creeps from her bedroom.

She puts on a dark-green Polarfleece jacket, rust-colored leggings, and a purple turtleneck. A pair of red woolen gloves, to hide her hands.

Faith tiptoes down the stairs. She's not running away, not really, since she's going to call her mother as soon as she figures out where there's a phone. She knows the number by heart. In case someone is listening, she will disguise her voice the way Inspector Gadget sometimes does and tell her mom to come to the movie theater where they saw *Tarzan*, because who will be expecting *that*? And then they'll go away, just the two of them and maybe Grandma, too, and leave all those dumb people sitting on the front lawn.

She is silent as a firefly when she sneaks out the sliding door.

Well, where the hell is she going *now*?

For once Ian's insomnia is a boon. Staring out the window of the Winnebago, he sees a bright flash that disappears into the woods around the White property. Carefully opening the door of the recreational vehicle, he steps outside. As he approaches the perimeter of the woods, he breaks into a run, trying to tune his senses to the sound of small feet falling like snow.

There—he sees again the flash that drew him to her in the first place, and he recognizes it as light bouncing off something. A triangle. The moon is reflecting off her jacket or sweatshirt, some safety device of L. L. Bean's. 'Hey!' he calls softly, and Faith freezes. She turns, spies him, and runs off again. With one swift leap, Ian tackles her and rolls simultaneously, so that she lands on the cushion of his body and knocks the breath out of him. He tightens his hold on the girl, who is kicking his shins. 'Cut it out!' he says, shaking her. 'You're hurting me.'

'You're hurting me, too!' Faith cries.

He relaxes his grip. 'If I let you go, will you run away?' When she solemnly shakes her head, he releases his arms. Immediately Faith scrambles to her feet and takes off into the forest.

'*Goddamn!*' He follows her and snags the sleeve of her fleece pullover, reeling Faith in like an angry, struggling fish. 'You lied.'

'No,' Faith says, the fight going out of her. 'I never did.'

Ian realizes that they are now talking about something entirely different. 'Isn't it a little late for you to be playing outside?'

'I'm running away. I don't like it here anymore.'

Ian feels his chest tighten. The end, he reminds himself, justifies the means. 'I guess your mom is okay with your leaving like this?'

Faith hangs her head. 'I'm going to tell her. I promise.' She glances around at the trees. 'Do you know where there's a phone?'

'In my pocket. Why?'

She looks at Ian as if he is very, very stupid. 'To call my mother when I get there.'

Ian brushes his hand over his coat, feeling the slender bulk of his cellular. At last he has a bargaining chip. 'If you want to call your mother when you get to wherever you're going, then you're going to have to keep my phone with you. And I don't go anywhere without my phone.' He pauses, making sure that she's following his logic. 'Besides, you probably shouldn't be wandering around alone in the dark.'

Faith looks down. 'I'm not supposed to go anywhere with strangers.'

Ian laughs. 'Haven't I been hanging around long enough to not be a stranger?'

She thinks about this. 'My mom says you're a menace.'

'Ah, you see. She didn't say I'm a stranger.' He holds out the cell phone, then drops it back in his pocket. 'Deal?'

'I guess,' Faith mutters. She begins to walk, and Ian strikes off beside her. He is thinking of all the things he is missing—sound and camera crew, foremost among them—but surely an off-the-record interview is better than none at all. If he figures out the catch in this story, he can blow it open publicly the next day.

They have been walking only a few moments when Faith, winded, sits down on a rotting log. This surprises him; he thought kids had more stamina than that. He tries to see her face by the moonlight that filters through the trees, but she looks pale and ghostly. 'You all right?'

'Yeah,' she says, her voice tiny. 'I'm just tired.'

'Past your bedtime. How'd you get by your mom anyway?'

'She's taking a shower.'

Ian is impressed. 'I ran away from home once, when I was five. I hid underneath the canvas cover of the barbecue for three hours before anyone found me.'

'That isn't really running away.'

Her voice is so weary, so rough with wisdom, that Ian again feels a pang of guilt. 'Don't you like being . . . important to so many people?'

Faith looks at him as if he is crazy. 'Would *you*?'

Well, actually, he would . . . that's the whole point of increasing his ratings share. But, admittedly, not everyone embraces that goal. Certainly not a child who's an unwilling pawn in someone else's machinations. He wonders if he might make an ally out of Faith White. 'Hey, can you help me with something?' Ian pulls a deck of cards out of his pocket—solitaire sometimes gets him through a long night. 'I'm working on this trick, and I'm not sure I'm doing it right.' He shuffles the deck, then asks her to pick a card. Faith slides it from the pack, the fingers of her gloves slipping. 'Now, remember which card you've got? You're sure? Slide it right into the middle again.'

Giggling, Faith does what he's asked. Ian silently thanks Uncle Beauregard for teaching him the one and only magic trick he's ever had the inclination to learn. He shuffles the deck impressively, making cards leap from palm to palm, and then tells Faith to tap the top of the deck. 'That's the seven of diamonds,' he announces. 'Your card.'

She lifts it and gasps. 'How'd you do that!'

'I'll tell you the secret to my magic,' he says, 'if you tell me the secret to yours.'

Faith's face falls. 'I don't know any magic.'

'Oh, I'm not so sure.' Ian sinks down beside Faith, clasping his hands between his knees. 'For starters—how did you heal your grandmother?'

He can feel Faith bristle beside him. 'I don't want to learn your stupid card trick anyway.'

'You know, I've met other people who think they can heal. Some of 'em were just hypnotists. They convinced the sick people that they were feeling better, when in fact their bodies weren't. And some of them really did manage to make people feel better, through some kind of electricity they just happened to carry along their skin.'

'Electricity?'

'A charge. Like the shock you get sometimes when you touch a TV set. *Bzzt*. You know.'

Faith stands up and stretches out her hands. 'Touch me,' she challenges.

Slowly, his eyes never leaving her face, Ian reaches toward her. 'You have to take off your gloves.'

Immediately Faith ducks her hands behind her back. 'I can't.'

Ian shrugs: *I told you so*.

'I really can't,' Faith pleads.

It has been a long time since Ian was seven. He tries to remember what worked in the playground. 'Liar.'

'I am not!' Faith insists, agitated. 'Ask me something else!'

'Okay.' Ian is not fighting fair—for Christ's sake, he's outsmarting a seven-year-old—but then again, he's never been known for his good sportsmanship. He has Faith right where he needs her to be: face upturned and eager, so desperate for a chance to prove herself that she can't help but slip up and reveal the ruse.

'Ask me,' she begs again.

Ian thinks of everything he wants to know: Who is in on this, who will profit, how did they manage to fool a medical staff? But when he opens his mouth, what he says surprises even himself. 'What does God look like?'

Faith's lips part on the answer. 'God—' she begins, and then she faints.

Quick reflexes make Ian reach out and catch the girl before she strikes her head on the log or a rock or tree root. 'Faith,' he says, shaking her gently. 'Wake up!' He lays her on the ground carefully and checks her pulse. He brushes leaves away from her face.

Then he goes to wipe off his hands on his raincoat and realizes it's smeared with blood.

Heart pounding, Ian checks his own chest and side. But he is fine, and a perfunctory examination of Faith's torso reveals no wounds. His gaze falls on her red gloves, bright against the mossy dirt and scattered leaves.

Gently he peels one away from her hand. 'Holy shit,' he breathes. Then he gathers Faith into his arms and runs as fast as he can to Mariah White.

The doorbell is ringing as she wraps a towel around her wet hair, cinches her robe at her waist, and flies down the stairs. It is ten-thirty at night, for God's sake. She has a child who's asleep. Who would have the nerve to bother them now?

As she reaches for the doorknob, the person on the other side begins to knock harder. Her jaw tight, Mariah swings open the door and finds herself staring at Ian Fletcher. But all her bluster dies the moment she notices that Faith is lying limp in his arms.

'Oh . . .' Mariah's voice trembles, and she falls back to let Ian enter the house.

'She was in the woods.' Ian watches Mariah touch Faith's temples, her cheek. 'She's bleeding. We need to take her to the hospital.'

Mariah covers her mouth, holding back a sob. She rucks up Faith's sleeve, expecting to find a cut across her wrist, but Fletcher tugs down her glove instead. 'Come on!' he says. 'What are you waiting for?'

'Nothing . . .' Mariah runs upstairs and dresses in the clothes that have already been thrown into the laundry hamper. Then she rips her car keys and purse from the Shaker pegboard beside the front door.

The far edge of the front yard is stirring with curiosity, most of the reporters having risen from their bored stakeout to notice Ian Fletcher, of all people, carrying the girl up to the house. Video cameras begin to whir, flashbulbs pop like firecrackers, and above all this is the thready refrain of people calling out to the unconscious Faith for help.

Mariah opens the back door of the car for Ian, and without a word of communication he climbs in with Faith, cradling her in his lap. Mariah gets into the driver's seat, hands shaking on the wheel, and tries to back out of the driveway without hitting one of the onlookers who insist on touching the car as it passes.

Mariah meets Ian's eyes in the rearview mirror. 'How did this happen?'

'I don't know.' Ian brushes Faith's hair from her forehead; this action is not lost on Mariah. 'I think she was already hurt when I found her.'

Mariah brakes down the long curve of a hill. Has Faith misguidedly been trying to kill herself? She does not ask Ian Fletcher what she wants to: Why were you with her? Why didn't my own daughter come to *me*?

She pulls into the Emergency entrance of the Connecticut Valley Medical Center. There, she leaves the car at the curb and precedes Ian into the building, toward the triage nurse. Mariah is ready to fight for Faith's priority as a case, but the nurse takes one look at the unconscious child and the blood on Ian's coat and immediately calls for a gurney and a doctor. Mariah can barely keep up with them as Faith is whisked away.

She does not think to ask Ian to follow her, but she isn't surprised to find him coming, too. And she is barely aware of how her body sways when the remaining glove is cut from Faith's fingers, of how Ian's hand reaches out to steady her.

'Vitals?'

'BP one hundred over sixty, thready pulse.'

'Let's drop a line and get bloods. I want a type and cross, a CBC, tox screen, 'lytes.' The doctor glances over Faith's still form. 'What's her name?'

Mariah tries to make her voice work, but she is unable to speak. 'Faith,' Ian offers.

'Okay, Faith,' the doctor says, his face inches from hers. 'Wake up for me, honey.' He glances up at a nurse. 'Get pressure bandages,' he orders, and looks at Mariah. 'Did she get into some pills? Drink something from under the kitchen sink?'

'No,' Mariah whispers, shocked. 'Nothing like that.'

Ian clears his throat. 'She was bleeding when I found her. Wearing the gloves, so I didn't realize it at first. And then she passed out.' He glances at his watch. 'About thirty minutes ago.'

A resident runs his hands along Faith's foot. 'No Kernig's or Brudzinski's signs.'

'These don't look like punctures to me,' a nurse says, and the doctor in charge takes up a position beside her and begins to press against Faith's upper arm. 'Bleeding's not slowing. I want a hand-surgery consult stat.' He looks at Ian. 'You the father?'

Ian shakes his head. 'A friend.'

To Mariah they seem like great vultures, swooping down on Faith's small body to get whatever untouched piece remains. A nurse lifts Faith's right hand, pressing hard on her upper arm at the brachial artery, and for a moment Mariah is able to see a pinprick of light through the wound—a tiny, clean tunnel passing right through the palm.

Suddenly Faith strikes out with her foot, catching a resident in the chin. 'Noooo!' she cries, trying to yank her arms away from the nurses who are pinning her down. 'No! It hurts!'

Mariah takes a step forward, only to feel Ian's hand on her shoulder. 'They know what they're doing,' he murmurs, as the doctor gentles Faith with his voice.

'How did you hurt your hands, Faith?' he asks.

'I didn't. I didn't hurt my—*Ow*! They just started bleeding and the Band-Aids wouldn't stay on and—*Stop*! Mommy, make them stop!'

Shrugging off Ian, Mariah runs toward the gurney, her hand falling on her daughter's thigh before she is yanked away.

'Get her out of here!' the doctor shouts, barely audible over Faith's shrieking. But the farther she's dragged from Faith, the more the sobs intensify, and it takes several moments in Ian's embrace before Mariah realizes that she is the one who's crying.

There is an insular peace to hospitals in the middle of the night, as if beneath the moans and sighs and muted beeps those people still roaming the halls or sitting at bedsides are united in purpose. You can meet a woman in the elevator and, just like that, know her sorrow. You can stand beside a man at the coffee-vending machine and tell he's coming off the high of having a baby. You find yourself asking for a stranger's story; you feel a connection to people you would ordinarily pass on the street.

Mariah and Ian stand like sentries at the foot of Faith's bed in the pediatric ward. She is sleeping easily now, her bandaged hands fading into the white sheets. 'Q-tips,' Ian murmurs.

'Excuse me?'

'Her arms look like Q-tips. It's that puffy thing on the end.'

Mariah smiles, the movement so unlikely after these past few hours that she can feel her face crumple as it happens. Faith turns and settles again on the bed, and Ian points to the door, his brows raised in question. Mariah follows him outside and begins to walk down the hall, past the quiet patter of the nurses' station and the elevator portal. 'I haven't thanked you for bringing her to me.' She crosses her arms, suddenly chilled. 'For not whipping out a camera and taking pictures of Faith when it happened.'

Ian meets her gaze. 'How do you know I didn't?'

Her mouth, her throat, is dry. She pictures Ian in the backseat of the car, holding Faith. 'I just do,' Mariah says.

They have stopped in front of the neonatal nursery, where the newborns, pastel-wrapped and swaddled, sit side by side like grocery items on a shelf. One infant bats a hand from his blanket and unfurls the petals of his fingers. Mariah cannot help but notice that his palm is new and pink and whole.

'Do you believe?'

Ian is staring at the newborns, but speaking to her. It is not a question she should answer; it is not a topic to discuss with Ian Fletcher, who—for all his chivalrous behavior tonight—will still be the enemy tomorrow. But there has been a connection in the past few hours, something that makes Mariah think of spiders throwing the thinnest silken line across incredible distances, something that makes her wonder if she may just owe Ian an answer.

'Yes. I don't know what Faith's seeing, I don't know why she's seeing it—but I do believe that she's telling the truth.'

He shakes his head almost imperceptibly. 'What I meant is, do you believe in God?'

'I don't know. I wish I could just say, "Oh, yes." I wish it was as easy as all that.'

'You have your doubts, though.'

Mariah looks up at him. 'So do you.'

'Yeah. But the difference is, that if you had the choice you'd want to believe. And I wouldn't.' He presses one palm to the glass in front of him, staring at the babies. '"Male and female created He them." But you can watch, under a microscope, an egg being fertilized. Y'all can take a tiny camera and watch cells dividing, or a heart being formed. You can see it happen. So where is God in that?'

Mariah thinks of Rabbi Solomon in his hippie T-shirt, negotiating a path between the Bible and the Big Bang theory of creation for Faith. 'Maybe in the fact that it happens at all.'

Ian turns. 'But we're talking about scientific proof here.'

She considers the circumstances that led to her placement at Greenhaven. 'Sometimes you can see things happen right in front of your eyes and still jump to the wrong conclusions.'

Their eyes lock for a moment. Mariah blinks first. 'You probably want to go home. Get some sleep.'

He massages the back of his neck and smiles faintly. 'Do I ever,' he agrees, but he makes no move to leave.

Mariah finds herself cataloging Ian Fletcher the way another woman might: the silky black hair, so straight that it spikes across his forehead; the reach of his spread fingers on the glass; the light behind his pale blue eyes. 'What were you?' she blurts out.

He laughs. 'Before being reincarnated as an asshole, you mean?'

'No.' Mariah blushes. 'Before you were an atheist. I mean, you were probably born *something*. Episcopalian or Methodist or Catholic.'

'Baptist. Southern Baptist.'

'You have the voice for it,' Mariah says, before she can censor herself.

'Just not the stomach.' Ian leans his shoulder against the nursery's glass wall and crosses his arms. 'I didn't take to the idea of Christ.'

'Maybe you should have tried Judaism or Islam.'

'No, it isn't the Messiah thing. It's the thought that any parent—including God—would make his child suffer intentionally.' He stares at the babies, nestled in a line. 'I can't worship someone who lets that happen.'

Mariah is so surprised, she is speechless. Put that way, how can she not agree? She is still trying to come up with a response when Ian smiles at her, scattering all her thoughts. 'I'll tell you one thing I believe,' he says softly. 'I believe that Faith is going to be just fine.' He leans forward, brushes a kiss against Mariah's cheek, and starts down the hall.

seven

All hell broke loose.

—John Milton,
Paradise Lost

October 15, 1999

TWO DAYS LATER Faith is still in the hospital. As far as I'm concerned, she's fine, with the exception of the open wounds on her hands. But even these, she says, no longer hurt. Dr Blumberg, the hand surgeon, has escorted in a parade of experts to confer on Faith's diagnosis. He won't give us a straight answer about that, and he won't discharge Faith until he does.

I've tried to reach Colin, but his voice mail said only that he'd gone out of town, without specifying where. I've tried calling every few hours, but nothing has changed.

My mother thinks I should worry about Faith, not Colin. She has spent every day here with us and wants to know why I'm in such a rush to get home. In the hospital, at least, none of the reporters or religious zealots can get to Faith.

I have been home myself, of course, to shower and change. The number of people has not really changed—the cult's still there, and the Winnebago—although I have seen neither hide nor hair of Ian Fletcher. This doesn't surprise me. What *does* surprise me is that he's had a live broadcast since Faith was admitted to the hospital, yet he did not mention her injuries.

'Ma,' Faith whines, 'that's the third time I've called you!'

I smile at her. 'Sorry, honey. I didn't hear.'

'No, you were too busy brooding,' my mother mutters.

I ignore her. 'What did you need, Faith?'

'One of those Popsicle thingies. The red kind.'

'Sure.' Rather than bother a nurse, I'll get it from the refrigerator at the end of the hall. I open the door and find Ian Fletcher on the other side, arguing with the policeman who's been thoughtfully stationed to keep Faith from being accosted by any media that might slip past hospital security unannounced.

'I'm telling you,' Fletcher demands. 'You ask her, and she'll let me in.'

'Ask her what?'

He smiles at me and indicates a bouquet of roses. 'I was hoping to see the patient.'

'My daughter isn't available right now.'

Right on cue, Faith's voice pipes up through the open doorway. 'Hey, Mom, who's here?' She scurries to the end of the bed, spies Ian Fletcher, and blushes. 'I guess I'm supposed to thank you for carrying me home the other night.'

Fletcher pushes his way into the room and holds out the roses to Faith. 'No need. White knights like me are always looking around for damsels in distress.'

Faith giggles, and my mother takes the roses. 'Aren't these just to die for?' she exclaims. 'Faith, what should we put them in?'

With an apologetic shrug to the policeman, I step back inside the hospital room and close the door. 'I never did meet a lady who wasn't partial to flowers,' Ian says.

'They make my mom sneeze,' Faith answers.

'I'll have to keep that in mind, then.' Fletcher turns to me. 'So, how is she doing?'

'Much better.'

His eyes remain locked on mine. 'Yes,' he says. 'She looks wonderful.'

We are interrupted by my mother, who bustles between us with the water pitcher full of roses. As she settles them on the nightstand, Ian sinks down onto the edge of the bed. 'Anyone tell you when you can go home?'

'Not yet,' I answer.

'I want to go now,' Faith says. 'It smells bad in here.'

'It smells like a hospital,' Ian agrees. 'Like someone's always cleaning toilets.'

'Were you ever in the hospital?'

A shadow falls across Ian's face. 'Not for myself.' He glances up at me. 'Could I speak to you for a second?'

Again he gestures to the hall. With a silent nod to my mother, I follow him out. This is where the other shoe is going to drop, I tell myself. This is where he will tell me that in spite of his exemplary behavior and yellow roses, I can expect a camera crew ready to record Faith's exodus from the hospital. 'You wanted to talk?'

He stands just a foot away, our shoulders leaning against opposite sides of the doorjamb. Ian clears his throat. 'Actually—'

'Mrs White.' The sound of Dr Blumberg's voice startles me. 'I'm glad you're here. I'd like to speak to you about Faith. Would you join me in the lounge at the end of the hall?'

Although this is what I've been waiting for, I begin to tremble. Somehow I know it is bad news; doctors always want to talk about bad news when they invite you to sit down. If Faith were well, he would have come right into the room. He is going to tell me that Faith has cancer, that she has three weeks to live, that it is somehow my fault. If I'd been a more competent mother, I would have noticed something before now—a lump behind her ear, a slow-healing cut on her knee.

'Mariah,' Ian asks quietly. 'May I?'

He glances down the hallway, where the doctor has already begun to walk, and then back to me. He is asking a thousand questions, catching me at my weakest, and, at the same time, offering his arm so that my legs feel a little less shaky. He should not be privy to this—and yet he was with Faith when it happened; he has seen all there is to see. My need for support edges out my better judgment. 'All right,' I whisper, dazed, and together we begin to walk.

• • •

Beside me, Ian is fussing with something, but I do not look. If it's a tape recorder or a notepad, I don't want to see. It is an effort to keep my eyes trained straight ahead, but when Dr Blumberg asks Ian to borrow his pen, it sparks my interest. He pulls a plastic-wrapped package from his pocket. 'You see this danish?'

It's a tart layered with cherry filling and cheese. Dr Blumberg takes Ian's pen and spears the danish, right through the Saran Wrap and all the fillings and out the other plastic-coated side. 'This is a pretty good example of a penetrating trauma. A puncture wound.' He hands Ian back his pen, now dripping and sticky, and points to the hole in the center of the danish. 'See how the tart is ragged? How the layer of cheese runs into the layer of cherry? And the cherry, it's oozing. A penetrating trauma to the hand tears and distorts tissue. There's skin torn in the periphery or pushed into the wound. Blood clots and mangled tissue from adjacent injured areas fill the wound. More often than not we find hematomas or shattered bones.' Dr Blumberg lifts his eyes to me. 'Your daughter's wounds looked nothing like this.'

'Maybe they weren't . . . penetrating traumas,' I suggest.

'Oh, they were. Went clean through. The operative word there being "clean." X-rays—I've got them in my office—showed these perfectly round little wounds, with perfectly round little gaps in the tissue and the bones . . . but no actual trauma.'

Now I am completely lost. 'That's a good thing?'

'It's an inexplicable thing, Mrs White. I've spent the past two days, as you know, in consultation with colleagues regarding Faith's diagnosis. We all agree: There is no way an object can enter the palm and exit the other side of the hand without causing substantive damage, or at the very least tearing some tissue.'

'But she was bleeding. She passed out because of it.'

'I'm aware of that,' Dr Blumberg says. 'Yet her hands were bleeding slowly. As opposed to a laceration, she hadn't lost enough blood to account for her loss of consciousness. Your daughter's wounds act like punctures . . . but don't look like them.'

'I don't understand.'

'Have you ever read of people who suffer head trauma and can suddenly speak fluent Japanese or French?' the doctor asks. 'They crack their heads on a telephone pole, and for some reason they can understand a language they've never understood before. It's not something you see every day, but it happens. Medically, it's very difficult to explain.' He takes a deep breath. 'After careful consideration, several physicians and myself raised the question of whether Faith actually injured her hands with anything—or if she just started to bleed.'

Fletcher whistles softly beside me. 'You're authenticating stigmata.'

'I am *not* conclusively offering that diagnosis at this juncture,' the doctor heatedly insists; at the same time I say, 'Stigmata?'

Dr Blumberg hesitates, clearly embarrassed. 'As you know, stigmata are supposedly replications of the crucifixion wounds of Christ, Mrs White, medically inexplicable instances where people bleed from the hands, feet, and side without any actual trauma to the body. Sometimes they accompany religious ecstasy. Sometimes these wounds vanish and reappear, sometimes they're chronic. They're almost always reported to be painful. There are apparently several historical instances where physicians have indeed gone on record with that as a diagnosis.'

'You're telling me my daughter—*No.*' Faith is not in religious ecstasy, whatever that is. And why would she have crucifixion wounds when she doesn't know what crucifixion *is*? I hunch my shoulders. 'Those historical instances . . . were from when?'

'Hundreds of years ago,' Dr Blumberg admits.

'This is 1999,' I say. 'Those things don't happen anymore. Those phenomena get x-rayed and carbon-tested and scientifically proven to be fakes.' I turn to Ian Fletcher. 'Right?'

But for once he doesn't say a word.

'I want to see her hands,' I announce. Agreeing, Dr Blumberg gets to his feet and walks back toward Faith's hospital room. 'Honey,' I say brightly as I follow him through the swinging door, 'the doctor wants to examine you.'

'Then can I go home?'

'We'll see.' I stand at Dr Blumberg's side as he unwinds the thick bandages. They've been changed daily, but after Faith's scene in the ER, medical personnel are very careful to keep her from getting a glimpse of the wounds. Gently tugging at the gauze with tweezers, the doctor switches on a gooseneck lamp beside the bed and maneuvers his body so that Faith's view will be blocked. He peels back the last of the bandages on Faith's right hand.

It is just a couple of millimeters wide, the hole, but it is there. The skin surrounding the edges is purple and bruised; there are arrows of dried blood radiating outward. Faith flexes her fingers and, inside, I can see the flash of a needle-thin bone. Yet the wound does not begin to bleed again.

Dr Blumberg probes the edges of the wound. Every now and then Faith winces, and at one point he inadvertently moves out of the way enough to let her get a look at her own hand. She lifts it to her face, peering at the pinhole of light coming through from the other side, while we all hold our breath.

Then she starts to scream.

Dr Blumberg rings for a nurse, and Ian Fletcher struggles along with my mother to hold Faith down. 'Faith,' I soothe. 'It's all right. The doctor's going to make it all right.'

'Mommy, there's a rip in my hand!' she shrieks. A nurse comes running into the hospital room with a Styrofoam tray that holds a syringe. Dr Blumberg firmly grasps Faith's arm and plunges the needle into her thin biceps. After a moment of fighting, she goes limp.

'I'm sorry about that,' Dr Blumberg murmurs. 'I think we ought to continue to keep her here. My suggestion for treatment is to get a psych consult.'

'You think she's crazy?' I say, my voice rising hysterically. 'You saw her hand. She's not making this up.'

'I didn't say she was crazy. It's just that the mind is a powerful organ. It can make a person ill just as easily as a virus. And frankly, I don't know the protocol in this sort of situation. I don't know if the mind can cause the body to bleed.'

Tears fill my eyes. 'She's *seven*. Why would she want to do that?'

I sit down beside Faith on the hospital bed, smoothing her hair while her face relaxes in sleep. Her mouth parts, a bubble rising between her lips. Behind me I hear the doctor speaking softly to my mother. I hear the door open and close twice.

Little girls, they dream of being princesses. Of owning ponies. Of wearing jewels and ball gowns. Not of bleeding for no reason at all, just to be like Jesus.

Ian Fletcher's voice falls quietly at my temple. 'I interviewed a nun once,' he says. 'Seventy-six years old, a Carmelite. She'd been cloistered since she was eleven. According to the Reverend Mother, Sister Mary Amelia had been blessed with stigmata.' Slowly I turn so that I can look him in the eye. 'Everyone thought it was a miracle. Until I found a sewing hook used for ripping out stitches slipped into the hem of Sister Mary Amelia's habit. Turned out there was a very fine line between religious ecstasy and religious insanity.'

You think she did this to herself. I don't have to speak the words; he knows what I am thinking. 'Her hands—the sister's—looked nothing like Faith's.'

'What are you saying?'

He shrugs. 'That this is different. That's all.'

All in all, Allen McManus figures it's a cheap trade. A pepperoni pizza and a six-pack for young Henry, who works part-time in production at the *Globe*, and in return the kid will get on the computer and hack his way into the privileged information of the White family.

'How come it's taking so long?' Allen asks, gingerly moving a piece of sweaty athletic clothing so that he can sit at the edge of the bed in Henry's room.

'My modem's only twenty-eight-point-eight,' Henry says. 'Cool your jets.'

But Allen can't. The more he's learned, the more he's felt anxious. Lately Allen has been remembering quotes from

Revelation, hideous stories told by Sister Thalomena in fifth grade about sinners who went to hell. It has been years since he personally went to confession or took communion, and religion for Allen will always be scarred by the bestiality of the nuns who taught his parochial-school classes. But Catholicism runs deep, and this girl has made him rethink his choices. What if, all these years, he's been wrong? How many Hail Marys and Our Fathers comprise a penance for turning one's back on God?

Suddenly the computer screen begins running with a stream of information. 'Credit-card purchases. This is the missus's card.'

Allen leans forward. Lots of groceries, kids'-clothing stores, a couple of L. L. Bean catalog buys. Nothing dicey. 'Jeez, they even paid the bill off every month.'

'She did. Let's check out her husband.' Henry's fingers fly over the keyboard, pulling up a business American Express card. Slowly, he whistles. 'Looks like Mr White did a bit of socializing on his business trips. Check this out—Lily's Palace of Dancing.'

Allen grunts. 'So he was screwing around on his wife. Big deal.' Infidelity doesn't naturally lead to setting up one's daughter as a fake Messiah. You do something like that to make yourself look better, to draw attention. Or else you're just plain nuts.

'Hey, bingo!' Henry shouts. 'The legal search turned up a name. It's from the records department of the state of New Hampshire. The courts have to file away all the injunctions and crap—just about anything that's brought before a judge. Looks here like Mr White tried to have the missus locked up. No, correction: Looks like he succeeded.'

'Let me see.' Allen sits down and scrolls through the page. 'Holy cow! He had her committed to a mental hospital.' He glances at the original order that landed the woman at Greenhaven, at the repeated hearings Millie Epstein instigated to try to get her daughter released.

Henry lounges on the bed, picking pepperoni out of his teeth. 'Lots of fucking crazy people in the world, man.'

But Allen does not hear him. A mental hospital. Now it makes sense. Seven-year-olds don't just start talking to God; someone puts them up to it. And someone who's crossed the edge once, he figures, is more than likely to do it again.

Getting up from the chair, Allen reaches into a paper sack for a Rolling Rock and tosses one to Henry. 'Cool,' Henry says. 'What are we celebrating?'

Allen smiles slowly. 'Atheism.'

Somehow word has gotten through the hospital grapevine about Faith. Nurses come on the pretense of checking Faith, only to wind up sitting by her side and speaking to her and, in one case, giving Faith a medal of Saint Jude to hold in her mittened hands for a moment.

Faith does not seem to know what to do. When she is awake, she politely answers questions about school and her favorite Disney movies; when she is asleep, these strangers touch her hair and her cheek as if even that small contact will preserve them.

My mother has been in a state all day. 'This doesn't mean anything,' she tells anyone who will listen. 'Stigmata, shmigmata. Jews have been waiting fifty-seven hundred years for a Messiah; we're not going to start believing in Jesus now.' At one point, when Faith is asleep, she pulls me aside. 'Doesn't this bother you? This thing with Faith?'

'Well, of course,' I whisper heatedly. 'You think I want her to go through this?'

'I mean the Catholic thing. Catholic, for God's sake! All these people parading in and out of here like Faith's some saint.'

'Bleeding from her hands doesn't make her Catholic.'

My mother nods emphatically. 'I should hope not.'

The one good thing that happens is this: My mother is in the cafeteria, in search of Jell-O for Faith, when Father MacReady walks through the door that afternoon.

'Charlotte,' he says to the nurse who's brushing Faith's hair—and pocketing strands when she thinks I'm not looking. 'How are you? And the children?'

'We're fine, Father,' the nurse says. 'I guess you've heard what's going on?'

'One of the hospital volunteers works in the church's business office.' The priest waits until the nurse leaves, then sits down in the chair she's vacated. 'Hi. I'm Father MacReady.'

'Why are you wearing that white thing around your neck?' Faith asks.

'It's a special shirt that says he works in a church,' I explain.

'I thought he was someone's father,' Faith says, her brow wrinkling.

The priest grins. 'Actually, that's the most confusing thing of all.' He gently lifts Faith's bandaged hand. 'I hear you speak to God. I like to do that myself.'

'Did she make your hands hurt, too?'

I stare at Faith. Until now, I had not known that this God of hers had told her what would be happening. I hadn't thought to ask.

'No, Faith,' the priest answers. 'God didn't make my hands hurt.'

Is that regret I hear in his voice?

At that moment my mother walks in bearing a tray of lemon Jell-O. 'No red today, Faithele, but—*Oh*.' Her gaze rakes over the priest. 'Already it's starting,' she says sourly.

'You must be Mrs Epstein,' Father MacReady greets her. 'It's a pleasure to meet you.'

My mother purses her mouth. 'I wish I could say the same.'

'Mother!'

'Well, it's true. I'm living life one day at a time now, you know, and I'm not going to cozy up to a man who's trying to convert my granddaughter.'

'Believe me, I have no intention of converting your granddaughter—'

'Of course not! You think it's half done already, what with the bleeding from the hands. Stigmata, my Aunt Fanny!'

I roll my eyes and take the priest's elbow. 'Ma, maybe you could watch Faith and help her with the Jell-O.'

'Good,' my mother announces. 'In the meantime, you get rid of him.'

As soon as Father MacReady and I are in the hallway, I apologize. 'I'm so sorry. My mother isn't exactly taking this well.'

'And you?'

'I'm still getting used to the idea of Faith talking to God. Taking it a step further—well, I can't even get my head around that.'

Father MacReady smiles. 'Stigmata—if that's what they are—are a gift.'

'Some gift. To leave you in constant pain, and make you a freak show.' There is a reason, I know, that the word 'stigmata' is rooted in 'stigma.'

'Millions of people would say your daughter is blessed.'

'*She* doesn't believe she's blessed.' To my embarrassment, my voice wavers. 'Do you know she put on dark gloves when it first happened? She was too ashamed to show me that she was bleeding.'

Father MacReady seems interested by this. 'From what little I know of stigmatics, they don't show their wounds to the world. They hide them.'

After a moment of silence, I stop walking. We have wandered to the end of the pediatric ward, to the infant nursery where I stood with Ian Fletcher. 'I have a confession to make.'

'I seem to bring that out in people.'

'I sneaked into confession once.'

'A confession about confession?' Father MacReady laughs.

'I was only ten. I wanted to see what it was like. But I thought some buzzer would go off, you know, some sensor to show I wasn't Catholic.'

'Nah, the Protestants are the ones with the fancy technology.' Leaning against the wall, he grins. 'Actually, I've always admired the Jews for their lack of confession. You can pass that along to your mother, as a matter of fact.'

'I just might.'

'See, a Catholic sinner confesses, says a few prayers, and gets the shame wiped away. It seems to me Jews carry guilt like camels, forever. Which do you think is the more effective deterrent?' Sobering, Father MacReady turns. 'I don't know if God is speaking to Faith, Mrs White. I'd like to believe it, though. I don't care what other clergymen say; I've never believed that spirit comes from religion. It comes from deep inside each of us; it draws people to us. And your daughter has a lot of it.

'Okay, so it's not Judgment Day. There's no Lake of Fire yawning in front of the green at the town hall. No Book of Life with a list of names in it. So she's a Jewish child with wounds that might be stigmata; so she happens to see a female God. I have to tell you that, although my superiors would probably disagree, I don't find it all that shocking. Maybe this is God's idea of a winning ticket—a way to get many different personalities to worship Him at once. To worship Him at all.'

'But she never agreed to it,' I say. 'She's not anybody's savior, or anybody's martyr. She's just a scared little girl.'

Father MacReady stares at me for a long moment. 'She's also God's child, Mariah.'

I cross my arms to hide the trembling. 'You know, that's where you're wrong.'

Father MacReady locks the door that leads from the rectory to his private quarters. He walks slowly into the kitchen, sitting down at the scarred table and watching the sun play through the dust motes on a thin spotlighted ray. On second thought, he stands up and gets a bottle of Sam Adams out of the refrigerator. He's not one to overdrink, but he feels that his dinnertime beer might be better served right now, in the middle of the afternoon.

The hell of it is that Father MacReady really, truly likes Mariah White.

But he also really, truly loves his church.

'I'm not doing this *to* them,' he murmurs to himself. 'I'm doing it *for* everyone else.' Then he finishes the entire beer.

In the decades he has been a priest, he's counseled on visions twice. The first time was in Vietnam, a soldier who said that the Virgin Mary had come to him in the jungle. The second time was much more disturbing—a sixteen-year-old inner-city girl who claimed that the Holy Ghost had impregnated her. That time Father MacReady had called in the authorities, who all waited with bated breath until the girl delivered a perfectly ordinary baby with a DNA match to the recently hired choir director.

He's never run across stigmata.

With a sigh he removes a battered book from a shelf beneath the telephone and looks up the number of the Chancery in Manchester.

From The Boston Globe, *October 17, 1999*

Mother of Visionary 'Mentally Unbalanced'

New Canaan, NH—If you see it, they will come.

Or so might be the slogan of the seven-year-old New Canaan girl who is allegedly envisioning God. The pious and the curious have flocked to the small New Hampshire town for a glimpse of the child who can work miracles.

But the basis for such heavenly sightings might be far more earthbound than these onlookers might imagine. Sources have revealed that the mother of the girl was hospitalized for mental illness several years ago. A psychiatrist formerly employed by the private psychiatric institution Greenhaven, who wishes to remain unnamed, confirmed that Mariah White was a patient at the Burlington, Vermont, facility for four months during 1991. When asked the nature of her illness, the psychiatrist declined to comment.

According to Dr Josiah Hebert, chairman of the department of psychiatry at Harvard University, some of the most common adult psychotic delusions involve religion. 'If Ms White's illness involved hallucinations about God, it does not necessarily follow that her daughter would experience the same sorts of things,' Hebert said. 'However, in the normal parent-child relationship, parental approval is key, and the behaviors that bring it about are infinitely varied. What we have may not be a case about a visionary, but about a little girl desperately trying to gain

> her mother's attention.' When asked about the alleged miracles effected by the girl, Dr Hebert was dismissive, calling such phenomena beyond the range of both logic and science.
>
> As for the hoopla surrounding the girl's visions, Hebert urges caution. 'I don't think you can seriously credit the claims of a child without examining the formative influences on that child. Which in this case may be more abnormal than paranormal.'

When I least expect it, Rabbi Daniel Solomon sneaks through my defenses.

We have only recently arrived home, Dr Blumberg's having discharged Faith that afternoon. I've just finished tucking Faith into bed and washing up the dishes from dinner when there is a knock at the front door. I am so astonished by the fact that Rabbi Solomon has managed to slip past everyone outside that I step back to let him in before I realize what I'm doing.

He is wild-eyed and disheveled, his long ponytail straggling and his dashiki twisted around his waist. He nervously fingers a string of amber beads at his throat. 'I'm sorry,' he says. 'I realize this must be a bad time—'

'No, no,' I murmur, gesturing to his clothes. 'It's the least I can do for someone who manages to run the gauntlet.'

He looks at his muddy shirt and jeans as if surprised to find them in this condition. 'They don't call us the Chosen People for nothing,' he quips, and glances up the stairs.

Immediately my face tightens. 'She's asleep.'

'Actually, I came here to see you. Do you get *The Boston Globe*?'

'The newspaper?' I ask stupidly. I wonder if he's had the nerve to speak on record about Faith. Almost angrily I grab the copy that he's holding out to me. There on page four is a headline staring me in the face: MOTHER OF VISIONARY 'MENTALLY UNBALANCED'.

The thing about having something hidden in your past is that you spend every minute of the future building a wall that makes the monster harder to see. You convince yourself that the wall is sturdy and thick, and one day, when you wake up and the horrible thing does not immediately jump into your mind, you give yourself the freedom to pretend that it is well and truly gone. Which only makes it that much more painful when something like this happens, and you learn that the concrete wall is really as transparent as glass, and twice as fragile.

I sink onto the stairs. 'Why did you bring this to me?'

'I knew eventually you'd see it. At the time, I thought bringing it here in person would be a *mitzvah*. I figured it was easier to get bad news from a friend.'

A *friend?* 'I was hospitalized,' I hear myself admit. 'My husband had me committed after I tried to kill myself. But I wasn't psychotic like this . . . Hebert idiot says. And I never had hallucinations about God. I certainly didn't pass them along to Faith.'

'I never thought you did, Mrs White.'

'What makes you so sure?' I ask, bitter.

Rabbi Solomon shrugs. 'There's a theory that there are thirty-six people in every generation who are truly righteous people. They're called the *lamed vavniks—lamed* for 'thirty,' and *vav* for 'six.' Usually they're quiet people, gentle, sometimes even unlearned—not unlike your little girl. They don't push forward. Most people don't know about them. But they exist, Mrs White. They keep the world going.'

'You know this for a fact. And you know that Faith is one.'

'I know that the world's been around for a very long time. And yes, I'd like to believe that Faith is one.' Above us, the hall clock chimes. 'Wouldn't you?'

Monsignor Theodore O'Shaughnessy does not get a chance to return Father MacReady's phone call until the following night. He's been busy untangling the administrative nightmares in his little diocese—overseeing the fiscal woes of parochial schools and Catholic hospitals, researching competitive insurance premiums, and, in one particularly overwhelming chunk of time, dealing with a nasty trial involving a Manchester priest and a group of preteen boys at a retreat in the summer of

1987. He sits down in his favorite brown cracked-leather wing chair, picks up the piece of paper with Father MacReady's message, and dials the phone.

'Joseph!' he says jovially when the priest answers on the other end of the line. 'It's Monsignor O'Shaughnessy. Been a while, hasn't it?' In fact, it has been a very long while. The monsignor can conjure a face in his mind, but he's not sure if it belongs to Father MacReady of New Canaan or Father MacDougal of New London. 'You wanted to speak about a youth mission?'

'No,' Father MacReady says. 'A youth's *vision*.'

'Ah. I'm afraid that Betty's a bit old for the secretarial job. She's lost most of her hearing, matter of fact, but I can't bear to let her go. So—it's a vision? As in apparition?' A youth mission—say, building houses for Habitat for Humanity—is one thing. It might even defray some of the bad press the diocese is getting through the sexual-abuse trial. This . . . well, this is only going to make them look even worse. 'What kind of vision?'

'There's a local child here, a seven-year-old girl, who is apparently seeing God.' MacReady hesitates and then adds, 'Technically, she's of the Jewish faith.'

'Then it's not our problem,' the monsignor says, greatly relieved.

'She may also have stigmata.'

Monsignor O'Shaughnessy thinks that, all in all, this has been a very tough week. 'You know what I'm going to do for you? I'm going to call Bishop Andrews. This is really out of my range of expertise.'

'But—'

'No buts,' the monsignor says magnanimously. 'My pleasure.'

He hangs up before Father MacReady can tell him that God, to Faith White, is female. Exhaling heavily, Joseph sets the phone back in its cradle and thinks that maybe this omission is not such a bad thing at all.

• • •

October 17, 1999

THE THING COLIN WHITE LIKES about Las Vegas is this: It never shuts down. As a sales rep, he's spent time in Washington, Seattle, St Paul, San Diego—all of those cities roll up their sidewalks by midnight. Las Vegas throbs like an artery, sucks you in, seduces.

The thing Colin White does not like about Las Vegas is this: He can't get a good night's sleep. He doesn't know if it is because the city burns just outside the hotel window, neon casino signs bright enough to create an artificial day. Or because he cannot get used to his new wife's shifting in his bed all night long. Or maybe he is thinking of Faith, of how he's left her hanging, of what sort of father that makes him.

He leaves Jessica buried in the spiral curl of sleep and walks into the adjoining living-room of the suite, letting his eyes adjust to the darkness. There is a half-eaten apple from the complimentary fruit basket balanced on the arm of the couch. With a sigh Colin sinks onto the cushions and picks up the core, gnawing as he points the remote control at the television set.

There is a commercial promoting vacations in New Hampshire. Colin stares at the wash of fall colors and the profile of the Man in the Mountain, the steep ski runs. With a pang of homesickness he sets down the apple and leans forward, elbows balanced on his knees.

If it were not certain to upset Jessica, he would cut the honeymoon short. There is so much he needs to do to settle his previous life before forging ahead with this new one. He would like to apologize to Mariah for the simple fact that they were not meant to live together. He would like to feel the weight of Faith settled in his arms, the sweet scent of her hair when he leans close to pull up the covers as he puts her to sleep. He would like to be able to say the word 'family' without his gut twisting like a sailor's knot.

On television there's an aerial view of the Mount Washington Hotel.

Snatching the telephone from its receiver, Colin pushes in nearly all the digits of his former number before realizing that in New Hampshire it is four-thirty in the morning. He sets the phone down. Surely Faith is asleep right now.

The familiar theme music of *Hollywood Tonight!* fills the small room. Figures they'd air that crap in the middle of the night. He stretches out on the couch and closes his eyes, opening them just a slit when he hears the voice of Petra Saganoff. He might be tired, but he isn't *dead*.

Her smoky voice rolls over him like a blanket, as a bright-blue banner fills the screen: THE LITTLEST SAINT? 'As you can see,' Saganoff says, 'we're on location, following a story that began last week with Rafael Civernos, the pediatric-AIDS baby who was miraculously cured after playing with a little girl in the yard right behind me.' Squinting, Colin tries to figure out what's so familiar about Petra Saganoff—something he can't quite put his finger on.

'*Hollywood Tonight!* has now discovered that the seven-year-old miracle worker has been hospitalized herself, for a mysterious, inexplicable ailment.' The footage changes to stock photos of stained-glass windows. 'For centuries, Christian saints have manifested religious ecstasy by receiving stigmata—medically impossible wounds on the hands, side, and feet that mirror those of Jesus on the cross.' Saganoff's voice-over begins to lull Colin to sleep. 'For one New Hampshire child, this is only the latest in a growing list of proof that God has somehow touched her.'

Petra Saganoff is back again, standing in front of a stone wall that is lined with people in blankets and sleeping bags, carrying flowers and rosaries and cameras. 'As you can see, Jim, the public acceptance of the girl's claims is growing by the hour. By now there are over two hundred people here who've heard about the visions and miracles of this little girl and want, somehow, to come in contact with her.'

The screen pulls back to reveal the *Hollywood Tonight!* anchor. 'Any word on the girl's medical condition to date?'

'We know she came home from the hospital, Jim. It remains to be seen if this pint-sized healer will now be able to heal herself. This is Petra Saganoff, on location for *Hollywood Tonight!*'

Colin sits up, suddenly realizing why this all looks so

familiar: Petra Saganoff is standing on the eastern edge of his own driveway.

October 18, 1999

'YOU KNOW WHAT?' Ian interrupts, leaving David with his mouth gaping. 'I don't give a flying fuck. All I know is that it's your job to tell me what's going on between the pages of *The Boston Globe*, and this one crucial tidbit was something you managed to overlook.' His voice has risen with each word, to the point where he's backed young David to the narrow door of the Winnebago. Grabbing yesterday's paper from the media assistant's shaking hand, he barely has to scowl in the boy's direction before David flees from the RV.

Ian sinks onto the uncomfortable couch and scans the small piece again, searching for something he's missed. It is an article that should be sending him over the moon with joy—an indirect dig at Faith's credibility that doesn't put Ian himself in the position of muckraker. Allen McManus did a better job than he'd anticipated, not only accessing the records of the court injunction that locked Mariah away but also getting confirmation from a psychiatrist that she was indeed a patient. If this were any other case, Ian would be on his cell phone inviting McManus to come speak at an impromptu press conference. He would be subtly suggesting other routes the reporter might use to slander the White family in general.

Instead all Ian can do is wonder why the hell he ever anonymously phoned McManus's office in the first place.

Ian closes his eyes and knocks his head against the wall of the Winnebago, trying to remember when he'd set that particular ball rolling. Ah, that's right—Millie Epstein's return from the dead. Well, Ian almost excuses himself for that; it's hard to beat. And if he's going to be honest, he's done this sort of thing a hundred times before. In his mind, the more doubts you sow, the more followers you reap. The problem here isn't that he set the reporter on the trail, it's that he set him on the trail of Mariah White.

The hell of it is, he *likes* her. He knows he shouldn't; he knows that it interferes with his judgment—but there it is, all the same. A physical attraction he could dismiss, but it goes beyond that. There are times he's found himself wishing she weren't involved in this case, so that in the end she would not be the one hurt. And that foreign feeling scares him to death.

A knock at the door interrupts his thoughts. Ian yanks it open, expecting to find a penitent David begging for his job, but instead there's someone he's never in his life seen before. The man is middle-aged, with a slight belly and thinning blond hair. He wears a baseball jacket with stains near the line of the zipper. 'Hey! I see you're already a fan of mine,' says the stranger.

Ian glances at his fist, still clutching the *Globe* article.

'Allen McManus,' the man says, holding out his hand. 'It's an honor to meet you. I came here to continue the series, and saw the Winnebago, and . . . what can I say? I guess we're all after the same story. Great minds think alike.'

Ian ignores the man's hand. 'And you're not one of them.'

'But you—'

He grasps McManus's fingers tightly in what would look like a handshake to a passerby, while actually causing great pain. 'I work alone,' Ian says through his teeth. 'And if you ever suggest that I'm in any way affiliated with the bullshit you're printing, I will find so many skeletons in your closet that your boss won't let you write the alphabet, much less the obits.' Then, with great satisfaction, he slams the door in the reporter's face.

At age seven Constantine Christopher Andrews sewed bits of barbed wire into the linings of his clothes, figuring that the only way out of the neighborhood he'd been born in and would probably die in was to do enough penance for God to notice him. His mother, who never bothered to learn English after coming over on the boat from Sicily, always assumed he'd become a priest—the premonition having something to do with a strawberry birthmark in the shape of the cross that clearly marked his belly upon birth. Constantine grew up hearing of his imminent ordination so often that he, too, grew to accept it as fact.

He loved Catholicism. It was a weekly dose of color and gilt and grandeur in a piss-poor immigrant ghetto. His dedication was duly rewarded, and he moved up the ranks of the Catholic hierarchy to the point where, for the past fifteen years, he's served as a bishop. He wanted to retire five years ago, but the Pope wouldn't let him. It's been so long since he's mingled with grassroots Catholics—so long, in fact, since his religion has meant anything more than oiling the wheels in major fund-raising campaigns—that when Monsignor O'Shaughnessy calls with the story of an alleged stigmatic, he is momentarily thrown for a loop.

'What are we talking here?' he asks, exasperated because taking this call means he's going to be late to the Heritage Breakfast at the Italian Center, with some of the richest Catholic businessmen in Manchester. 'Hands, feet, sides?'

'As far as I know,' the monsignor says, 'hands only. Apparently the child is Jewish.'

'Well, that's that. Let the rabbis take care of her.'

'They could. Except there's already been press attention. According to Father MacReady, about three hundred practicing Catholics have visited the site.' He clears his throat. 'There's also the small matter of an alleged resurrection.'

'Press attention, you say?' Bishop Andrews considers. One of the phenomena he's noticed as a member of the Catholic hierarchy is that donations to the Church get more frequent when the faith is promoted as a result of good PR. If he reaches his fund-raising goal by December, perhaps he'll be able to take a little time golfing in Scottsdale.

He wishes, not for the first time, that he were the bishop of a big city like Boston, rather than a small, poor diocese in southern New Hampshire. 'I sent three candidates down to St John's this year. They ought to be able to spare us a seminary priest to look into the matter.'

'Very good, Your Excellency. I'll let Father MacReady know.'

The bishop hangs up the phone and then places a call to the Rector of St John's Seminary in Boston, talking about the

Celtics game for a minute before getting down to business with the same calculated charm he usually saves for glad-handing. It takes less than ten minutes for the rector to cough up a name, which Andrews writes on a slip of paper and routes to his assistant. By the time he leaves his office, he's thinking about whether he'll have the waffles or the French toast, having completely erased the young girl with stigmata from his mind.

The way Faith knows it is not going to be a very good day is that her mother has made banana pancakes for breakfast. She likes pancakes, on the whole, but when the bananas hit the griddle they smell like feet, and the whole time she's trying to swallow, she finds herself thinking of sweaty socks instead, which at breakfast is enough to make you throw up. She must have told her mother a gazillion times that she doesn't like banana pancakes, but, like most things she says, it doesn't stick, causing Faith to wonder if she's really making noise when she speaks or if the volume is turned up only inside her head.

'Ma,' she says, sliding into place at the table, 'I want something else.'

Without speaking, her mother sidles over and removes the banana pancakes. Faith's jaw drops. Whenever her mother goes to the trouble of whipping out more than a cereal box for breakfast, it means that she's put enough time and effort into the meal for Faith to eat whatever is on her plate, thank you very much. Faith watches her mother dump the pancakes into the garbage disposal and absentmindedly flip the switch.

'What am I supposed to eat?'

Her mother blinks at her. 'Oh,' she says, coming back to earth. 'I don't know. Oatmeal?' Without waiting for Faith's approval, she rips open a packet and dumps it into a bowl, then adds water from the Insta-Hot tap. Faith hears the bowl ring as her mother sets it down, and she sniffs. *Banana.*

'I bet Daddy wouldn't make me eat stuff that's totally gross like this,' she mutters.

Her mother whips around. 'What did you say?'

Faith lifts her chin. 'I bet if I lived with Daddy, he wouldn't make me eat this.'

Her mother's eyes are droopy and red, and her voice is so soft that it hurts Faith just to listen to it. Immediately she feels as if she's been kicked in the stomach. She watches her mother swallow hard, as though the banana oatmeal were stuck in her throat. 'Do you want to live with Daddy?'

Faith bites her lip. She loves her father, that much is true, but there is something different about her mother—something easier and more involved—and after all these years of living on the fringe of her mother's life, Faith is not willing to give up a precious second.

'What I want,' Faith says carefully, 'is to stay here.'

It is worth it, the way her mother rushes the space between them to gather Faith in her arms. What is even better is that her mother sticks her elbow in the banana oatmeal. 'Damn,' she says, and then blushes. 'I guess I'd better get you something else.'

'I guess.'

She watches her mother rinse out her sleeve and wet a sponge. 'I'm not very good at this,' she says as she begins to wipe down the table.

Globs of oatmeal spill over the edge, landing on Faith's lap and the floor. She looks up at the way her mother's hair curtains half of her face, at the little dimple in her cheek. As a toddler, Faith would touch that spot on her mother's cheek and then wait for it to cave in when she grinned. She loved that, the way she could fall right into her mother's smile.

'You're doing great,' Faith says, and shyly rises off her seat to kiss the bow of her mother's neck.

Father MacReady sneaks a glance at the priest in the passenger seat of his old Chevy and thinks that having a graduate degree in pastoral psychology isn't what makes you an expert. Father Rourke, fresh from St John's Seminary, is still wet behind the ears. He's so young that he probably wasn't even born when Father MacReady was overseas in 'Nam. And being stuck in Boston, in seminary, only makes him an ivy-tower type. He wouldn't know how to counsel a parishioner if one fell into his lap.

But of course Father MacReady doesn't say anything of the sort. 'Pastoral psychology,' he says amiably, turning onto Mariah White's road. 'What made you get into that?'

Father Rourke crosses his leg, a Polarfleece sock and Birkenstock sandal peeking out from beneath his black trousers. 'Oh, a gift for people, I guess. I would have been a psychiatrist, I suppose, if I hadn't felt another calling.'

And the profound need to tell everyone about it. 'Well, I don't know how much the rector told you about Faith White.'

'Not a lot,' Rourke says. 'Just that I'm here to check out her mental state.'

'For the record, that's been done. By lay psychiatrists.'

Rourke turns in his seat. 'You do realize that the chance of this child's being a true visionary is basically nonexistent?'

Father MacReady smiles. 'Don't you ever see a glass as half full?'

'If it's a mind we're talking about, half isn't nearly as good as whole.'

Father MacReady parks in the field across from the Whites' driveway, in between a camper and a group of elderly women on folding stadium chairs. The seminary priest glances around, his jaw dropping. 'Wow! She's already got quite a following.'

They chat for a while with the policeman at the end of the driveway, another parishioner, thank the Lord, who easily lets Father MacReady pass when he says they've made an appointment to see Mrs White.

'Have we?' Rourke asks as they walk up the driveway. 'Made an appointment?'

'Not exactly.' Father MacReady approaches the front door and knocks, to find a small, elfin face peeking out at them from the sidelight. There is the sound of tumblers falling as a key is turned in a lock, and then the door swings open. 'They're better,' Faith says, holding up her hands for the priests' perusal. 'Look, I only need Band-Aids.'

Father MacReady whistles. 'And they're Flintstone Band-Aids. Very cool.'

Faith glances at the second priest and shoves her hands behind her back. 'I'm not supposed to talk to you.' She suddenly remembers.

'Maybe we could talk to your mother, then.'

'She's upstairs taking a shower.'

Rourke steps forward. 'Father MacReady here was telling me how much he liked talking to you when you were in the hospital, and I was really looking forward to doing that, too.'

Father MacReady realizes Faith is wavering. Maybe there's something to pastoral psychology after all. 'Faith, your mother knows me. Surely she wouldn't mind.'

'Maybe you'd better wait here till she comes down.'

Rourke turns to Father MacReady. 'Well, I don't know what I'm going to do now with all those games I brought.'

Faith rubs her sleeve on the doorknob, bringing it to a high polish. 'Games?' she says.

Upstairs, I have just towel-dried my hair when I hear the sound of male voices. 'Faith!' I dress quickly, my stomach knotting as I race downstairs.

I find her sitting on the floor with Father MacReady and another unfamiliar priest, using a green crayon to circle answers on what is clearly a psychological-assessment test. Gritting my teeth, I make a mental note to call the chief of police and have him send out a Protestant patrolman. 'Faith, you weren't supposed to answer the door.'

'It's my fault,' Father MacReady smoothly answers. 'I told her you wouldn't mind.' He hesitates, then nods in the direction of the second priest. 'This is Father Rourke, from St John's Seminary in Boston. He came all the way up here to meet Faith.'

My cheeks burn with disappointment. 'How *could* you! You were supposed to be on *our* side.' Father MacReady opens his mouth to apologize, but I won't let him. 'No. Don't think you can say something that makes this all right, because you can't.'

'Mariah, I didn't have a choice. There's a certain procedure we follow in the Catholic Church, and—'

'We're not Catholic!'

Father Rourke gets to his feet quietly. 'No, you're not. But your daughter has attracted the attention of a number of Catholic people. And the Church wants to make sure that they're not being led astray.'

I have visions of crucifixions, of martyrs being burned at the stake. 'Mariah, we're not taking pictures,' says Father MacReady. 'We're not going to broadcast the brand of Faith's breakfast cereal on the evening news. We just want to speak to her for a little while.'

Faith stands up and slips her hand into mine. 'It's okay, Mom. Really.'

I look from my daughter's face to the priests'. 'Thirty minutes,' I say firmly. Then I fold my arms over my chest, sit beside her, and prepare to bear witness.

Father Rourke might just as well pick up his diagnostic tests and his inkblots and head back home on the next Amtrak. He does not need the computer analysis to tell him that Faith White is not a child who has lost touch with reality, that hers is not the behavior of a psychotic.

He glances at Father MacReady, picking through a decorative bowl of M&M's on the coffee table and extracting the yellow ones to pop into his mouth. The mother's barely moved a muscle in over twenty minutes. Rourke is at a loss. The girl is not mentally ill, but she doesn't seem to be particularly problematic from a religious standpoint either. It's not as if she yaps about what God's told her, like the woman he was sent to Plymouth to examine. In fact, mostly Faith White doesn't say anything at all.

Trying to figure out his next course of action, he pulls his rosary from his pocket and absentmindedly fingers it. 'Oh,' Faith breathes. 'That's pretty.'

He stares at the polished beads. 'Would you like to see it?'

Faith nods, slipping the rosary over her head like a necklace. 'Is this how it goes?'

'No. It's for praying to God.' At Faith's blank look, Rourke adds, 'Our Father, who art in Heaven, hallowed be thy Name . . . ' He is interrupted by Faith's laugh.

'You've got that wrong.'

'Got what wrong?'

Faith rolls her eyes. 'God's a mother.'

'I beg your pardon?'

'A lady. God's a lady.'

Rourke's face reddens. A female God? Absolutely not. His head swings toward Mrs White, who raises her eyebrows and shrugs. Father MacReady, on the other hand, is the very picture of innocence. 'Oh,' MacReady says. 'Did I forget to mention that?'

Just after 10:00 P.M., the doorbell rings. Hoping not to wake Faith, I scramble down the stairs and yank open the door to find myself staring at Colin.

He looks terrible. His hair is flattened on one side, as if he's been asleep on it; his raincoat is wrinkled; his eyes are bloodshot with lack of sleep. His mouth is a thin slash, pinched tight with disapproval.

He glances over his shoulder at the vans and cars parked in the cornfield across the road, illuminated by a full moon. Faith stumbles sleepily down the stairs and skids to a a stop beside me, her arms wrapped around my waist.

When Colin sees her, he crouches and reaches out a hand. Faith hesitates, then dashes behind me. 'What in the name of God,' he says tightly, 'have you done to my daughter?'

'Actually,' Mariah answers, 'it's funny you should put it that way.'

Colin uses every bit of his self-control to keep from pushing her aside so that he can get his hands on his daughter. Until he got here, he did not really know what he would find. Certainly those trashy telemagazines bent the truth, in the same way the *National Enquirer* supposedly stuck Elizabeth Taylor's head on Heather Locklear's body. Colin thought maybe he'd find that Faith had burned her palm on the stove. Maybe she'd fallen off her bike and needed stitches. There were a multitude of ways to explain a bad camera shot of a little girl's bleeding hands.

But Colin had reserved a coach ticket on the first flight out of Las Vegas, fought with Jessica over coming, traveled all day by plane and rental car, only to arrive at the driveway of his former home and find it blockaded by the police, lined with shrines and tents and hordes of curious people.

'I'm coming in,' he says tightly, and Faith lets go of her mother and skitters upstairs.

'I don't think so. This is my house, now.'

Colin needs a minute to pull himself together. Mariah, telling him no? He shoves forward, only to have her stop him with a bracing hand.

'I mean it, Colin. I'll call the police if I have to.'

'Go ahead!' he yells with frustration. 'They're just at the goddamned end of the goddamned driveway!'

He is tired, crabby, and overwhelmed. When he set their divorce in motion, he had not thought twice about giving custody of Faith to Mariah. He'd never assumed that she would balk when he was ready to introduce Faith to the new mix of his life. She was fair, and when she wasn't, she was a pushover.

Was. 'Look,' he says calmly. 'Can you just tell me what this is about Faith's hands?'

Mariah looks down at her bare feet. 'It's not that easy.'

'*Make* it easy.'

She hesitates, then pushes the door wider so that he can walk inside.

After tucking Faith in again, I explain it all to Colin—the imaginary friend, the medicines for psychosis, the steady parade of priests and rabbis, the resurrection of my mother. For a moment he just stares at me; then he begins to laugh. 'You had me going there for a while.'

'I'm not kidding, Colin.'

'Right. You really think that Faith has some hotline to God.' He laughs again. 'She's always had a hell of an imagination, Rye, you know that. Remember the time she got the whole nursery-school class to believe that when they went outside for recess, they'd be in Disney World?'

I'm having trouble concentrating. There's an anger brewing just below the surface in me, resentment that Colin feels he can walk back in here and issue commands, when he clearly relinquished that right months ago. But there are other emotions, too. Just being in the same room with Colin still feels like a homecoming, as if my body knows the right of it and is reaching for him before I can convince my mind to do the same. A tornado starts in the pit of my belly—one that whirls with the assumption that he's come back for good and sucks my good sense right down through its center.

I watch the play of Colin's mouth, listen to him call me by my nickname, and wonder if I am going to live through being this close to him knowing that he no longer wants me.

'Whatever happened, it's out of control. Do you think it's normal that she can't go to school? That there are a bunch of people sleeping under the rhododendrons who think our daughter—' He snaps his fingers beneath my nose. 'Hey . . . are you even listening to me?'

I stare at his long fingers. In spite of the fact that there was a divorce decree, Colin is still wearing a wedding band.

Then I realize it isn't the one *I* gave him.

'Oh,' Colin says, coloring. 'That.' He covers the ring with the palm of his other hand. 'I, um, got married. To Jessica.'

When I shake my head, my vision of Colin reconfigures. He is no god, no tender memory, but simply someone I will never understand. 'You married Jessica,' I repeat slowly.

'Yes.'

'You married Jessica.'

'Rye, we never would have made it work. I am sorry truly, truly sorry for that.'

My anger returns full force. 'We never could have made it work? How could you know that, Colin, when I was the only one willing to try?'

'Yes, you were. But, Rye—I wasn't.'

He reaches for my hand, but I pull it away and tuck it between my knees. 'You were willing to try again, Colin. Just not with me.'

'No, not with you.' He looks away, embarrassed. 'That's not important right now.'

'It's not? God, what could be more important?'

'Faith. It's not about you this time. You always twist it so it's *your* problem, *your* issue.'

'It *was* about me!' I cry. 'How can you say Greenhaven wasn't about me?'

'Because we're not talking about Greenhaven! Jesus Christ, we're talking about our daughter!' He rakes his hand through his hair. 'It's been eight years, for God's sake. I did what I thought I had to do. Aren't you ever going to forgive me for that?'

'Apparently not,' I whisper.

'I know,' Colin says after a moment. 'I'm sorry.'

'I'm sorry, too.'

He holds out his arms, and I move into them. With detachment I marvel at how you can know someone's body so well, even after a separation, like a land you visited as a child and return to years later, with an eye toward the unfamiliar but a feeling of confidence in your footing. 'I never meant to hurt you,' he murmurs into my hair.

I plan to say the same to him, but it comes out all wrong. 'I never meant to love you.'

Surprised, Colin draws back, a rueful smile on his face. 'That's the hell of it, huh?' He touches my cheek. 'You know I'm right, Rye. Faith doesn't deserve this.'

It strikes me then why he has come: not to make his peace with me, but to take my daughter away.

Suddenly I remember how, years ago, I would sometimes wake him in the middle of the night and ask him a ridiculous question: 'What do you like best about Cracker Jacks—the peanuts or the popcorn?' 'If you were going to be a day of the week, which one would it be?' And others, as if I expected to be a contestant on the *Newlywed Game*. Colin would pull a pillow over his head, ask why I needed to know. I see now that I was storing away the answers, like a squirrel. To give myself a modicum of credit: I did not know that Colin was sleeping with another woman, but I did know that he likes the yolks broken in his eggs. That the smell of wallpaper paste makes him dizzy. That given the choice to learn a new language, he would choose Japanese.

Now Jessica will learn these things. Jessica will have *my* husband, *my* daughter.

Faith didn't deserve this, Colin had said.

And I think, *Neither did I*.

The thought makes my heart catch—what if I couldn't keep Faith?

Suddenly I feel strong enough to move a mountain. To single-handedly sweep away all the people who have stolen my privacy. To carry Faith to where nobody has the chance to touch her in passing or snag pilled wool from her sweaters or sort through her discarded trash.

I am strong enough to admit that maybe I'm doing all right as a mother, all things considered. And I am certainly strong enough to admit that, for the first time in my life, I wish Colin would just go away.

'You know,' I say, 'if Faith told me, without a doubt, that the sky was orange, I'd entertain the notion. If she says so, there's a reason for it, and I'm going to listen.'

Colin stills. 'You believe she's talking to God, and raising the dead, and all of this garbage? That's crazy.'

'No, it's not. And neither was I.' I stand up. 'You made a decision to give me custody of Faith. You have a visit coming up at Thanksgiving. But until then I don't want to hear from you, Colin.'

I walk to the front door and hold it open, although it takes a moment for Colin to get over the shock of being dismissed. He moves briskly to the door. 'You won't hear from me,' he says softly. 'You'll hear from my lawyer.'

In spite of my newfound bravado, I tremble for hours after Colin leaves. I turn on all the lights downstairs and walk from room to room, trying to find a comfortable place. Finally I sit down at the dining-room table, gingerly playing with the shutters on the model farmhouse I made years ago. It isn't accurate now. The wallpaper in the master bath has changed, and Faith has a bed instead of a crib, and—of course—it is now a residence for two instead of three.

I'm furious at Colin for what he's done, what he's threatened. My rage propels me up the stairs, down the hall, to the doorway of Faith's room, where I hover like a ghost. Did he mean it? Would he fight to have Faith taken away?

He would win; this I know. I don't stand a chance. And if it is not Colin who comes for Faith, it will be someone else: another official from the Catholic Church . . . the tabloid-TV reporter whose national coverage brought Colin running . . . or the thousands of others who also saw the broadcast and want a piece of her.

I tiptoe into the room and stretch out beside Faith on the narrow bed, staring down at the slope of her cheek and the spiral of her ear. How is it that you never realize how precious something is until you are about to lose it?

Faith shifts, turns, and blinks at me. 'I smell oranges,' she says sleepily.

'It's my shampoo.' I smooth the covers over her. 'Go back to sleep.'

'Is Daddy still here?'

'No.'

'Is he coming back tomorrow?'

I stare at Faith and make up my mind. It is not what I want to do, but I don't really have a choice. 'He can't,' I say. 'Because you and I are going away.'

eight

Ian Fletcher is a man destined for hell, if ever there was one—unless he manages to prove it doesn't exist before he gets there.

—Op-ed page,
The New York Times, August 10, 1999

October 19, 1999

'FOR THE RECORD,' Millie says, 'I'm against this.'

'I'm not,' Faith announces as Mariah zips her jacket. 'I think it's cool to be a spy.'

'You're not a spy. You're a sneak.' Mariah pats down the placket of the zipper. 'You ready?'

She knows Faith is; she's been ready since 6:00 A.M., when Mariah told her what was going to happen. Of course, she'd couched it in the vocabulary of suspense and adventure, so that Faith would feel more like a young Indiana Jones than a child being taken into hiding. And so far the escapade has lived up to Faith's anticipation—stealing into the car with little more than a knapsack apiece, driving forty-five minutes to the mall, blending into the crowds to lose the two dogged reporters who'd tailed them there. The reporters will no doubt stake out her Honda, waiting for the three of them to appear. But by the time Millie walks to the parking lot to drive the car back home, Mariah and Faith will already have changed clothes and met a taxi at an exit on the far side of the mall, headed toward the airport.

Now all she has to do is say good-bye.

Mariah glances at the mirror in the bathroom at Filene's and catches her mother's gaze. Millie walks forward and puts her arm around Mariah's waist. 'You don't have to let them chase you away,' she says softly.

'I'm not, Ma.' Mariah swallows the lump in her throat. 'I'm getting a head start.' She cannot stand the thought of leaving her mother behind—not only because of the recent heart trouble, but also for the simple fact that Millie is Mariah's closest friend, as well as her mother. Then again, even Millie would agree—you do what you have to do to keep Faith. With it put that plainly, Mariah cannot let herself be steamrolled—again—by people and circumstances beyond her control.

She has not told Millie about Colin's custody threat, nor has she mentioned where she plans to go. This way, when the lawyers get in touch with her . . . or the reporters, or Ian Fletcher—her mother will not be forced to lie. Mariah turns and throws her arms around her mother's neck. 'I will call you. When I can, when I know it's all right.'

Faith burrows between them. 'Get dressed, Grandma! We're going to miss the taxi.'

Mariah touches Faith's hair. 'Honey, Grandma has to stay here.'

'Here?'

'Well, not *here*. But at our house, to watch over . . . things.'

The words do not register. 'Grandma has to come with us,' Faith insists.

Mariah has not told Faith this part of the plan, for exactly this reason; it is the one thing that will make her balk. 'Faithele,' Millie says, crouching down, 'there's nothing I'd like more than to go with you in the taxi on your trip. But I can't.'

'Because someone has to drive our car home,' she says after a moment. 'But you'll come later?'

Millie glances at Mariah. 'You bet.' She zips Faith's spare clothes into the knapsack, then pulls the straps over her granddaughter's arms. 'Be good,' she adds, then kisses Faith on the forehead. She watches Mariah take Faith's hand and lead her out of the bathroom, Faith turning at the last minute to blow a kiss. Then Millie sits down in an empty toilet stall, imagining a thousand things that could go wrong now that Mariah and Faith have run away, imagining a thousand things that could have gone wrong even if they hadn't.

Malcolm Metz spreads his capable hands on the surface of his highly polished desk. 'Let me get this straight, Mr White. You voluntarily relinquished custody of your daughter ten weeks ago. And now you want her to move in with you and your new wife.'

Colin nods. He tries not to feel daunted by the offices of Walloughby, Krieger and Metz, but they were far less intimidating six months earlier when he retrofitted the entire place with electroluminescent exit signs. Of course, back then he was only taking care of business. This visit is far more personal, and there's much more at stake.

'That's correct.' He assesses Metz slowly, from the man's close-cropped salt-and-pepper hair to his Italian loafers. Known for his bulldozing drive to win, Metz is something of a New Hampshire litigating legend.

The attorney taps the tips of his fingers together. 'Why the change of heart?'

Colin feels the beginnings of a slow burn. 'Because my ex-wife is crazy? Because my daughter's been turned against me? Because I'm worried about her welfare? Take your pick.'

Metz has heard it all before. As a matter of fact, he has a court appearance in less than two hours as the divorce attorney for a reputed Mafia wife, and he would much rather be in the executive washroom perfecting his demeanor for the cameras that are sure to be there. A custody case like this—well, he should be able to win it in his sleep.

'What has your ex-wife done to endanger your daughter?'

'What have you heard about the little girl who's seeing God?'

Malcolm stops drumming his fingers on his desk. 'That's your kid?'

'Yeah. No.' Colin sighs. 'Ah, shit. I don't even know anymore. There are a couple hundred people at the end of the driveway, and they all believe that Faith's turned into some prophet, and her hands are bleeding and . . . Christ.' He looks at the attorney. 'This is not the little girl I left.'

Malcolm silently extracts a yellow pad from a drawer of his desk. The potential for media coverage of this case is extraordinary—far beyond the narrow range of New Hampshire. He uncaps a pen and decides to sink his teeth in. 'You believe that you would be better able to serve the interests of this child. You believe that living with her mother, as it stands, is adversely affecting your daughter.' Colin nods. 'Can you tell me why you didn't believe these same things just four months ago?'

'Look, if I'm going to pay you a twenty-thousand-dollar retainer and five hundred dollars an hour over that, then I don't have to explain anything. I want my daughter. I want her now. I heard that you could help me. Period.'

Malcolm holds his client's gaze for a moment. 'You want full custody?'

'Yes.'

'At all costs?'

Colin does not have to ask what Metz means. He knows that the surest way to prove himself the better parent is to make Mariah look worse. By the time this is over, Mariah won't lose only Faith. She'll also have lost her self-respect.

He shifts uncomfortably. It is not what he wants to do, but he doesn't really have a choice. Just as when he made the decision to have Mariah committed, the ends here justify the means. Just as then, he is only concerned for the safety of someone he loves.

He has a painful flashback of the night Mariah tried to kill herself—the blood everywhere, his name still bubbling on her lips. He forces himself to imagine Faith hiding when he appeared yesterday at the door. 'I want my daughter back,' Colin repeats firmly, convincing himself. 'You do whatever it takes.'

Last Tuesday Ian Fletcher flew out of Manchester, a little airport trying to pretend it was several shades more cosmopolitan than it actually was. It was, in a word, a nightmare.

Not only was his flight to Kansas City delayed, but there was no Admiral's Club to lounge in before the flight, meaning that he'd spent the better part of an hour hiding in a bathroom stall to avoid recognition. This week he was flying out of Boston. It meant a longer limo ride to the airport, but a considerably less stressful journey.

'Sir? What airline are you traveling?'

At the sound of the chauffeur's voice, Ian leans forward. 'American.' He gathers his briefcase as the limousine snakes into a spot at the curb, signs the credit-card receipt, and hands the clipboard back to the driver without saying another word. Keeping his head low, he ducks to the right, toward the bank of elevators that he knows will take him to the private first-class passenger club, where he can wait in a secluded room until his flight is called.

Mariah stands in front of the departures board, skimming the list of destinations. So many places; how is she to pick? It is not as if one destination holds any edge over another—no matter where they wind up, they will be starting from scratch.

'Mom?' Faith asks, tugging at her arm. 'Can we go to Vegas?'

A smile tugs at Mariah's mouth. 'What do you know about Vegas?'

'Daddy went there once. You can push buttons, and money just comes flying out at you. I saw it on TV.'

'Well, it's not quite like that. You have to be very, very lucky. And anyway, I don't even see a flight to Las Vegas listed here.'

'So where *are* we going?'

Good question. Mariah smooths her hand over her purse, considering how much money she has inside. Two thousand dollars in cash—God, she feels like a walking target. But she knows better than to leave a paper trail, and this was as much money as she could get out of a local bank on short notice. If they are frugal, she and Faith should be able to remain undetected for a little while at least. And if they manage to elude the media, maybe the interest in Faith will just die down.

Without a passport, she's limited to the United States. Hawaii—she's always wanted to go to Hawaii, but the tickets are sure to be phenomenally expensive and eat into their budget. Mariah's eyes run down the columns again. There is a flight to Los Angeles at noon. One to Kansas City, Missouri at eleven-fifteen.

She leads Faith to the line where they can purchase standby tickets, deciding that their destination, quite simply, is whatever plane leaves this airport first.

As they board, Mariah finds herself thanking God that the story about Faith has only just gone national, meaning that most people with whom they come in contact—the flight attendant, the nice man who offers to stuff their knapsacks into the overhead compartment—look at them and see a mother and her child, instead of a pair of media fugitives.

Faith has only been on a plane twice before, once as a baby when her grandfather died and once when they all went to Washington D.C., for a family vacation. She bounces in her seat, craning her neck to get a better peek at the first-class cabin, which they are seated directly behind. 'What's in there? How come the seats are a different color?'

'It's where businessmen and people who have a lot of money sit. They pay more for those seats.'

'Why didn't we pay for them?'

'Because . . .' Mariah throws an exasperated look in her daughter's direction. 'Just because,' she says as the flight attendant unsnaps a blue curtain to shield the cabin from view.

'Final boarding call for Flight 5456 to Kansas City . . .'

Ian strides toward the gate and presents his boarding pass. 'Mr Fletcher,' the airline representative says, 'I enjoy your show.'

He nods brusquely and hurries toward the plane, handing the flight attendant his coat and settling into his seat. 'Good morning, Mr Fletcher. Can I get you something to drink before takeoff?'

'Bourbon, straight.'

There are three other passengers in first class, a pain in

the ass, but not a tragedy. It would have been worse if one of them had been seated beside him. The flight attendant returns with his liquor. This weekly flight, like everything else about his visits to Michael, is a routine. He sets down the glass and closes his eyes, drifting into a dream in which cards fall red and then black, red and then black, in endless succession.

'I have to pee,' Faith announces.

Mariah sighs. The drink cart is directly behind them, blocking the route to the lavatories in the rear; there's no way Faith will be able to hold it in until the flight attendants finish the beverage service. She eyes the blue curtain that leads to the first-class cabin. 'Come here.'

She leads Faith through the short aisle strip quickly, hoping that she can get her into the little bathroom before a flight attendant busts them for trespassing. 'Here,' she says, nearly hauling Faith into the cubicle. 'Don't forget to lock the door so the lights come on.' Then she leans against the humming wall of the plane, glances around first class.

And finds herself staring at Ian Fletcher.

Oh, God. There is nowhere to go on a plane. Mariah takes the coward's way out, hustling Faith back to their seats after she comes out of the lavatory and thoroughly avoiding Ian Fletcher's gaze the entire way. She closes her eyes in disgust. There must have been—what, fifty flights?—leaving Logan Airport this hour, and she managed to blindly choose the one with Fletcher on it. The person who had the most to gain from giving up her and Faith's whereabouts.

Then it strikes her: This was no chance meeting. Somehow Ian Fletcher managed to follow them to the airport. She doesn't know why he doesn't get it over with, just stomp back here to steerage and tell her he's got her number. Maybe he's using one of those little AirPhones even now to arrange for a producer and a camera crew to meet them in Kansas City.

She feels tears constricting her throat. Her grand plan is over before it's even started.

• • •

For a full minute after Mariah White flees like a frightened rabbit into the back of the plane, Ian entertains the thought of calling James Wilton and directing the hounds to the fox; he even goes so far as to take a credit card out and read the AirPhone instructions, but then remembers why he cannot. The very last thing he wants to do is bring the media crashing down within a hundred miles of Michael.

Mariah White doesn't know it, but she has just as much of an edge on Ian as he has on her.

Ian finishes his bourbon and signals the flight attendant for another. The easiest way out of this is to go along with what Mariah is no doubt thinking: that he tailed them from New Canaan to the Boston airport. Otherwise she'll wonder why he's on a plane bound for Kansas City. It is one thing for him to learn all her secrets, another thing entirely for her to learn his. His entire trip will have to be changed now.

A thought takes root in Ian's mind. What if he can watch Faith put on her private healing show at close range? What if he handpicks the target of her so-called miracle, so that she can't help but fail? The grandmother and the woman with the AIDS baby, they could have been in on the action somehow. But Michael—well, no one knows better than Ian himself that Michael isn't part of their charade . . . and that Michael can't be cured.

All he has to do is whittle away at their sympathies, so that they agree to try to fix Michael as a personal favor to Ian. And while Faith White is attempting to pull off her hoax, he gets an up-close, personal look at how it's being done. Even Michael's anonymity is preserved; Mariah White's not about to go blabbing if it means revealing her location.

The ludicrous image of Faith laying hands on Michael in some charlatan revue that's been choreographed by her mother gives way in Ian's head to the image he's tucked so far away that it aches to bring it to the surface: Michael looking him in the eye, Michael reaching for him of his own volition, Michael clapping him on the back in an embrace.

Ha—more likely he'd see Mariah White scrambling to explain that the moon is out of alignment or some other crap like that to excuse the fact that her miraculous daughter couldn't heal an autistic man.

If Ian were a man who believed in destiny, he'd think it was fate that brought the Whites to this particular plane. Instead he considers it an opportunity that's dropped into his lap, one that could potentially become the story of a lifetime. He only has to charm Faith and her mother into thinking that a cynic like him might not be the enemy after all, might actually pin his hopes on a child with the alleged power to heal, might stand by and act devastated when Faith ultimately fails.

But would that really be an act?

Mariah isn't surprised when she steps off the plane to find Ian Fletcher waiting for her, nor is she surprised to have him ignore her—entirely—for Faith. 'Hey, there,' he drawls, getting down to her level. 'Did y'all come out on this plane, too?'

Faith's eyes widen. 'Mr Fletcher!'

'The one and only.' He stands up and nods. 'Ma'am.'

Mariah squeezes Faith's hand, a warning. 'We're here for a wedding. My cousin's wedding. Tonight.' Her voice is too high, staccato, and the moment she volunteers information Fletcher didn't even solicit, she feels as if she could kick herself.

'That so? Don't believe I ever heard of a wedding that took place on a Tuesday night.'

Mariah's chin lifts a notch. 'It's . . . part of their religion.'

'Seems there's a lot of that goin' around.' He smiles at Faith. 'On account of us running into each other, what do you say we get an ice cream?'

Faith, clearly excited by the idea, turns to Mariah. 'We don't have time,' Mariah says.

'But we don't have any—'

'Faith!' Mariah interrupts, then sighs. 'All right. We can get an ice cream.'

Ian leads them to an airport cafeteria. He orders a cone for Faith and Cokes for himself and Mariah. 'Faith, your mama and I want to have a talk. How about eating your ice cream over there at that table?'

As Faith runs off, Mariah tries to call her back, but is stopped by Ian's hand on her arm. For a moment she cannot breathe, cannot move, until he takes it away. 'Let her go. You've got a clear view, and you're fifteen hundred miles away from the people who want to get to her.'

Mariah defiantly turns. 'We could just walk away from you. You can't stop us.'

'You gonna call the police? I doubt it. First of all, that'd leave a paper trail. And something tells me you don't want to leave one of those.' He smiles sadly. 'Would you believe me if I said I was here for any reason other than you and Faith? I didn't think so. The hell of it is, Miz White, that I admire you for this. And I'd like to offer you some advice.'

'Said the fox to the gingerbread man,' Mariah mutters.

'What was that?'

'Nothing.'

'Huh. Well, what I was about to say was that you can't be too careful. Have you given any thought as to where you and Faith will be staying?'

Refusing to let him in on their plans, Mariah tightens her mouth.

'A motel, I'll bet,' Ian continues breezily. 'But sooner or later it'll cross your mind that a lady staying with a little girl for some time in a dingy motel will stick out like a sore thumb. On the other hand, moving from motel to motel is going to be awful hard on a child. So that'll leave you at the mercy of a local friend—of which I'm willing to bet you don't have too many—or leasing some cheap apartment. Thing is, Miz White, any landlord worth his salt is gonna want some references. And they're hard to come by when you're anonymous. Plus, that doesn't even address the problem of how to rent yourself a car, when your driver's license and credit card are surely items you don't want recorded for posterity.'

Having had about enough of this, Mariah starts to move away. The hell with Ian Fletcher. The hell with Kansas City. There are at least a hundred connecting flights leaving this afternoon; all she has to do is manage to slip past him once more. She turns toward Faith, but he grabs her wrist, holds her. 'I will find you,' he whispers, reading her mind. 'You know that.'

Still, her eyes flicker toward the corridor, the bathrooms, all the possible exits. 'You said you were going to give me some advice.'

'That's right. I think you ought to look up an acquaintance while you're in town.'

Mariah chokes on a laugh. 'Wait. Let me think of all the sorority sisters I have in Kansas City.'

'I meant me,' Ian says softly. 'I think you should stay with me.'

For a long moment Mariah only stares at him. 'Are you crazy?'

His eyes are as blue as a pool, as inviting to fall into. 'I just may be, Miz White,' he admits. 'Because if I wasn't, I surely would have told my producer about your little girl's hands last week. I would have had a bunch of cameras waiting to meet you when you got off that plane, instead of just me. I would have spent that flight thinking I was out to expose you to the world, instead of thinking that maybe, this one time, I could do the right thing and help hide you away.' He glances at Faith. 'It's the ultimate cover. The very last place anyone would ever expect you'd go underground . . . is with me.'

'Unless you told them so yourself.' Mariah's gaze is unflinching. It is impossible for her to trust this man, whom she never even would have met if not for his interest in Faith as a juicy story. But then again, she cannot fault his claims. As blustery and vindictive as the public image of Ian Fletcher is, in private, he has often been sympathetic. And yet to run away from the eyes of the press and into Fletcher's residence seems like a direct and suicidal jump from the frying pan into the fire.

He has not released her wrist, and his thumb grazes the skin along the ridge of her scar. 'You have my word that I won't give away your hiding place. And you will have your privacy.' Then he smiles. 'What's worse, Mariah? The devil you don't know . . . or the devil you do?'

• • •

They're buying it. Ian is nearly giddy with relief as Mariah walks toward Faith and speaks to her daughter about the change in plans. She's still wary, but that's all right. Let her think he has a hidden agenda. After all, he does. It's just not what Mariah White thinks. Getting Faith to the point where she willingly comes to meet Michael—and getting her mother to the point where she allows this—will take the bulk of Ian's thespian skills.

As she walks back with her daughter in tow, Ian is struck again by her features. It's the contradictions that draw him: the stunning green eyes, puffy and tired; the soft mouth bracketed by lines that have been carved by pain. 'So,' she says hesitantly, 'you have a home here?'

At that, Ian almost laughs. He wouldn't live in this state if it were the last place on earth. 'Give me an hour and I will.'

He leads them to an Avis dealership and rents a car, signing it out on a Pagan Productions corporate credit card. Mariah remains in the background near a bank of phones, unwilling to risk being seen by someone who might later identify her or Faith. As he returns with keys in hand, Ian checks his watch and scowls. He has less than an hour to get to Michael.

'Do you know where you're going?' Mariah asks as they turn onto the interstate.

'West. I thought it might be better to get outside the city.' And closer to Lockwood.

'You drive like you know your way.'

'I come here a fair amount on business,' Ian lies. 'There's a little place in Ozawkie that rents cabins on Perry Lake. I've never stayed there, but I must have passed their sign a hundred times. I figured we could stop up there and give it a try first.'

'Can we go swimming?'

Ian grins at Faith in the rearview mirror. 'Don't think your mama's gonna let you swim when it's this cold. But I can't imagine she'd get angry at a little fishing.'

In a while they turn off and drive across the flats from Missouri into Kansas. Mariah glances out the window, staring at stubbled fields where corn was recently harvested. Faith's nose is pressed to the glass. 'Where are the mountains?'

'Home,' Mariah murmurs.

As Mariah looks at the beaten shacks that comprise Camp Perry, she tells herself that beggars can't be choosers. She and Faith might have found more luxurious accommodations, but, as Fletcher has said, they'd also be easily traced. She watches him circle the manager's office and knock on the door, then step up and peer into a window. When no one answers, he shrugs and walks toward the car. 'Looks like—'

'Can I help you?'

A little old lady with the look of a wren about her opens the door of the manager's office. 'Why, yes'm, you can,' Fletcher says, his voice dripping with charm. 'My wife and I were hoping to rent one of your charming establishments.'

Wife?

'We're closed for the season,' the woman says. 'Sorry.'

Fletcher stares at her for a moment. 'Surely a good Christian woman like yourself would be willing to make an exception if it furthered the work of Our Lord.'

Mariah nearly chokes on her tongue. 'Mommy,' Faith whispers from the backseat, 'how come he's talking weird?'

She cranes her neck back. 'Ssh. He's putting on a show. Like a play for us to watch.'

'Jesus told me to pack it all up October first,' the woman says.

'That is a pure shame, ma'am.' Ian shakes his head. 'Because He told me to listen to His voice right here at Camp Perry.' He comes forward, extending a hand. 'Forgive me for not introducing myself sooner. I'm Harry Walters, a preacher from Lou'ville. This here's my lovely wife, Maybelle, and my daughter Frances.'

'Frances is a fine name,' the woman says. 'My maiden aunt's name.'

'We thought so ourselves.'

The woman cocks her head. 'You say you're a preacher?'

'That I am. And a musical one at that. I'm the director

of the Greater Kentucky Hymn Sing, and this year the Lord's called me to fashion a few new tunes in His name.'

'I been to those hymn sings myself. Always did believe in offering up a joyful noise.'

'Amen, ma'am,' Fletcher says.

The woman throws up her hands. 'Well, who am I to stand in the way of the Lord? I can't promise you regular housekeeping, but I imagine I can poke around and find some sheets yet.' She walks back into the manager's house, presumably to find a key.

Ian Fletcher turns toward Mariah and Faith and gives a nearly imperceptible bow. Mariah bursts out with a startled laugh. The nerve of the man! He approaches the car and opens her door. 'Maybelle, honey,' he says, smiling hugely, 'looks like I got us a temporary home.'

'*Maybelle?* You couldn't have picked Melissa, or Marion, or—'

'I like Maybelle. It seems . . . bovine.'

Mariah glares at him, then turns to the backseat. 'Come on, Faith—'

'Frances,' Ian interrupts.

'Whatever.' She helps Faith tug her knapsack from the car as the old lady comes out of the manager's house.

'You got bungalow seven. I go to bed at nine o'clock, and I don't care if it is Jesus you're singing to—you make sure it's quiet then.' She turns and leaves them to their cabin.

Crossing the threshold, Ian becomes another person entirely. 'Christ. Did someone *die* here last summer?'

Mariah, standing in the doorway, cannot fault his observation. To call the cabin rustic would be a stretch of flattery. A ratty braided rug with numerous stains graces the floor. Off the central room are two doors, one leading to a bathroom the size of a closet and one leading to the only bedroom. There's a coffee table, a frayed plaid couch, and a battered kitchen table, on which rests an assortment of mismatched, dusty Tupperware.

'This is gross.' Faith scowls. 'I don't want to stay here.'

Mariah immediately forces herself to smile. 'It's an

adventure. Like camping out, except we have a bed.' She peers into the bedroom. 'Well, one of us has a bed.'

Ian snorts. 'You and Faith can sleep in it. I'll risk the communicable diseases growing on the couch.' He sits down heavily on it and bows his head, his shoulders shaking in silence. For a stunned moment Mariah thinks he might be crying, but then a guffaw spills out of him as he tips back his head. 'God, if my producer could see me now,' he says, wiping his eyes. 'The Winnebago is a goddamned *palace* compared to this.'

It is at the mention of his producer that Mariah realizes what's been niggling at the back of her mind. She's terrified of being recognized, although she and Faith are still far from familiar faces. However, Ian Fletcher is a household name, a celebrity. And yet he can walk up to the Avis counter without causing a rush of fans; he can pretend to be Preacher Harry Walters and no one recognizes him. 'How come?' she asks quietly. 'How come she didn't know you?'

Ian grins. 'This is the Bible Belt, sweetheart. We got hymn sings and little old ladies who want to please Jesus, but not a huge population of atheists. I've got a built-in disguise here, because I'm not real high on the must-see-TV list of most of these religious folk.'

Mariah raises a brow. 'You couldn't have known by looking at her that that old lady's never seen your show.'

'I'd stake my bets.'

Annoyed by his certainty, she crosses her arms. 'Because she's elderly? Because she couldn't see through your snow job?'

'No, Miz White.' Fletcher leans forward and flicks on the battered TV set to reveal a screen of static. 'Because she doesn't have cable.'

By the time Ian gets to Lockwood he's an hour and seventeen minutes late. He's left Mariah and Faith at the cabin with the excuse that he's going to find food at the market. Now he flies into the recreation room, where he usually finds Michael. Peering through the door, he sees Michael still sitting in his usual corner, tossing down cards.

Tempered with the wash of relief that Michael's waited

for him is the bitter realization that there's nowhere for him to go.

'Hey.' Ian pushes inside and draws up a chair. Sweat runs down his temple, but he doesn't remove his coat just yet. He knows the routine; first Michael has to acknowledge him.

A red card falls. Then a black one. Ian rubs his temple against his collar.

'Three-thirty,' Michael says quietly.

'I know, buddy. I'm an hour and . . . twenty minutes late.'

'It's four fifty-one. Twenty seconds. Twenty-two seconds. Twenty-four—'

'I know what time it is, Michael.' Irritated, Ian shrugs off his coat.

'Three-thirty. Three-thirty on Tuesday. That's the time that Ian comes.' Michael begins to rock gently in his seat.

'Ssh, Michael. I'm sorry now. I won't let it happen again.' Recognizing the warning signs, he moves slowly, holding his hands up as he comes closer.

'Three-thirty!' Michael yells. 'Three-thirty on Tuesday. Not on Monday. Not Wednesday Thursday Friday Saturday Sunday! *Tuesday Tuesday Tuesday!*' As quickly as the outburst has come, it's over. He pulls his chair away from Ian, into the corner of the room, his shoulders hunched over his deck of cards.

'You were late.'

Ian turns to find one of the psychiatrists who come daily to Lockwood standing a few feet away. His smile twists. 'So I've been told.'

'Michael has a gift for that, doesn't he?' The doctor laughs. 'Your flight was late?'

'No. I got hung up on my way here.'

'Well, in his world there's no room for mistakes. Don't take it personally.'

Ian calls the man as he turns to go. 'What do you think would happen if I came back tomorrow? Or a couple of days after?'

'You mean other than Tuesday at three-thirty?' The psychiatrist considers Michael, in the corner. 'I think it would set him off again.'

Ian nods and looks away. He'd thought so, too. It means that he has seven days, exactly, to get Faith White back here.

He sighs and pulls up a chair directly behind Michael. Ian can see the crown of his head, peppered with gray now, and it depresses him. What kind of life has it been here, for so long?

A better one than it almost was. The voice in his head is an absolution. Lockwood is a supervised-care facility, just one step away from a residential group home, and considerably better than an institution. One day, maybe, Michael will be ready to live on his own. Until then, this is the best care money can buy.

Wearily, Ian glances at his watch, and sits in silence for the rest of the hour, because even if Michael is not speaking to him directly, he's fully aware of how long Ian stays. He watches Michael rock, a metronome, and wonders how a man like himself, who has no use for the Bible, has become his brother's keeper.

By the time Ian returns to the cabin, the sun has set. Still rattled by Michael's outburst, he absently walks up the gravel path, lets himself inside, and stops dead. The small open room of the cabin is lit by candles, the scarred kitchen table covered with a checked table runner. Clean silverware and chipped dishes are laid out at place settings. Mariah has moved some of the furniture around to hide watermarks on the wooden floor and suspicious streaks on the walls. It's still not the sort of room to which he's accustomed, but it looks . . . almost cozy.

Mariah and Faith freeze on the couch like two deer caught in headlights. After a moment Mariah gets to her feet and wipes her palms on her thighs. 'I figured if we were going to be here awhile . . .' she says, letting her voice trail off.

Ian's gaze falls to Faith and to the battered game of Yahtzee sprawled across the coffee table in front of her. The girl draws her knees up, hiding her face, and rattles the dice in her cupped palm. He fights the urge to sit beside her, to kick off his shoes and set his stockinged feet beside the Yahtzee tumblers.

'. . . in the car?'

It is a moment before Ian realizes Mariah is speaking to him. What stuff in the car? Groaning, he remembers his excuse for leaving—the groceries. 'I, uh, haven't gotten around to it yet,' he says, backing toward the door. 'I'll head out now.' He all but flees outside, before Mariah can ask him where he's been all this time, before he breaks down and simply tells her.

It begins to rain as he drives away from the cabin. In the rearview mirror he sees Mariah standing in the doorway, silhouetted by the yellow light from the candles. Where did she find those candles? Or the board game? Or any of the other stuff, for that matter? Ian's hands tremble on the steering wheel as he tries to remember the way to the nearest Piggly Wiggly. The frayed rugs, the battered games, the woman waiting on him—they circle in his mind. He forces himself to make a mental list of what he'll buy: milk and juice and eggs, cereal and soda pop and macaroni, item after item crowding out the unsettling thought that the life he has been leading, for all its luxury, is nowhere near as fine.

Her mother keeps skipping the good parts. It's bad enough that Faith has no books for a bedtime story—in spite of what her mother said, *Reader's Digest* doesn't count—but now her mom can't even get through a memorized version of Little Red Riding Hood without telling it wrong. 'The basket of food,' Faith prompts. 'For Grandma. Remember?'

'Right.' Her mother keeps looking at the door. Faith guesses it's because she's hungry. Ian Fletcher was supposed to bring dinner, but he'd spaced out, and so all Faith had was a handful of Tic-Tacs from her mother's purse. If she closes her eyes and tunes out her mother's voice, she can hear her stomach gurgling, like the falls down by the New Canaan Dam.

'So Red Riding Hood gets to the door and knocks and the wolf—'

'You didn't even talk about the wolf yet,' Faith complains. 'He has to eat Grandma.'

'For God's sake, Faith, if you know it so well, why don't you just tell it to yourself!'

When she was getting into her nightgown, Faith had said something like she hoped God could find her all the way out here in Kansas, and her mother had jumped at her and said she absolutely, positively couldn't talk about God in front of Ian Fletcher. Now her mother doesn't even want to tuck her in. Faith rolls onto her side. If she cries right now, she doesn't want anyone to see it. 'Fine,' she mutters.

She feels her mother's hand on her arm. 'I'm sorry. I shouldn't have snapped at you.'

'Whatever.'

'No, it was wrong of me. I'm hungry and I'm tired, but that's not your fault.' Her mother scrubs the heels of her hands into her eyes and sighs. 'I'm not up for a bedtime story right now, Faith, okay?'

'Okay,' she murmurs.

Her mother smiles and kisses her hair. 'Thanks.'

As she gets up, Faith reaches for her sleeve. 'I don't like it here.' Her voice catches in her throat, which embarrasses her, but she doesn't know how to stop it. And before she even has a chance to try to stop them, the tears come. 'It smells funny and they don't have the Disney Channel and there's nothing to eat.'

'I know, honey. But Mr Fletcher's going to fix that.'

'How come he's even here? How come we have to stay with him?'

Her mother suddenly looks so upset that Faith wishes she'd never even asked the stupid question. 'We'll go one day at a time,' her mother says. 'If living with Mr Fletcher doesn't work out, we'll just take a plane somewhere else. Las Vegas, maybe.'

That soothes Faith. She feels her mother curl up behind her. It makes Faith think of a hammock in their yard, a web of rope that she thought would unravel the first time she leaned back on it, but that managed to support her all the same. 'Maybe we'll get lucky,' Faith answers, yawning.

Her mother's arms come around her, hold fast. 'Maybe we will.'

First thing, he smells the smoke. Twin towers of fire reach up as far as he can see, making black spots before his eyes, but he knows that he has to get through them. His parents, Christ, they're burning— He dives headfirst into the heat, ignoring the pain that races up his arms and legs and flays the skin off his back. His eyes swell with the heat and the soot, but he can see five fingers, the outline of a hand, and he stretches toward it, slips palm against palm, and closes around a wrist. A yank—they're tumbling free now, and he lands clear, only to find that he's holding tight to his brother. His brother, who cannot be touched, who cannot bear to be touched, who stares at Ian's hands on his shoulders and screams loud, loud, loud –

'Mr Fletcher.' He jerks away, sweating, the covers pooled onto the floor. Mariah White kneels beside the hideous couch, touching his arm. 'You were having a nightmare.'

'It wasn't a nightmare,' Ian insists, although his voice is still hoarse. It wasn't a nightmare, because that would mean he's been asleep for a while, and the chances of that are next to nothing. He shrugs away from her and huddles at the far end of the couch, wiping his sweaty face with the edge of his T-shirt.

He should have known better than to try to stay in Kansas City and pretend that it would be all right. The town holds nothing for him but rotten memories. Even if his ploy to get Faith and Michael together works, it's inevitable that he'll experience some of the fallout.

Mariah offers him a glass of tap water. Hand shaking, he takes it and drinks deeply. His eyes follow hers to the counter, where he's set the nonperishable groceries. When he'd come home last night, the door to the tiny bedroom had been closed and a stack of sheets and blankets left on the couch. He'd told himself that rather than bang around cabinets and wake the Whites, he'd just get to it all in the morning. Then he'd pulled out a pad and scribbled notes for next week's broadcast. It is the last thing he remembers, until finding Mariah White by his side.

'You were saying something about a fire,' she says hesitantly.

'I'm sure I was saying a whole lot of things.'

'I wouldn't know. I only just came out.'

'I didn't wake your daughter, did I?'

Mariah shakes her head. 'Faith sleeps like a rock.'

'Then I apologize for waking you.'

'Well, you didn't exactly wake me.' A smile ghosts over her lips. 'That mattress was a torture device in a previous life.'

Ian laughs. 'They probably used it to finish off the prisoners who didn't succumb to this couch.'

His eyes meet hers. 'I should check on Faith,' Mariah says softly.

'Right. You go on ahead. And I'm sorry.'

She reaches for the sheets, tangled on the floor, and snaps them into the air so that they billow over Ian and settle like a whisper onto his lap. Then she gives a quick, smooth tug at the satin edge of the blanket, bringing it up to cover him. A simple, instinctive move, a routine any mother knows by heart, and yet Ian finds himself holding his breath until she steps away, for fear he might break the spell.

'Good night, Ian,' she says, and he nods at her, unable to find his voice. He watches the small, smooth curves of her bare heels as they strike the floor, watches as she pulls the bedroom door shut behind her. Then he picks up his pen and pad again and smiles, realizing that, for the first time, Mariah White has used his given name.

New Canaan, New Hampshire

MILLIE IS GOING CRAZY. Would it have been so much trouble for Mariah to at least call from a pay phone and say they were all right? She's held up her part of the bargain—driving the car home, and taking care of the house in their absence, but she's on borrowed time and she knows it. Everyone saw her get out of the car alone. Sooner or later, when Faith and Mariah don't turn up, they're going to start asking questions.

Millie gets out of bed and draws back the curtain, noting the small Sterno campfires and portable lights of the TV reporters' cameramen. Is it her imagination, or have they nearly doubled in number?

Millie knows *Hollywood Tonight!* is still here; unlike most of the TV reporters, who have about three or four people around when they make their daily broadcasts, Petra Saganoff seems to need eight or ten. She's got lights and makeup people and men carrying machines that do God knows what. Personally, Millie could do without Petra Saganoff. If there's going to be reporting, she'd rather see that nice Peter Jennings, in the bush vest he wears when he goes on location.

It's just as well that Faith and Mariah are gone. From the looks of things at the end of the driveway, they're going to need a second policeman before long, to keep order. Mariah was unsettled by a handful of people; how would she react to *this*? With a sigh, Millie gets back into bed. She shuts off the light, then flicks it on and lifts up the receiver of the telephone beside the bed to make sure the dial tone is working, just in case.

Lake Perry, Kansas—October 20, 1999

TO MARIAH'S SURPRISE, Ian leaves shortly after breakfast. 'Gotta earn a living,' he says, grabbing the car keys and striding out the door as if spending another moment in their company were too painful to bear. He has not mentioned his nightmare, and Mariah decides that this must be the reason he's running—embarrassment can't rest easily on the shoulders of a man like him.

'How come *he* gets to go somewhere?' Faith grumbles. 'And *we* have to stay in this ugly place where there's nothing to do?'

'Maybe we'll take a walk. Find a phone and call Grandma.'

This sparks Faith's interest. 'Then she'll come here?'

'In a little while, maybe. We need her to watch our house right now.'

Faith empties more cereal into her bowl. 'There's a whole bunch of people watching our house. She doesn't have to do that, too.'

Mariah stands at the window as Ian drives away. He's taking the car, granted, but that wouldn't stop them from walking to town and hailing a taxi, returning to the airport and hopping on a new flight. Mariah assumed, when he'd offered his protection, that his good intentions were really much more selfish—what better way to observe Faith than to live in close quarters? Still, she'd figured that Ian would see of Faith only what she let him see—so she'd acquiesced. However, she had expected him to stick to her and Faith like glue.

Instead, he seems almost to . . . trust them.

She watches Faith lift the cereal bowl to her mouth to drink the remaining milk and starts to warn her about manners, but then stops. With so many rules to follow now that they are hiding, letting this one small thing slip cannot hurt.

She's reasoned out what dangers Faith has to face living with Ian Fletcher, but not herself. What she'd forgotten was that it was much easier to dislike a television character than an ordinary man. To see Ian's shoes tucked under the edge of the couch or his papers strewn over the coffee table—even to walk into the bathroom and smell the faint mixture of cedar and soap that clings to his skin—well, it makes him real. It changes him from a two-dimensional cultural icon with a hell-bent desire to expose Faith into someone with feelings, doubts, even nightmares.

If Ian Fletcher is able to trust them enough to leave them alone, can't Mariah trust him enough to believe that renting this cabin for them was not a selfish act, but a kind one?

She turns to Faith. 'Let's get dressed. We're leaving.'

It nearly breaks Ian's heart to buy clothes at Kmart. A man who owns Armani suits and Bruno Magli shoes shouldn't be reduced to shopping off the bargain rack for jeans and tennis shoes, but he knows that he's less likely to be recognized there by a dull-eyed clerk than by a salesperson at a more exclusive boutique. He stands at the checkout, behind a mother with three children screaming for candy, and surveys the collection of items in his basket.

'Did you find everything you needed?' the clerk asks.

It's blissfully quiet; the mother has succumbed and is wheeling out her children, their fingers digging into packets of M&M's. On impulse, Ian grabs another one off the shelf and tosses it onto the checkout counter, for Faith. 'I believe so.'

At the sound of his voice, the woman looks up. She squints a little, trying to connect the Southern drawl with the face. For a moment, Ian thinks the jig might be up . . . but then she returns to scanning the items. She must have decided he's a look-alike. After all, what would the illustrious Ian Fletcher be doing in a Kmart?

'Oh, I love this,' the woman says, holding up a shirt-and-legging set with Tweety Bird screen-printed on the front. 'Got one for my own daughter.'

Ian's picked it out for Faith. He realized last night that they couldn't have much in those knapsacks, and would need clothes for this unexpected stay just as much as he did. Unfortunately, he's confounded by children's sizes. What the hell is the difference between a 7 and a 7X?

It was easier to find clothing for Mariah. All he had to do was imagine how high she came up on his chest, how wide her hips were and how small her waist, and he could easily match her body type to one of the many women he'd dated. She has a lovely figure, actually, but he found himself tossing into the shopping cart baggy jeans and flannel shirts, oversized sweatshirts—things that would keep her covered, that wouldn't draw his attention.

'That comes to one twenty-three thirty-nine,' the clerk says.

Ian unfolds his wallet and withdraws a stack of twenties. He carries the bags to the rental car, gets inside, and then takes out his cell phone to call his producer.

'Wilton here.'

'Well, it's a damn good thing one of us is,' Ian jokes.

'Ian? Christ, I've been going crazy. You want to tell me where the fuck you are?'

'Sorry, James. I know I said I'd be back last night, but there was . . . a family emergency.'

'I thought you didn't have any family.'

'All the same, I'm going to be tied up for a while.' Ian taps his fingers on the steering wheel, knowing that there's nothing James can do. Without Ian, there isn't a show.

'How long is a while?' James says after a moment.

'I don't know just yet. I'm definitely going to miss the Friday broadcast, though. You'll have to do a rerun.'

He can practically see James seething. 'Well, that's just fabulous, Ian, because we've already run the promos for a live show. Plus, there are about ninety reporters here, including a few national affiliates, who are dying to get the story. Maybe I ought to go ask one of them to stand in for you.'

Ian laughs. 'By all means, try Dan Rather. He did a real fine impression of me on *Saturday Night Live*, once.'

'I'm glad you're so fucking congenial today. Because you're not gonna have more than a smile left to pitch when your show goes down the toilet.'

'Now, James, you relax before you bust a gut. Faith White isn't even there, right?'

There's a beat of silence. 'How did you know that?'

'I have my sources. And I'm only doing what I told you I'd be doing—following a story on the road.'

James draws in his breath. 'Are you saying you're with her?'

'I'm saying that just 'cause I'm not three feet away from you doesn't mean I'm not still on top of things.' He glances at his watch. Christ, by now Mariah and Faith could be halfway across Missouri—but it was a chance he had to take. He'd learned long ago that the best way to catch a butterfly was not to chase it at all, but to remain so still that it made the choice to light on your shoulder. 'Gotta go, James. I'll be in touch.'

Before his producer has a chance to protest, Ian turns off his phone and slips it into his coat pocket again. Then he drives back toward Camp Perry, slow enough to keep a watch out for a woman and a child who may have decided to leave on their own.

Mariah's sweating. Although it's fairly cool outside, Faith balked at walking about a mile down the road, so she had to carry her daughter piggyback all the way to the gas station. Then she called home, reversing the charges and speaking to her mother, while Faith whined about getting candy.

'You're with *who?*' her mother had said.

'I know, I know. But we're going to leave.' At that point Mariah had spotted the number of a local taxi service, etched into the wall of the pay-phone booth. 'I'll call you when we find a place to settle.'

As she speaks to the taxi dispatcher, she feels a thread of guilt drawing tight. Ian Fletcher has been nothing less than solicitous up to this point. For whatever reason, it is possible that his TV persona's ruthlessness is only an act.

Still, she isn't going to stick around to find out.

Faith is sitting on the floor, picking at dead bugs, when Mariah hangs up. The taxi will arrive in ten minutes. 'What are you doing? You're going to be filthy.'

'I want candy. I'm hungry.'

Mariah digs into her pocket for fifty cents. 'That's it. Get whatever you can for this amount.' She wipes the sweat off her forehead and watches Faith choose peanut M&M's, hand them to the man working behind the counter. He smiles at Mariah; she smiles back.

'You're not from around here,' the man says.

Mariah thinks she's going to be sick. 'What makes you say that?'

He laughs. 'I pretty much know everyone in town, and you're not one of those people. You get your taxi all right?'

He must have overheard her conversation. Mariah feels her mind spin into action. 'Yes . . . my, uh, husband had an errand to run, and he was supposed to pick us up here after I made a phone call. But I think my daughter's running a fever, and I want to get her back to the motel . . . so we're just going to take a cab.'

'I'd be happy to tell him where you went, when he comes looking.'

'That would be great,' Mariah says, edging toward the door, wanting nothing more than to cut short this conversation. 'Honey, why don't we wait outside?'

'Good idea,' the man says, although she hasn't included him in the invitation. 'Wouldn't mind a little fresh air myself.'

Resigned, Mariah walks out the glass door of the gas station and stands next to the pump, shading her eyes to see down the road for anything that remotely resembles a cab. But from the opposite direction a car speeds into the station, stopping a few feet away from them.

Ian gets out of the passenger seat, thrilled to have spotted Mariah and Faith. 'Hey there.' He smiles at Mariah. 'Looking for a ride home?'

'Hope you got some roses, brother,' the gas-station attendant says. 'You're in the doghouse.'

Ian continues to smile, puzzled, but all he can think of is something Faith once said, that her mother sneezes at roses. Before Mariah can stop her, Faith gets into the backseat of the car and sees the pile of bags on the floor. 'What's this?'

'Presents. For you and your mama.'

Faith pulls out the Tweety legging set, and a package of barrettes, and a sweatshirt with hearts all around the neckline. Then she tugs free a shirt that is clearly the right size for Mariah.

This is where he went this morning? To buy them all clothes?

'Guess you won't be needing the taxi,' the attendant says. 'I'll call the dispatcher.'

'That . . . would be wonderful,' Mariah manages.

Ian waves at the man, then gets into the car. Mariah slides into the front seat as well. 'Guess y'all wanted to take a little walk around town,' he says evenly. 'I just happened to see you as I was driving by.'

Faith pipes up from the backseat. 'Good, because I was getting tired of walking.'

Mariah tries to read an accusation in his words, tries to make him into the sort of man she had naturally assumed he was. He turns to her. 'Course, I can take Faith back, if you'd still like to walk a spell.'

'No,' she says, to him and to herself. 'This'll be just fine.'

• • •

New Canaan, New Hampshire—October 22, 1999

SOME PEOPLE BLAMED IT on the taxi driver who took the young Father Rourke to the train station. Others said it was clearly a reporter snooping. Months later, no one clearly remembered how word leaked from the visiting priest's files to those gathered outside Mariah White's house, but suddenly they all knew that the God Faith White was seeing happened to be female.

The Associated Press reporter's three-paragraph story ran in newspapers from L.A. to New York. Jay Leno did an irreverent monologue about a female Jesus being worried about the fashion statement made by a crown of thorns. A new group of devotees arrived on the edge of the White property, letting their dismay over Faith's absence only slightly dampen their enthusiasm. Numbering about one hundred, they came from Catholic colleges and church ladies' guilds and taught at parochial schools. Some had fought to be ordained as female priests, but had not succeeded. Armed with Bibles and texts by Naomi Wolf, they unrolled a hastily painted MOTHERGOD SOCIETY banner and very loudly chanted the Lord's Prayer in unison, changing the pronouns where necessary. They held up posters with photos retouched to look like holy cards and others that read YOU GO, GIRL!

They were bonded and raucous, like a women's hockey team, although most of the other followers camped outside did not consider them dangerous.

But then again, they did not know that the MotherGod Society had left another hundred members spread up and down cities on the East Coast, handing out pamphlets emblazoned with their amended Lord's Prayer and Faith White's name and address.

Manchester, NH—October 22, 1999

'WHAT IN THE NAME of Saint Francis is *this?*' Bishop Andrews asks, recoiling from the pink pamphlet as if it were a rattlesnake. '"Our Mother, who art in Heaven?" Who wrote this garbage?'

'It's a new Catholic group, your Excellency,' says Father DeSoto. 'They're promoting an alleged New Hampshire visionary.'

'Why does this sound familiar?'

'Because you spoke to Monsignor O'Shaughnessy about her a week ago. Father Rourke—the pastoral psychologist from St John's—sent you his report by fax.'

Bishop Andrews has not read the report. He spent the morning marching in the Pope Pius XII Parochial School's homecoming parade, positioned in an antique Ford in front of a very large percussion band that gave him a headache that has not yet gone away. Father DeSoto hands him a piece of paper. '"Definite lack of psychotic behavior . . ." He's too open-minded for his own good,' Andrews mutters, then picks up the phone and dials the Boston seminary.

A female God. For Pete's sake!

Why send a pastoral psychologist, when this is clearly a case for a theologian?

Lake Perry, Kansas—October 22, 1999

THAT AFTERNOON, Ian and Faith are playing hearts when Mariah falls asleep on the couch. One moment she is talking to them, and then the next, just like that, she's snoring. Ian watches her neck swan to the side, listens to the soft snore from her throat. God, he's jealous. To just be able to drift off like that . . . in the middle of the day . . .

Faith shuffles the cards and manages to send them flying. 'Hey, Mr Fletcher,' she says, scrambling to pick them up, her voice strident.

'Sssh!' Ian nods toward the couch. 'Your mama's asleep.' He knows that having Faith in close, confined quarters with Mariah means it's more likely than not to be a quick rest. 'How'd you like to go outside?' he whispers.

Faith pulls a face. 'I don't want to play in the grass again. I did that this morning.'

'I recall promising you some fishing.' Ian remembers seeing an old rod and reel gathering dust in the shed beside the manager's office. 'We could give that a try.'

Faith glances from Ian to Mariah. 'I don't think she'd want me to go.'

Of course not, Ian thinks. Faith might unwittingly tip her hand. 'A quick trip, then. What your mama doesn't know isn't gonna hurt her.' He stands up and stretches. 'Well, *I'm* gonna do some fishing anyway.'

'Wait! I just have to get on my shoes.'

He shrugs, pretending not to care whether he has company. But this is the first time he's been alone with Faith White, except for the night she ran away bleeding. There's so damn much he wants to know about her, he doesn't even know where to start.

It's crisp and cool outside, and the sun is hanging heavy in the sky. He walks with his hands in his pockets, whistling softly, pretending not to notice how hard Faith is huffing and puffing to keep up with him. Retrieving the fishing rod and a small gardener's spade, Ian strikes out toward the lake.

He squats at the edge near a patch of cattails and offers Faith the small shovel. 'You want to dig, or shall I?'

'You mean, like, for worms?'

'No, for buried treasure. What'd you think we were gonna use as bait?'

Faith takes the spade and makes a halfhearted attempt to overturn the thick marsh grass. Ian stares at the Band-Aids still on her hands, one on the outside and one on the inside of each palm. He, of course, has studied case histories of alleged stigmatics—in his profession, you have to know the competition. He remembers reading how painful the wounds are supposed to be, not that he really ever bought it. Still, he wrests the shovel from Faith. 'Let me,' he says gruffly.

He unearths a chunk of grass, peeling it back like a scalp to reveal several purple worms pulsing through the dirt. Faith wrinkles her nose. 'Gross.'

'Not if you're a largemouth bass.' He gathers a few in a small plastic bag and directs Faith toward the dock. 'You go on over there. Take the rod with you.'

He finds her sitting with her bare feet dangling in the water. 'Your mama finds you like that, she's going to pitch a fit.'

Faith glances back over her shoulder. 'The only way she'd find out is if you told her I'd come out here with you, and then she'd be too angry at *you* to yell at *me*.'

'Guess we're partners in crime, then.' Ian reaches out a hand to help her stand. 'So—you know how to cast? Your daddy ever take you fishing?'

'Nope. Did yours?'

Just like that, his hand stills on Faith's. She's squinting up at him, her face partially hidden by shadows. 'No,' he says. 'I don't reckon he did.' He puts his arms around Faith from behind and closes his hands on hers. Her skin is warm and impossibly soft; he can feel her shoulder blades bumping against his chest. 'Like this.' He tips back the rod and lets the line fly.

'Now what?'

'Now we wait.'

He sits beside Faith as she digs her thumbnail into the grooves in the planking of the dock. She lifts her face toward the setting sun and closes her eyes, and Ian finds himself mesmerized by the tiny beat in the hollow of her throat. There's a quiet between them he is almost unwilling to break, but his curiosity gets the better of him. '"Follow me,"' he says softly, watching for her reaction, '"and I will make you fishers of men."'

She turns her head toward him. 'Huh?'

'It's a saying. An old one.'

'It's stupid. You don't fish for men.'

'You ought to ask God about it sometime,' Ian suggests, leaning back and covering his eyes with his forearm, just enough that he can peek out and still see her.

Faith frowns, on the verge of saying something, but then she stops and picks at the wood of the dock again. Ian finds himself straining forward, waiting for a confession, but whatever Faith might have said is lost to the sudden jerk of the rod and her squeal of delight. He shows her how to reel in her catch, a beauty of a fish that's every bit of three pounds.

Then he unhooks the bass and rounds open its mouth, so that Faith can grab hold.

'Oh,' she breathes, the tail of the fish snugging against her stomach. *She's a picture*, Ian thinks, smiling. With her hair caught in the late sun and dirt streaked across her cheek, he looks at her and truly sees her not as a story, but simply as a little girl.

The fish starts to thrash its tail, fighting for freedom. 'Look at how— *Oh!*' Faith cries, and she drops the bass—the last thing Ian sees before she loses her footing and falls from the dock into the freezing water.

Mariah awakens to her worst nightmare: Ian Fletcher has disappeared with Faith. Bolting upright on the couch, she screams for her daughter, knowing by the stillness in the small cabin that they are gone. A deck of cards lies scattered across the rug, as if he's taken her in the middle of everything, as if he's taken her by force.

She will have to call the police, but that seems like an easy sacrifice if it means Faith's safe return. With her heart pounding, Mariah races outside, so distraught that she does not even notice the car still sitting in front of the cabin. She runs toward the manager's office, the nearest phone, cursing herself for putting Faith within reach of Ian Fletcher. When she rounds the corner, two figures are silhouetted against the lake, one tall, one tiny. With intense relief, Mariah stops short, her knees buckling. She cups her hands around her mouth to call out to them, but then before her very eyes, Faith falls into the lake.

Oh, shit! That's all Ian has time to think before the water swallows Faith, and Mariah's scream echoes. It's freezing in there, and he has no idea if the kid can swim, and the very worst part of it is that he can't just jump in and grab her because there's every chance that he'll land on top of her, push her farther down. He is distantly aware of Mariah scrabbling down the slope, yelling, but with intense focus he stares at the murky water until a pale streak of silver unfurls beneath the surface. He leaps in a few feet to the left of where he's seen Faith's hair, opens his eyes to the gritty underworld, and tangles his fingers in a silky skein.

He can see her, her eyes wide and terrified, her mouth open, her hands pushing at the underside of the dock that she's trapped beneath. Dragging her by her ponytail, he yanks Faith free and pulls her up. She crawls onto the wood, choking and sputtering, her cheek pressed against the planks as she spits up water.

Ian hauls himself onto the dock as well, just as Mariah reaches them and folds Faith into her arms, soothing and cuddling. Only now does he let himself breathe, let himself think of what might have happened. He notices that he's soaked and shaking; his clothes must weigh fifty pounds wet, and they're freezing to boot. With a glance in Faith's direction to make sure she is all right, he stands and slowly sets out toward the cabin to change.

'Don't you move!'

Mariah's voice, vibrating with anger, stops him. Ian turns and clears his throat to speak. 'She'll be fine,' he manages. 'She wasn't under for more than a few seconds.'

But Mariah isn't ready to give up. 'How dare you take her out here without my permission?'

'Well, I—'

'Were you waiting for me to fall asleep so that you could sneak her out with a . . . a candy bar and ask her questions up one side and down the other? Did you get your precious tape? Or did you forget to take it out of your pocket when you jumped in?'

Ian feels his lips draw away from his teeth, an involuntary snarl. 'For your information, the only thing I asked your daughter was if her daddy ever taught her how to cast a fishing line. I didn't tape a frigging word of our conversation. She fell into the lake by accident and got stuck under the dock. All I did was go in after her.'

'She would never have gotten stuck under the dock if she hadn't been standing on it in the first place! For all I know, you might have pushed her.'

Ian's eyes glitter with rage. This is what he gets for saving the child's life? He takes a step back, breathing hard. 'For all I know,' he sneers, 'she might have walked on water.'

Long after Mariah has fed Faith hot soup, bathed her, and tucked her into bed for the night, Ian still has not returned to the cabin. She finds herself pacing, staring blindly at the static on the television. She wants to apologize. Surely now that they've both had time to cool down he realizes that it was the fear talking, not really her, but she'd like to tell him so herself. After all, if Faith had wandered down to the dock by herself, she could have just as easily fallen in—and drowned.

She waits until her daughter is sleeping deeply, then goes to sit on the edge of the bed. Mariah touches the curve of Faith's cheek, warm as a ripe peach. How do other mothers go about keeping watch? How do they shut their eyes with the certainty that in that moment, something won't go wrong? Being in water that cold could have had far more serious effects, yet Faith seems absolutely fine.

For whatever it is worth, Faith's God wasn't the one to haul her out of the water; that was done by Ian himself. For this at least, Mariah owes him her gratitude.

She sees the swinging beam of headlights cut across the small room. Walking out of the bedroom to the front door of the cabin, she waits for Ian to come inside. But a minute passes, and then another, and finally it is five minutes later. She peeks through the window—yes, the car is there—and then opens the door.

Ian is sitting at her feet. He's been leaning against the door. 'I'm sorry,' Mariah says, coloring.

'Nah. It's a stupid place to sit.'

They look at the night sky, the rotting porch, the chipped paint on the door—anywhere but at each other. 'I mean that I'm *really* sorry.'

'Well, so am I. This isn't the first time I've done something involving Faith without getting your permission first.' Ian rubs the back of his neck. 'She liked fishing, though. Right up till the end there.'

They each imagine a picture of Faith with that bass, and

it forms a bridge between them. Then Mariah sits down beside Ian, drawing a circle absently on the dirt of the porch floor. 'I'm not used to letting her out of my sight,' she admits. 'It's hard for me.'

'You're a fine mother.'

Mariah shakes her head. 'You might be the only one who thinks so.'

'I doubt that. I bet there's a little girl inside that thinks so.' He leans against the side of the cabin. 'I figure I owe you an apology, too. You got me riled up, or else I wouldn't have said all that about Faith walking on water.'

Mariah considers his words. 'You know,' she says finally, 'I don't want her to be some . . . Messiah figure . . . any more than you do.'

'What do you want?'

She takes a deep breath. 'I want her to be safe. I want her to be mine.'

Neither of them speaks the thought that crosses their minds: that these two wishes might not both be able to come true. 'She sleeping now?'

'Yes.' Mariah glances at the cabin door. 'Went to bed without a problem.' She watches Ian draw up one knee and hook a wrist over it, and lets herself wonder what this moment might be like if she hadn't met Ian over a war of religious convictions, but when she dropped her purse in the grocery store, or when he gave up his seat for her on the bus. Her mind scrambles over territory she's deliberately left untraveled, marking the raven's wing of his hair and the brilliant blue of his eyes, remembering the night in the hospital when he kissed her on the cheek.

'You know,' he says quietly. 'Even during the world wars they had a cease-fire on Christmas.'

'What?'

'A truce, Mariah,' Ian says, his voice running over her name like a waterfall. 'I'm saying that, just for here, just for now, maybe we could give each other the benefit of the doubt.' He grins at her. 'I'm probably only half the monster you think I am.'

She smiles back. 'Don't sell yourself short.'

He laughs out loud, and in that moment Mariah realizes that if Ian Fletcher is intimidating when he's scowling, he's positively threatening when he lets down his guard.

In the middle of the night, when Faith and Mariah are long asleep, Ian sneaks into their room. He stands at the edge of the bed with all the gravity of a man on the edge of a precipice. Mariah holds Faith in her arms, like an ingredient that's been folded into a batter. Their hair is woven together on the pillow. From where he's standing, it looks almost as if they are not two people, but different incarnations of one.

Tonight had gone better than he'd expected, considering his outburst at the lake. The truce is going to buy him some time, make Mariah predisposed to trust him. And, of course, he'll have to act as if he trusts her. Which, in a way, comes almost too goddamned easy. Sometimes she looks like any other mother, and Faith looks like any other little girl. Until you add God to the mix.

Lake Perry, Kansas—October 23, 1999

FAITH SITS DOWN next to Mr Fletcher at the breakfast table and watches her mother at the counter. 'We've got a selection this morning of Cheerios, or Cheerios . . . or, if you'd rather have them, Cheerios,' her mother says brightly.

'I'll have Cheerios, then.' Mr Fletcher smiles at her mom, and right away Faith can tell there's something different. Like the air is easier to take into your lungs.

'How are you feeling?' Mr Fletcher asks her.

'Okay.' But then she sneezes.

'Wouldn't surprise me if she caught a cold,' her mother says to Mr Fletcher, who nods. She sets a bowl of cereal in front of Faith.

'Give her vitamin C. You can ward off a cold if you take enough of it.'

'That's an old wives' tale. Like wearing garlic on a string around your neck.'

Faith looks from one to the other and wonders how she

managed to go to sleep last night and wake up this morning and somehow, in that short time, miss the entire world's turning upside down. The last time she'd seen Mr Fletcher and her mom together, they were shouting so loud it made her head pound.

They're still talking about medicines and getting sick, as if Faith isn't even in the room. Quietly, she stands up and crosses the small kitchen, dragging a stepstool to the counter. She reaches for the bowls on the middle shelf of the cabinet and takes down a second one. This she fills with Cheerios and places in front of an empty seat at the table.

'Well,' Mr Fletcher says. 'At least you're still hungry.'

Faith stares at him, challenging. 'It's not for me. It's for God.'

Her mother's spoon clanks against her cereal bowl. Faith watches the two grown-ups look at each other for a long time, a staring contest to see who'll fold first. Her mother, especially, seems to be hanging on the edge of the table, waiting for Mr Fletcher to speak.

After a moment he reaches for the jug of milk and passes it down the table. 'Here,' he says, calmly taking another spoonful of his own Cheerios. 'Just in case She doesn't like it dry.'

October 24, 1999

THE NEXT NIGHT Ian is sprawled on the couch, writing on a pad, while Mariah sits at the kitchen table. The heady scent of rubber-cement fumes wafts across the room, and although he cannot see her hands, he knows she's busy gluing something together. Thankless job, he thinks. Everything in this damn cabin is falling apart.

Suddenly she stretches, her breasts rounding out against one of the shapeless flannel shirts. She turns to him and smiles hesitantly. 'What are you working on?'

'General notes for a broadcast.'

'Oh. I didn't know you were still doing them.' She blushes

at her own words, the subtext loud and clear: I didn't know that you could be kind, and cross us at the same time.

'Gotta make a living.'

At the mention of employment, Mariah groans. 'I've probably lost all my clients.'

Surprised to discover she is more than a stay-at-home mom, Ian raises his brows. 'Clients? What do you do?'

She seems flustered for a moment, then gestures toward the table. 'I do this.'

He walks over and stands behind her chair. Spread across a paper towel is a fan of toothpicks, glued side by side. Beside it is a tiny structure, and as he watches, Mariah curls the fan into a thatched roof for the top of a tiny hut. But rather than looking silly, like a child's camp craft, it is remarkably realistic. Strategically breaking bits of wood here and there, she's created a door, a window, the feel of an aboriginal home. 'That's amazing,' Ian says, surprised by the extent of her talent. 'You're a sculptor?'

'No, I make dollhouses.' She rolls a bead of rubber cement between her fingers.

'What is the hut for?'

'Me.' Mariah laughs. 'I was bored. The toothpicks were the first thing I could find.'

Ian grins. 'Remind me to hide the wooden spoons from you.'

She leans back in her chair and looks up at him. 'Your broadcasts—who's doing them?'

'Me. In living color. We're doing reruns while I'm here.'

'The ones you're writing . . . ?'

'For when I get back,' Ian says softly. 'Whenever that is.'

'Are they about Faith?'

'Some parts.' Even as he says the words, he wonders why the hell he's told her the truth. Wouldn't it be easier, smarter, to say that he's stopped focusing on Faith entirely?

But he can't. Because at some point during this past week Mariah White has stopped being a story and somehow turned into a person much like himself. Sure, there have been some bizarre moments—Faith getting cereal so that her hallucination could eat breakfast; Faith sitting on the porch, holding a conversation with absolutely nobody. But most of these incidents Mariah had tried to hide from Ian, seemingly embarrassed, instead of flaunting them as proof. He tells himself that she's acting every bit as much as he is, that she's playing dumb in the hopes that Ian will become a convert like the rest of the poor fools who've been suckered in by Faith. He tells himself this because the alternative—unthinkable!—is that his hunch about Mariah is incorrect. And if he's misjudged her, then what else might he be wrong about?

'If I asked you what you were going to say about her,' Mariah asks, 'would you tell me the truth?'

Ian thinks of Michael, of the story he will have when this is all over. But he schools his face into a furrow of confusion and looks away. 'I'd tell you if I could, Mariah. But the fact of the matter is, right now, I don't know *what* I'm going to say.'

New Canaan, New Hampshire

JOAN STANDISH HAS listened to the news reports and the growing coverage of Faith White's mysterious absence from New Canaan. Petra Saganoff begins each *Hollywood Tonight!* report with a countdown: Day Three Without Faith, Day Four. The local NBC affiliate, a respectable channel, has even featured a live broadcast during which a caller said that he'd seen Faith in line for a movie in San Jose, California—and then ruined his credibility by shouting out something about how Howard Stern rocks. All in all, she hasn't paid much attention to the story, apart from feeling sympathy for the little girl caught in the middle of it.

But then Malcolm Metz's high-profile Manchester law firm called to say that they'd been trying to serve papers to her client since Tuesday, a motion to change custody on behalf of Colin White. Her client? Who knew if Mariah White wanted Joan's representation? She hadn't talked to the woman since the divorce came through.

But for reasons she doesn't fully understand or want to analyze, she finds herself driving to the Whites' house during her lunch hour. None of the programming she's seen prepares her for the drive up the long, hilly road, lined on both sides with cars that have their hatches popped, and makeshift picnics and tailgates spread across their insides. People cluster in small groups—the media representatives and the others, the ones who think Faith can help. They line the edge of the stone wall that separates the White property from the road, caretakers bent over their wheelchair-bound charges, blind men with harnessed dogs, curious Christians wearing cameras around their necks that tangle in the chains of their oversized crosses.

God, there have to be at least two hundred people. Joan pumps the brakes on her Jeep at a small roadblock erected at the end of the driveway. Two local policemen are manning it; they recognize her as one of the town's few attorneys. 'Paul,' she greets him. 'This is something.'

'Haven't been here recently, huh?' the cop says. 'You ought to show up after lunch, when the cult gets to singing.'

Joan shakes her head. 'I don't suppose Mariah White is really at home after all?'

'No such luck. Course, then there'd be a hundred *more* loonies.'

'Is anyone here?'

'Her mother—holding down the fort, I guess.' He steps back so Joan can drive through. She parks at the edge of the lawn and walks up the porch stairs to knock on the front door. An older woman's face appears in the sidelight, clearly weighing whether or not to open up.

'I'm Joan Standish,' she yells. 'Your daughter's attorney.'

The door swings open. 'Millie Epstein. Come in.' The woman hovers around Joan as she steps inside. 'Did something happen to them?'

'To whom?'

'Mariah and Faith.' Millie anxiously worries her hands. 'They're not here, you know.'

'As far as I know, they're fine. But I do need to get in touch with your daughter.' Joan is a professional when it comes to reading the clues on a person's face, and Millie

Epstein clearly is hiding something. 'Mrs Epstein, this is incredibly important.'

'I don't know where they are. I swear it.'

Joan considers this for a moment. 'But you've heard from them,' she guesses.

'No.'

'Then you'd better hope Mariah calls soon, because I have a message. You tell her that her ex-husband is suing for custody of their daughter. And that no matter how noble her intentions were in taking Faith away from all this, what a judge is going to see is that she bucked the system by going underground when papers were being served. And frankly, Mrs Epstein, that pisses off judges. The longer she stays hidden, the greater the chance that Colin White will be given custody.' The older woman's face is white, her lips pressed tight. 'You tell her to call me,' Joan says softly.

Millie nods. 'I will.'

Lake Perry, Kansas—October 24, 1999

MARIAH FINDS HERSELF unable to sleep. She turns on her side and watches the night sky through the cabin's window, the moon rising and the stars three-dimensional, as if she could reach out and have them settle on her palm. She marks time by Faith's steady breathing and lets questions chase their own tails in her mind: *How long can we stay? Where do we go next? How is my mother coping? Will a reporter arrive here the next day, or the next, or the next?*

She sits up, tugging down the sweatshirt she's been using as sleepwear. Ian had bought Faith a nightgown, but not one for herself. She thinks of him rifling through serviceable flannels, slinkier silks, wondering what he might choose for her. Then, feeling her cheeks flame, she gets up and paces. No reason to dream about things that won't ever come to pass.

She would love to go for a walk now, but that would mean trekking through the living room, where Ian is sleeping. Instead she crosses to the window and gazes out. Ian is leaning against the hood of the car. The copper glow of a cigar paints his face in profile, as wide-eyed and preoccupied as Mariah herself. She stares unabashedly, wondering what keeps him up at night, willing him to turn.

When he does, when their eyes meet, Mariah's heart hitches. She presses her hands against the window sash, caught. They do not move, they do not speak, they simply let the night tie them tight. Then Ian crunches the cigar beneath his heel, and Mariah gets back into bed, each mulling over the thought that he or she is not the only one counting the minutes till morning.

Atlanta—CNN Studios

LARRY KING SMOOTHS down his scarlet tie and looks at his guest. 'You ready?' he asks, not waiting for an answer, and then the tiny light at the edge of the camera flickers to life. 'We're back with Rabbi Daniel Solomon, spiritual leader of Beit Am Hadash, which is affiliated with ALEPH, or Jewish Renewal.'

'Yes,' Rabbi Solomon says, still awkward after ten minutes on the air. 'Hello.' He is wearing a moth-eaten black jacket—the only one he has with lapels, instead of a mandarin collar—and his trademark tie-dyed T-shirt, but he might as well be naked. There are millions of people listening to him—millions!—after his years of fighting to be heard. He keeps reminding himself that he owes this fortuitous interview to Faith White, as well as to his own congregation. So what if King's brought in a Catholic prig of a professor to rebut whatever Solomon says? Even David managed to conquer Goliath, with God on his side.

'Rabbi,' King says, capturing Daniel's attention. 'Is Faith White the Messiah?'

'Well, she's certainly not the Jewish Messiah,' Rabbi Solomon says, rolling his shoulders in the familiar feel of his own theological turf. 'One criterion for a Jewish Messiah involves creating a sovereign Jewish state, according to the Torah. And nothing that Faith's heard from God indicates this.' He crosses his legs. 'The interesting thing about a Messiah is that it differs greatly from Judaism to Christianity. To Jews, the Messiah won't show up until we've managed to rid the world of all its evil and make it ready for a divine being. To Christians, far as I understand, the Messiah heralds the age of redemption. Brings it with Him. Jews have to work to get to a Messianic age; Christians have to wait.'

'If I can object?'

They turn at the sound of a voice on a TV monitor overhead. 'Yes, please do,' King says. 'Father Cullen Mulrooney, chair of theology at Boston College. You were saying, Father?'

'I find it irresponsible for a rabbi to tell me what Christians have to do.'

'Let's talk about that, Father,' Larry King asks, tapping a pen on the desktop. 'How come the Catholic Church is investigating the claims of a little Jewish girl?'

Mulrooney smiles. 'Because she's affecting a large group of Catholics.'

'The fact that she's only seven isn't an issue?'

'No. Visionaries younger than Faith White have been accredited by the Catholic Church. And actually, seven used to be called the age of reason, when a person was mature enough to be morally responsible for his own deeds. That's why the first confession takes place then.'

Larry King purses his lips. 'By the admission of her mother, this is not a girl who is schooled in formal religion—any religion. Let's take a caller.' He pushes a button. 'Hello?'

'Hello? I have a question for the rabbi. If she's not a Jewish Messiah, what *is* she?'

Rabbi Solomon laughs. 'A little girl who is exceptionally spiritual, maybe more skilled at opening herself up to God than the rest of us.'

A second caller's voice fills the studio. 'If she's Jewish, why does she have the wounds of Christ?'

'If I may I address that?' Father Mulrooney asks. 'I think it's important to remember that the bishop hasn't offered any official statement about the *alleged* stigmata. It may take years . . . decades . . . before the bleeding is authenticated by the Vatican.'

'But it's a good point,' Larry King says. 'We're not talking about a Carmelite nun here, just a kid, and a non-Christian one at that.' He turns to Rabbi Solomon. 'How come a Jewish girl would develop the wounds of a savior she doesn't believe in?'

'Faith White is a blank slate,' Father Mulrooney cuts in. 'If a religious innocent, a non-Christian, develops the wounds of Christ, surely that's proof that Jesus is the one true Lord.'

Rabbi Solomon smiles. 'I didn't see it like that at all. I think God's picked a little Jewish girl and tossed stigmata into the mix because it's the way to gather many different people. Christians, Jews—we're all watching her now.'

'But why now? Why wait thousands of years, and then just show up? Does it have to do with the millennium?'

'Absolutely,' the priest says. 'For years the turn of the century has been posed as the apocalypse, and people are looking for redemption.'

The rabbi laughs. 'Forget the millennium. According to the Jewish calendar, there's forty-three years to go before we even hit the turn of the *century*.'

'Caller?' King says, pushing another button.

'She's the devil's handmaiden. She—'

'Thank you,' King says, cutting off the line. 'Hi, you're on the air.'

'I say good for Faith White. Even if she's making the whole damned thing up, it's about time someone suggested God might be a woman.'

'Gentlemen? Is God male?'

'No,' say the rabbi and the priest, simultaneously.

'God is neither, and both,' Mulrooney says. But there's so much more to a vision than just physical attributes. There's the concrete, verifiable sign of proof apart from the vision, and the visionary's piousness and Christian virtue—'

'I've always resented that,' Rabbi Solomon murmurs. 'The idea that it's only Christians who have virtue.'

'That's not what—'

'You know what your problem is?' the rabbi accuses. 'You say you're open-minded. But only as long as your visionary happens to be seeing something you all like. You sit on a college faculty. You haven't even *met* the girl, but she's a round peg in a square hole, so you're discrediting her with your theology.'

'Now, just a moment,' Father Mulrooney says, fuming. 'At least I *have* a theology. What kind of radical hippie movement calls itself Jewish but uses chanting and Buddhism and Native American imagery?'

'Hey, there's room for a female God in Jewish theology.'

The priest shakes his head. 'Correct me if I'm wrong, but aren't Hebrew prayers addressed to *'adonai eloheinu'*—the *Lord* our God?'

'Yes,' Rabbi Solomon says. 'But there are many Hebrew names for God. *Hashem*, for example, which means "the name"—very unisex. There's God's presence, *Shekhinah*, traditionally considered to be a feminine term. My personal favorite word for God is *Shaddai*. It's always conjugated in the masculine, and for years rabbis have translated it to mean "the Hill God" or "the Mountain God." Yet *shaddai* is amazingly similar to the word *shaddaim* . . . which means "breasts."'

'Oh, for criminy's sake,' Father Mulrooney snorts. 'And "hello" minus the *o* is "hell."'

'Why, you—' Rabbi Solomon nearly comes out of his chair, until Larry King restrains him with a touch of his hand.

'Faith White, healer or hoax?' King says smoothly. 'We'll be back in a minute.' When the camera light blinks off, Father Mulrooney is an alarming shade of scarlet, and Rabbi Solomon's eyes are blazing with anger. 'Look, you guys are giving me terrific stuff, but try not to kill each other, all right? We've got to fill twenty more minutes of air time.'

Lake Perry, Kansas—October 25, 1999

A FULL KANSAS MOON is a remarkable sight, luminous and filled to bursting as it grazes the plains. It is the kind of moon that coaxes animals out of hiding, that makes cats dance on fenceposts and barn owls cry. It changes you, if only for the time you stare at it, making your blood beat thick and your head spin to a song played on bare branches and marsh reeds.

It is the kind of moon that thrusts its belly toward Ian and Mariah on Monday night, only hours before he will go to visit Michael.

This has become their habit, a moment to wind down before Mariah goes inside to bed and Ian goes back to work. On the porch they speak of easy things: geese they have seen flying south, the remarkable number of stars, the way winter already hangs in the air. They wrap up in plaid blankets and sit side by side until their cheeks pinken and their noses run and they surrender to the cold. Tonight Ian has been unusually quiet. He knows what he has to do—the acting job of his life, essentially—but he's putting it off. Every time he draws in a breath to start, he looks at Mariah and realizes that he does not want to set in motion the beginning of the end.

Mariah yawns. 'Well, I guess I'd better go in.' She glances around the porch for stray items that Faith might have left outside and reaches for a pair of shoes. 'I swear that girl sheds,' she murmurs, then picks up a worn leather Bible. Clearly assuming that Faith found it inside the cabin, she tries to tuck it into the folds of her blanket before Ian can notice.

'Actually, that's mine.'

'The Bible?'

He shrugs. 'It's a starting point for my speeches. It's great reading. Course, I see it as fiction, not fact.' He closes his eyes, tilts back his head. 'Ah, hell. I'm lying to you, Mariah.'

He can sense the moment she tenses, takes a mental step back. 'I beg your pardon?'

'I lied. I was reading the Bible tonight because . . . well, because I wanted to. And that's not all I lied about. I let you think I was on that plane because I followed you to Kansas City, but I was booked on the flight before you probably ever thought of running to the airport. I come here fairly often, matter of fact, to see someone.'

'Someone.' Her voice is cool, and although it's what Ian expected, it still smarts.

She is anticipating a producer, a documentary filmmaker, some other satellite person who might expose Faith. 'A relative who's autistic. Michael lives out here in an assisted-care facility, because he can't function by himself in the regular world. It's real private to me, which is why no one knows about him—not my producer, not my staff. When I saw you and Faith on that plane, I knew you figured I was tailing you. I wasn't, but I didn't want you to know why I *was* there. So I did what you expected—I followed you.'

He rakes his hands through his hair. 'What I didn't figure on was what might happen when I did that.' Ian glances away. 'Faith—I've seen her day in and day out, now. And the more time I spend with her, the more I wonder if maybe there isn't something to her story, if maybe I'm wrong.' He swallows hard. 'I go out during the day and I see Michael and then I'll come back home and see Faith, and— God, the two of them get all tangled up and my head starts spinning: *What if? What if she's telling the truth? What if she could cure Michael?* And then, just as quick, I'm ashamed of myself—me, the great disbeliever!—for even thinking such a thing.' Ian turns to Mariah, his eyes glistening, his voice broken. 'Can she do it? Can she make miracles happen?'

He can read Mariah's heart in her eyes; she sees him as a man in pain. She reaches for his hand. 'Of course we'll go see your relative, Ian,' she murmurs. 'And if Faith can do something, then she will. And if she can't, it's no different from what you've been saying all along.'

Without a word Ian lifts her hand to his lips, the very image of gratitude, even as the tiny microphone and tape recorder hidden in his clothing capture Mariah's promise.

October 26, 1999

LOCKWOOD IS AN UGLY PLACE. The halls and floors are the color of pistachio ice cream. There are doors lined up like dominoes, and each one has a little box outside with a chart stuffed into it. Mr Fletcher leads them to the end of a hall, where they enter a room that's a lot nicer than anything else Faith's seen. There are books on the walls and a bunch of tables with board games and even some classical music playing. It reminds her a little bit of the library in New Canaan, except the library doesn't have nurses walking around in their soft white sneakers.

Her mother hasn't told her much of anything, except that Mr Fletcher has a sick relative they are going to visit today. It's fine with her; that cabin is so boring. Plus, some of the rooms that they passed had TV. Maybe this person has the Disney Channel, and Faith can watch while the grown-ups all talk.

Mr Fletcher walks to the corner of the room, where a man is sitting with a deck of cards. The guy doesn't even turn around when they get close, but just says, 'Ian's here. Three-thirty on Tuesday. Just like always.'

'Just like,' Mr Fletcher answers, and his voice sounds strange to Faith, stiff and high.

Then the man turns around, and Faith's eyes go wide. Why, if she didn't know any better, she would have said it was Mr Fletcher himself.

Mariah's mouth drops open. His *twin*? Pieces begin to fall into place: why Ian would keep this a secret, why he visited on a regular basis, why he had such a vested interest in having Faith meet this Michael. She falls back to the periphery, where Ian has asked her to stand with Faith while he slowly approaches his brother.

'Hey, buddy,' Ian says.

'Ten of diamonds. Eight of clubs.' The cards fall in a pile, fanning out across the table.

'Eight of clubs,' Ian repeats, settling into a chair.

Ian has told her that Michael has been diagnosed as severely autistic. His survival strategy in the real world is to live by a routine. To break the routine sets him off. It can be as simple as someone's rearranging the order of the eating utensils on his napkin, or Ian's staying two minutes past the hourlong visit. And he cannot stand to be touched.

Ian has told her that this is the way Michael will always be.

Faith yanks at her hand. 'Let go,' she whispers.

Michael turns over an ace. 'Oh, no.'

'*Ace in the hole*,' the brothers say in unison.

There is something of the scene that moves Mariah greatly: Ian sitting inches away from a man who could be his mirror image, trying to connect with words that do not signify anything. She brings up her hand to wipe at her eyes and realizes she's no longer holding on to Faith.

Her daughter moves toward the card table. 'Can I play, too?'

Frozen, Ian waits for Michael's reaction. He turns from Ian to Faith and then back to Ian and begins to shout at the top of his lungs. 'Ian comes alone! Three-thirty on Tuesday. Not Monday Wednesday Thursday Friday Saturday Sunday; alone alone alone!' With his hand, he thrashes at the cards so that they scatter across his lap and the floor.

'Faith.' Mariah tries to draw her away as a member of the staff arrives to calm Michael down. But Faith is crawling around on the floor, picking up the fallen cards. Michael is rocking, throwing off the soothing words of the nurse who knows better than to lay a hand on him. Faith awkwardly sets the pack of cards on the table, staring curiously at the grown man with the mind of a child. 'It might be best if you and your friends go, Mr Fletcher,' the attendant says softly.

'But—'

'Please.'

Ian flings himself out of the chair and walks from the room. Mariah reaches for Faith and follows him, glancing over her shoulder once to see Michael reach for the deck of cards, cuddle it close to his chest.

Just outside the library, Ian closes his eyes and takes great, deep breaths of air. Just as whenever Michael has an episode, he finds himself shaking. But somehow this seems worse.

Mariah and Faith slip outside and wait beside him quietly. He can barely even stand to look at them. '*That* was your miracle?'

There is a phenomenal rage running through him, like a poison working its way through his system. He doesn't know why, or where it's come from. After all, this is what he had expected to happen.

But not what he'd hoped.

The thought catches him unawares, pulls the world out from beneath his feet. He feels himself spinning and has to lean against the wall. All the bullshit he'd fed to Mariah last night, all the little concessions he'd made during the week to make them think he was starting to believe in Faith . . . they weren't really lies. Professionally, Ian may have wanted Faith to fail today. But personally, he had wanted her to succeed.

Autism isn't something you can fix with a blink or a touch of your hand; he's known that all along. Faith White, for all her claims, is a fake. But being right, this time, doesn't bring him any sense of satisfaction. This little girl, who's been playing everyone for a fool, has managed to show Ian he's only been fooling himself.

Mariah touches his arm, and he shrugs it off. *Like Michael*, he thinks, and he wonders if his brother cannot stand to be touched because he cannot bear such open, honest pity. 'Just go away,' he mutters, and he finds himself walking off. By the time he reaches the doors, he's nearly running. He circles around to the back of Lockwood, to the small pond with its brace of swans. Then he rips the microphone from beneath his lapel. He takes the microcassette recorder out of his pocket, tape still turning. He throws them both as hard as he can into the water.

It is nearly three-thirty in the morning before Ian returns to the cabin. Mariah knows exactly what time it is; she's been waiting up the whole night, worried. After running from Lockwood, Ian had driven off in the car, leaving her and Faith to find their own transportation back. And even after the taxi had dropped them off and the car was nowhere in sight, Mariah assumed Ian would return by dinnertime. By nine o'clock. Midnight.

She's been picturing the car in a ditch, wrapped around a tree—clearly, he is too upset to be out driving. Relieved that he's safe, she walks from her bedroom to the living room. The fumes of alcohol reach Mariah before she even sees Ian lounging on the couch with his shirt unbuttoned, gripping a bottle of Canadian Club by the neck. 'Please, just go away.'

Mariah wets her lips. 'I'm so sorry, Ian. I don't know why Faith was able to help my mother but not Michael.'

'I'll tell you why,' he says tightly. 'Because she is a goddamned hoax. She couldn't heal a fucking paper cut, Mariah! Just give up the act already, will you?'

'It's not an act.'

'It is. It's all an act.' He waves the bottle, sloshing liquor on the couch cushions. 'I've been acting since the minute I saw y'all on the plane, and God knows your daughter's gunning for a goddamned *Oscar*, and you . . . you—'

He leans so close to Mariah, she can taste the Canadian Club on his breath. She hesitates, then leans forward and kisses him.

It is slow at first, a gentle rubbing of his lips against hers. She reaches around his head and brings him closer, kissing him deeply, drawing out whatever is hurting him so badly.

Ian's throat works for a moment before he can speak. 'What was that for?'

'I'm not acting, Ian.'

Setting his palms on her cheeks, Ian tips his forehead to hers. 'You don't understand.'

Mariah stares at his haunted features, but sees instead Ian sitting beside his twin, trying to play by the odd rules of engagement because it's better to have that than nothing at all. Ian's wrong. She knows him better than he might think.

'I'd like to understand,' she says.

Ian Fletcher had been born two and a half minutes before his brother Michael: bigger, stronger, more active than his twin, a circumstance for which he'd been paying for the rest of his life. Clearly, Ian had taken the lion's share of nourishment and space in the womb, and although no doctor ever said so, he felt responsible for his brother's ill health and slow responsiveness, perhaps even for the autism that Michael was diagnosed with as a toddler.

Their parents had been rich, jet-setting socialites from Atlanta who married late in life and held their Learjet, their restored plantation manor, and their condo on Grand Cayman in much higher esteem than they did their twin sons. Ian and

Michael had been a mistake, and clearly one they didn't talk about, since something was obviously not quite right with one of the boys. They lived high off the hog, traveling around the world for months at a time and leaving Ian and Michael in the hands of whatever tutor or nanny had been hired to deal with them. Ian knew he was responsible for Michael; he understood that as soon as he was able to understand the differences between them. Privately tutored, Ian did not have friends or playmates. What he had, what he'd always had, was his brother.

When Ian was twelve, his father's lawyer arrived in the middle of the night with the local sheriff. His parents' plane had crashed in the Alps, and there were no survivors.

Overnight the world changed. Ian learned that the lifestyle to which they'd been accustomed was courtesy of an immense credit-card debt, one that left the boys bankrupt before an inheritance could even be considered. Ian and Michael were placed in the reluctant custody of his mother's sister and her Bible-thumping husband, and uprooted to Kansas. But his aunt and uncle had no intention of trying to understand Michael's pyschological problems, and they didn't have the resources to hire someone else to do so. The state's public-education system would have paid to send Michael anywhere in Kansas, but no one researched the choices, and so Michael was sent to the nearest institution with an open bed, a place that reeked of feces and urine, a place where Michael was the only patient even able to talk.

Ian visited him, even when his aunt and uncle stopped coming. He went to the library and found out which residential homes had the best reputations, but no one would listen. He spent six years wondering what horrors Michael had suffered that made him regress, unwilling to dress himself in the morning and rocking more often in silence and absolutely, positively refusing to be touched.

On the day that Ian and Michael turned eighteen, Ian dressed in a secondhand suit from a thrift store and petitioned a Kansas City court for custody of his brother. He got a scholarship to Kansas State and worked around the clock to pay for his books and to save money. He learned all about group homes for autistic adults and met with doctors who told him Michael was not capable of such an independent arrangement yet. He learned about assisted-care facilities—how they took both federal and state aid, and would take some indigent cases, but very few. How you had to know someone in the right place at the right time, or you'd be told there were no beds available. How you then paid for a quality of care, and continued to pay, lest that precious bed be given to someone else.

Ian's drive to succeed was fueled by his brother. It dovetailed naturally with the fact that a long time ago, he'd stopped believing in God. What God would have taken away his parents, his childhood? Most important, what God would have done this to his brother? Ian was angry, and, to his surprise, people wanted to listen: first, grade-school English teachers, then theology professors, then radio listeners, and then TV producers and viewers. The more famous he became, the easier it was to pay Michael's board at Lockwood. The more outspoken he became, the more quickly he clawed his way back to a lifestyle he had only barely remembered.

When Michael was twenty-two, he began to feed himself again. At twenty-six he was able to button his own shirt. At thirty-seven he still refuses to be touched.

Suddenly Mariah understands what has fashioned a man like Ian Fletcher. He spent years making himself into someone other than that lost little boy—into someone whose cornerstone is disbelief in God—and with good reason. How painful it must have been to find himself hoping—*praying*—that a miracle might come about after all.

She also realizes that Ian might have gotten his brother into Lockwood, and might have reached the financial peak he'd staked out in order to pay for his brother's care, but her intuition tells her that Ian hasn't gotten what he needs most of all. He's been taking care of Michael all his life—but it has been years since anyone has taken care of Ian.

Mariah starts out slowly, running her hand over his hair, then flipping it over so that her knuckles graze his throat and his jaw. She raises her palms to his cheeks and draws them down the slope of his shoulders, watching him close his eyes like a cat in the sun. Then she wraps her arms around him tightly, fits her face into the crook of his neck, and feels him shudder.

His arms close about her with such force that she cannot breathe, cannot do anything but ride out the crest of his need. His hands map her back and her shoulders, his lips falling at her ear. 'Thank you,' he whispers.

Mariah draws back and kisses him. 'My pleasure.'

Ian smiles. 'Let's hope so.' He kisses her and lets his lips silver her skin. He undresses her, reaches into his wallet for a condom, and uses his hands and his tongue to navigate her body.

Is it her imagination, or does he linger at her wrists, the places that still make her ashamed? Mariah pictures herself shrinking, small and malleable beneath Ian's hands, until she feels that surely she would be able to fit inside one of her dollhouses, walk on its pristine floors and look into its spotless mirrors. She opens her eyes as Ian moves over her, into her.

It has taken years to find out, she thinks, but this is what it was like to be a perfect fit.

Ian's rhythm becomes stronger. Mariah strains toward him, her fingers clutching his shoulders, her mouth round on the salt of his skin. She stops thinking about Ian's past, about Faith's future, about anything at all. And just before Mariah splinters around him, she hears Ian's voice fanning past her temple. 'Oh,' he cries, lost in her. 'Oh, God!'

'I didn't,' Ian says, chuckling.

'You did.'

'Why do you think that is? I mean, it happens all the time, but if it's just you and me in bed, why would I call out God's name?'

Mariah laughs. 'Force of habit.'

'For you, maybe.' He wraps his arms around her, still amazed by the lull of peace inside him now, steady as a flat-line. 'I'm thinking it has more to do with divinity.'

Mariah turns in his embrace. 'Does it?' she says, her eyes darting away. 'Was it . . . okay?'

Ian's brows rise. 'You have to ask?'

Her shoulders rise and fall, and his body instinctively tightens. 'It's just—well, I always wondered what would have happened if I was thirty pounds lighter, or platinum blond, or sexier. I thought that might have kept Colin's interest.'

Ian is quiet for a moment. 'If you were thirty pounds lighter, you'd blow away in the wind. If you were platinum blond, I wouldn't recognize you. And if you were any sexier, you'd probably kill me.' He kisses her on the forehead. 'I've seen your handiwork. You told me how you make those miniature houses. You made one hell of a daughter. So what is so hard about believing that anything you make . . . including love . . . might be any less exquisite?'

Ian frames Mariah's face in his hands, effortlessly sliding between her legs again. 'You're not perfect. You have this freckle here.' He points to her collarbone. 'You can be downright stubborn. And your hips are—'

'I had a baby!'

Ian laughs. 'I know. I'm just trying to show you that if you want to get clinical about perfection, none of us would pass muster. Me least of all.' He strokes her hair. 'Colin is an idiot. And I do mean it this time when I say: Thank God.'

Mariah smiles and snuggles closer on the nest of blankets they've made on the rug. 'Do you know what the most beautiful word in the English language is?'

'Let me think on it a minute.' Ian wrinkles his brow in concentration. '"Mellifluous."'

Mariah shakes her head. '"Uxorious,"' she breathes. 'Excessively fond of one's wife.'

In his whole life, Ian cannot remember ever feeling this sense of peace, right here in this hellhole of a Kansas cabin. This is his temporary reprieve, he knows. His truce. Tomorrow he will have to tell Mariah that he has been lying all along, that he cultivated her sympathy from the moment they stepped off the plane just so that he'd be able to set Faith up for a fall. Tomorrow he'll have to tell her that he intentionally recorded Faith's disastrous meeting with Michael, even if he no longer has the tape. Tomorrow he'll have to decide how much to reveal to his producer.

Tomorrow will be soon enough to have her hate him.

'Penny for your thoughts,' she says, yawning.

A penny? They're worth a far piece more. 'I don't think we get a choice in who we fall for,' Ian whispers. 'I think we just *do*.'

But Mariah's breathing is even and regular, and Ian realizes she's already drifted off. He savors the weight of her numbing his arm and warming his skin, and moments later—for the first time in years—Ian falls into a deep, easy sleep.

It is just after five in the morning when Ian slips away from Mariah. He covers her with the blanket, unsure of whether or not she sleeps naked as a matter of course and not wanting Faith to come bounding in to find her sprawled that way. He dresses quickly and writes Mariah a quick note that says when he'll be back, where he is going, and nothing important at all.

He drives to Lockwood. Why he is returning, he cannot say. Clearly, if his brother was set off by the presence of Mariah and Faith interrupting the regular schedule, then a 6:00 A.M. visit isn't going to go smoothly. It's just that things had been left so rough. Michael shouting, and Ian storming off . . . He doesn't want a week to pass before he sees him again. If Michael is asleep, Ian can just peek in, make sure he's all right, and get on his way.

The staff gives Ian a wide berth as he walks to his brother's room and pushes open the door. Michael is snoring softly, his face relaxed, his big body sprawled over the covers. 'Hey, buddy,' Ian whispers, and then hesitates before he touches his brother's hair.

Michael's eyes open with a start. 'Ian?'

'That's right.' He quickly withdraws his hand and glances at the clock over the door, certain that Michael is about to start screaming, but instead his brother yawns and stretches.

'How come you're here so early?' Michael says. Ian blinks at him, stunned. 'What, you've got no place better to go?'

His brother, who has not spoken about anything but cards for the past three years, is *teasing* him. Ian narrows his eyes, taking in the spark of understanding, of connection, in his brother's eyes. 'God, Ian. And they say *you're* the smart one.' Michael holds out his arms, an invitation.

'Michael,' Ian breathes, folding his twin into an embrace. When Michael's hand pats him clumsily on the back, he loses the power of speech.

Gaining control, he draws back to talk—really talk!—to his brother, but finds Michael's expression remote. Ian watches him take the deck of cards from the nightstand. 'Four of diamonds. Three of spades. Seven of diamonds. Ian comes at three-thirty on Tuesday. Not Monday Wednesday Thursday—'

Dumbfounded, Ian steps back from the bed. He walks out of Michael's room before a full-blown tantrum begins, certain that he's imagined the whole surreal encounter, that his brother was actually asleep the entire time. With a sigh Ian digs for his car keys and pulls something unexpected from his breast pocket—the jack of hearts, slipped there minutes before by someone close enough to truly touch him.

nine

Spirits when they please
Can either sex assume, or both.

—John Milton, *Paradise Lost*

THE FIRST TIME Colin kissed me, I was a college junior, sitting in an empty gymnasium, conjugating the French verb *vouloir*. 'To want,' I had said, a test, and I tried to concentrate on the hard plane of the bleachers beneath me, instead of the light reflecting off Colin's face.

He was, quite simply, the handsomest boy I'd ever seen. He was from the South, a member of the good-ol'-boy network; I was a Jewish girl from the suburbs. His granddaddy had endowed a chair in the history department; I was at the school on an academic scholarship. I had learned his name from the Saturday football rosters: COLIN WHITE, QB, 5′11″, 185 lbs, HOMETOWN: VIENNA, VA. I braved the cold and my own ignorance of football to watch him flash across the deep-green field like the needle of a skilled embroiderer.

But he was just a daydream for me; our worlds were so far apart that finding common ground seemed not only unlikely, but ludicrous. Yet when the coach of the team called the Student Tutoring Service and asked for someone to help Colin pass French, I snatched up the assignment. And then spent three days gathering the nerve to call and set up a tutoring schedule.

Colin turned out to be unfailingly polite, always pulling

out my chair and holding open doors. He was also the worst French student I'd ever met. He ruined the melody of the language with his Virginia drawl and stumbled over the simplest forms of grammar. I was doing him no good, although I didn't mind. It meant that I would get to keep coming back.

'*Vouloir*,' I had said that day. 'It's irregular.'

Colin shook his head. 'I can't. I don't get this the way you do.'

It was one of the nicest things I'd ever been told. Although I would have been entirely out of place in Colin's sports or social world, I was in my element right here. '*Je veux*.' I sighed. 'I want.' I pointed at the book, to show him.

His hand came over mine, and I went absolutely still. Afraid to look him in the eye, I found something fascinating about that page of the textbook. But I could not stop myself from feeling the heat of his body as he leaned closer, hearing the swish of his jeans as he stretched out his legs, imprisoning me. And then his face was all I could see.

'*Je veux*,' he murmured. His mouth was softer than I'd dreamed, and then he pulled away, waiting to see what I would do.

I glanced at him long enough to realize that the invincible Colin White, Star Quarterback, was nervous. My heart pounded like a timpani, so loud in my ears that for a moment I did not hear the distant sound of catcalls, of someone clapping.

I stood up and ran out of the gym.

October 27, 1999

THE NIGHT AFTER Ian and I make love, I dream that we are getting married. I'm wearing the gown from my wedding to Colin and carrying a bouquet of wildflowers. I walk down the aisle by myself and smile at Ian, and then we both face the person officiating. For some reason I am expecting Rabbi Solomon, but when I open my eyes I am standing in front of Jesus on the cross.

Faith is cuddled beside me. 'How come you're naked?' she asks. 'And how come you slept out here?'

With a start I glance around the living room, searching for Ian. When I realize he's missing, all my doubts creep in: He is used to one-night stands. He makes a living out of seducing people in one form or another. I am one of those people, for more than one reason. I remember our discussion about a truce; was last night a way of saying that it is over?

'Ma-a!' Faith whines, yanking my hair.

'Hey!' I rub my scalp and try to focus on her. 'I got hot, so I took off my nightgown. And *you* were snoring.'

Faith seems to accept this. 'I want breakfast,' she announces.

'Get dressed and we'll find something to eat.'

With Faith gone, a thousand thoughts run through my mind, none of them with happy endings. I am not sophisticated enough for someone like Ian. He's left because he cannot look me in the eye. He's gone back to New Hampshire, and he's going to tell the world everything he has learned about Faith, from her shoe size to her bumbling experience with Michael. He does not even remember what happened last night. I close my eyes, disgusted. I have already lived this story. I have already fallen in love with a man whom my mind inflated to such mythic proportions that I could stare right at him and still not see him clearly.

'I didn't mean it,' Colin told me years ago, after our first kiss. He admitted that two of the wide receivers had bet twenty dollars he couldn't seduce me before the end of that first tutoring session. Then he shook his head. 'No, I take that back. I *wanted* to kiss you. For the money at first, but then it happened, and it wasn't about that at all. I would really like it,' he said, 'if you'd go out with me sometime.'

We went to a movie three nights later. And then to another movie. And out to dinner. And soon, as unlikely as it seemed, when Colin was walking across campus, I was wedged beneath his arm. For someone small and skinny and brainy, someone who had never moved in popular circles, it was a heady feeling. I would pretend that I did not hear cheerleaders snickering as we passed, teammates asking when he'd switched over to screwing little boys.

Colin liked me, he said, because I was sweet and could talk about nearly anything with knowledge and conviction—unlike most of the Magnolia Queen debutantes who had always been trotted out in front of him. But Colin was accustomed to that type of girl all the same. And whether it was unconscious or by intent, he turned me into one of them little by little—bringing me headbands to pull the hair off my face, introducing me to Bloody Marys on Sunday mornings, even buying me a cheap strand of fake pearls, to wear with everything from the Izod knit shirts I borrowed from his dresser to my own corduroy jumpers. I did whatever he asked, and more, intent on being as good a student at turning into a WASP as I had been at any academic subject. It never occurred to me that Colin was interested in what he could make me into, instead of what I already was. What struck me, then, was simply that he was interested.

The night of Winter Formals I put on a simple black dress and hooked on my pearls and even wore a special bra that made it look as if I had something to support. We were going to Colin's fraternity, and I was bound and determined to pass muster. But fifteen minutes before Colin was supposed to pick me up, he called. 'I'm sick. I've been throwing up for an hour.'

'I'll be right over,' I said.

'Don't. I just want to sleep for a while.' He hesitated, then said, 'Mariah, I'm sorry.'

I wasn't. I could not be sure of myself at a fraternity dance, but I knew how to take care of someone ill. I got into my faded jeans again and walked into town, where I bought chicken soup at the grocery store, fresh flowers, and a crossword-puzzle book. Then I went to Colin's dormitory room.

Which was empty.

I left the chicken soup still steaming on the threshold of the door and wandered aimlessly around the campus. Hadn't I expected this, deep down? Hadn't I told myself this was coming? Snow began to settle on the shoulders of my coat as I turned onto Fraternity Row. The parties were loud, with steam and laughter and fumes of grain alcohol spilling through the open windows. I edged to the back of Colin's frat house, stood on a milk crate, and looked inside.

A group of football players and their dates formed a Gordian knot—black tuxedos threaded with splashes of colored satin on a lap or draped over a neck. Colin was facing me, laughing at a joke I had not heard. His arm was looped around the waist of a beautiful redhead. I stared for so long that it took me a moment to realize that Colin was looking at me, too.

He chased me across campus to my room. 'Mariah! You've got to let me explain!'

I yanked open the door. 'You were *sick*,' I said.

'I was! I swear!' His voice turned low and smooth. 'When I woke up, I tried to call you, but you weren't here. The guys came by and convinced me to go over to the House for a while. Annette . . . well, she's nothing. She was someone who was hanging around.'

Was *I* nothing? Was *I* someone who was hanging around?

Colin's fingers framed my face. 'But I left her to be here with you,' he said, reading my thoughts. His breath fell onto my mouth, a curious mix of mint and scotch, and I remembered how Colin had described gentling the horses he'd worked with in Virginia—by blowing into their nostrils, so that they would not fear his scent.

'Colin,' I whispered, 'why me?'

'Because you're different from them. You're smarter, and better, and—I don't know—I just keep thinking that maybe if I'm with you, it's going to rub off, so I'll be different, too.'

It was an amazing concept—that somehow Colin had a new explanation for why I'd always remained on the fringe: not because I wasn't good enough for others, but because I was just waiting for others to flock around *me*. I leaned forward and kissed him.

Later, when we were undressed and Colin was rising over me like a great bird blocking out the sun, he asked, 'Are you sure you want to do this?'

I was not only certain, I'd been waiting my whole life for this first time with a man who knew me better than I knew myself. I nodded and reached toward him, expecting magic.

When Ian comes into the cabin, we both freeze. With great precision I lay my spoon down beside my cereal bowl; he methodically closes the door behind him.

This time, I tell myself, *I am not going to let it happen*. I clasp my hands in my lap so that Ian cannot see them trembling. He's not Colin, but I am just as powerless now as I was then.

Suddenly I realize why I could not have turned Colin away years ago. I realize why I am getting involved, once again, with a man bound to hurt me. In my experience, falling in love has little to do with wanting someone. It is much more enticing to me to be wanted.

Without saying a word, Ian meets me halfway across the kitchen and pulls me into his arms. Inside, I am tumbling. He doesn't kiss, or stroke, or do anything but hold me, until I give in to the urge to close my eyes and let him lead.

Ian hands Mariah his cell phone and watches her disappear into the bedroom for privacy while she calls her mother. He can't blame her. As wonderful as it is to touch her, they are still strangers of a sort. He has not told her about his morning visit to Michael; she prefers to be alone when she speaks to Millie.

'So,' he says amiably to Faith, 'how about a game of gin?'

She looks up from her coloring book, wary. Well, he can respect that, too. The last time he was with her—at Lockwood—he'd practically snarled. He widens his grin a little, determined to be charming, if only for Mariah's sake.

Suddenly Mariah is standing at the doorway of the living room, her face white. 'We have to go home,' she says.

Boston, Massachusetts

IN THE VATICAN there is an official whose sole responsibility is to find the holes in each proposed case of sainthood. He examines every action and writing and word spoken by the allegedly virtuous person in an effort to find one slip, one swear, one lapse from the faith that might prevent canonization. For example, he might unearth the fact that Mother Teresa missed vespers on July 9, 1947. Or that she took the Lord's name in vain when seized with fever. The Catholic Church even has a certain name for this position: Promoter of the Faith, or more irreverently, the Devil's Advocate.

It is a job Father Paul Rampini thinks he'd fill splendidly.

He doesn't live in Rome, though. And he is hardly important enough to be chosen for such a critical job, since he's only taught at seminary in Boston for sixteen years. But still, Father Rampini has met his fair share of the falsely venerated. As one of the foremost theologians in the Northeast, he's been called in to consult on many occasions when visionaries began spouting claims. Of the forty-six cases he's examined, not one received a favorable report to the bishop from Father Rampini. And most of them only chattered on about the usual: glowing images of Mary, a crucifix appearing in the mist over a valley, Jesus telling people the hour of reckoning was at hand.

The idea of a female God does not sit well with Father Rampini.

He turns off the ignition in his Honda and opens his briefcase. The pink pamphlet from the MotherGod society lies on top. Father Rampini can barely stand to look at it. It is one thing for someone like him—a priest who teaches at seminary, a man who has devoted his life to theology—to reconsider the procession of persons in the godhead. It is another thing entirely for a seven-year-old girl—Jewish, at that!—to start proclaiming God as a mother.

It is said that she's a healer. Well, that he might even accept, with the proper sorts of proof. And that she has stigmata—again, he'd like to see it with his own eyes. But to say that God is visiting her in a clearly female form . . . certainly it is heresy.

Father Rampini checks his reflection in the rearview mirror before opening the door of his car. He tucks the leather portfolio beneath his arm and steps out, smoothing the placket of his black shirt and adjusting the white collar.

The door to the rectory sweeps open, and Father MacReady stands on the threshold. For the briefest of moments they size each other up: parish priest to seminary priest, confessor to researcher, Irish to Italian. Father MacReady steps forward, filling the doorway, making it impossible for the visiting priest to enter.

Just as quickly, he steps back. 'Father.' He nods. 'I hope your trip was all right?'

'A little bit of rain near Brattleboro,' Paul says, the mutual antagonism vanishing into professional politesse like smoke.

'Come in,' Father MacReady says, glancing around. 'Can I get your bag for you?'

'That's all right. I don't imagine I'll be staying.'

This is news to Father MacReady. Although he isn't thrilled to share his home with some pompous, published yahoo from St Joseph's, he knows that it will reflect poorly on himself if he fails to offer enough hospitality. 'It's no trouble.'

'No, of course not. I just believe I'll be able to wrap this case up in a matter of hours.'

At that, Joseph MacReady laughs. 'Do you? Maybe you'd better come inside.'

On the plane home from Kansas City Ian sits apart from Faith and me, since we don't want to attract attention by being seen together. An hour into the flight, while Faith is busy listening to the movie, I hesitantly creep into the darkened first-class cabin and take the seat beside him. He reaches over the seat divider and squeezes my hand. 'Hi.'

'Hi.'

'How's everything back there?'

'Fine. We had cereal for breakfast. You?'

'Waffles.'

'Oh,' I answer politely, thinking that this is not the conversation two people who made love so magically the night before ought to be having.

'Have you thought about the hearing?'

I've told Ian everything my mother told me: Joan Standish has received word that Colin's suing me for custody of Faith. 'What can I do? He'll say that Faith shouldn't have to live with a hundred people shoving to take her picture and ask her questions every time she leaves the house. Who's going to disagree with that?'

'You know I'll do what I can to help,' Ian says, but I do not know that, not at all. Now that we are headed home, the differences between us have sprung up, a minefield that makes it impossible to recall the seamless landscape of the night before. When we step off this plane, by necessity, Ian and I will be on very different sides of a controversial issue.

We both sit silently, brooding. Then Ian reaches for my hand, turning it over in his own before he starts to speak. 'I have to tell you something, Mariah. I wanted Faith to fail. I thought you were putting her up to this . . . prophet show for the attention. I deliberately set out to win your sympathy, so that you'd take her to Michael.'

'You already said this to me the other—'

'Hear me out, all right? I did and said whatever I could to get you there—including when I told you I was starting to believe in Faith. That was a lie, just one more thing to make sure you'd go to Lockwood. I was hot-miked that night. I taped you saying that Faith would give her healing powers a try. And when we got to Lockwood, I taped that whole damned fiasco. I was going to show the way you two ran your sting.'

Stricken, I have to force my lips to move. 'There's your proof, then.'

'No. After Michael pitched his fit and I realized Faith hadn't been able to work a miracle, I was furious. I had my story, and it didn't make a heap of difference so long as Michael was still rocking back and forth. I lied to you, Mariah, but I lied to myself, too. I didn't want Faith to be a fraud, not when it came to my brother.' He looks at me. 'I tossed the tape into the pond in Lockwood's garden.'

I glance into my lap, one question tumbling through my mind. I have to know, I *have* to. 'Last night . . . Were you lying to me, then, too?'

Ian lifts my chin. 'No. If you believe nothing else I've told you, believe that one thing.'

I let out the breath I've been holding and pull away from

him. 'I would just ask you one favor—if you could hold off on your show until after the preliminary hearing . . .'

'I'm not going to get on the air and say Faith couldn't work a miracle.'

His voice is so soft that I realize what I've overlooked: Any reference to Faith is going to circle right back to Ian's own brother. 'You don't want anyone to know about Michael.'

'That's not why. It's because Faith *did* work one.'

I sit back, stunned. 'She did not. I was there. I watched you leave the room.'

'When I went back this morning, Michael and I had a real conversation. He made fun of me. And he reached right up and hugged me.'

'Oh, Ian.'

'It didn't last for long, and at first I thought I'd just dreamed it. But I didn't. I really had that minute with him, Mariah. One minute in twenty-five years.' He smiles sadly. 'One hell of a minute.' His expression clears as he turns to me. 'Autism . . . it isn't like that. It doesn't switch on and off like a faucet. Even on Michael's good days, he's always been . . . apart. But this morning he was the brother I'd always wanted to have—and that's beyond the power of science. I can't tell you that I believe in God. But, Mariah . . . I *do* believe Faith can heal.'

The wheels of my mind turn. I imagine Ian stepping onto the front lawn and convoking the press. I imagine them hanging on his every word. I imagine the furor that will ensue when Ian, the most influential doubting Thomas of them all, announces that he's found the real thing.

They will never let go of Faith.

'Lie,' I say quickly. 'Tell everyone Faith couldn't do it.'

'I don't lie. That's the whole point of the show.'

By now I am on the verge of tears. 'You *have* to lie. You *have* to.'

Ian takes my hand and brings it to his mouth, kisses each finger. 'Hush, now. We'll figure it all out.'

'We?' I shake my head. 'Ian, there is no "we." There's you and your show, and there's me and custody. If one of us wins, the other one loses.'

He tucks my head onto his shoulder, his voice soothing. 'Ssh. Let's pretend it's six months from now. And I already know the name of the high school you went to, and your favorite Disney dwarf, and how you take your coffee.'

I smile hesitantly. 'And we sit around on Saturday nights watching videos.'

'And I wear my boxers to breakfast. And you let me see you without makeup.'

'You already have.'

'You see?' Ian brushes his lips across my forehead, erasing the worry. 'We're halfway there.'

North Haverhill, New Hampshire

A. WARREN ROTHBOTTAM LIKES his show tunes. He likes them so much, in fact, that he's personally paid to have his judge's chambers at the Grafton County Superior Court rewired with a state-of-the-art stereo system and cleverly hidden Bose speakers, which make it seem as if Carol Channing is robustly singing from behind the neat row of New Hampshire Procedural Law books. The music, however, is too big for the room, and often spills into the hall or through the walls. Most people do not mind. If anything, it gives a certain character to the courthouse that the squat, unremarkable building in the middle of nowhere does not manage by itself.

Today, before settling down behind his desk, Judge Rothbottam selected *Evita*. He closes his eyes and slices his hands through the air, humming loudly enough to be heard in the hall.

'Your Honor.'

The timid voice cuts through his orchestration, and Rothbottam scowls. Punching a button on his intercom, the music dulls. 'What, McCarthy? This better be good.'

The clerk of the court is shaking. Everyone knows that when Judge Rothbottam puts on an original-cast recording, he isn't to be disturbed. Something about the sanctity of the music. But then again, an emergency motion is an emergency motion. And Malcolm Metz is too famous a lawyer to be put off by a county clerk.

'I'm sorry, Your Honor, really. It's just that Mr Metz called for the third time in response to his emergency motion.'

'You know what you can tell him to do with his emergency motion?'

McCarthy swallows. 'I can guess, Your Honor. Would that be a denial, then?'

Scowling, Rothbottam reaches beneath his desk, and the glorious voice of Patti LuPone cuts off in the middle of a high C. The judge has never met Malcolm Metz, but one would have to be blind, deaf, and dumb to move in the circles of the New Hampshire legal system and not know about him. A highly paid rainmaker in a prestigious Manchester law firm, Metz has managed to reel in case after case receiving plenty of TV coverage: the custody battle for Baby J that resulted in a nasty courtroom war between a surrogate mother and an adoptive family, the sexual harrassment suit won by a secretary against her senator boss, the current fiasco involving the split between a Mafia don and his bimbo wife. Rothbottam does not care for grandstanding; he leaves that to the legitimate theater. If his courtroom has to be violated by some asshole like Metz, the counselor will damn well play by the judge's rules.

'Just a second,' Rothbottam says to the clerk. He thumbs through the motion to modify custody that Metz has filed that morning and the accompanying brief requesting an ex parte hearing. According to Metz, the child is in grave danger and needs to be removed from the mother's influence immediately; the ex parte motion is necessary before the defendant even gets wind of the motion to modify custody.

Just the kind of dramatic bullshit he'd expect from Malcolm Metz.

Rothbottam scans the brief. *White* v. *White*. He just heard the divorce a month ago, and there hadn't been any custody issues then. What the hell is going on?

He does not realize that he's spoken aloud until he hears McCarthy on the intercom. 'Well, Your Honor, she's that girl. The one who's been on the news.'

'Who is?'

'The one the father wants custody of Faith White.'

The seven-year-old who is raising the dead and speaking to God and showing stigmata. Rothbottam groans. No wonder Metz is deigning to come to New Canaan, New Hampshire. 'You know, I don't know Metz at all. I don't even *want* to know him, although I guess I'm not going to be so lucky. But I do know Joan Standish, who represented the mother in the divorce. Call Metz and tell him to be here at three o'clock. Let him know that Joan and her client will be joining him. I'll listen to his argument about the child being in danger, and we'll set a date for the custody hearing.'

'All right, Your Honor.' The clerk beeps off the intercom after agreeing to find the judge the latest newspaper stories about Faith White. Rothbottam sits at his desk for a moment, then walks to the bookshelves and extracts a new original-cast recording from the many stacks.

The music from *Jesus Christ Superstar* fills his chambers, and Rothbottam smiles. There is nothing wrong, nothing at all, with getting in the mood for what is yet to come.

Manchester, New Hampshire

MALCOLM METZ MOVES so gracefully in the leather swivel chair that he looks like a twentieth-century version of a centaur as he gestures to his three minions and finishes telling the joke. 'So Saint Peter opens the gates of heaven and lets in a pope and a lawyer. "Come in," he tells them. "I'll show you to your new quarters."' Metz glances around. A skilled litigator, after all, is at best a superb actor.

'Saint Peter stops off at a tremendous golden penthouse, built on top of a cloud. He leads them inside and shows them the gold faucets in the bathrooms and the silk bedding and the expensive rugs in the halls. Then he turns to the lawyer and says, "This is your new home." He leaves with the pope, and takes him to a tiny cell with a little twin bed and a washstand. "And this," he says, "is where you are going to live from now on."'

Metz adopts a lilting Italian accent. '"Now, wait a second!" the pope cries. "I've lived a pious life and led the Catholic Church—but I have to live here while that lawyer gets a penthouse?" Saint Peter nods. "Yes," he says. "See, we've got plenty of popes up here. But this is the first time we've ever had a lawyer!"'

The conference room erupts into laughter—no one likes lawyer jokes more than lawyers. But Metz is equally aware that he could have read a perfectly dull legal statute aloud, and if he'd expected his associates to find it funny, they would have been rolling on the floor. At the sound of the intercom, he holds up a hand, and the younger lawyers fall silent. 'Peggy,' Metz says to his secretary, 'put him through.'

They watch him with expectant faces. 'All right. Yes, I see.' Metz hangs up the receiver and folds his hands on the polished table. 'Gentlemen and lady,' he says, 'the ex parte motion has been denied.'

He turns to Hunstead, his first associate. 'Call Colin White. Tell him to get himself into a good suit and meet me at the Grafton County Courthouse at two-thirty P.M. Lee,' he says to a second man, 'tip off the media. I want them to know the father thinks his daughter's in danger.'

The two associates run off, leaving Metz alone with the third. 'I'm sorry, Mr Metz,' Elkland says. 'A lucky break would've been nice.'

Metz shrugs, collecting his papers and files. 'Actually, I never expected the judge to rule in my favor.' He taps the legal pads on their edges, aligning them. 'I only filed it so that the judge could deny it, and get that out of his system. Let's face it—no small-town judge wants someone like me cruising into his courtroom. I'd much rather have Rothbottam use this motion as a pissing contest to show me who's boss, instead of something intrinsic to the case.'

The associate is surprised. 'Then this was just strategic? Isn't the kid in danger?'

'Hell, who knows? Filing an ex parte motion keeps the father happy. Denying it keeps the judge happy. And you know what makes me happy?'

'Knowing that you're going to win?'

Metz pats her shoulder. 'I knew I hired you for a reason,' he says.

New Canaan, New Hampshire

'THE MOTHER ISN'T GOING to let you near Faith,' Father MacReady says, watching the visiting priest move about the rectory's tiny guest room. 'I can't blame her.'

Father Rampini turns in a smooth motion. 'Why not?'

'She's Jewish. We've got no right to be there.'

'She's spouting heresy,' Father Rampini corrects. 'If we don't have jurisdiction over the person making the claims, we at least can control what she says that misleads good Catholics.' He lifts a jacket and hangs it in the closet. 'Surely you take issue with a female apparition?'

'No. The Church has accredited plenty of visions of Mary.'

'Are we talking about Mary? No. God in a dress, God as a mother.' Rampini frowns. 'You have no problem with this?'

Father MacReady turns away. He has taken vows that hold him to helping others for the rest of his life, but that doesn't take away the occasional urge to plant a facer. He sits at the small table and drums his fingers on its surface, casually glancing at the stack of books Rampini has placed there and the Saint-A-Day desk calendar, open to November 7. *Saint Albinus*, he reads. If he remembers correctly, Saint Albinus killed an evil man by breathing into his face.

'Maybe God just looks different to a seven-year-old,' Father MacReady muses.

'Tell that to the children at Fatima,' Rampini says. 'Three kids, who—unlike Faith White—all saw the same vision of Mary. They didn't say she was wearing pants or smoking a hookah. They saw the Blessed Virgin the way she's traditionally pictured.'

'But not everyone has traditional visions. Saint Bernadette said the Virgin spoke to her in French patois.'

'Cultural resonance isn't part and parcel of a vision. So what if the Virgin was speaking French to Bernadette? She was still too uneducated to know what Mary meant when she referred to herself as the Immaculate Conception.' Rampini zips his duffel bag and slides it beneath the bed. 'Everything you've told me and everything I've read suggests that this is a crock. It's a hallucination, one the girl's managed to pass along into a mild hysteria. If Faith White *is* seeing God, there's no way He would appear in the form of a woman. Either an apparition is Jesus Christ or it is not.' He shrugs. 'I'm more likely to consider the visions satanic than divine.'

MacReady runs his finger along the tabletop, scattering a fine layer of dust. 'There's concrete, objective proof.'

'Right. The resurrections and the healing. I'll let you in on a little trade secret: I've read about Lourdes and Guadalupe and a hundred others, but in my lifetime I've yet to see a bona fide miracle worker.'

Joseph MacReady meets his gaze. 'For a good Catholic, Father, you sound an awful lot like a Pharisee.'

I am still half asleep when I hear Ian, speaking from the plane seat beside Faith. 'I didn't get to thank you.' I will my eyelids to stay slitted, and just listen.

Faith doesn't answer him. 'You did it, didn't you?' Ian presses. 'You gave Michael those few minutes.'

'I didn't do anything.'

Ian shakes his head. 'I don't believe that.'

'You don't believe a lot of stuff.'

He grins. 'Call me Ian.'

'Okay.' They stare at each other. Faith smooths down the front of her shirt, and Ian uncrosses his legs. 'Ian? You can hold my mother's hand if you want.'

Ian nods gravely. 'Thank you.' He hesitates for a moment. 'Can I hold yours?'

Faith slowly extends her hand, with the Band-Aid at its center. Ian slips his fingers around hers carefully. He does not examine the Band-Aid, doesn't even give the supposed stigmata a second glance.

Maybe, just maybe, Faith has worked a miracle after all.

Millie Epstein opens the front door, expecting to see Mariah and Faith back from their flight, and instead lays eyes on yet another man in a black shirt and backward collar. 'What are they doing in Rome? Cloning you fellows?'

Father Rampini draws himself up to his full five feet ten inches. 'Ma'am, I'm here to speak to Faith White at the request of His Excellency, Bishop Andrews of Manchester.'

'Who asked him?' Millie says. 'I don't mean to be rude, but I find it highly unlikely that my daughter or granddaughter called His Highness—'

'His Excellency—'

'Whoever,' Millie interrupts. 'Look. We've had more priests around here than the St Patrick's Day parade in New York. I'm sure that one of them has the information you want. Have a nice day.'

She begins to wedge the door closed but is stopped by the priest's foot. 'Mrs . . .?'

'Epstein.'

'Mrs Epstein, you're interfering with the process of the Roman Catholic Church.'

Millie stares at him for a moment. 'And your point is?'

By now Father Rampini is sweating. He wonders if he should have taken the insufferable Father MacReady up on his offer to accompany him to Faith White's home. At the time, the thought of twenty minutes on back roads with the ridiculously liberal priest had seemed like more penance than any man of God should have to face. Of course, he hadn't known about this particular dragon at the gate.

'All right,' he says, 'why don't you just get it over with?'

'I beg your pardon?'

'You don't like me, Mrs Epstein. You don't like priests. Go ahead and tell me why.'

'You see? You hear my name, know I'm Jewish, and assume I'm prejudiced.'

Father Rampini grits his teeth. 'My apologies. Is Faith available?'

'No.'

'What a surprise,' he says dryly.

Millie crosses her arms. 'Now I'm a liar? Next you're going to assume I'm some kind of shyster moneylender, I suppose?'

'No more than I'm a Bing Crosby look-alike who drinks

too much and seduces altar boys,' Rampini says tightly. 'Now, I could always go ask for the cooperation of that police captain at the end of the driveway.'

'Fortunately, we already fought the war to separate church and state,' Millie says. 'My granddaughter isn't home, thanks to all of you.'

Rampini feels a muscle tic at the base of his jaw. This is the resurrected grandmother? And what did she mean by 'all of you'? Who had driven the girl away?

He looks into her feisty, lined face and sees, in a flicker of her eye, a monumental sadness that it has come to this. For a moment he even feels guilty. 'Mrs Epstein, maybe if you set forth some guidelines, I can take them back to the bishop and we can compromise on the best way to examine Faith without upsetting her . . . or you.'

The woman snorts. 'You think I was born yesterday?'

'Actually, from what I've heard, that's not so far off the mark.'

'Where's the other one? The nice priest?' Millie looks around the front yard for a sign of Father MacReady. 'Mariah likes him.' Then she narrows her eyes. 'Are you two doing a good-cop/bad-cop thing?'

By now Father Rampini has a headache. He thinks this woman might have done very well on their side, during the Inquisition. 'We aren't partners. I swear to God.'

'Oh?' Millie says. 'Yours or mine?'

It has been a two-hour ride from Boston, but the heating system in the silver rental car has not warmed me at all. In the rearview mirror I can see Ian's rental, a black Taurus, driving behind me. We decided that it would be best to arrive separately. Otherwise, how do we explain why we're coming home together?

'Lies,' I mutter. 'More and more lies.'

'Ma?' Faith's voice comes, drowsy and rich.

'You have a good nap?' I capture her attention in the mirror and smile. 'There's something we have to talk about. When I get home, I'm going to have to leave you with grandma and go visit the lawyer.'

Faith sits up. 'Does it have to do with Daddy again?'

'In a way. He wants you to live with him. And I want you to live with me. So a nice judge is going to decide where you ought to be.'

'How come nobody wants to know what *I* think?'

'I want to know,' I say.

But now that she's on the spot, Faith hedges. 'Do I have to pick just one of you forever?'

'I hope not, Faith.' Hesitating, I consider how best to phrase this next sentence. 'Since a lot of people are going to be watching us while the judge decides, it might be best if you . . . told God . . . that you need to keep Her a secret for a little while.'

'Like when we were at the cabin.'

Not quite, I think. Faith failed pretty miserably at keeping her light under a bushel.

'God says it's no one's business.'

But that's wrong. It is a business, a booming one of donations and salvation and even atheism. 'Just do this for me, Faith,' I say wearily. 'Please.'

She is quiet for a moment. Then I feel her hand slip through the narrow slat of the headrest, into my hair, to rub the muscles of my neck.

Ian arrives at the house a half hour before Mariah, having driven straight through during the time she stopped at McDonald's to get Faith a snack. He turns his car into the street, stunned at how the crowd has grown. All the network affiliates have vans there, there's some group with a banner, and the cult hasn't given up its stronghold around the mailbox. And that doesn't even take into consideration the sea of eager faces that have come to be healed or touched or blessed.

He slips into his own small knot of production personnel unobtrusively, simply because it is so crowded. James is nowhere to be seen. His assistants fall into file behind him, but he shoos them away when he reaches the Winnebago. 'Not now, y'all. Let me catch my breath.'

But inside, he only paces. He waits until the commotion

outside reaches him like a current on the air, and then he exits the Winnebago and watches, from a distance, as Faith and Mariah get out of their car.

She's dazed, he can see from here. She hustles Faith to the house, shielding her from view, although there is no way to block out the roar of a crowd that has waited on the child for a week. But she only trades her daughter off to Millie, and then an unfamiliar woman—the lawyer?—marches Mariah right back to the driveway and into a Jeep.

Ian pushes his way to the front of the crowd, a swarm of people who touch the fenders and doors of the Jeep as it slows to a stop at the end of the driveway. The police push them out of the way, and the SUV inches forward. Ian stares at the passenger window, willing Mariah to look up. As the Jeep pulls out of the driveway, she does. He smiles at her for encouragement, and she cranes her neck as the car continues to move, turns in her seat, taps her fingers to the glass as if she would touch him.

Book II

THE NEW TESTAMENT

ten

When love begins to sicken and decay,
It useth an enforced ceremony.
There are no tricks in plain and simple faith.

—William Shakespeare, *Julius Caesar*

October 27, 1999

MARIAH STANDS BESIDE Joan in the middle of the judge's chambers, terrified of making a wrong move. She is uncomfortably aware that she's wearing leggings and an oversized sweatshirt, while Joan is wearing an olive suit, and both Colin and his attorney are dressed in Armani. She stands ramrod straight, as if posture might count when it comes to deciding who will retain custody of Faith.

'Mariah,' Colin whispers behind his lawyer's back, but the man hushes him.

The judge has been diligently scribbling away at his desk, and although it is past three o'clock, neither Joan nor the other lawyer has made any move to remind him that the hearing was supposed to start. Mariah realizes that the judge is wearing earphones. Very tiny ones, like news anchors wear—the kind that snake over the shell of the ear like a hearing aid. He reaches beneath his desk, pushes at something, and then tugs the tiny plugs from his ears. 'All right,' he says, turning to Colin's lawyer, whom Mariah thinks she may have seen on the regional news. 'Mr Metz, what do you have to say?'

The man smooths his tie with a feline preening that makes Mariah think of a ferret. 'This is a matter of life and death, Your Honor. Mariah White is endangering my client's child.'

Mariah feels everyone's eyes settle on her. A flush works its way up her neck.

'Your Honor, my client only recently became aware of the dog-and-pony show that has become his child's life, and the constant threat of physical endangerment. He's in a position now to provide her with the safety and security she needs, and he feels that it is of the utmost importance that she get out of her mother's household. It's why we felt strongly about an ex parte hearing, and it's why we're confident that you'll decide my client should have full custody. But in the interests of safety, we want her removed from the home right now, before any more irreparable damage is done.'

Judge Rothbottam purses his lips. 'Six weeks ago your client legally ceded custody to his ex-wife, which leads me to believe he didn't consider her a threat to the child's welfare then. As far as I can see, the only thing that's changed is a little press activity on the front lawn. What's life-threatening about that?'

'In addition to the psychological stress of being paraded in front of the media daily, my client's daughter has been hospitalized for intense trauma to the hands.'

'Trauma?' Joan sputters. 'Your Honor, there's absolutely no medical proof that Faith's injuries were caused by trauma. In fact, several doctors have gone on record saying as much, and, as I'm sure you know, there's an issue here that Mr Metz is conveniently ignoring, which is that the child is apparently performing miracles and speaking to God. And as for the media—well, their descent on the household has absolutely nothing to do with my client. She has done everything humanly possible to provide her daughter with a normal life in spite of them. Mr Metz's charge of endangerment is nothing but a thinly veiled attempt to turn a weak case into the sort of wildly dramatic spectacle in which he prefers to be involved.'

Mariah cannot take her eyes off Joan Standish. She's

never heard the woman string together that many words, and so compellingly.

Judge Rothbottam snorts. 'Well, Ms Standish, that was some pretty histrionic grandstanding yourself.'

Metz sits forward at the edge of his seat, a pit bull ready to spring. 'Your Honor, the issue that Ms Standish is trying to obscure is that a child is in jeopardy. Three months ago, when my client left, his daughter was a well-adjusted little girl. Now she's a victim of psychotic hallucinations and serious bodily injury. I urge you to err on the side of safety here, and give my client temporary custody of the child until the hearing.'

Joan completely ignores Metz. 'Judge, the divorce has been hard enough on Faith. The last time she saw her father, he was half naked and carousing with some other woman.'

'I beg your pardon!' Metz says, livid.

'Don't beg *mine*. The last place Faith White should go is to her father's house, Your Honor. Please let her stay with my client.'

Judge Rothbottam picks up his earphone and begins to laboriously wind the wires into a tight sailor's noose. 'I think I've had enough for one afternoon. It doesn't appear to me that the child is in any immediate crisis, Mr Metz. We'll have a custody hearing in five weeks. I trust that's enough time?'

'The sooner the better, Your Honor,' Metz says. 'For Faith's sake.'

The judge does not bother to look up from his calendar. 'I'm appointing a psychiatrist, Dr Orlitz, whom I want to evaluate your client, Metz; and your client, Standish; and their daughter as well. It's a court order, which means that you all *will* cooperate. You're free to get your own psychiatrists, of course, but you'll also speak to Dr Orlitz. I'm also appointing Kenzie van der Hoven as guardian ad litem, and I'll expect you to give her any information she needs. If you have an objection to Ms van der Hoven, I want to hear it now.'

Joan whispers to Mariah, 'She's good.'

Metz feels his client's eyes on him, and shrugs. He doesn't know jackshit about GALs in New Canaan, New Hampshire. Manchester is one thing, but for all he knows Kenzie van der

Whatever is Joan Standish's sister. 'We think that's fine, Your Honor,' Metz announces in a strong, clear voice.

'We do, too,' Joan adds.

'Marvelous. The custody hearing will begin Friday, December third.'

'I have a conflict,' Metz says, poring over his calendar. 'I'm scheduled to be taking a deposition in the case of a boy who's divorcing his parents.'

'Is that supposed to impress me, Mr Metz?' Judge Rothbottam asks. 'Because it really doesn't. Find someone else to do it. You're the one who wants this case tried expediently.'

Metz folds the leather binding of his Filofax. 'I'll be here.'

'Joan?'

'I don't have any conflicts.'

'Excellent.' The judge pushes the earphones into place. 'I can't wait.'

Joan pulls into the driveway and touches Mariah's arm. 'Remember what I told you. This isn't the end of the world.'

Mariah's smile does not quite reach her eyes. 'Thank you. For everything.' She folds her hands in her lap. 'I was impressed.'

'Girl, you ain't seen nothing yet.' Joan laughs. 'I might have taken on this case for free, just to stand up to Malcolm Metz. Now, you go on inside and play with your daughter.'

Mariah nods and gets out of the Jeep, flinching at the questions hurled from distant reporters, and at the sight of a tremendous poster of Faith's face held by a large group of women. She feels fragile, an ornament made of spun sugar, but she steels her composure while she climbs the porch steps. As soon as she opens the door, her mother and Faith come running into the parlor. After a searching look at Mariah's face, Millie turns to her granddaughter. 'Honey, I left my reading glasses on the arm of the couch. Could you get them?'

As soon as Faith is out of hearing range, Millie closes in. 'So?'

'In five weeks we have to go to court.'

'That son of a bitch. I knew you—'

'Ma,' Mariah interrupts. 'Don't do this now.' She sinks

down on the stairs and scrubs her hands over her face. 'This isn't about Colin.'

'It's not about you, either, Mariah, but I'll bet five weeks from now it will be.'

'What's that supposed to mean?'

'That your Achilles' heel, unfortunately, is a target as big as a barn. And that Colin and his fancy lawyer are sure to strike there.'

'By then Joan will have come up with something,' Mariah says, but she knows she is trying to convince herself as well as Millie. What court would pick *her* as the better parent?

Maybe Colin's right—maybe it *is* her fault. She has made poor choices before regarding Faith; this could be yet more proof of her inadequate parenting: one rash decision, one selfish move, one conversation that took root in Faith's imagination and brought her to this point. There have been times, after all, when Colin questioned Mariah's judgment with good reason.

'Oh, no you don't,' Millie mutters, pulling Mariah upright. 'You go right upstairs and steam that look off your face.'

'What—'

'Take a hot shower. Clear your head. I've seen you get like this before, all full of doubts about whether you've got the good sense God gave a beetle, much less a competent mother. I swear, I don't know how Colin does it, but the man's a Svengali when it comes to your mind.' She pushes Mariah up the stairs as Faith comes into the parlor with her grandmother's eyeglasses. 'Oh, good,' she says to the girl. 'Let's go see if we can find Sunday's comics.'

Aware of Faith's eyes following her, Mariah smiles with every step. She deliberately shoves aside the thoughts that batter away at her: what Joan will say in court, what the judge will make of Mariah's hasty escape to Kansas City, what Ian will say and do now that they have returned. She undresses and turns the shower on so that a white mist fills the bathroom. Inside the stall, the water pounds heavy and hot, but Mariah cannot stop shivering. Like the survivor of an accident, the close call hits all at once, and she is by turns frightened and stunned. What if, five weeks from now, her daughter is legally removed? What if, once again, Colin gets his way? Mariah slides down to the tiled floor, arms crossed tight, and lets herself fall apart.

After Faith is bathed and put to bed, Mariah walks into the living room to find Millie peering out from the edge of the curtains. 'Like Yasgur's Farm,' she murmurs, hearing Mariah come up behind her. 'Look out in the field. You can see all those little flickering lights . . . What were they holding up back then—candles?'

'Cigarette lighters. And how would *you* know about Woodstock?'

Millie turns and smiles. 'Don't underestimate your mother.' She reaches for Mariah's hand and squeezes. 'You feeling better yet?'

At the simple, sweet concern, Mariah almost breaks down again. She lets her mother lead her to the couch and lays her head in her lap. As Millie begins to smooth Mariah's hair back from her brow, she can feel some of the tension ebb, some of the problems fall by the wayside. 'I wouldn't say I'm feeling better. Numb is more like it.'

Millie continues to stroke her daughter's hair. 'Faith seems to be holding up all right.'

'I don't know if she understands what's happening.'

There is a moment of silence. 'She isn't the only one.'

Mariah sits up, color flooding her face. 'What do you mean by that?'

'When are you going to tell me the rest?'

'I already told you everything that happened in court.'

Millie tucks a strand of Mariah's hair behind her ear. 'You know, you look just the way you did when you stayed out with Billy Flaherty two hours past curfew.'

'It was a flat tire. I told you that almost twenty years ago.'

'And I still don't believe you. God, I remember sitting up in bed watching the clock and wondering, What on earth does Mariah see in him, with his brooding and his moods?'

'He was only sixteen, and his father was an alcoholic, and his parents were in the middle of a divorce. He needed someone to talk to.'

'The thing is,' Millie continues, as if Mariah has not spoken, 'the other night I was lying in bed watching the clock and wondering, Why on earth is Mariah staying with Ian Fletcher? And you come home, and you've got that same face on all over again.'

Mariah scoffs and turns away. 'I don't have any face on.'

'Yes you do. It's the one that says it's already too late for me to keep you from going over the edge.' She waits for Mariah to look at her again, slowly, and with great reservation. 'So you tell me,' Millie says softly. 'How hard was the fall?'

A stillness settles over Mariah as she realizes that her mother is no more prescient than Mariah herself. All the moments she's awakened in the middle of the night a split second before Faith's cries fill the dark, all the times she has looked at her daughter's face and cleaved a lie in half with a single look. This is the codicil of motherhood: Like it or not, you acquire a sixth sense when it comes to your children—viscerally feeling their joy, their frustration, and the sharp blow to the heart when someone causes them pain.

'Fast.' Mariah sighs. 'And with my eyes wide open.'

As Millie opens her arms, Mariah moves into them, drawing close the comfort of childhood with a great rush of relief. She tells her mother of Ian, who was not following her when she thought he was, who was not the person he made himself out to be. She describes the way they would sit on the porch after Faith went to sleep, and how they would sometimes talk and sometimes just let the night settle over their shoulders. She does not tell Millie of Ian's brother, of what Faith might or might not have briefly done for him. She does not tell Millie how it felt to have Ian's body pressed against hers, heat from head to toe, how even during hours of sleep, he held on to her hand as if he could not bear to let her go.

To her credit, Millie does not act surprised or ask if they are speaking of the same Ian Fletcher. Instead she holds Mariah close and lets the explanations fall where they may. 'If this happened between you,' she says carefully, 'where do things stand?'

Mariah glances through the gauzy curtains at the smattering

of lights that attracted her mother. 'With him out there and me in here,' she answers, smiling sadly. 'Just like before.'

Sometimes in the middle of the night Faith thinks she can hear something crawling under her bed, a serpent or a sea monster out of water or maybe the tiny, hooked feet of rats. She wants to toss off her covers and run into her mother's room, but that would mean touching the floor, and there's a very good chance that whatever is making the noise will wrap itself around her ankle and eat her with its rows of sharp teeth before she ever makes it into the hall.

Tonight Faith wakes up, certain it's coming for her, and screams.

Her mother comes rushing into the room. 'What's the matter?'

'They're biting me!' she cries. 'The things that live under the bed!' But even as she speaks, the world comes back to her, strange black shapes turning into lamps and dressers and other ordinary things. She glances down at her hands, still fisting the covers, Band-Aids covering the small holes beneath the knuckles. They don't hurt at all now. They're not bleeding either. They tingle a little, as if a dog were pushing his wet nose into them.

'You okay?'

Faith nods.

'Then I think I'll go back to sleep.'

But Faith doesn't want her mother to leave. She wants her to be sitting here, on the edge of the bed, thinking of nothing but Faith. 'Ow!' she cries impulsively, clutching her left hand.

Her mother turns quickly. 'What? What happened?'

'My hand hurts,' Faith lies. 'A big, sharp, needle pain.'

'Here?' her mother asks, pressing.

It doesn't hurt at all. It feels sort of nice, actually. 'Yes,' Faith whimpers. 'Ow!'

Her mother crawls into the bed, gathering Faith into her arms. 'Try to rest,' she says, her own eyes closing.

In the dark, Faith falls asleep smiling.

October 28, 1999

CLEARLY, HER MOTHER has been eating like a pig.

That's the only explanation Mariah can come up with to make sense of the absolute dearth of food in the house. Having been gone for a week, she'd have expected the fruit and the milk to go bad, but there's no more bread, and even the peanut-butter jar is empty. 'God, Ma,' she says, watching Faith pick at a dry bowl of Rice Krispies. 'Did you host a party?'

Affronted, Millie sniffs. 'That's the kind of gratitude I get for keeping house?'

'I would have expected you to replenish the pantry, that's all. For your own comfort.'

Millie rolls her eyes. 'Oh, and of course the vultures out there would have just waved politely as I went on my merry way.'

'If they harassed you, you could have harassed them right back.' Grabbing her purse, Mariah strides to the door. 'I'll be back in a little while.'

But eluding the reporters is not as simple as Mariah expects. Inching out of the driveway, she nearly hits a man who pushes his daughter's wheelchair in front of her car. Police notwithstanding, hundreds of hands pat her windows, her bumpers, her trunk. 'God,' she breathes, astounded by the sheer numbers of people, gratefully picking up speed a quarter mile past her own driveway.

She believed that, without Faith in tow, there was less of a chance that she'd be pursued, but three cars tail her as she makes her way into the grocery store in a neighboring town. Keeping careful track of them in the rearview mirror, she deliberately takes side streets instead of main roads, hoping to lose them before she reaches her destination. Two of the cars are gone by the time she leaves the outskirts of New Canaan. The third follows her into the parking lot but turns in a different direction, leading Mariah to realize sheepishly that this might have been a neighbor or ordinary citizen, rather than a reporter on her trail.

In the grocery store she keeps her head ducked, reaching

for melons and lettuce and English muffins and not making eye contact with other shoppers. She rounds the aisles with grim determination, set on making it through the checkout line without being noticed. But she has just reached into a frozen-food locker when a hand closes around her wrist and pulls her behind a tall display of ice-cream cones.

'Ian.'

He is dressed down in jeans and a tattered flannel shirt, a baseball cap pulled low over his face. He has not shaved. Mariah touches his cheek. 'This is your disguise?'

His hand slides from her wrist to her shoulder. 'I wanted to know what happened in court.'

A small light goes out inside Mariah. 'Oh.'

'And I wanted to see you.' Ian's fingers curl around the soft skin of her inner arm. 'I needed to.'

She looks up at him. 'We go back to the judge in five weeks.' She can just make out his eyes beneath the bill of his cap, pure Arctic blue and focused with the most singular intensity, pinning her like a butterfly.

Another shopper rounds the corner, toddler twins hanging on either side of her cart like docking buoys. She glances dismissively at them, then continues down the aisle. 'We can't be here like this,' Ian says. 'One of us is bound to get recognized.' But he makes no move to leave, and instead strokes his fingers under her chin, making her arch like a cat.

Just as suddenly, he steps away. 'I'll do anything I can to make sure Faith stays with you.'

'The only way the judge is going to let me keep her is if he thinks her life's perfectly normal,' she says evenly. 'So the best thing you could do, Ian, is leave.' She grants herself permission for one more glance at him, one more touch of his hand. 'The best thing for Faith, and the worst thing for me.' Then she reaches for the handle of her shopping cart and continues down the aisle, her heart tripping, yet her face as serene as if she'd never seen him at all.

The telephone rings when Mariah is nearly asleep. Groggy and dazed, she reaches for it assuming that Ian is on the other end, and too late realizes that even before dreams descend, he has already claimed a part in them.

'I am so glad to hear that you're still answering the phone.'

'Father MacReady,' Mariah says, sitting up in the bed. 'Isn't it a little late?'

He laughs. 'For what, exactly?'

'Calling.'

There is a beat of silence. 'I've been led to believe that it's never too late for a calling. Sometimes they just catch you behind the knees and knock you down like a linebacker.'

She swings her legs over the edge of the bed, pleats the edge of the top sheet. 'You're twisting my words again.'

'For what it's worth, I prayed for you,' Father MacReady admits quietly. 'I prayed that you'd be able to take Faith and get away.'

'Your hotline is apparently a little rusty.'

'It may be, you know. Which is why I wanted to talk to you. Your mother had the pleasure of turning away a colleague of mine today who'd like to take a look at Faith.'

'My daughter isn't the Catholic Church's lab specimen, Father,' Mariah says bitterly. 'Tell your colleague to go back home.'

'That's not up to me. It's his job. When Faith starts saying things that don't match up with two thousand years of teachings, they have to come evaluate it.'

It makes Mariah think of that old adage—if a tree falls in the woods and no one's there to hear it, does it make a sound? If you do not want religion, do you have the right to send it away?

'I know you're not going to want to hear this,' Father MacReady says, 'but I'd consider it a personal favor if you'd allow Faith to speak with Father Rampini.'

There are people at the edge of her property now who have gathered in the name of Christianity. She did not ask them to come; she would certainly like them to leave.

The judge would consider it a mark in her favor if she managed to get them to leave.

The simplest way to do that is for them to hear, straight

from the mouth of their Church, that Faith is not who they would like her to be.

But then again, it means exploiting Faith, and Mariah is not sure she wants to do that even if it leads to a greater good. 'Faith and I don't owe you any favors. We're not Catholic.'

'Technically,' Father MacReady says, 'neither was Jesus.'

Mariah sinks back into her pillow, feels it brush against the sides of her face. She thinks about those trees falling in the woods, silent and unobserved, until one day someone comes along and notices with a start that the entire forest is gone.

October 29, 1999

FATHER RAMPINI KNOWS many ways to make a statue weep, none of which have anything to do with Jesus. You can rub the marble face with calcium chloride, which makes water condense from the air in false tears. You can press small balls of lard into the eyes, which melt when they warm to room temperature. You can even use sleight of hand, dabbing at the statue with a sponge to make moisture when your audience is distracted. He's seen fake magician's blood hidden up a sleeve, stigmata spontaneously bursting with a flick of the wrist. He's watched rosaries go from silver to gold, scientifically explicable metallurgic reactions.

His gut feeling? Little Faith White is full of crap.

He believed, at first, that it would be easy to discredit the child. A couple of discreet inquiries, a tearful admission, and he'd be back at the seminary before supper. But the more he learns about Faith White, the more difficult it is becoming to dismiss her out of hand.

Yesterday he interviewed many of the reporters on the front lawn, trying to uncover a secret book deal the mother might have made or word of a TV exclusive. Historically, true prophets didn't profit—either by money, esteem, or comfort. Had he found even the subtlest hint of self-aggrandizement, he'd have been on the Mass Pike that afternoon.

All right, so she wasn't trying to become rich and famous by acting like a visionary. But neither was there proof apart from Faith White's alleged vision—like the spring at Lourdes that cures ailments, or the picture of the Virgin not made by human hands, given to Blessed Juan Diego and still hanging four hundred years later in the shrine in Mexico City. He said as much to Father MacReady, who—maddeningly enough—barely looked up from the sermon he'd been writing in his office. 'You're forgetting,' MacReady said. 'She's a healer.'

That morning Father MacReady accompanied him to the medical center. While the parish priest visited members of his congregation who were recuperating on the patient floors, Father Rampini spent hours reading the reports about Millie Epstein, with no firm conclusions. Medically, the woman had died. Certainly she was alive and kicking now. And yet rumor had it that Faith touched the woman to bring her back—a laying-on of hands smelled a little fishy.

The only way to prove that Faith White was an out-and-out liar would be to interview her directly. And that is what he's slated for today. Father Rampini has decided on a three-pronged attack: First, he will narrow down the truth regarding this female vision—Mary maybe, but certainly not God. Second, he will prove that the vision is inauthentic. Finally, he'll examine the alleged stigmata and list the reasons they aren't the genuine article.

Father MacReady asks him to remain silent during his introduction to Mariah White, and out of professional courtesy Father Rampini agrees. 'If you wait here,' the woman says, 'I'll get Faith for you.'

Father MacReady excuses himself to use the bathroom—Lord knows, he eats enough breakfast sausage to fell a horse, much less upset his bowels—while Rampini idly glances around. For a farmhouse, it is in remarkably good shape, the exposed beams of the ceiling straight and sanded, the floors buffed to high polish, the steely milk paint and flocked wallpaper meticulous. It looks like a residence featured in *Country Home*, except for the glaring evidence that real people abide here: a Barbie doll wedged between the bananas of a decorative fruit bowl, a child's mitten snugged like a skullcap over the knob of the banister. He sees no Palm Sunday crosses tucked behind mirrors, no Sabbath candles on the dining-room table, no evidence of religion whatsoever.

He hears footsteps on the stairs and draws himself erect, ready to stare down this heretic.

Faith White skids to a stop three feet in front of him and smiles. She is missing one of her front teeth. 'Hi,' she says. 'Are you Father Rampenis?'

Mariah White's face goes scarlet. 'Faith!'

'Rampini,' he corrects. 'Father Rampini.'

The parish priest appears in the doorway, laughing. 'Maybe you should just call him Father.'

'Okay.' Faith reaches for Rampini's hand, pulling him toward the stairs. Rampini is aware of two things at once: the rasp of Band-Aids against his own palm, and the extraordinary magnetism he feels when their gazes connect. It reminds him of being a child and seeing the first big snow stretch over his family's Iowa farm—so diamond-bright and pure that he could not tear his eyes away. 'C'mon,' she says. 'I thought you wanted to play.'

MacReady folds his arms across his chest. 'I'll stay down here. Have a cup of coffee with your mom.'

Rampini can see by the look on the woman's face that she believed she'd be present for the interview. Well, good. It will be easier to get out the truth in her absence.

Faith leads him to her bedroom and sits down in the middle of the floor with a Madeline doll and a collection of interchangeable outfits. Pulling out his notepad, Rampini jots down several ideas. If he remembers correctly, Madeline lived in a parochial school. It is possible that this so-called religious innocent knows more than people think.

'Do you want her skating clothes,' Faith asks, 'or her party dress?'

It has been so long since he's played with a child—since he's done more than examine hoaxes and heretics and write lengthy dissertations on his findings—that for a moment he is nonplussed. Once this might have come easily to him. Now he is an entirely different man. 'What I'd really like is to play with your other friend.'

Faith's mouth pinches shut. 'I don't want to talk about her.'

'Why not?'

'Because,' she says, and jams Madeline's leg into a set of tights.

Well, Rampini thinks, surprised. The visionary who chatters away about what she's seen is usually lying. Genuine seers, in fact, often have to be coerced into discussing their visions. 'I bet she's very beautiful,' he urges.

Faith peeks up from beneath her lashes. 'You know Her?'

'I work in a place where a lot of people study and learn about God. That's why I wanted to talk to you so badly, so that we can compare what we know. Does your friend have a name?'

Faith snorts. 'Duh. It's God.'

'Your friend told you this. She said, "I am God."'

'No.' Faith slides a shoe onto the doll's foot. 'She said, "I'm *your* God."'

He writes this down, too. 'Does she come whenever you need her to?'

'I guess.'

'Could she come now?'

Faith glances over her shoulder. 'She doesn't want to.'

Against his better judgment, Rampini looks toward the same spot. Nothing. 'Is she wearing a blue dress?' He struggles for a term for Mary's mantle that would be familiar to a seven-year-old. 'One with a hood?'

'Like a raincoat?'

'Exactly!'

'No. She wears the same thing over and over. It's a brown skirt and top, but it's all together in one piece, and it looks like the things people from olden times wear on TV. Her hair is brown and comes to here.' Faith touches her shoulders. 'And she has those shoes that you can wear on the beach and even into the water and everything without your mom getting mad. The ones with Velcro.'

Father Rampini frowns. 'She has *Tevas*?'

'Yeah, except hers don't have the Velcro and they're the color of throw-up.'

'I bet you wanted to see this friend of yours for a while, before she first appeared to you.'

But Faith doesn't answer. She rummages in the closet, returning with the Lite-Brite box. Father Rampini feels a pang of sentiment—he remembers giving the toy to his own son, long before he was ordained. Has it been around so many years?

Faith is watching him curiously. 'I'll let you do the yellows.'

Rampini shakes his thoughts back to center. 'So . . . you asked to see her?'

'Every night.'

Father Rampini has seen enough alleged visionaries to make comparisons. The religious devotees who pray to see Jesus for years and then have Him suddenly appear are always the ones who've simply gone off their rockers. Even, sad to say, in the case of that very sweet elderly nun from Medford whom he was sent to evaluate the previous winter. Compare that to the Fatima children, who were simply tending sheep when Mary appeared, unexpected. Or Saint Bernadette, who was gathering wood near a garbage dump when Our Lady materialized.

Heavenly visions come from heaven, but out of nowhere. Yet, according to Faith, she'd been asking for one—religiously, one might say.

'I wanted a friend really bad,' Faith continues. 'So every night I wished on a star. Then she came.'

He hesitates before writing on his notepad. Desiring a friend wasn't quite the same thing as praying for a miraculous appearance, but there were cases of child visionaries who'd played, so to speak, in the fields of the Lord. Saint Herman-Joseph romped with Mary and a boy Jesus; Saint Juliana Falconieri had visions where the Christ Child wove her a garland of flowers.

His eyes fall on Faith's hands, grasping the tiny pegs and stuffing them into the gridded holes of the Lite-Brite. 'I heard that you hurt yourself.'

She quickly hides her fists behind her back. 'I don't want to talk anymore.'

'Why? Is it because I asked about your hands?'

'You'll make fun of me,' she whispers.

'As a matter of fact,' Father Rampini says gently, 'I've seen other people who have the same kinds of cuts you do.'

This catches Faith's attention. 'Really?'

'If you let me take a look, I can tell you if yours are the same or different.'

She takes one hand and places it on the floor between them, uncurling her fingers like the petals of a rose. With her other hand she peels back the Band-Aid. In the center of her palm is a small hole. The flesh around it isn't mangled on either side of the hand, and neither are there protuberances such as Saint Francis of Assisi had, as if nails were stretching the skin from beneath its surface. 'Do they hurt?' Rampini asks.

'Not now.'

'When your hands are bleeding,' he asks slowly, 'do you sometimes think about Jesus?'

Faith frowns. 'I don't know anyone named Jesus.'

'That's the name of God,' the priest explains.

'No it's not.'

A seven-year-old can be very literal. Is Faith saying this because God specifically told her He is not Jesus? Or simply because He hasn't said His name at all? Or is it because this vision, far from being heavenly, is satanic?

Rampini wants to ask her more about God's name—like the story Rumpelstiltskin, guessing until he gets it right. It is not Mary, not Jesus. But is it Beelzebub? Yahweh? Allah? Instead he hears himself say, 'Can you tell me what it feels like when God talks to you?'

Faith looks down into her lap, not speaking. Father Rampini stares at her and thinks of the time he first saw his son. He remembers watching the baby fingers spider over Anna's breast as she rocked him. Although he has learned, in ascetical theology training, that feelings are not important, and that celebrating mass and administering the sacraments are the moments one is closest to God, he is not thinking about it now. That fullness of heart, a divinity spilling over, he's only felt twice in his fifty-three years. Once watching his wife after childbirth. And then again six years later, when the Holy Spirit settled over him like one of those early Midwestern snowstorms, numbing him to the pain of the car accident that had taken his family, and leaving forgiveness in its place.

It takes Father Rampini a moment to notice that Faith has taken one of the Lite-Brite pegs, a red one, and pushed it into the hole on her right hand. The peg sticks at the halfway point. The wound doesn't reopen, though, and as Faith flexes the muscles of her hand, it eventually falls out. Then she plugs in the Lite-Brite, and Father Rampini is jolted by the incandescent blaze of the flower. 'When She talks, I feel it here,' Faith says, making a fist and bringing it up to his heart.

Father Rampini has known for a long time that he moves in a world skeptics consider to be impossible, but, to him, Catholicism—specifically, its theology—has been a haven of logic. The *world* makes no sense—what other reason could there be for the drunk driver who picked his family's station wagon to plow into, instead of the other three hundred cars he passed that night? Religion, with its godhead, its order, and its salvation, has literally been Rampini's saving grace.

He runs the cold water in the bathroom sink and splashes it on his face. As he dries himself off and looks up into the mirror of the medicine cabinet, he hesitates for a moment. What is he going to say about Faith White? On the one hand, she has the humility of the blessed, and she's not gaining anything but a notoriety she does not seem to want. On the other hand, she's spouting heresy.

He begins mentally to chronicle the pros and cons. Rampini has yet to see a verified case, but Faith may indeed suffer from stigmata.

However, she's also seeing something that no one else has ever seen. Technically, God isn't a man. But that does not mean He is a woman.

He sits back down on the lid of the toilet and stares blankly at the collection of naked Barbie dolls in the bowl of the tub. Faith White is, for all intents and purposes, a perfectly ordinary secular girl. She doesn't structure her life around prayer; she probably couldn't tell a Hail Mary from the Pledge of Allegiance. It is in her favor that verified visionaries like the Fatima children and Saint Bernadette weren't likely candidates for visions either.

But at least they were Christian.

Rampini sighs. Father MacReady was correct—there are many compelling things about Faith. But, ultimately, her vision isn't one of them. She's saying things that quite simply are completely out of line.

Father Rampini opens the bathroom door and starts back down the hall, his decision made. Yet with each step he thinks of the saints of the sixteenth century, who were scorned and vilified for their radical beliefs. Saints whose autopsies, years after the persecution, revealed strange scars etched onto the walls of their hearts that looked like the letters of Jesus' name.

Malcolm Metz looks at the beat-up Honda that belongs to Lacey Rodriguez, one of a battalion of excellent private investigators his firm has used over the years. He points to a tiny statue of Mary glued to the dashboard with a piece of double-edged tape. 'Nice touch.'

'Yeah, well.' Lacey shrugs. 'I didn't know if someone might see the car.'

'From the way it sounds, you'll probably have to park a mile away. You'll be in touch with me later?'

'This afternoon, when I get there. And twice a day after that.'

Metz leans against the rusted hood of the car. 'I don't need to tell you how imperative it is for you to dig up dirt on the mother.'

Lacey lights a cigarette and offers one to Metz, but he shakes his head. 'How hard could this be?' she says, exhaling. 'The woman was in a freaking mental institution.'

'Unfortunately, possession is nine tenths of the law, and the child is still living with her mother. I want to hear if she keeps the girl up too late or feeds her something with Red Dye Number Two or talks on the portable phone too close to the tub when the kid's in it. I want to know what the hell she's saying to those priests and rabbis who keep coming to the house.'

'You got it.'

'Just don't do anything that won't be admissible in court. No dressing up like the plumber's assistant and going to check the pipes, only to come out with evidence seized without a warrant.'

'I only did it once,' Lacey says, chagrined. 'Are you going to bring it up forever?'

'I might.' Metz claps her shoulder. 'Go to work.' He watches the Honda weave down the street, and then walks toward the building that houses the law office. His eyes flicker toward his name, carved on the stone plaque outside. The glass-and-chrome doors swing open on sensor, as if they have been waiting for him all along.

Mariah takes refuge in the basement workshop. With determination she picks up a thin block of maple, intent on turning it into a miniature kitchen table, but she is too distracted to do it well. Frustrated, she sits beside her half-finished dollhouse and rests her head in her hand.

She can see the tiny bathroom fixtures and the knotty-pine floors in the bedrooms and the kitchen cabinet that is still ajar. She can see into the most private parts of this house without even having to try.

This is what it's like, she thinks, *to be God*.

She considers this for a moment, thinking of all the young girls who play so easily at being a divine being—able to put their dollhouse families through their paces. Mariah glances up at the ceiling and wonders if God is doing the same thing to her and Faith.

She remembers, suddenly, why as a child she never had people in her dollhouses. The family dog would butt up against the house and the miniature baby would tumble down the stairs before Mariah had a chance to grab him. Or the mother figurine would be facedown on the bed, and Mariah would think that the doll had been sobbing her heart out all night while she herself slept. It made her feel guilty—she couldn't play with all of the dolls at once, couldn't take care of all their needs. It was no great bargain to be godlike, to have the power to help and soothe and comfort and know that she couldn't save everyone all the time.

So she grew up to build houses without dolls, places where furniture was bolted down and glued into position, homes where nothing was left to chance. And yet, Mariah realizes that she still didn't make a clean escape.

Manipulation, responsibility, watchfulness. It is not so different, really, from being a mother.

From the Manchester Diocese of the Catholic Church

> **Manchester, NH, October 29, 1999**—His Excellency the Bishop of Manchester has issued a notice in response to the queries by priests, religious, and laity regarding the activity of Faith White, resident of New Canaan, NH, who claims to be allegedly hearing and seeing heavenly revelations.
>
> A serene and attentive examination of the matter was undertaken by the diocese, and Faith White's visionary claims have been ruled false. It is our duty to underline one major doctrinal error: erroneous language regarding Christ, who is not and should not be referred to as a woman or mother of any kind.
>
> The MotherGod Society, which has been primarily responsible for transmitting the message of Faith White via pamphlet and preaching, is spreading teachings which are not regarded as Catholic dogma and which must be ignored.

That night, when the MotherGod Society first hears of Bishop Andrews's official denunciation of Faith White, they hand out apples. They dispense more than three hundred Jonagolds from a local orchard and invite people to take a bite out of the myth of male religion. 'The Garden of Eden was just the beginning,' they shout. 'Eve didn't cause the fall from grace.'

The woman who has become their leader, Mary Anne Knight, mills through the crowd shaking hands. She knows this is not as radical and new a movement as people might think. Twenty years ago, she'd studied at Boston College with Mary Daly, who went on to leave the Catholic church after saying it was rooted in sexism. But Mary Anne loved Catholicism too much to renounce it. *One day*, she prayed, *there will be room for me in the Church*.

Then she heard about Faith White.

She stands on an overturned apple crate, her cohorts gathering around and waving half-eaten cores. Pulling her fleece jacket tighter, she covers a T-shirt provocatively printed MY GODDESS GAVE BIRTH TO YOUR GOD. 'Ladies,' she cries out, 'we have the pastoral letter from Bishop Andrews here.' She extracts a Zippo lighter from her pocket. 'And this is what we have to say in response.' With a flourish, she sets fire to the corner of the missive and lets it burn all the way to her fingertips.

As the crowd of enthusiastic women cheers, Mary Anne smiles. Let the Manchester diocese think that a gaggle of women are just letting their petticoats hang out; let the stuffy old bishop write warnings till he's blue in the face—there are some things His Excellency hasn't taken into consideration. The MotherGod Society still has Faith White. And two representatives en route to the Vatican, planning to launch a formal protest.

Mariah is brushing her teeth and flipping through the late-night channels on the television when she sees Petra Saganoff's face, and the backdrop of her own house. '*Hollywood Tonight!* has uncovered a new development in the case of Faith White. In an unexpected move, the father of the child, Colin White, has reappeared in New Canaan to seek full custody of his daughter.'

Millie, wearing cream on her face and a flannel nightgown, comes rushing into the room. 'Are you watching this?'

The screen changes to shots of the courthouse, where Colin and his attorney appear to speak into several microphones at once, their shoulders hunched against the bitter wind. 'It's a tragedy,' Colin says to the cameras. 'No little girl should be raised like that—' His voice breaks, seemingly unable to continue.

'Oh, for crying out loud,' Millie says. 'Did he hire an attorney or an acting coach?'

Petra Saganoff's face reappears. 'Malcolm Metz, the attorney for Mr White, alleges that being placed in Mariah White's custody is physically and psychologically endangering Faith. Of course, the pending custody case is now a matter of public record. We'll have more on this story as it unfolds. This is Petra Saganoff, for *Hollywood Tonight!*'

Millie walks to the television set briskly and turns it off. 'It's drivel. No one with a brain is going to believe anything Colin says.'

But Mariah shakes her head and spits toothpaste into the sink. 'That's not true. They're going to see him crying over his daughter, and that's what they're going to remember.'

'The only person who you should worry about is the judge. And judges don't watch garbage TV like that.' Mariah, rinsing out her mouth, pretends not to hear. She wonders if Joan saw it, if Ian saw it, if Dr Keller saw it. Her mother is wrong. You can reach a lot of people, without even trying—Faith is proof of that. She keeps the water running, until she hears Millie walk out of the room.

He knows when to call her, because he has repositioned the Winnebago so that it faces Mariah's bedroom. After the light goes out, Ian closes his eyes, trying to imagine what she is wearing to bed, whether her legs scissor between the cool sheets. Then he picks up his cell phone and dials, his gaze on the small pair of windows. 'Turn on the light,' he says.

'Ian?'

'Please.' He hears her shift, and then there is a golden glow to the room. He cannot see her, but he pretends he can; he imagines her sitting up and gripping the phone and thinking of him. 'I've been waiting on you.'

Mariah settles into her bedding—he can tell by the soft sigh of the fabrics. 'How long?'

'Too long,' Ian answers, and there is more to the words than easy flirting. Watching her walk away from him in the grocery store without being able to follow took all his self-control. He pictures her hair, spread over the pillow like a spray of gold, the curve of her neck and shoulder a puzzle piece made to fit flush against him. Curling the phone closer, he whispers, 'So, Miz White. You gonna tell me a bedtime story?'

He expects to hear a smile in her voice, but instead it is thick with tears. 'Oh, Ian. I'm all out of happy endings.'

'Don't say that. You have a long way to go between here and that custody battle.' He stands up, willing her to come toward the window. 'Don't cry, sugar, when I can't be there.'

'I'm sorry. I— Oh, God, what you must think of me! It's just this whole thing, Ian. One nightmare after another.'

He takes a deep breath. 'I'm not going to do a story on Faith, Mariah. I may even pull out of here entirely, make it look like I'm onto something else. At least until after the hearing.'

'It won't make a difference. There are plenty of other people left around to turn Faith into some kind of martyr. Did you see *Hollywood Tonight!*?'

'No—why?'

'Colin was on, breaking down and saying that Faith can't live like this.'

'He's putting the media to work for him, Mariah. His lawyer's just savvy enough to get his client's face out in front of the public for sympathy.' He hesitates for a moment. 'It's not such a bad idea, actually. You ought to turn right around to *Hollywood Tonight!* and invite them to hear the other side of the story. Give ol' Petra an exclusive.'

Mariah goes absolutely silent. 'I can't do that, Ian.'

'Why, of course you can. I'll coach you through it, just like the lawyer did for your ex.'

'It's not that.' Her voice is small and suddenly distant. 'I can't have a reporter asking me all kinds of questions, because there are things that have happened to me that I don't want spread around. Things I haven't even told you.'

He learned long ago that sometimes the wisest course is to keep quiet. Ian sits on the edge of the Winnebago's couch and waits for Mariah to tell him what he learned weeks before. 'I was suicidal seven years ago, and Colin had me sent to an institution.'

'I know.' Ian thinks of *The Boston Globe*, and feels his gut twist.

'You . . . you do?'

'Well, of course,' he says, aiming for a light tone. 'Before I was smitten by your considerable charms, I *was* doing a story on you and your daughter.'

'But—but you didn't say anything.'

'Not in public, no. And not in private, because it didn't make any difference to me. Mariah, you're the sanest person I know. And as for not having anything to live for anymore, well, I'm doing my damnedest to keep you from thinking that these days.'

He hears it then, the joy breaking over her. 'Thank you. Thank you so much for that.'

'I aim to please.'

'If memory serves, you hit the mark,' Mariah says, and they both laugh.

Then there is a comfortable quiet between them, punctuated by the distant calls of owls and barking dogs. 'You should do it, though,' Ian adds after a moment. 'Have Petra Saganoff over. It's the best way to show a great number of people that your little girl is just a little girl. Tell Petra she can shoot B-roll and do a voice-over as she sees fit, but no interviews.' He smiles into the phone. 'Fight back, Mariah.'

'Maybe I will,' she says.

'That's my girl.' He sees a shape appear at the window of the bedroom. 'Is that you?'

'Yes. Where are you?'

He watches her turn, scan the darkness for a face she cannot see. Ian flickers the lights in the Winnebago. 'Here. See?' Her hands come up to press against the glass, and Ian remembers them against the flat of his chest, cool and curious. 'I wish I was with you now.'

'I know.'

'You know what I'd do if I were with you now?'

'What?' Mariah asks breathlessly.

Ian grins. 'Go to sleep.'

'Oh. That wasn't what I had in mind.'

'Maybe that, too, then. But I haven't had a night's rest like I did with you in . . . God, well, years.'

'I think . . . I think I'd like to wake up with you,' Mariah says shyly.

'That would be a fine thing, too,' Ian agrees. 'Now, get away from that window. I don't want the whole crowd out here laying eyes on you.' He waits until he hears the covers rustle, Mariah pulling up the sheets to cover herself. 'Good night.'

'Ian?'

'Hmm?'

'About what you said before—you won't leave now, will you?'

'I'll stay as long as you like,' he says, and then watches the small square of light in her bedroom go black.

Mariah has no sooner put the phone on the cradle than she realizes her mother is standing in the slightly open doorway. She does not know how much Millie has heard, how long Millie was standing there.

'Who was calling so late?' her mother asks.

'No one. Wrong number.' With the weight of Millie's gaze thrown over her like another quilt, Mariah turns onto her side, toward the window, toward Ian.

For reasons Father MacReady does not understand, Father Rampini has not hightailed it back to Boston after sending along his recommendation that afternoon to Bishop Andrews. He has spent several hours in the guest room at the rectory, not packing but instead tying up the telephone line with faxes he sends from his laptop computer. So it is a surprise when Father MacReady comes downstairs for a glass of milk before bedtime and finds the visiting priest sitting at the kitchen table with a bottle of wine.

'Chianti?' Father Rampini says, a corner of his mouth lifting. 'Why, Joseph,' he jokes in an Irish brogue, 'where are you hidin' the good malt whiskey?'

Father MacReady grins. 'I find it useful to break across cultural barriers every now and then.'

'Want some?' Rampini hands the other priest a glass filled

to the rim with wine, then lifts his own and downs it in one swift motion.

Well, it's not milk, but it'll put him to sleep all the same. Father MacReady tips his own glass and finishes every drop.

Rampini laughs. 'Wanna have a spitting contest now?'

'No thanks. I already feel sick. But I was taught it's not good manners to let someone drink you under your own table.'

The other priest smiles. 'I'll be a good guest. I promise to pass out neatly in my chair.'

MacReady drums his fingers on the tabletop. 'How long do you think you'll *be* a guest?'

'If you need—'

'No, no,' he says placatingly. 'Stay as long as you want.'

Rampini snorts. 'You're trying to think of a nice way to ask why I'm still here.'

'The thought did cross my mind.'

'Mmm.' The visiting priest scrubs his hands over his face. 'I've been asking myself that, too. Do you know what I was doing all afternoon?'

'Ringing up a tremendous telephone bill?'

'Yes, but the diocese will pay for it. Actually, I was reading the work of a psychiatrist who talks about a young child's image of God. There's a theory that the earliest roots for God are tied to an infant looking up at his mother and knowing that it's okay to close his eyes and imagine her, because when he opens his eyes she'll still be there.'

Father MacReady nods slowly, unsure of where this is going.

'Then a kid gets to be six, seven. He hears about God on TV, sees pictures of angels. He doesn't know what God is, really, but he knows from context that God is big and powerful and sees everything. There are two people the kid knows who fit that bill—his mom and dad. So he uses them as raw material. If he was cuddled a lot, he may come up with a representation of an affectionate God. If he was raised strictly, God might be more stringent.' Father Rampini tips the Chianti bottle over his glass again. 'Conversely, the kid might attribute to God the things she wishes she had in a parent—unconditional love, protection, whatever.'

He rubs a small circle of condensation into the tabletop. 'So now we look at Faith White, whose mother—by her own admission—hasn't always been the most devoted of parents. What happens to a child who's always wanted her mother's attention? And then winds up, miracle of miracles, with only a mother in her life? What is she most likely to imagine God to be?'

'A loving mother,' Father MacReady murmurs, and then picks up the Chianti and drinks straight from the bottle. He wipes his mouth with the back of his hand. 'I thought you already wrote your recommendation to the bishop.'

'I did.' Rampini winces. 'There's just . . . something.' He leans back in his chair, his gaze roaming the worn walls of the rectory kitchen. 'If I could just make sense of why she's seeing a woman. Why. That would tip the scales, you know? I mean, that crap I just told you—it's psychology. Not theology. I can read it, but I can't believe it in my heart.'

'Maybe it's not what she's seeing,' Father MacReady says slowly. 'Maybe it's the way she's interpreting it.'

'How is that any different from what I just said?'

'It is. Did you ever see that drawing, the one that if you look at it one way, turns into a bottle, and if you see it a different way, looks like two people kissing?'

Father Rampini takes the wine away. 'I think it's time for you to stop.'

'I'm perfectly sober. You know . . . whatchamacallits . . . optical illusions! Well, it could just be Faith's frame of reference that's wrong, not her vision.' At Father Rampini's blank look, MacReady continues. 'Say you're a little girl who knows *nothing* about religion. Any religion. And you live in the nineties, in a fairly conservative town, where most people look the same. Then one day someone appears out of thin air. The person is about so tall, and has long brown hair, and is wearing a dress and sandals like your mother. What do you assume you're seeing?'

'A woman,' Father Rampini murmurs. 'But it's Christ—maybe young, without the beard—in traditional clothing.'

'There's no reason to assume that a little girl from New Canaan would know what men wore in Galilee two thousand years ago.' Father MacReady is smiling so hard, he thinks his face might split. He feels himself being yanked to his feet as Father Rampini grabs him in a bear hug.

'Do you know what this means? Do you?'

'That you're going to make another long distance call on my phone,' Father MacReady says, laughing. 'Go ahead. Call Bishop Andrews on my dime.'

He follows Rampini to the guest room, where the other priest scrabbles around his cluttered desk for the Manchester phone number. 'Of course,' Rampini mutters, 'the Bishop's Conference will say that Christ would make Himself known as the Lord fairly quickly, dress notwithstanding . . . but at least it'll go to conference. Ah, here we are. Hand me the phone?'

Father MacReady is not listening. He holds the portable phone in one hand and Father Rampini's Saint-A-Day desk calendar in the other. He's ripped off the page, so that the display is for tomorrow. Wordlessly, he hands it to the visiting priest.

> Saint Elizabeth of Schonau. Died 1146. *Saint Elizabeth beheld a vision of a young woman sitting in the sun and asked an angel to tell her what it meant. The angel said, 'The young woman is the sacred human nature of our Lord Jesus.'*

Father Rampini dials the phone. 'I know,' he says after a moment into the receiver. 'Wake him up.'

eleven

To whom then will ye liken God?
or what likeness will ye compare unto him?

—Isaiah 40:18

WHEN I WAS Faith's age, I learned that I was going to hell.

Ursula Padrewski sat behind me that year in school. She was tall for seven, with long braids that her mother coiled on top of her head like a sleeping rattlesnake. Her father was an assistant rector at the Episcopal church. One day on the playground she took each girl's Barbie and plunged it headfirst into a puddle of rainwater. She came up to me with her hands on her hips and said Malibu Barbie had to get baptized.

'What's baptized?' I asked.

She gasped, as if this were a word I should have known. 'You know. Where you get dunked underwater for God.'

'God didn't dunk me underwater,' I told her.

'They do it in church when you're a baby,' she said, but not before she took a step back. 'If you don't get baptized,' Ursula confided, 'you get thrown into a pit of fire and go to hell.'

I was old enough to understand that my family didn't go to church, which meant I probably had not been baptized, after all. That left in my mind the image of the ground opening up and flames reaching as high as my throat.

I started screaming so loud that even after the playground monitor had wrestled me to the nurse's office, no one could calm me enough to figure out what was wrong. My mother, summoned with a phone call, arrived ten minutes later. She skidded to a stop on the worn linoleum, laying her hands on my body to check for broken bones. 'Mariah, what's the matter?'

She motioned the nurse away. 'Mommy,' I asked, breath hitching, 'did I get baptized?'

'Jews don't get baptized.'

I burst into tears again. 'I'm going to hell!'

My mother wrapped her arms around me, and muttered something about prayer in public schools and Reverend Louis Padrewski. Then she tried to tell me about the Jews being the Chosen People, that I had absolutely nothing to worry about, and that there was no pit of fire.

But I knew that my family was nothing like Joshua Simkis's, who were also Jewish but worked very hard at it. Joshua, in third grade, couldn't have milk whenever the cafeteria served hamburgers. And he wore a little crocheted yarmulke to school, tucked into his hair with a bobby pin. My family, well, we didn't go to church—but we didn't go to temple either. I hadn't been baptized, but I didn't think we were going to be Chosen.

Eventually I was ready to go home. But as we walked to the car, I was careful to leap over the cracks of the sidewalk, thinking that at any moment they would split to reveal Ursula's pit of fire. And that night, when my parents had long been asleep, I filled the bathtub with water and dunked Malibu Barbie. Then I stuck my head in and repeated a bedtime prayer I'd heard Laura Ingalls say on the TV show *Little House on the Prairie*. Just in case.

October 30, 1999

IN THE MORNING, Joan calls me. 'Just wanted to make sure you're still alive,' she says, and although she is joking, neither of us laughs. 'I thought I might stop by this afternoon, talk about a defense strategy.'

The very concept makes me think of what Ian said the

night before, about fighting back. Self-defense, by definition, involves putting oneself on the line. 'Joan, did you happen to see *Hollywood Tonight!?*'

'I'd rather do a bikini wax than sit through that show.'

Not for the first time, I wonder who *is* responsible for their huge number of viewers. 'Colin was on. With Malcolm Metz. They spoke outside the courthouse yesterday, and Colin talked about how Faith's in danger and then started to cry.'

'Well, you don't have to worry about the media distorting your case. Thank God, the only person who will be hearing it is the judge, and—'

'I think I ought to let *Hollywood Tonight!* come into my house and film Faith.'

'You *what?*' It takes Joan a minute to get over her surprise, and I can fairly hear her stiffen. 'As your legal counsel, I highly recommend against that particular course of action.'

'I know it has nothing to do with the hearing, Joan. But the judge needs to see Faith as a normal little girl, playing with dolls and Legos and what have you. And for that matter, so do the other people who think she's some saint. I don't want to look like I'm hiding anything.'

'You should never mix the media with the courtroom, Mariah.'

'I shouldn't sit here and let Colin walk away with my daughter either. I don't want him planting ideas in people's heads about me and Faith, when we're perfectly capable of speaking for ourselves.' Hesitating, I add, 'I've been at this point before, with Colin. And I'm not going to let him do it to me again.'

I can hear her tapping something—a finger? a pencil?—against the edge of the phone. 'No interviews, with either you or Faith,' she says at last, starting to hammer out a list of conditions. 'Fifteen minutes of film footage, tops, and only in rooms that have been contractually agreed upon beforehand. And you don't sign a goddamned thing until I see it.'

'All right.'

'You know this means I'm going to have to watch that damn show.'

'I'm sorry.'

Joan sighs wearily. 'Yeah,' she says. 'So am I.'

Lacey Rodriguez believes in starting at the beginning. And as far as she can see, the furor surrounding Faith White blossomed after the incident with her grandmother's resurrection. She takes a small notebook from her tote bag and smiles at Dr Peter Weaver, the cardiologist in charge of Millie Epstein's case.

For an attractive man, he's a pill. He flattens his hands on the surface of his desk and glares at Lacey. 'I understand that you're only doing your job, Ms. Rodriguez. Which is why you must see that I can't divulge any information about my patient.'

She turns up the wattage on her smile. 'And I wouldn't ask you to. In fact, the attorney with whom I'm working is more interested in your knowledge of Faith and Mariah White.'

Dr Weaver blinks. 'I don't know them at all. Except, of course, for the rumors that we've all heard about the child. But medically, I can't substantiate any claims of healing. For me the issue was not how Mrs Epstein was resuscitated, but simply that she *was*.'

'I see,' Lacey says, pretending to record every single word on a page of her notebook, when in fact the man's said nothing at all of value.

'The only times I've even come in contact with Mrs White were at her mother's bedside and subsequent checkups.'

'Did she seem . . . fragile to you at the time? Emotional?'

'As much as anyone would have been, given the circumstances. I'd have to say that, overall, my impression of her was one of concern and protectiveness for her mother.' He shakes his head, his thoughts spooling backward. 'And her daughter.'

'Could you give me an example?'

'Well,' Dr Weaver says, 'there was a moment during Mrs Epstein's stress test, when the cameraman must have gotten the little girl in his range and—'

'Pardon me—you *filmed* the stress test?'

'No, not me. Ian Fletcher. That television guy. Mrs Epstein and the hospital had signed waivers to allow it. I'm sure it's already been aired. But the point was, Mrs White clearly didn't want her daughter filmed, and did everything in her power to stop it. Went after the cameraman, even, screaming and pushing at him. The very picture of a fierce maternal instinct rearing its head.' He smiles apologetically. 'So, you see, I don't really have much to say that is going to help your case.'

Lacey smiles back at him. *Don't be so sure*, she thinks.

November 2, 1999

KENZIE VAN DER HOVEN COMES from a long line of legal-minded men.

Her great-grandfather had started van der Hoven & Weiss, one of the first law firms in Boston. Her father, her mother, and her five older brothers were all currently partners there. When she was born, the last of the lot, her parents were so sure she was another boy that they simply gave her the name they'd already picked out.

She grew up as Kenneth, confusing the hell out of schoolteachers and doing everything she could to shorten her name to a diminutive, although her parents never bowed to her wishes. Following in the deep treads of everyone else in her family, she went to Harvard Law and passed the bar and litigated exactly five trials before deciding that she was tired of being what other people wanted her to be. She legally changed her name to Kenzie, and she turned in her shingle to become a guardian ad litem, a court-appointed child's advocate during custody cases.

She's worked for Judge Rothbottam before, and considers him a fair man—if a little partial to Broadway musicals that have starred Shirley Jones. So when he called her yesterday with the White case, she accepted on the spot.

'I should warn you,' the judge said. 'This one's going to be a doozy.'

Now, as Kenzie walks wide-eyed around the White property, she understands what he meant. At the time she had not connected the name with the religious revival occurring in New Canaan—most of the papers she read referred to Faith simply as 'the child,' in some semblance of protecting a minor's privacy. But this—well, this is indescribable. There are small knots of people camped out under pup tents, heating lunch over Sternos. Dotting the crowd are the ill in their wheelchairs, some spiraled with MS, some trailing intravenous lines, some with their eyes wide and vacant. Black-habited nuns patter across the fallen leaves like a flock of penguins, praying or offering service to the sick. And then there are the reporters, a breed apart with squat vans and cameramen, their chic suits as unlikely as blossoms against the frozen November ground.

Where on earth is she supposed to start?

She begins shoving through the crush of bodies, determined to get to the front door so that she can see Mariah White. After five minutes of tripping over sleeping bags and extension cords, she finally quits. Somewhere around here there must be a policeman; she saw the marked car at the edge of the property. It would not be the first time she's had her guardian-ad-litem status enforced by an officer of the law, but crowd control has never before been the reason.

Turning to a woman beside her, Kenzie laughs breathlessly. 'This is something, isn't it? You must have been here a pretty long time to get such a plum spot. Are you waiting for Faith?'

The woman's thin lips stretch back. 'No Eng-lish,' she says. '*Sprechen Sie Deutsch?*'

Great, Kenzie thinks, *hundreds of people and I pick the one who doesn't understand me*. She closes her eyes for a moment, remembering the judge's schedule. The custody hearing will be in five weeks. In that time, she has to interview everyone who's had contact with Faith since August and possibly earlier, she has to get to the bottom of the grandmother's resurrection, and she has to win Faith over and convince her that she is an ally.

Basically, she needs a miracle.

• • •

As I am sticking Faith's shoes in the closet, I realize someone is taking photographs through the sidelight of the front door. 'Excuse me,' I say, yanking it open. 'Do you mind?'

The man lifts his Leica and takes a picture of me. 'Thanks,' he says, and scurries away.

'God,' I mutter to myself, standing in the open doorway. My mother's car inches along the driveway, finally parking halfway down when people begin milling too close for her to continue safely. She's gone home to pack a valise and return, deciding to move in for a while. It's easier than trying to shake off the reporters who trail her on the short drive to her home. The man with the Leica is right in her face, too, when she leaves the car. Groupies chant Faith's name. For some reason, today they are all much closer to my house than they ought to be.

My mother stumbles up the porch steps with her suitcase and turns around. 'Go,' she says, waving her hands at the masses. 'Shoo!' She stalks past me, shuts and bolts the door. 'What is *with* these people? Haven't they got something better to do?'

I peek out the sidelight. 'How come they're all the way up to the porch?'

'Accident in town. I passed it coming in. A lumber truck jacknifed on the highway exit ramp, so there's no policeman at the end of the driveway.'

'Great,' I murmur. 'I guess I ought to be thankful they're not rushing the door.'

My mother snorts. 'It's early yet.'

Prophetically, the doorbell rings. Standing on the threshold, with more chutzpah than I've imagined possible, is Petra Saganoff. She has a cameraman behind her. Before I can shut the door in her face, she manages to wedge a red pump inside. 'Mrs White,' she says, the cameraman recording her words, 'do you have any response to your ex-husband's claims that Faith is in danger living here with you?'

I think about Ian's idea to invite this bitch into my home, about my own reluctant agreement, and I almost choke. This is not the time to grant her access—it must be on my terms, Joan's made that clear. I turn to my mother, whom I can always count on to put someone in their place, but she has disappeared. 'You're on private property.'

'Mrs White,' Saganoff repeats, but before she can finish, my mother returns, carrying the antique Revolutionary War rifle that hangs over the living-room fireplace.

'Mariah,' she says, carelessly waving the muzzle at Petra Saganoff, 'who's here?'

I have the satisfaction of watching the cameraman blanch and Saganoff step back. 'Oh,' my mother says sourly. 'It's her. What were you telling Ms Saganoff about private property?'

I close the door and lock it again. 'God, Ma,' I moan. 'What on earth did you do *that* for? She'll probably take her videotape to the judge and tell him Faith's crazy mother waved a gun in her face.'

'Faith's crazy mother didn't do it, her crazy grandmother did. And if she takes it to the judge, I bet he'll ask why she's violating a police-enforced restraining order.' She pats my shoulder. 'I just wanted to give the big-city girl a little scare.'

I grimace. 'It's a black-powder rifle that hasn't worked in a couple hundred years.'

'Yes, but *she* didn't know that.'

The doorbell rings again. My mother looks at me. 'Don't answer it.'

But whoever is there is insistent; the bell rings over and over. 'Mom!' Faith yells, running into the foyer. 'Someone's doing that thing to the doorbell that you told me not to do—'

'Christ!' I tell my mother to call the police station and demand an officer at the end of the driveway. I tell Faith to play in her room, where she cannot be seen. Then I throw open the door with so much force it slams into the wall.

The woman is dressed in a conservative suit and is carrying a pad and a microcassette recorder. I have no idea what newspaper or magazine she's from, but I've seen enough like her to recognize the breed. 'You people have absolutely no respect. How would you like it if I showed up at your house uninvited when you . . . when you were in the middle of taking a bath? Or celebrating your child's birthday? Or— God, why am I even speaking to you?' I slam the door.

The bell rings again.

I count to ten. I take three deep breaths. Then I open the door just a crack. 'In sixty seconds,' I bluff, 'a cop is going to be here to haul you off to jail for trespassing.'

'I don't think so,' she says coolly, shifting her recorder and notepad so that she can extend a hand. 'I'm Kenzie van der Hoven. The court-appointed guardian ad litem.'

I close my eyes, hoping that when I open them this will not have happened, that Kenzie van der Hoven will not still be standing just outside my front door bristling with all the insults I've just hurled at her. 'I'd like to speak to you, Mrs White.'

I smile weakly. 'Why don't you call me Mariah?' I suggest and, as graciously as I can, let her into the house.

'Faith's in here,' I say, directing the guardian ad litem toward the living room, where my daughter is watching TV, a reward for having finished the math worksheets I made up for her. My mother sits beside her on the couch, idly smoothing Faith's hair. 'Faith,' I say brightly, 'this is Ms van der Hoven. She's going to spend some time with us.' My mother's eyes meet mine. 'Ms van der Hoven, this is my mother, Millie Epstein.'

'Nice to meet you. Please call me Kenzie.'

'And this,' I add, 'is Faith.'

Kenzie van der Hoven rises leagues in my estimation as she squats down beside Faith and stares at the television. 'I love *Arthur*. D.W.'s my absolute favorite.'

Faith cautiously edges her bandaged hands beneath her thighs. 'I like D.W., too.'

'Did you ever see the one where she goes to the beach?'

'Yeah,' Faith says, suddenly animated. 'And she thinks there's a shark in the water!'

They both laugh, and then Kenzie stands again. 'It's nice to meet you, Faith. Maybe you and I could talk a little bit later.'

'Maybe,' Faith says.

I lead Kenzie into the kitchen, where she declines a cup of coffee. 'Faith doesn't usually watch TV. Two hours a day, that's it. Disney Channel or PBS.'

'Mariah, I want to make something perfectly clear. I'm

not the enemy. I'm just here to make sure Faith winds up in the best possible place.'

'I know. And I'm not usually . . . the way I was when I opened the door. It's just that there's supposed to be a policeman around to keep everyone away, and—'

'You were being careful. I can certainly understand that.' She looks at me for a moment, holds up her tape recorder. 'Do you mind? I have to write up a report, and it helps to replay the conversations I have with people.'

'Go right ahead.' I slip into the seat across from hers at the kitchen table.

'What do you think the judge should know?'

For a moment I'm silent, remembering years ago when there was so much I had to say and no one willing to hear me out. 'Will he listen?'

Kenzie seems a little startled by this. 'I'd like to think so, Mariah. I've known Judge Rothbottam for a while, and he's been very fair.'

I pick at a cuticle on my hand. 'It's just that I haven't been very lucky in the court system before,' I say carefully. 'It's hard for me to tell you this, because you're *in* the court system, and it's probably going to sound like sour grapes. But it feels the same: Colin's word against mine. Colin's quick; he's better at thinking on his feet. Seven years ago he managed to convince everyone he knew what was best for me. Now he says he knows what's best for Faith.'

'But you think that *you* do?'

'No,' I correct. 'Faith does.'

Kenzie makes a note on her pad. 'So you let Faith make her own decisions?'

Immediately I can tell that I've said the wrong thing. 'Well, no. She's seven. She's not getting M&M's for breakfast, no matter what she says, and she can't wear a tutu to school when it's snowing out. She isn't old enough to know everything, but she's old enough to have a gut feeling.' I look down at my lap. 'I'm worried that Colin is so sure he knows Faith better than she knows herself, he'll convince her he's right before anyone can stop him.'

'That's why I'm here,' Kenzie says crisply.

'Oh—I didn't mean to tell you how to do your job . . .'

'Relax, Mariah. Everything you say isn't going to be used against you.'

I lower my gaze and nod. But I don't quite believe her either.

'What do *you* want to happen?'

After all these years, someone is finally asking. And after all these years, the answer is still the same. What I want is a second chance. But this time, I want it with Faith.

Out of the blue comes the memory of something Rabbi Weissman said the day I took Faith to see him: You can be an agnostic Jew, a nonpracticing Jew . . . but you're still a Jew. Just as you can be an unsure parent, a self-absorbed parent . . . but you are still a parent.

I stare at Kenzie van der Hoven. I could make myself out to be the Mother of the Year. I could tell her what I know she wants to hear. Or I could tell her the truth.

'I tried to kill myself seven years ago, after I found my husband in bed with another woman. All I could think was that I wasn't a good enough wife, I wasn't a beautiful enough woman, I just . . . wasn't. Colin had me committed to Greenhaven by telling a judge it was the only way to keep me from trying to kill myself again.

'But, see, he didn't know I was pregnant when he had me sent away. He took away four months of my life, and my home, and my confidence, but I still had Faith.' I take a deep breath. 'I'm not suicidal anymore. I'm not Colin's wife. And I'm certainly not the woman who was so under his spell that I let him lock me up in an institution. What I am is Faith's mother. It's what I've been for seven years. But you can't be a mother, can you, if your child is taken away?'

Kenzie has not written down a single word that I've said, and I do not know if this is good or bad. She closes her notebook, her face revealing nothing. 'Thank you, Mariah. I wonder if now would be a good time to speak to Faith.'

As the guardian ad litem walks into the living room, my mother comes to join me in the kitchen. I try not to watch them through the doorway, even when Kenzie sits down on the couch beside Faith and says something that makes her laugh. 'So?'

'So.' I shrug. 'What do I know?'

'Well, what you said to the woman, for example. You must have formed some impression of what she thinks of you.'

I have, of course, but I am not going to tell my mother. Even if I hadn't told the guardian ad litem about Greenhaven, it would have come out at the hearing. By then, though, maybe the woman would have found something to admire about me, something to balance the fact that I was sent to an institution. The truth doesn't always set you free; people prefer to believe prettier, neatly wrapped lies. Kenzie van der Hoven might feel pity for me, but that's not going to make her let me keep Faith.

'I'm going to lose her, Ma,' I say, burying my face in my hands. I feel her touch my back. And then I am in her arms, where I have always fit, listening to that incredible heart of hers beat beneath my cheek. Suddenly I can feel her strength, as if resilience were something one can gift to another. 'Says who?' my mother murmurs, and kisses the crown of my head.

Kenzie has only one firm rule as a guardian ad litem: Do not expect anything. That way, she cannot be disappointed. It is a rare child who warms during the first meeting; she has had numerous cases where days go by before her charge even mutters hello. Until a child has seen and poked at Kenzie's good intentions, he rarely believes she is a friend.

Then again, a child who can believe God is paying her a visit ought to be able to accept that Kenzie's on the up-and-up.

Kenzie is practical enough to realize that chances are rather slim Faith is the mystic others think she is. Children Faith's age love dinosaurs and whales because they're so big and powerful, when seven-year-olds are not. Playing God has the same psychological roots.

Faith sits beside her like a lamb that's been led to the slaughter, her head bowed and her hands carefully hidden in the shadow of her lap. Clearly the child has been dragged out before to be observed, questioned, or studied. 'Faith, do you know why I'm here?'

'Uh-huh. Don't *you*?'

Kenzie grins. 'Actually, yes. Someone explained it to me.'

With resignation, Faith faces her. 'I guess you want to ask me some questions.'

'You know . . . I bet you've got some things you'd rather ask *me*.'

Faith's eyes widen. 'For real?' Kenzie nods. 'Well, am I going to keep living here?'

'Do you want to?'

'You said *I* could ask the questions.'

'You're right, I'm sorry. I don't know the answer, Faith. It's going to depend on a lot of things, including what you want to happen.'

'I don't want to hurt my mother,' Faith whispers, so softly that Kenzie has to lean closer. 'And I don't want to hurt my father.' She turns away. 'I want . . .'

Kenzie takes a deep breath, waiting. But instead of speaking, Faith curls her hands into fists and tucks them beneath her armpits. Kenzie stares at her fine-boned wrists, wondering if the girl's hands hurt, if she ought to call Mariah, if she just ought to come back another time.

Kenzie knows nothing about stigmata—alleged or real. But the one thing she understands inside out is what it feels like to be a little girl who doesn't fit in.

'You know,' Kenzie says casually, 'I don't want to talk anymore.'

Faith pops to her feet. 'Does that mean I can go?'

'I guess so. Unless you'd like to come outside.'

'Out . . . side?' Faith's voice breaks with delight.

'It's beautiful out. Just cold enough that your throat tickles when you breathe in deep.' She cocks her head. 'I'll tell your mom where we're going. What do you say?'

Faith stares at Kenzie for several seconds, evaluating whether this is a cruel joke. Then she tears out of the room. 'I gotta get my sneakers. Wait for me!'

Grinning, Kenzie draws on her coat. Faith's fear of hurting her parents could mean many things, but Kenzie knows that at the very least it suggests that the girl feels a heavy responsibility—and why shouldn't she? Her family has broken apart, her yard is beset with people who think she's the Messiah. Being a child advocate in this case means lightening the load, allowing Faith the freedom to be a simple seven-year-old.

As spontaneous hunches go, it isn't a bad one. Kenzie will get the opportunity to see Faith react to the press barrage that is sure to follow them at a distance. She pokes her head into the kitchen and tells Mariah her intentions, then walks into the parlor before Mariah can voice an objection. 'You ready?' she asks as Faith returns, then twists the lock and steps onto the porch.

Faith hesitantly crosses the threshold. With hands tucked into the pockets of her fleece coat, she kicks tentatively at a pile of leaves. Then she stretches out her arms and spins in a circle, her face lifted to the sky.

It doesn't take long for the reporters to creep to the edge of the stone wall, regulated once again by the fortuitous arrival of the local police. But even from a distance, long-range lenses allow them to photograph Faith, and they cup their hands around their mouths to call out to her. Faith is halfway to the swing set beside the farmhouse when she hears the first questions, lobbed like softballs to smack her off guard: 'Is the world coming to an end?' 'Does God want something from us?' 'How come God picked you?'

She stumbles over a woodchuck's hole, and would have fallen if Kenzie weren't there to steady her. Ducking her head, Faith murmurs, 'Can we go back in?'

'You don't have to answer them,' Kenzie says softly.

'But I still have to hear.'

'Ignore them.' She takes Faith's hand and leads her to the swing set. 'Play,' Kenzie urges. 'I won't let them do anything to you.'

The media begin to react en masse—photographing and running video and shouting out questions. 'Close your eyes,' Kenzie yells over their voices. 'Tip back your head.'

To illustrate, Kenzie does it first on the swing beside Faith's. She watches Faith watch her, and finally sees the little girl tentatively begin to move back and forth, a smile gracing her face.

The press keeps yelling, and in the distance a rich, vibrating alto begins to sing 'Amazing Grace,' and still Faith swings. And then, suddenly, her eyes are open as she goes back and forth, back and forth. 'Kenzie!' Faith cries. 'Watch what I can do!' In one heart-stopping moment she lets go of the chain links of the swing and jumps into the air.

Collectively, the questions stop. They all hold their breath, including Kenzie. A hundred cameras capture the girl with her arms outstretched, her body an arrow, flying.

And then, in a thud and a giggle and a scrape of knee, Faith falls, just like anyone else.

I watch them from the living room, peeking between the horizontal slats of the blinds. I can feel it growing inside me like a tumor, something I haven't felt since I came home to find someone else beside Colin, where I was supposed to be.

I am so jealous of Kenzie van der Hoven that I am having trouble breathing.

My mother comes up behind me. 'Some people use a duster to clean their blinds.'

Immediately I fall back. 'Do you see what she's doing? Do you?'

'Yes, and it's driving you crazy.' My mother smiles. 'You wish you were the one to think of it. So why weren't you?'

She leaves before I can come up with an excuse. Why haven't I taken Faith outside to play? There's the obvious reason, of course—the glut of reporters waiting like barracudas for the smallest bit of bait—but then again, so what? They have managed to televise stories about Faith whether or not she appears to fuel the frenzy. They broadcast when she was all the way in Kansas City. How could footage of a little girl being, well, a little girl be turned into something any more insidious?

Minutes later, Faith is standing at the sliding door. Her cheeks are pink with the cold, her leggings are muddy at the knees. She proudly shows me the new scrape on her elbow.

'I brought her back,' Kenzie van der Hoven says. 'I've got to be going.'

It takes all my strength to look her in the eye. 'Thank you. Faith needed this.'

'No problem. The court—'

'You and I both know,' I interrupt, 'that what you did today had nothing to do with a judge's order.'

For a moment I see a light in Kenzie's eyes, and I know that I have surprised her. Her face softens. 'You're welcome.'

Faith tugs at my sweater. 'Did you see me? Did you see how high I went?'

'I did. I was impressed.'

She turns to Kenzie. 'Can't you stay just a couple more minutes?'

'Ms van der Hoven has other places she needs to go.' I tweak Faith's ponytail. 'On the other hand, I bet *I* could swing as high as you did.'

The look of surprise on Faith's face is almost comical. 'But—'

'Are you going to argue with me, or are you going to accept the challenge?'

I barely have time to register the wide smile that splits Kenzie van der Hoven's face before I'm tugged across the yard, following in my daughter's footsteps.

Ian stands outside his Winnebago, drawn by the clamor that ensues when Faith comes out to play. He watches her kick up her heels on the swing set and stifles a grin—whoever this woman is with her, she's doing Faith a good turn.

'I'm surprised you're not at the front line.'

Ian turns at the sound of a voice. A woman stands beside him. 'And who might you be?' he asks dryly.

'Lacey Rodriguez.' She extends a hand. 'Just another worshipper from afar.'

'You're with an outfit,' Ian speculates. 'Which one?'

'What makes you think I'm with an outfit?'

'Call it a hunch, Miz—Rodriguez, is it?—but most of the faithful fanatics, as you pointed out, are too busy calling out hosannas to be shooting the breeze back here. Now, don't go telling me where you work . . . it must be *Hard Copy*. Or *Hollywood Tonight!*—they've got some inspired underlings there.'

'Why, Mr Fletcher,' Lacey drawls. 'You'll turn my head with all this flattery.'

At that, Ian laughs. 'I like you, Miz Rodriguez. Definitely *Hollywood Tonight!* You stick to your guns, and one day you'll bump Saganoff off her throne.'

'I'm not in the entertainment business,' Lacey says quietly. 'I deal in information.'

She watches his eyes narrow as he runs through the options: FBI, CIA, Mafia. Then he raises his brows. 'Metz sent you. He should have known I'm not inclined to share.'

Lacey takes a step closer. 'I'm not asking you to be a bit player on some TV newsmagazine. I'm talking about the wheels of justice—'

'Thanks, Lois Lane. I'll pass. If and when I feel like exposing Faith White it'll happen on my own terms and my own agenda.'

'How much more credibility can your word carry than when it's used in a court of law?'

'What you mean to say,' Ian corrects, 'is that Metz can't dig up jackshit, and wants my proof that she's a hoax.'

'You have proof,' Lacey breathes.

'Would I still be here if I didn't?'

After a long moment Ian reaches into his pocket and extracts a card, then scrawls a phone number on it. 'Tell Metz that I just might be willing to talk.'

No sooner has Lacey Rodriguez left than James Wilton approaches Ian. 'There's a reason we're not filming this,' he says slowly. 'Right?'

His eyes, like everyone else's, are at the front door, where Faith is standing with her mother and the woman Ian doesn't recognize. Ian feels himself begin to sweat. His producer, of course, will expect him to continue his investigation of Faith, no matter how he feels personally. And, to be honest, he doesn't want to sacrifice his show and his reputation. He turns to James and smiles. 'Of course there's a reason. I'm waiting for . . . this.'

The strange woman gets into her car, and Mariah and Faith start off down the porch steps. 'Tony! You ready yet?' Ian calls, startling the cameraman, who he knows would never have the nerve to mention to Ian that he hadn't been summoned at all. Slinging the camera on his shoulder, he follows Ian through the crowd, nodding as Ian gives him directions for filming. Ian checks back one more time, to make sure that James is watching, and then to the audible surprise of the crowd, hops the police barricade and strides toward Mariah and Faith.

Behind him, he can sense the policeman on guard pushing through the mass of bodies in an effort to get to him. He hears other reporters murmuring praise for his go-to-hell brand of journalism, and some contemplating following him. But what he keeps his eyes on is Mariah, standing beside the swing set, watching him approach.

Startled, her eyes dart from his face to the crowd behind him. 'What are you doing?'

Ian reaches out and grasps her arm. It will look, he knows, as if he were trying to keep her from running away. But right now, it only feels wonderful to have her close enough to touch, close enough to smell the soap on her skin. 'They're all watching,' he says softly. 'Act like you want me to go away.'

The policeman, a young boy really, comes to a halt a few feet behind them. 'Miz White,' he pants, 'you want I should arrest him for trespassing?'

'No,' she says, in a voice that wavers before it gets stronger and carries. 'I just asked Mr Fletcher to get off my property, since my daughter and I do not wish to be disturbed.'

The policeman grabs hold of Ian's other arm. 'You heard her.'

Ian's eyes burn into hers. 'This isn't over,' he says, words for the camera that speak differently to Mariah. 'Not by a long shot.' His thumb, hidden, strokes the soft underside of her upper arm, leaving Mariah trembling with what will later be described by reporters on numerous broadcasts as righteous indignation.

The telephone wakes me up from a deep sleep, and I breathe Ian's name.

'Well, of course it's me,' he says, irritated. 'How many other men call you in the middle of the night?'

I wrap my arms around myself. 'Hundreds,' I say, smiling. 'Thousands.'

'Really? I'll have to make you forget the competition.'

'What competition?' I whisper, and I am only half joking. When Ian surrounds me I do not think about anything else—not of the press just outside the house, not of Colin and the custody battle, not even of Faith. When I loved Colin, it was because he anchored me. But Ian—well, he does for me what Kenzie van der Hoven did for Faith. He takes me away.

My blood begins to move more quickly, making me restless. 'I'm too old to be feeling like this.'

'How do you feel?'

I close my eyes. 'Like I'm going to jump out of my skin.'

For a moment all I can hear is his breathing on the line. When he speaks, his voice is higher, tense. 'Mariah, about this afternoon.'

'Yes. What was that?'

'My producer. He expects something to be happening, some sense that I'm still with the story.'

'Are you?' I ask, suddenly cold.

'I'm with you,' Ian answers. 'I also knew that if I jumped the police line, I'd get to touch you.'

I turn onto my side, hoping to see the lights on in the Winnebago, and then cry out softly as I start to tumble off the edge of the bed and drop the telephone. 'Sorry,' I explain a moment later. 'I lost you.'

'Never,' Ian says, and with all my defenses down, I believe it.

twelve

I have long time holden my peace; I have been still,
and refrained myself: now will I cry like a travailing woman;
I will destroy and devour at once.

—Isaiah 42:14

November 8, 1999

JESSICA WHITE ADJUSTS a pale-green glass vase an inch to the right, making lavender tulips sway. Beside her, Colin White relaxes against throw pillows in increasing degrees of purple. I have fallen into a catalog, Kenzie thinks, and I can't get out.

'Ms van der Hoven,' Jessica says, 'can I get you more seltzer?'

'No, thanks. And it's Kenzie.' She smiles at the couple. 'I hear that you're going to have a baby.' Is it her imagination, or does Colin lean the slightest bit away from his wife?

Jessica's hand steals over her abdomen. 'In May.'

'We're hoping his big sister is here for the event,' Colin adds.

She knows exactly what he's trying to get across. 'Yes. Well. Maybe you can tell me, Mr White, why you've suddenly developed an interest in your daughter's custody.'

'I've always wanted custody of Faith,' he says quietly. 'I was just trying to get myself back on my feet first. I didn't think that ripping Faith away from her home was smart, right after the shake-up of the divorce.'

'So you had her best interests in mind?'

Colin offers a remarkable smile, and thoughts scatter through her head—this was a man who could sell sand in the desert, who could charm the shoes off a horse. 'Exactly!' He leans forward, relinquishing his wife's hand to clasp both of his together. 'Look. This is a messy situation, and I'm not going to look like a saint. I didn't expect Mariah to come home that day with Faith, and I know that's not an excuse, but clearly you can see it wasn't just some . . . some passing fling. I love Jessica; I married her. Whatever problems I was having in my relationship with Mariah, they had nothing to do with Faith. I'm her father, I'll always be her father, and I want to give her the kind of home she deserves.'

Kenzie taps her pencil. 'What's wrong with the kind of home she's in now?'

He seems startled for a moment. 'Well, you've been there! Is it normal for a little girl to have an entire press corps follow her when she opens the door? Is it normal for her to believe, for Christ's sake, that she's having conversations with God?'

'It's my understanding that your ex-wife made an attempt to remove Faith from media scrutiny.'

'Is that what she told you?' Colin's jaw sets. 'She made an attempt to buck the legal system. The day after I told her I was going to sue for custody, she disappeared.'

Kenzie sits up at this. 'She knew she was going to be subpoenaed?'

'I said, "You'll hear from my lawyer." And—bam—she went into hiding.'

Kenzie makes a note on her pad. As a woman nearly weaned on the value of the law, the very thought of stepping outside the system immediately raises her suspicions. 'Mariah did come back, though,' she says.

'Because her attorney put the fear of God into her. Can't you see now why I want Faith out of her reach? If things start to look bad for Mariah during the hearing, she's going to pack up and run away with Faith again. Mariah doesn't stick around for a fight; it's not in her nature. In fact, she's been in therapy for that for years.'

'Are you an advocate of psychotherapy?'

'Sure,' he says. 'When it's warranted.'

'And yet your ex-wife says it wasn't an option you considered after her suicide attempt.'

Colin's mouth tightens. 'Forgive me, Ms van der Hoven, but you don't seem very objective.'

Kenzie meets his gaze. 'It's my job to turn over stones.'

Jessica interrupts by standing suddenly and clearing her throat. 'Wouldn't now be a lovely time for cake?'

They both watch Jessica go into the kitchen. As soon as she is out of earshot, Colin begins to speak, clearly agitated. 'Don't you think it upset me to send Mariah to Greenhaven? God, she was my *wife*. I *loved* her. But she was . . . she was . . . Well, almost overnight she became someone I didn't recognize. I didn't know how to talk to her or take care of her. So I did what I thought I had to do, to help her. And now it's like history's repeating itself. My little girl isn't acting like my little girl anymore. And I can't stand to see this happening again.'

Kenzie learned a long time ago that sometimes the wisest course of action is to say nothing at all. She sits back and waits for Colin White to continue.

'Right after Faith was born, I used to walk around the house at night with her when she fussed. She was this tiny little thing, with all the right pieces, and sometimes she'd just stop crying and look at me like she already knew me.' Colin looks down into his lap. 'I love her. Whatever happens, whatever the court does, you can't take that away.' Kenzie has stopped taking notes. 'Have you never in your life made a mistake, Ms van der Hoven?' he asks softly.

She glances away and notices a large box hidden behind the dining room table. From its label, she sees it is a plastic easel. Clearly not a toy for the baby on its way—and yet, clearly new. Colin follows her gaze and reddens. 'I'm an optimistic man,' he says, and smiles shyly.

Kenzie realizes that—out of sympathy for Mariah White—she has been expecting a monster. But this man has his reasons for setting a battle in motion. And they are not vengeful, or vindictive—he's simply seen something that scares him, and he wants to fix it.

Then again, Colin White may be a consummate actor.

November 9, 1999

FATHER RAMPINI STANDS in a nicely appointed office at the Diocesan Chancery with his hands clasped behind his back, staring at a bookshelf and idly wondering why His Excellency the Bishop of Manchester would have sixteen copies of the biography of Saint Theresa, the Little Flower. As the door opens, he whirls around, surreptitiously wiping the sweat from his palms before nodding at Bishop Andrews. 'Father,' the bishop grunts, settling down in a burgundy leather wing chair.

'Your Excellency.'

'Please.' Andrews gestures, and Rampini edges into a smaller chair and fixes his eyes on the swaying chain of the pectoral cross tucked into the bishop's pocket.

Rampini has examined alleged visions before to make sure there was nothing in them contrary to faith. In every case to date, even the promising ones, he's recommended a wait-and-see policy. He has been careful not to make a hasty judgment, lest he come off looking foolish.

And that, in a nutshell, is why his hands keep shaking. He's going out on a limb here. Because he really believes that Faith White may just be envisioning God.

Bishop Andrews takes off his glasses and polishes them before slipping them back on. 'According to the rector at St John's, you're the most esteemed theologian in the Northeast.'

'If you say so, Your Excellency.'

'On behalf of the diocese, I'd like to thank you for coming.'

'Perfectly all right,' Rampini says.

The bishop nods graciously. 'I only have a couple of questions, Father.'

'With all due respect, Your Excellency, I've already submitted my report.'

'Yes, in fact . . . two of them. The original recommendation and—what did you call it?—ah, the revised update. You know, I can't quite figure out why a theologian—the most esteemed theologian in the Northeast, that is—would file two completely contradictory reports within a few hours' time, regarding the substantive miracles of Faith White.'

At Rampini's affronted silence, Andrews gets impatient. He reaches into his pocket and fingers his rosary—it makes a handy set of worry beads. 'I'm certain a man of your credentials has been called in for consultation on a wide number of religious sightings.'

'Often.'

'Yet you've never before given your personal endorsement.'

Father Rampini tightens his mouth. 'That's true. And yes, the revised report indicates that this time I am.'

The bishop decides to play dumb. He scratches his head. 'I'm a little confused, Father. Now, I don't presume to be half the theologian you are, naturally, but it seems to me that a Jewish child seeing a female God goes against traditional Catholic dogma.'

Father Rampini crosses his arms. 'Are you asking me to justify my findings?'

'No, no. But for my own . . . edification . . . I'd love to know your thought process.'

Rampini clears his throat. 'There are a variety of supporting criteria. The fact that Faith White isn't Catholic is unorthodox, Your Excellency, but not inauthentic. One would be more leery of the elderly ladies who pray for sixteen hours a day and then confess Jesus appeared to them at the kitchen table. Faith wasn't asking for this vision, but it came. She's also very closemouthed about her conversations with God, and she tries to hide episodes of stigmata.'

'Stigmata,' the bishop says. 'Did you see them?'

'I did. I'm not personally familiar with Holy Marks, of course, but the general consensus of the medical community is that they aren't self-inflicted.'

'She could be a hysteric.'

'Entirely possible,' Rampini agrees. 'Except that in addition to the wounds, there's proof apart from the person of the seer. In this case, healing.'

'You're the expert, of course, but I have to admit—it would bother me a bit to know she's running around saying God's a woman.'

'Actually, she's not. The MotherGod Society is spreading the propaganda. Faith isn't saying much of anything at all. In addition to the fact that—as I said in my second report—she isn't seeing God as a woman. She's seeing Our Lord Jesus Christ, in His traditional form and clothing, yet interpreting Him as a female figure.'

Bishop Andrews raises a brow. 'That's a stretch, son.'

'Surely you're not telling me, Your Excellency, how to do my job.' Father Rampini speaks softly. 'You meet her. And then come talk to me.'

They stare at each other silently. 'You feel this strongly,' the bishop finally says.

'I do.'

'You think I should take this to the U.S. Bishops' Conference.'

'I wouldn't presume to tell you what to do.'

Bishop Andrews taps his forefingers together. 'You know, this isn't *The X-Files,* Father. No matter what the public wants, some fantastic display isn't the way to get the flock back to the Church. Even if I were to go along with your recommendation, I'd be wary of the haste with which you made it. The last thing I want is to be exposed as some loony on a supernatural scavenger hunt—can you imagine what that would do to the diocese? To Catholicism in general? There's a reason these evaluations take years, Father. It's so that in the event Faith White is a charlatan, you and I will be dead and buried and blissfully unaware of the backlash.' Bishop Andrews tilts his head. 'Has this child ever even been in a Catholic church?'

'Not that I know of, Excellency.'

'Has she been raised according to the Jewish faith?'

'No. Since her mother isn't a practicing Jew, she felt taking the child to temple would be hypocritical. I confirmed with a rabbi, however, that if the mother is Jewish, so is the child. Regardless.'

'And that,' the bishop says, 'is the stumbling block. We have no jurisdiction over a child who isn't Catholic.'

A muscle tics in Rampini's jaw. 'Then why did you ask me to come?'

He watches the bishop walk to his desk, and suddenly realizes that Andrews is going to hedge his bets. He won't use Rampini's endorsement of Faith White—unless the tide turns and he needs it. He'll keep both contradictory reports, so that he's ready for either contingency; and Father Rampini won't be able to say a thing about it without making himself look indecisive. Heat floods the priest's face, moving up from his white collar. 'You will disregard the first report,' Rampini orders. 'I'm officially submitting the second one, and only the second one, for your consideration.'

Without taking his eyes off the younger man's face, Bishop Andrews slides the paper he's holding into a desk drawer. 'Which one was that?' he says.

November 10, 1999

WHEN IAN ENTERS Malcolm Metz's office, the attorney doesn't get up from his seat. 'Well,' he says instead, leaning back in his chair. 'This certainly is a pleasure. I'm a big fan.'

Ian stares at him squarely. 'My fee's ninety thousand. It's what advertisers pay for a commercial during my shows. I'm envisioning your trial in much the same way—an interruption bracketing the things I'm planning to say anyway.'

To his credit, Metz doesn't even blink. 'I don't foresee that being a problem,' he says. In truth, he has no idea whether or not his client can come up with the money, but he's not about to squash negotiations before they even really begin. 'As long as you remember that this isn't a television show. A little girl's life is as stake.'

'Save your bullshit for the court,' Ian says. 'I know what you want.'

'Which is?'

'Proof that Faith White is a charlatan. And hints that her mother is the puppeteer.'

Metz smiles. 'And you, of course, have all this information.'

'Would you have asked for me if I didn't?'

Metz considers this for a moment. 'I don't know. Just on

your Q-rating alone, you could probably convince a judge that the sun isn't going to rise tomorrow.'

At that, Ian laughs. 'Maybe you are a fan after all.'

'Why don't you tell me what you've got?'

'Some decent hidden-camera footage of Mariah White coaching the kid before she bows and scrapes for the crowd. A testimonial from a woman who went on national TV saying that her baby had been cured of AIDS by Faith, admitting that Mariah White paid her three thousand dollars to make up the story. Couple of experts who've signed off on a written scientific explanation for Millie Epstein's corpse coming back to life—has to do with electrical currents and bodily tissue, or some such like that.'

'What about the hands?'

'The alleged stigmata? It's an optical illusion.'

'An optical illusion?'

'Come on now, certainly you've seen fire-eaters at the circus, or magicians passing objects through their fists.'

'How could they fool a bunch of doctors?'

'Well, I'm still working on that. My theory is that they didn't. That when it came to medical personnel taking a look-see, Faith truly poked herself with something or other.'

Metz looks skeptical. 'Why? What's the point?'

Ian leans back in the chair. 'I'm surprised you'd even have to ask, Mr Metz. For the attention, of course.'

Metz narrows his eyes. 'If you don't mind my asking, how come none of this has made it to your show as of late?'

'Because there's something even bigger I'll be using to blow this case open, and before you even ask, it's not negotiable.' Ian steeples his fingers. 'Way I see it, your courtroom can do just as good a job as any of my teaser broadcasts, leading up to the grand finale. For the fee I mentioned, you are welcome to the information and signed testimonies I just described, as well as my considerable reputation in the field and my stage presence. But that's all you're damn well gonna get.'

Slowly, Metz nods. 'I see.'

'The other thing you have to understand is that I'm a busy man. I'll be happy to go over testimony regarding any of that information I just gave you . . . but we're gonna do it here, and we're gonna do it now.'

'Absolutely not. I'm not ready. I have to—'

'You have to do half as much as you would with any other witness. I already know how to act. All you've gotta do is set down the facts you want in the order you want them.'

For a moment there is silence, two men who are larger than life considerably cramped in such close quarters. 'Another rehearsal the day before your testimony,' Metz bargains.

Ian grins. 'Sir,' he says, 'you have yourself a deal.'

Mariah opens the door a crack to find Kenzie van der Hoven on the threshold. 'Can Faith come out and play?'

Against her better judgment, Mariah laughs. 'It's a little cold out. Maybe you two could stay in.' This prearranged visit with the GAL comes as a relief. Mariah has been snapping at Faith all day for getting underfoot, something completely understandable while they are cooped up in the house.

Faith races into the room on rollerblades. Mariah watches the wheels leave black tracks on the tile and bites her tongue to keep from yelling at her daughter for the twentieth time that day, especially in front of the guardian ad litem. Catching Faith's eye instead, Mariah raises a brow and then glances down at the skates, clearly annoyed.

'Oops,' Faith says, plopping onto her bottom and ripping open the Velcro fastenings of the skates. 'Kenzie, did you come to see me?'

'Yup. Is that okay?'

'It's awesome.'

Mariah smiles. 'I'll be making dinner if you need me.'

Kenzie watches her walk into the kitchen, and then feels five tiny fingers reach around her hand. 'Come see my room,' Faith says. 'It's really cool.'

'Oh?' Kenzie allows herself to be led upstairs. 'What color is it?'

'Yellow.' Faith pushes open a door to reveal sunny walls and a white canopy bed. She leaps onto it and starts jumping, her hair flying in an arc behind her. Then she bounces onto her bottom and off the bed, playing hostess. 'These are my Legos. And my art set that Santa brought last year, and this picture was taken of me when I was only two hours old.'

Kenzie dutifully peers at a photo of a tiny, tomato-faced infant. 'Do you spend a lot of time in your room?'

'It depends. Mom won't let me have a TV up here, so I can't watch videos or anything. Sometimes I feel like drawing at the kitchen table, so I take my art set down there. And sometimes I just color on the floor.' She raises her arms over her head. 'I used to take ballet.'

Kenzie watches her twirl in a slow circle, her arms lifted in a pirouette. 'Not anymore? How come?'

'Things happened.' Faith picks at a loop of the throw rug and shrugs. 'Mom got sick.'

'And then what?'

'Then God came.'

Kenzie feels herself freeze. 'I see. Was that a good thing?'

Faith flops backward and stretches out her arms, curling the edges of the rug around her. 'Look, I'm a cocoon.'

'Tell me about God,' Kenzie prompts.

Faith rolls toward her. Wrapped in the blanket like the chrysalis she's mentioned, her face is the only visible part of her body. 'She makes me feel good, all warm, like when I get to sit in the pile of clothes that just came out of the dryer. But I don't like it when she hurts me.'

Kenzie leans forward. 'She hurts you?'

'She says she has to, and I know she doesn't want to, because she tells me after that she's sorry.'

Kenzie stares at the little girl, at her hands with their definitive marks. As a guardian ad litem she has seen many things, most of them not very pleasant. 'Does God come to talk to you when it's dark in your room?' she asks, and Faith nods. 'Can you touch her? Or see her face?'

'Sometimes. And sometimes I just know it's her.'

'Because she's hurting you?'

'No . . . because she smells like oranges.'

At that, Kenzie gives a startled laugh. 'Really?'

'Uh-huh.' Faith picks up a figurine in her dollhouse. 'Want to play?'

Kenzie looks at the replica of the farmhouse. 'This is beautiful,' she says, running her forefinger over the delicate curve of the oak banister. 'Did Santa bring this, too?'

'No, my mom made it. It's what she does for work.'

Kenzie knows from years of experience that the most likely explanation for Faith's wounds is either self-infliction or infliction by someone close to her. Someone who's convinced her that she's making Faith suffer out of love for her. Kenzie stares at the dollhouse, precise and perfect, thinking hard. Even after all the times she's seen it happen, it is difficult to believe that parents who seem otherwise normal might be monstrous to a child. 'Honey,' Kenzie says, 'is your mommy doing this to you?'

'Doing what?'

Kenzie sighs. It is almost always impossible to get an abused child to admit who's abusing her. In the first place, she lives with the fear of retribution promised for breaking her silence. In the second place, there's a twisted gratification system in place—the child finds, on some sad level, that the episodes are measures of attention.

Then again, sometimes kids don't point a finger because there's nothing to point to. A select few really do walk into doors and get black eyes, or tumble off a table and get concussions . . . or maybe even spontaneously bleed. Mariah certainly doesn't harm her daughter in full view; Faith doesn't exhibit aversive behavior around her mother. Maybe press exposure isn't the best thing in the world for a little girl, maybe Faith could stand to socialize more—but these things alone do not constitute abuse.

The door opens suddenly. Mariah stands there holding a pile of sheets, surprised to see Faith and Kenzie. 'I'm sorry,' she says awkwardly. 'I thought you were in the playroom.'

'No problem. I was just admiring your dollhouse. I've never seen anything like it.'

Mariah nods, blushes. Setting the sheets on the dresser, she heads for the door. 'I'll give you two some privacy.'

'Really, it's fine if—'

'No,' Mariah interrupts. 'It's all right.' And she leaves, trailing the faint scent of citrus perfume.

Kenzie's last case involved a nine-year-old girl who lived with her grandparents because her mother had abandoned her. They were a couple that went to church every Sunday and made sure she had nice clothes for school and a hot breakfast each morning. And roughly once a week the little girl would wake up in the middle of the night to find her grandfather raping her. He told her if she said a word to anyone, she'd be out on the street.

This is running through her mind as she pulls onto the highway, heading away from the Whites' house. Although there is no proof that this new case of hers is anything like the last one, there are resonances that Kenzie cannot put from her mind.

There is something being hidden here. It's written all over Mariah White; it's why she makes it a point not to be in the same room as Kenzie for longer than five minutes. Sighing, Kenzie pulls down the visor to block the sinking sun. Maybe it's embarrassment over the institutionalization. Maybe it's only what Colin White told her—that Mariah intentionally went into hiding to avoid prosecution. But then, why would she have come back? And could there be more to it than that?

In her two sessions with Faith, Kenzie has the sense that the child would prefer to stay with her mother. But she doesn't know if that's because she dislikes Jessica White or because Mariah has blackmailed her into staying.

On the other hand, maybe Mariah White left New Canaan ignorant of Colin's plans to change custody. Maybe she was fleeing in the best interests of her child. There has been no hint from any medical personnel she's interviewed that Mariah White is a possible catalyst for any of Faith's physical or psychological problems. Maybe Faith is just a little girl with a particularly overactive imagination.

A car cuts Kenzie off, sending her swerving into the breakdown lane. Pumping her brakes, she rolls to a stop, and passes her hand over her eyes. Focus, focus. So many close calls.

She gently eases back into traffic, wondering if the worst

thing Mariah's done is to simply, blindly, believe that her daughter is telling the truth.

November 14, 1999

IT WAS JAMES'S IDEA, initially, to run a Sunday-morning show—just on the principle that airing an atheist's views on the most common day of Christian worship was sure to create controversy. And although Ian has at least seven scripts ready to go, none seem appropriate anymore. He's talking impromptu, off the cuff. There is only so much he can say before it will be used against Faith, and Mariah. And then again, there is only so much he can say that is neutral, before raising the suspicions of his executive producer.

The lights are hot on his face now, and the wide mouth of camera one pivots in front of him as he tosses—deliberately—a Bible onto the grass behind him. Unlike most of his studio tapings, this one—on location—has an audience. It's a small one, since the lion's share of the people congregated around Mariah's home are zealous believers, rather than atheists. But that's exactly why he's chosen a biblical text as the subject of his diatribe.

'"Take now thy son, thine only son Isaac, whom thou lovest, and . . . offer him there for a burnt offering."' Ian glances around at those listening. 'Yeah, you heard it right. Abraham is supposed to kill his child, just to prove that when God says "Jump!" he asks "How high?" And what happens? Abraham does it. He puts a knife to Isaac's throat, and at the last minute God shows up and basically says he was just foolin'.' Ian snorts. 'This is the sort of God you worship? A Supreme Being who looks at his subjects like pawns? You ask any of those fine men of the cloth just over yonder and they're gonna tell you this here is a story about faith, about putting yourself in the hands of the Lord and letting him make it work out for the best. But this isn't a story about faith. This isn't even a story about Abraham. This here's a story about Isaac.

'What I want to know, what the Bible doesn't bother to

tell me, is what Isaac thought when his father set him down on that altar in the middle of nowhere. What he felt when his father touched a blade to his neck. Whether he cried, whether he wet his pants. The person who got lost in this story is a child. Now, as a good Christian, you're supposed to respect Abraham for doing what he was told. But I'll tell you something. As a *human being*, I do not respect that man at all. I have contempt for a God that uses a child in such a manner. And I'd be a far piece more likely to pledge myself to a parent who stands between a despot—even an allegedly heavenly one—to keep him from reaching a child.' He raises his brow as the camera moves in for his close-up. 'I only hope that Miz White—mother of Faith—pays heed to this.'

Someone calls out 'Cut!' and Ian turns away, grabbing a towel from an assistant and wiping the makeup and sweat from his face. He collects his notes from another assistant and stalks back toward the Winnebago, oblivious to the murmuring of the crowd that was listening.

Either they got it or they didn't.

There are two ways to read his broadcast, and Ian damn well knows it. Either people will believe that his final line was meant to accuse Mariah of being like Abraham, prostituting her child just because God and the media want it that way. Or else people will hear Ian praising Mariah for *not* being like Abraham, for taking her daughter away, even fleetingly, from these same greedy powers.

He doesn't much care how his fans perceive it, actually. The only reactions he cares about are Mariah's and James's. He wants Mariah to have heard it one way, and James to have heard it the other.

The door opens and closes behind his executive producer. James sits down at the table and props up his feet. 'Nice broadcast,' he says easily. 'But I thought you might talk more about the kid.'

'Isaac?'

'Faith White.' James shrugs. 'Just on account of us being here for a few weeks now. I think viewers are expecting more.'

'More what?'

'More . . . . I don't know. More heart. More guts. More proof than theatrics.'

Ian feels a muscle tic in his jaw. 'Just say what you mean to say, James.'

The producer holds his hands up. 'Jesus H. Christ, don't jump down my throat here.'

'You know that rumor about me being a temperamental asshole? I'd like to cash in on it right now.'

'All I'm telling you, Ian, is that you called me from the road and intimated that you were onto something regarding the White case. And then you come home and do two live shows and barely mention it. Faith White is the cash cow here, Ian. The mother lode. Isaac and Abraham? Yeah, they're nice, but you can save them for when you've got a contract renewed with a network.' He peers into Ian's face. 'There better be something going on. Something that's going to go up like a bottle rocket, with you holding right onto its tail.' When Ian remains impassive, James scowls. 'You hear me?'

Ian's head swivels slowly, his eyes connecting with James's. 'Boom,' he says.

'That's Betelgeuse,' Faith says, pointing. 'The red one that's part of Orion.' From her position on the ratty football blanket, Kenzie blinks at the night sky. She wraps her winter coat more tightly around her. 'That's Taurus,' Faith adds. 'The reason it's so close is because Orion is trying to shoot it.'

'You know a lot about stars.'

'We studied them in school before I stopped going. And my dad used to show me constellations sometimes, too.'

It is the first time Faith has ever brought up Colin without being prompted. 'Did you like looking at stars with your father?'

'Yes,' Faith murmurs.

Kenzie draws up her knees and tries a different tack. 'My father used to play hockey with me. Ice hockey, actually.'

Faith laughs, surprised. '*You* played ice hockey?'

'Yeah, I know. I pretty much sucked at it. But I had five older brothers, and I don't think my father ever actually noticed that I was a girl.' At Faith's giggle, she's glad she's said it, but that doesn't keep Kenzie from recalling the sting of feeling unwanted by her family.

'Were you the goalie?'

Kenzie smiles. 'Most of the time I was the puck.'

Faith rolls to her side, propping up on an elbow. 'Does your dad still live around here?'

'He lives in Boston. I don't see him very often.' She hesitates only a moment before adding, 'I miss him.'

'I miss my dad, too.' The words are as quiet as the night, absorbed into the sway of the trees around them. 'I don't want to, but that doesn't keep it from going away.'

'Why don't you want to?'

'Because he did something awful,' she says, low. 'Something that made my mom cry.'

'And what was that?'

Faith doesn't speak. After a moment Kenzie realizes that she is weeping silently. 'Faith?'

The girl turns away, burying her face in her own shoulder. 'I don't know!' she sobs. 'I was talking to him, and then there was this other lady in the bathroom, and he left. He left, and I think it was because I said something wrong.'

'You said nothing wrong, honey. It was a problem between your mom and your dad.'

'No, he just doesn't want to live with me.'

'Your father does want to live with you,' Kenzie explains. 'And so does your mother. They both love you very much. That's why a judge and I have to help decide which house you should go to.' Involuntarily, she recalls the Sunday-school legend of King Solomon. When two women claimed they were both the mother of one baby, he suggested cutting the infant in half with a sword, to discover which parent would relinquish her claim on the child rather than see it hurt. Textbook wisdom: problem solved, and no drop of blood shed. But that was just a story. In the real world, often both parents were completely worthy, or completely unworthy. In the real world, there were mitigating circumstances. In the real world, children were often the ones who swept up the messes their parents had left behind.

November 15, 1999

MALCOLM METZ COMES into the conference room where Lacey Rodriguez has been told to wait and props a hip against the edge of the table. 'You bring me any?' he asks.

She pauses, her turkey and coleslaw on rye hovering before her mouth. 'Nope. As it is, you're funding this one.'

Malcolm grunts. 'What's black and tan and looks good on a lawyer?'

'I don't know. What?'

'A doberman.' He grins, takes the sandwich from her hand, and stuffs one end into his mouth. 'Very nice. I never would have thought of the coleslaw.' He wipes his lips with her napkin and hands back the sandwich. 'So what have you got?'

She taps a sheaf of papers. 'What do you know about Kansas City?'

'Everything's up to date there. Hell, I don't know. Isn't that why I'm paying you?'

Lacey grins. 'Not nearly enough, Malcolm. My contact at the airlines came through. Guess where Mariah White went into hiding last week?'

Metz takes the list she offers, scans the list of names. 'Big deal,' he says. 'The whole world knows she was gone with the girl.'

Lacey stands up and flips to the first page of the list, to the first-class passengers. 'Does the whole world know that Ian Fletcher was on the same plane?'

'Fletcher?' Metz considers his earlier meeting with the man, the teleatheist's assertion that something big, something Metz was not privy to, would be used to expose Faith as a sham. They'd gone over testimony, and Fletcher had never mentioned this little morsel. Clearly, this trip has something to do with his grand plan.

Metz smiles, silently filing this trump card in his mind. Fletcher might think his secret is safe, but he isn't thinking along the lines of the law. Once Fletcher's on the witness stand, Metz can ask him anything at all. Once Fletcher's under oath, he has no choice but to tell the truth.

Mariah has made a dedicated attempt to stay out of Kenzie's way when she's visiting Faith. If Kenzie is in the kitchen, Mariah finds something to do in the living room. If they head upstairs, Mariah goes to the basement. She is too nervous around the guardian ad litem, too certain she will say something she will later regret.

Today Kenzie has promised to French-braid Faith's hair. 'We're playing beauty parlor today,' she tells Mariah. 'You're welcome to join us.'

'Oh, that's all right.'

'No—really. I'd like you to. Part of my evaluation involves watching you interact with Faith.'

Mariah ducks her head. It will only be for a little while. And surely it will look worse if she refuses. 'Okay,' she says, and then she grins. 'As long as you don't give me a perm.'

Kenzie follows her up the staircase to Faith's room. As soon as she knocks, the door swings open. 'I'm ready!' Faith shouts. 'I washed my hair and conditioned it and everything.' Kenzie sits on the bed and begins to stroke Faith's hair. It slides through her hands like silver. 'You want an outside braid or an inside braid?'

Faith glances at her mother, and they both shrug. 'We're about at the ponytail stage,' Mariah confesses. 'Anything would be a treat.'

Kenzie separates the hair at Faith's crown into three segments. 'When I was Faith's age, my hair was about an eighth of an inch long all the way around my head.'

'Her father wanted her to be a boy,' Faith whispers to Mariah.

Kenzie nods. 'It's true. Of course, the first thing I did when I got old enough was grow my hair down past my butt.'

Faith giggles. 'Ma,' she says in a stage whisper. 'Kenzie said *butt*.'

'Oops.' She braids sections of hair, feeding in a strand from the side of Faith's head. Mariah watches intently, as if she will be called upon to recite the procedure from memory.

'I grew up in Boston,' Kenzie says breezily. 'You ever been to Boston, Faith?'

'No.' Faith squirms on her heels. 'But I went to Kansas City.'

Kansas City. The words strike her like a blow, so much so that Mariah finds herself short of breath. Mariah hasn't been dishonest with Kenzie, but she hasn't volunteered information about her attempt to take Faith away either. She is certain that the things she does not want to tell Kenzie are written all over her face—her involvement with Ian, Ian's brother, Faith's effect on Michael. 'You went to Boston when you were little, sweetie,' she says, desperate to change the subject. 'You just don't remember.'

'I remember Kansas City,' Faith says.

'Honey . . . we don't need to bore Kenzie with that.'

'Oh, I'm just braiding. Go right ahead. When did you go to Kansas City?'

'Last week,' Faith says.

Kenzie lifts her head. 'I took her away from here. From this,' Mariah adds softly.

'What made you decide to leave then, rather than earlier?' Kenzie asks.

Mariah turns away. 'It had been going on too long. It was time.'

'It would have nothing to do with the fact that your ex-husband said he'd be filing for a change of custody?'

Mariah scrambles to think of what she can tell the guardian ad litem without making herself look as if she had been dodging the law. Which, of course, would be the truth. She glances at Faith, intent to steer off the topic before her daughter blurts out that they stayed with Ian. 'It wasn't intentional,' Mariah answers. 'I just wanted to make things easier.'

'Why Kansas City?'

'It was the first plane that left the airport.'

Faith bounces on the bed. 'Yeah, and guess who was in first class—'

'*Faith*.' The word, sharply spoken, brings the little girl up short. Mariah tightens her mouth, fully aware of Kenzie's stare set square on her, of Faith's confusion. 'We came back; that's what matters. When I heard about papers being served, we came back.'

Kenzie does not blink. Mariah feels sweat bead under the collar of her shirt; she reads the GAL's eyes as clearly as if her impression were written across them: *This woman is lying*. But to tell Kenzie more is to admit to running from Colin's threat of a lawsuit. To make public her relationship with Ian. To violate his privacy. She stares at Kenzie, unwilling to back down this time.

To her surprise, Kenzie does. She doesn't whip out a notepad or ask more questions or rebuke Mariah at all, but instead shifts the slightest bit away from Mariah on top of Faith's bed. Then she bends back toward her task, humming softly, winding Faith's beautiful hair through her fingers like yarn through a loom. And all Mariah can do is watch as Kenzie wraps together all the loose ends.

'Ian, oh, God. I'm so glad you called.'

He curls his hand around the receiver, smiling. 'That's one hell of a reception, sugar.'

'I think she knows. The guardian ad litem. She was asking questions today and Faith blurted out something about Kansas City and—'

'Mariah, calm down. Take a deep breath. . . . There you go. Now, what happened?' He listens, frowning as she recounts the conversation with Kenzie van der Hoven. 'Well, I don't think that's anything conclusive. All she knows is that someone who struck Faith's fancy was on the plane. That could mean one of the Backstreet Boys, or Prince William.'

'But she knows what day we left, and when Colin filed the papers.'

Ian gentles his voice. 'She was gonna find that out anyway. The best defense you have is that you came back with Faith.' He hesitates, thinking of his meeting with Metz. 'I told you not to worry, Mariah. I told you that I'd figure this out. Don't you trust me?'

For one horrible moment, she does not answer. And then Ian can feel it, a rush of warmth that reaches through the phone connection before her voice does. 'I do, Ian.'

He tries to respond, and finds that there are no words.

'I'm sorry that I brought you into this,' Mariah adds.

Ian closes his eyes. 'Sugar,' he says, 'there's nowhere else I'd rather be.'

November 16, 1999

ON THE DAY that Kenzie meets with Millie Epstein, the blue-plate special at the café in the center of New Canaan is fish and chips. 'Very bad,' Millie says, clucking over the menu. 'You don't even know if it's done in canola, or what.'

It seems like the perfect introduction, so Kenzie leans forward, elbows on the scarred table of the booth. 'I guess you're pretty careful about what you eat these days.'

Millie glances up. 'Why should I be? If I croak again, I'll just call for Faith instead of a paramedic.' Watching the younger woman's jaw drop, Millie smiles. 'I'm *kidding*. Of course I'm careful. But I was careful before the heart attack, too. I ate well, took my medicine like clockwork. Let me ask you something: Did you see my hospital records?'

'I did.'

'Do you believe I was resurrected?'

Kenzie flushes. 'I don't know if "resurrected" was the term for it, exactly—'

'Then what *is* the term for it? A miracle?'

'I was thinking more along the lines of an extremely irregular nervous-system response.'

'Aha,' Millie murmurs. 'Do you believe in God, Ms van der Hoven?'

'That's not the issue here. And I think I'm the one who's supposed to be asking the questions, Mrs Epstein.'

The older woman continues blithely. 'It makes me a little antsy, too. I'm not a praise-be-to-Jesus type—probably wouldn't be even if I was a Christian.'

'The issue in this custody hearing is where the best home is for Faith, ma'am. With all due respect, that doesn't leave a lot of room for God.'

'See, I don't agree with you.' Millie picks at her teeth

with her thumbnail and shakes her head. 'A more religious woman would say that there's always room for God, but that's neither here nor there. To me, you can't do your job without asking yourself whether or not you believe. Because if you don't, then Faith must be lying—and that's going to affect your decision about where she belongs.'

'Mrs Epstein, you aren't a guardian ad litem.'

Millie looks at Kenzie squarely. 'No. But you're not her grandma.'

Before Kenzie can respond, the waitress arrives. 'How you doing, Millie?' she says, with the familiarity of a town where one can walk down the street and actually recognize people.

'Irene, do they do up the fish and chips in canola oil?'

The waitress laughs. 'You think this is The Four Seasons? Far as I know, it comes out of a Mrs Paul's freezer box.'

Millie reaches across the table and pats Kenzie's hand. 'Go with the soup. It won't make you sick later.'

But Kenzie orders only a Coke. 'What we need here is a deli,' Millie muses. 'You have any idea how long it's been since I had good pastrami?'

Kenzie's lips twitch. 'A lifetime?'

Millie laughs. 'Touché,' she says, then runs her forefinger along the edge of a packet of Equal. 'I used to have tea parties with Faith when she was about three. She'd come over my house, and we'd take out all my grandmother's linens, and we'd dress up in old bathrobes I had from the forties—the ones with those pink feathers on the cuffs and collar, what is that called?'

'Marabou.'

'That's right. Marabou. Isn't that some kind of reindeer?'

'That's *caribou.*' Kenzie smiles. 'Mrs Epstein, I appreciate your concern for your granddaughter. You can rest assured that I'm only trying to make a decision in her best interests.'

'Well, if you think Faith's lying, then it must be pathological and contagious. Because her mother believes her, and so do about five hundred people camped outside, not to mention a host of doctors who saw my heart stop beating.'

Kenzie is silent for a moment. 'Remember the broadcast of *War of the Worlds*?'

'Of course. My husband and I were just as scared as anyone.'

'That's all I'm saying, Mrs Epstein. People hear what they want to hear. They believe what they want to believe.'

Millie slowly sets down her glass of water and unconsciously rubs her hand over her heart. 'What do you want to believe, Ms van der Hoven?'

Kenzie does not hesitate. 'That whatever I recommend will be right for Faith. And you, Mrs Epstein? What do you want to believe?'

That time can be turned back. That nightmares stop. That Colin never entered my daughter's life. 'I want to believe there's a God,' Millie says clearly. 'Because I sure as hell know there's a devil.'

'Hunstead,' Metz calls from his throne at the end of the conference table, 'you and Lee get confirmation. I want a copy of the ticket that got her to Kansas City—'

'Sir?' an associate asks. 'Are we talking about Kansas City, Missouri, or Kansas City, Kansas?'

'Where the fuck have you been for the past hour, Lee?' Metz asks. 'Hunstead, fill in your anamnesis-challenged colleague as to what we've been discussing while he's been dreaming of *Baywatch*.'

'How about rental-car agencies?' Hunstead suggests. 'If Fletcher was the one who provided the transportation, it should be in his name, or his production company's. Otherwise Mariah White would have just used a credit card.'

'Very nice,' Metz says. 'Go with it. I also want copies of local hotel registers.'

Two associates sitting to Metz's right at the chrome-and-glass conference table scrawl the directive onto their pads. 'Lee, I want to know all the cases in the past ten years where custody's been overturned and given to the father. And I want to know why. Elkland, start scouring our list of experts for psychiatrists. We need one who's willing to say that once someone's a nutcase, they're always a nutcase.' He glances up, palming an apple that's been sitting in front of him. 'What do you call a lawyer encased in concrete at the bottom of the ocean?'

The young lawyers glance at each other. Finally Lee raises his hand. 'A good start?'

'Excellent! You win the deposition this afternoon, with the court psychiatrist who's evaluated Colin White.'

'What are you going to do?'

Metz laughs. 'I'm going to fucking get down on my knees and pray to fucking Allah.' He jots several notes while the younger lawyers scatter to do his bidding, then pushes the intercom button. 'Janie, I don't want to be bothered.'

It used to be a joke between them; he used to say, 'I don't want to be bothered unless God calls.' What made it funny, of course, was that most people in the firm didn't discount that as an impossibility. But since taking on the White case, Metz has stopped using that tag line.

He does not like Colin White, but then again he does not particularly like any of the clients he defends. He admires White, though, for the challenge the man presents. Metz has a golden opportunity here to show law at its best—something that has little to do with justice, and more to do with seduction.

In a couple of weeks he will walk into a courtroom, take the life of a fuck-up like Colin White, and totally turn it around. He will do such a good job of re-creating his client that a judge and the press and maybe even the prosecutor will believe what he says.

Metz laughs to himself. And they say surgeons have a God complex.

He is not a religious man. In fact, the last brush with organized worship he can recall was at his own bar mitzvah. Metz remembers the red dress his mother wore, the boxy suit that hung on his frame, the surprising sound of his voice as it sang out the words of the Torah. He'd been so scared he nearly pissed his pants, and then later at the reception, when his aunts leaned over him in clouds of perfume to offer kisses and receive *nachas*, he'd come close to passing out. But it had been worth it when his father had come with him to the bathroom, stood beside him at the urinal, and said without meeting his eye, 'Now you're a man.'

It was the first time Metz had used his words to remake a person. In that case, himself.

He shrugs his attention back to the file before him. Colin White, Mariah White, Faith White. Those are the names on the legal documents; 'God' comes up nowhere. And according to Malcolm Metz's interpretation of the law, that's as it should be.

November 18, 1999

IN HER ENTIRE LIFETIME, Kenzie has never been inside a temple. She knows that she is gawking at the richly decorated Ark, at the unfamiliar Hebrew prayer books, at the *bema*. 'It looks just like a church,' she says, and then covers her mouth in embarrassment.

Rabbi Weissman grins. 'We gave up dancing naked around a fire about a year ago.'

'I'm sorry.' Kenzie meets his eye. 'I don't have much familiarity with Judaism.'

'Apparently you can still be an expert.' He gestures toward a pew. 'So you want to know if Faith White's really having conversations with God. Ms van der Hoven, *I* have conversations with God. But you don't see *Hollywood Tonight!* outside my office.'

'So you're saying—'

'I'm saying that God, in His infinite wisdom, hasn't shown up in drag to play checkers with me.' He takes off his glasses and polishes them on his shirt. 'Wouldn't you be a bit suspicious if a little girl with absolutely no legal training suddenly announced she could and would sit as a judge?'

'Is that the same thing?'

'You tell me. So she's talking to God. So what. I don't see God telling her that the Israelites are going to cream the PLO. I don't see God telling her to keep kosher. I don't see God even inspiring her to come to Friday-night services. And I have a very hard time believing that if God did choose to manifest Himself in human form to a Jew, He would choose one who hadn't followed a code of Jewish living.'

'As I understand it, religious apparitions don't appear only to the pious.'

'Ah, you've been talking to priests! Look at the Bible. The people who've been lucky enough to speak to God are either extremely religious or positioned to do the most good for the religion. Take an example: Moses wasn't raised Jewish, but he embraced his religion after speaking with God. I don't see that happening here.' He grins. 'As comforting as it is for us to nurse the fantasy that God might buddy up to the average Joe who doesn't go to church or temple and prays only to secure Super Bowl bets, it's not realistic. God's forgiving, but He's also got a long memory, and there's a reason Jews have been following a pattern of life for five thousand years.'

Kenzie looks up from her notebook. 'But I've met with Faith, and I don't think she's intentionally trying to take people for a ride.'

'Neither do I. Don't look so surprised. I've met with her, too, you know; she's a sweet kid. Which leads me to believe someone's putting her up to this.'

Kenzie thinks back to the moment in Faith's bedroom, when Mariah silenced her daughter with a single glance. 'Her mother.'

'That was my conclusion, yes.' He settles back against the pew. 'I know Mrs White isn't much of a practicing Jew, but some things stay with you. If repressed childhood traumas can come back to haunt you, why not religious practice? Maybe it was ingrained at an early age in Mrs White—preverbally, even—and she's somehow communicated this to her daughter.'

Kenzie scratches her chin with the top of her pencil. 'Why?'

Rabbi Weissman shrugs. 'Ask that fellow Ian Fletcher. God can be a very lucrative silent partner. The question isn't *why*, Ms van der Hoven. It's *why not?*'

• • •

November 19, 1999

'YOU CERTAINLY RAISE a good point,' Father MacReady says. He walks beside Kenzie on the grounds of the church, setting up small tornadoes of leaves with the toe of his cowboy boot. 'But I can raise a good one, too. Why would a child—or her mother, as you suggest—choose to be a stigmatic?'

'Attention?'

'Well, there is that. But seeing God isn't nearly as big a draw as, say, seeing Elvis. And if you want to stick to Catholicism, I'd have to say that visions of Mary have always attracted a bigger, more emotional crowd than sightings of Jesus.' He turns to Kenzie, the wind ruffling his hair. 'Stigmatics are subject to intense scrutiny by the Catholic Church. Far as I know, if you commune with Elvis, you only have to answer to someone like Petra Saganoff.'

'It doesn't seem odd to you that a little Jewish girl is having a vision of Jesus?'

'Religion's not a competition, Ms van der Hoven.' He looks at Kenzie carefully. 'What's really upsetting you about this case?'

Kenzie crosses her arms, suddenly cold. 'I'm convinced Faith isn't lying. Which means that I can't help but believe that maybe someone else is putting her up to this . . .'

'Mariah.'

'Yes,' Kenzie sighs. 'Or else . . . she's really seeing God.'

'And you have a problem with that.'

She nods. 'I'm a cynic.'

'So am I,' Father MacReady says. 'Every now and then, even up here, we get a crying statue or a blind man who can suddenly see, but these things don't usually happen unless you're David Copperfield. I'm the first person who'll tell you that devout faith can change a person. But work miracles? No way. Heal? Uh-uh. And the truth is, the only piety Faith's got going for her is in her name. She didn't grow up believing in God. She doesn't care even now, really, who God is. Except for the fact that God is a friend.'

Father MacReady stares toward the edge of the church's property. The sun has broken through the clouds, reflecting in blue and gold rays like a stock photo on religious paraphernalia. He can remember his mother pulling the car over to sigh at the beauty of a moment like this. 'Look at that, Joseph,' she'd say. 'It's a Jesus sky.'

'Ms van der Hoven,' he muses, still staring off into the distance, 'have you ever seen the sun set in Nepal?'

Kenzie follows his gaze to the dazzling palette of the sky. 'No, I haven't.'

'Neither have I,' Father MacReady admits. 'But that doesn't mean it doesn't happen.'

Vatican City, Rome

THE FORERUNNER OF the Office of the Sacred Congregation for the Doctrine of the Faith was instituted in 1231 by Pope Gregory IX, and occasionally carried out its mission by stretching suspects on the rack, searing them with live coals, flogging, and burning them at the stake. It has been a long, long time since the Inquisition, and the office is now devoted to furthering correct Catholic doctrine rather than censuring heresy. Yet Cardinal Sciorro sometimes walks through the halls and smells ashes; sometimes he wakes in the night because he's heard people scream.

The cardinal prefect likes to think of himself as a simple man, a holy man—but a fair man. Since the Sacred Congregation for the Doctrine of the Faith acts like a court of appeal, he knows he is well suited to his position. He wears responsibility as surely as he wears his mozzetta, and it weighs just as heavily on his shoulders.

He is in his office, sipping his morning chocolate and reading over paperwork that's been piling up, when he first comes across it. 'The MotherGod Society,' he says slowly, testing the words on his tongue; they leave a bitter aftertaste. He skims the brief: A group of Catholic women of significant numbers wish to appeal the censure of His Excellency the Bishop of Manchester, claiming that the words of one Faith White, who is *not* Catholic, are not heretical.

The cardinal prefect calls to his secretary, an attentive

monsignor named Reggie with the look of a beagle about him. 'Your Eminence?'

'What do you know about this MotherGod Society?'

'Well,' Reggie says, 'they were demonstrating in St Mark's Square yesterday.'

These militant Catholic women are becoming more and more of a force. For a moment, the cardinal feels a pang of nostalgia, for the way the world was before Vatican II. 'What did Bishop Andrews consider heresy?'

'From what I've gathered, the Jewish visionary says God is female.'

'I see.' The cardinal prefect exhales slowly, thinking of Galileo, Joan of Arc, of other victims of alleged heresy. He wonders what good it will do if, after this appeal, the MotherGod Society remains censured. He can stop these women from putting heresy into print, from spreading false dogma, because they're followers of Catholicism.

But Faith White—she'll still be out there, saying whatever she wants.

Lacey Rodriguez kicks off her shoes and slips the tape into the VCR. Not for the first time since she's been an investigator, she mulls over how thoughtless employers can be. A few more perks, a better benefits package—hell, maybe even a personal greeting every now and then . . . any of these things might have gone a long way to keep Ian Fletcher's cameraman from selling out a videotaped copy of Millie Epstein's stress test for a measly ten thousand dollars.

She pushes the fast-forward button on the remote control, not having the slightest interest in the old woman's cardiac rhythms or huffing and puffing on the treadmill. Then she sits forward, transfixed, her fingertips covering her slowly spreading smile.

thirteen

Be sober, be vigilant; because your adversary,
the devil, as a roaring lion,
walketh about, seeking whom he may devour.

—1 Peter 5:8

November 23, 1999

'THE MAN,' Joan announces, slinging her briefcase onto our kitchen table, 'is an asshole.'

Neither my mother nor I blink an eye. We've heard Joan rant this way about Malcolm Metz before. I sit down across from her as she shuffles through papers. 'The good news,' I say, full of false cheer, 'is that in a few weeks you'll never have to see Metz again.'

Joan looks up, surprised. 'Who's talking about Metz?' She leans back in her chair, massaging her temples. 'No, today I had the singular pleasure of deposing Ian Fletcher. The guy's twenty minutes late and wouldn't answer to anything beyond his name and address. Back in third grade he must have learned to say "I take the fifth," and he's been waiting for a chance to use it ever since.' Shaking her head, she hands Mariah a list. 'All I got out of him is that he's going to be a pain in the ass on cross.'

Mariah takes the paper, trying to get her head around Joan's comment. Ian, a witness for Malcolm Metz? For *Colin*?

'Besides Fletcher, is there anyone else on the witness list you can give me some information about?'

I try to answer, but my mouth is too dry to manage more than a puff of surprise. I am dimly aware of my mother, her eyes narrowed on my face; of the sea of letters that form and dissolve into names: Colin, Dr Orlitz, Dr DeSantis. 'Mariah,' Joan calls, her voice a long way away, 'are you all right?'

He has said, all along, that he will help me. He has said that he'll do whatever is in his power to make sure I keep Faith. And yet here he is, in league with Malcolm Metz, lying to me.

What else has he lied about?

With a great surge of adrenaline I stand, pushing my chair back from the table. Joan and my mother watch me walk out of the kitchen, follow me to the parlor. When it becomes clear to them what I mean to do, Joan rushes to intervene. 'Mariah,' she cautions, 'don't fly off the handle here.'

But I'm not thinking clearly; I don't want to think clearly. I don't care who sees me running across the yard with a speed born of hurt and fury. I barely even pay attention to the charge that electrifies the media as I close in on the Winnebago with single-minded purpose.

I don't even bother to knock. Chest heaving, I stand in the doorway and stare at Ian and three of his employees, gathered around a tiny table with papers strewn all over. For a beat, Ian's eyes speak to me: surprise, pleasure, confusion, and wariness registering one after the other. 'Miz White,' he drawls. 'What a very pleasant surprise.' He turns to the other three people and asks for a moment alone; they file from the Winnebago casting curious looks my way.

As soon as the door closes behind them, Ian comes around the table and grasps my shoulders. 'What's the matter? Did something happen to Faith?'

'Not yet,' I bite out.

He steps back, distanced by my anger. 'Well, it's got to be something. You can't imagine the kind of stories brewing in the heads of all the reporters who watched you walk on in here just now.' Then his face changes, slipping easily into a boyish smile. 'Or maybe you just couldn't live another moment without seeing me in person.'

I swallow hard. 'Why didn't you tell me you're testifying for Metz?'

I can't help it, the way my voice breaks in the middle. I have the satisfaction of watching Ian start, and then, to my surprise, he begins to laugh. 'Joan told you.' I nod. 'She let on how uncooperative I happened to be?' Then Ian reaches for me. 'Mariah, I'm testifying for *you*.'

I sniff into his shirt. Even now, when I should hate him, I notice the scent of his skin. Steeling myself, I draw away. 'Well, you may not have noticed, but Malcolm Metz is not my lawyer.'

'That's right. I went to him, made him think I'd give him examples to kingdom come about you being an unfit parent. When it's my turn to testify in court, though, he'll be in for a surprise, since my speech will be dramatically different.'

'But Joan—'

'I didn't have a choice, Mariah. I can go over my testimony with Metz to his face and then get up on the stand and start speaking Swahili without it being a big deal. After all, I'm his witness, and it just means I'm not behaving properly. But if I lie to Joan Standish in a deposition and then get up in a court of law and say something entirely different, I'll be committing perjury. I had to plead the fifth today—repeatedly—because it keeps her from getting in trouble, and me from getting in trouble, and Metz from getting suspicious of me.'

I want to believe him; God, I do. 'You would do this for me?'

Ian inclines his head. 'I would do anything for you.'

This time when he takes me into his arms, I don't resist. 'Why didn't you tell me you were doing this?'

His hand strokes my back, gentling. 'The less you know, the better. That way if it all blows up in my face, you won't be caught in the explosion.' He kisses the corner of my mouth, my cheek, my forehead. 'You can't tell Joan yet. If she finds out before the trial, she could get into a hell of a lot of trouble.'

In answer, I go up on my toes and kiss him. Shyly, at first; then I open my mouth on his, identifying coffee and something sweeter, like candy. Surely if Ian was lying to me, it would be evident. Surely if he was lying, I would have the good sense to see through him.

Like I did before? Closing my eyes, I firmly push away the thought of Colin and his indiscretions. I feel Ian's heat rising between us, his hips pushing against mine.

With a gasp, he breaks away from me. 'Sugar, there's a whole crowd of people out there waiting to see whether you're gonna make it out of this trailer alive. And if we keep this up, I can't make any promises.' He chastely kisses my brow and takes a deliberate step away, a grin tugging at the corner of his mouth.

'What?'

'You don't look like you've been fighting with me, exactly.' Flushing, I smooth my hands over my hair and touch my fingertips to my lips. Ian laughs. 'Just look angry, and get back to the house fast. They'll think you're still nursing a powerful mad.'

He cups my cheek in his hand, and I turn my lips into his palm. 'Ian . . . thanks.'

'Miz White,' he murmurs, 'it's my pleasure.'

Joan and my mother hover at the door and immediately surround me as I walk inside, making me think of circus performers who wait at the high rope ladder to make sure their companion on the trapeze returns to safety. 'Good God, Mariah,' Joan scolds. 'What were you thinking?'

My mother doesn't say a word. She stares at my mouth, red and kissed, and raises a brow.

'I wasn't thinking,' I confess, and at least this much is true.

'What did you say to him?'

'To be polite to my attorney in the future,' I lie, staring Joan right in the eye, 'or else he'll have to answer to me.'

A few minutes before Petra Saganoff and her film crew are due to arrive, I pull Faith aside into an alcove by the bathroom. 'You remember what we talked about?'

Faith nods solemnly. 'No talk about God. At all. And

there's going to be a big camera,' Faith adds. 'Like the ones outside.'

'That's right.'

'And I can't call Petra Saganoff the B word.'

'Faith!'

'Well, *you* called her that.'

'I was wrong.' I sigh, thinking that if I survive this day, I will never complain again in my life. Through Joan, I've arranged to have Petra Saganoff in to film what she calls 'B-roll'—background footage of Faith playing and of us just being us in our house, that she'll then go off and record over with her own narrative, before airing the segment on *Hollywood Tonight!* Joan made sure that Saganoff signed a release about what she is allowed to film and what she isn't, but I worry about her visit all the same. Although I think Faith will be able to act normally for a half hour, this could backfire . . . something Joan has pointed out to me ever since I suggested this exclusive. Our lives haven't exactly been predictable lately. What if Faith starts bleeding again? What if she forgets, and starts talking to God? What if Petra Saganoff makes us all look like fools?

'Mommy,' Faith says, touching my arm. 'It'll be okay. God's taking care of it.'

'Excellent,' I murmur. 'We'll make sure to give her a good seat.'

The doorbell rings. I pass my mother on the way to answer it.

'I still don't like this. Not a bit.'

'Neither do I,' I say, scowling at her. 'But if I don't say something, people are going to assume the worst.' I pull open the door and fix a smile on my face. 'Ms Saganoff, thank you so much for coming.'

Petra Saganoff, primed and in person, is even more attractive than she is on television. 'Thanks for the invitation,' she says. With her are three men, whom she introduces as a cameraman, a sound man, and a producer. She does not make eye contact with me; instead her gaze darts around the hall, looking for Faith.

'She's just inside,' I say dryly. 'Why don't you follow me?'

We have agreed to allow her access to Faith's playroom. What better way, I figure, to show that a child is just a child, than to watch her with her dolls and puzzles and books? But by the time the cameraman and the producer have decided where to set the camera and arranged the lighting for the shot, nearly thirty minutes have passed. Faith's getting fidgety; the cameraman even gives her a 'gel'—a colored piece of plastic that he's affixed to the lights with clothespins. She takes it and peers through it, screening her world yellow, but I can tell that she's reached the end of her patience. At this rate, Faith will be ready to leave her toys and go somewhere else by the time Petra's just getting started.

I am thinking of the time Ian filmed Faith at my mother's stress test, of how even with limits in place, there is still so much that can go wrong—when suddenly a fuse blows. 'Ah, damn it,' the cameraman says. 'Circuits are overloaded.'

Another ten minutes until we fix the fuse. By now Faith is whining.

The cameraman turns to the producer. 'You want continuous time code or time of day?' Then the sound man holds up a white card in front of Faith's face. 'Give me some tone,' the cameraman says, and a few moments later, 'Speed.' The producer looks at Petra Saganoff. 'Whenever you're ready.'

When filming begins, I'm on the floor helping Faith play with a felt board. As per Joan's instructions, I don't talk to Petra or the camera; I do only what I would normally be doing with Faith. I try to keep Faith's attention from the little red light on top of the camera, a place she seems to want to fix her gaze. Petra watches from the corner.

'I'm hungry,' Faith says, and I realize it's already lunchtime.

'Come on. We'll go into the kitchen.'

Well, that creates a quandary. Technically we haven't filmed for thirty minutes, but the crew is off limits to the rest of the house. I suggest that the crew take a break and continue filming after Faith eats. Graciously, I invite Petra into the kitchen.

'You have a nice place here, Mrs White,' she says, the first words she's really addressed to me since her arrival.

'Thank you.' I reach into the refrigerator and pull out the peanut butter and jelly, set it on the table—Faith likes to spread her own sandwiches.

'I imagine this has been hard for you,' Petra says, and then smiles at the expression on my face. 'Want to frisk me? See if I'm wearing a mike?'

'No, of course not.' Joan's ultimate command: Keep your cool. I choose my words carefully, sure that the voice-over narrative Saganoff does will somehow come back to whatever conversation we are about to have. 'It has been difficult,' I admit. 'As you've probably noticed, regardless of what the people outside think, Faith's just a little girl. That's all she wants to be.'

Behind Petra's back, I see Faith holding up her palm. She's spread jelly all around the Band-Aid, so that it looks as if she's oozing blood, and she's waving her hand in the air and silently pretending to moan. My mother, catching my look, rushes over to Faith and wipes the jelly off her hand with a paper towel, firmly waggling a finger in her face in warning. I focus my attention on Petra again and smile brightly. 'What was I saying?'

'That your daughter's just like any other little girl. But, Mrs White, there are a lot of people who'd disagree with you.'

I shrug. 'I can't tell them what to think. But I don't have to believe what they believe either. First and foremost, Faith is my daughter. Plain and simple, and whatever else is going on really has nothing to do with us.' Proud of myself, I stop while I'm ahead. Even Joan couldn't find fault with that last statement; I almost wish the camera had been rolling.

I take a head of lettuce out of the refrigerator. 'Would you like some lunch, Ms Saganoff?'

'If it's not too much trouble.'

For years afterward, I will never be able to figure out what made me say what I say next. It bursts out of me like a belch, and leaves me just as embarrassed. 'No trouble at all,' I joke. 'We're just having loaves and fishes.'

For a single, horrifying moment, Petra Saganoff stares at me as if I've grown another head. Then she breaks into laughter, steps up to the counter, and offers to help.

November 24, 1999

ON WEDNESDAY, *Hollywood Tonight!* runs teasers, promising an inside look at the White household: 'Home with an Angel.' To my surprise, I begin to get nervous about the broadcast. I do not know, after all, what Saganoff is going to say about us. And millions of people are going to hear it, no matter what.

At six o'clock, we eat dinner. At six-thirty, I make a bowl of microwave popcorn. By twenty to seven, my mother, Faith, and I are sitting on the couch, waiting for Peter Jennings to stop talking so that *Hollywood Tonight!* will come on. 'Oh, shoot,' my mother says, patting her chest. 'I left my glasses at home.'

'What glasses?'

'My glasses. You know, the ones I need to see.'

I raise a brow. 'You were wearing them this afternoon. They're probably in the kitchen.'

'I wasn't wearing them; you're mistaken. I clearly remember leaving them on the kitchen counter in my house.' She turns to me. 'Mariah, you know how I hate driving in the dark. You have to get them for me.'

'Now?' I ask, incredulous. 'I can't leave when this show's about to go on.'

'Oh, please. My house is five minutes away, even less. You'll be back before the news is over. And if you aren't, you can always turn on *my* TV and watch, too.'

'Why can't you just pull a chair up close to the television set?'

'Because she'll hurt her eyes,' Faith pipes in. 'That's what you always tell me.'

Frustrated, I press my lips together. 'I cannot believe you're making me do this.'

'If you hadn't complained to begin with, you'd be back by now.'

I throw up my hands and grab my purse, speeding out of the driveway so quickly that the reporters don't have time to jump in their cars and follow me. I rip through the streets of New Canaan until I reach my mother's house.

Not only has she forgotten her glasses, she's left the light on in the kitchen, as well. I unlock the door and step inside and see Ian.

'What . . . what are you doing here?'

He smiles, reaches for my hands. 'A little birdie gave me the key.'

I shake my head. 'A little birdie about yea high, fifty-something, with a blond bob? I can't believe it.'

Ian slides his arms around my waist. 'She wanted to play fairy godmother, Mariah. Don't ruin it for her.'

I move around, shutting curtains, locking the door, checking to make sure that no telltale car lights are hovering outside waiting for me. Ian's car is nowhere to be seen. 'But I have to get back home . . . the show . . .'

'It's on in the other room. Your mama came to the trailer yesterday and asked me if I would mind coming down here, watching it with you. I guess she figured you might want some moral support.'

'*She* could have given me moral support,' I say.

Ian looks affronted. 'But it wouldn't have been nearly as much fun.'

That brings me up short. 'Are you telling me that my mother . . . that she wants us . . .'

He touches my hair. 'She's heard you talking to me at night, on the phone. And she said that you deserve a little bit of happiness about now.' He grins at me. 'She also told me to tell you that she'll put Faith to bed, which sounds like she's certainly giving us her blessing, in addition to her house.' Twining his fingers with mine, he leads me into the living room, where the anchors of *Hollywood Tonight!* have just appeared on screen.

I am barely aware of Ian settling beside me on the couch as the television fills with pictures of my home, my daughter. Petra Saganoff's rich voice seems oddly out of place, superimposed on the scene of Faith arranging figures on her felt board. 'For weeks now we've heard of the miracles brought to pass by this little girl, Faith White.' The scenes cut away to pictures of the hospital, where Petra mentions my mother's resurrection, and to a close-up of the infant with AIDS who had played in our yard. Then Faith is on the floor of the playroom again, but this time I'm with her.

'Don't you look fine on the small screen,' Ian whispers.

'Sssh.'

Petra continues. 'Perhaps the greatest miracle, however, is the way Faith's mother, Mariah White, is struggling to keep a level head and a loving home for her daughter in spite of the maelstrom just outside their doors.'

'Oh,' I gasp, a smile breaking over my face even as tears come to my eyes. 'Oh, Ian, did you hear?'

He opens his arms, and I launch into them, laughing and crying and so very, very relieved. I am not listening to *Hollywood Tonight!* anymore; it fades in the wake of Ian's hands on my shoulders and back, pulling me even closer. Cradling his face between my palms, I kiss him deeply, until I am lying flush against him on the couch and breathing just as hard as he is.

He unbuttons my shirt and presses his lips to the skin revealed at my throat. 'I like the effect this show has on you.'

He is teasing, but I have moved past that point. I want to feel him, take him, celebrate him. I am shaking as I lock my hands behind his neck.

Sensing the change in me, Ian draws back enough to look into my eyes. 'I have missed you so,' he whispers, and he kisses me. With his hands he builds a fire in me. *This is love,* I think. A place where people who have been alone may lock together like hawks and spin in the air, dizzy with surprise at the connection. A place you go willingly, and with wonder.

Then my hands are freeing him and as Ian moves inside me, our fingers lace together, so that we hinge on each other. *Mine, mine, mine.* His hair falls over my eyes, and when I turn my face against my own shoulder, I realize that I smell of him, as if he has already taken root under my skin.

The television hums, a kaleidoscopic test pattern splashed over the screen. I touch my hand to the base of Ian's neck, to the small knot of collarbone beneath his shirt, all places that I am beginning to know by heart. 'Ian . . . do you ever think about going to hell?'

He pulls back and smiles quizzically. 'What brought this on?'

'Do you?'

Running a hand through his hair, he leans against the headboard. 'Believing in hell means believing in some religious construction, so I'd have to say no.'

'You'd have to say no,' I agree slowly, 'but that doesn't tell me what you think.'

He covers me with his body and breathes against my neck. 'What made you think of hell? Was it this?' He scrapes his teeth over my shoulder. 'Or this?'

No, I want to tell him. This is heaven. This must be heaven because never in my life have I imagined that someone like you would want to be with me, here, doing this. And on the heels of this thought comes another: that such pleasure, surely, comes with a price.

Then Ian tips his forehead to mine and closes his eyes. 'Yes,' he whispers. 'I think about going to hell.'

Metz scowls at the television set and turns it off in the middle of the videotape. 'This is crap,' he announces to an empty room. 'Crap!'

Mariah White one-upped him by giving *Hollywood Tonight!* a backstage pass to her home, and frankly, from what Colin White has told him about the woman, it's surprised him. Traditionally, she's rolled over and played dead at the first sign of confrontation. This media courting, after weeks of hiding away, is clearly a positioning strategy—one that Metz unfortunately admits is paying off. With the trial a week away, a press corps that's in love with Faith White, and a very anxious client in the wings, he has his work cut out for him.

There is a knock on the door. 'Yeah?'

Elkland, one of his young female associates, sticks her head in. 'Mr Metz? Have you got a minute?'

Hell, he's got a minute. He's got a whole evening full of them, since he doesn't seem to be using them to any advantage stacking the odds in his favor in the White case. 'Sure.' He gestures to a chair and wearily rubs his hands over his face. 'What's on your mind?'

'Well, I was watching that show *Nova* on PBS last night.'

'Congratulations. You want to be an attorney or a Nielsen family?'

'It's just that it was about this disease. It's called Munchausen Syndrome by Proxy. Basically, if you've got it, you make someone else look physically or mentally ill.'

Metz sits up, intrigued. 'Tell me those papers in your hand are some preliminary research,' he murmurs.

She nods. 'It's a clinical disorder. Usually, it's a mother doing it to her kid, in secret. And the reason is to get positive attention—to look, ironically, like a good mother because she's dragging the child into the ER or to a psychiatrist. Of course, since the mom made her sick in the first place, that's a crock.'

Metz frowns. 'How do you make someone else have a hallucination?'

'I don't know,' admits Elkland. 'But I found someone who does. I took the liberty of interviewing an expert on Munchausen Syndrome by Proxy over the phone. He wants to talk to you about the case.'

Metz taps his fingers on his desk. The chances of Mariah White's having this Munchausen disorder are probably rather slim, but that's neither here nor there. His strongest cases usually have nothing to do with the truth, but simply with being able to blow smoke the right way. The best strategy for Colin White will be to make the judge find fault in Faith's mother, so that he has no choice but to award custody to the father. Metz could hint that Mariah has leprosy, schizophrenia, or this Munchausen by Proxy—anything, just so long as it makes Rothbottam sit back and reconsider.

In a way, he's only fighting fairly, using the same tactic Mariah White did when she invited *Hollywood Tonight!* to her home. The fact of the matter is, in this case, perception is everything. Judges don't traditionally give custody to fathers, unless the mother is proven to be a heroin addict or a whore. Or, perhaps, crazy as a loon.

'I like this,' he says guardedly.

Elkland grins. 'I haven't told you the best part. These mothers? The ones who really have Munchausen by Proxy?

They're pathological liars—it's part and parcel of having the syndrome. If you ask them to their faces whether they've hurt their children, they'll deny it, they'll act outraged, they'll get very hostile.'

Metz smiles slowly. 'Just like Mrs White is bound to do when we cross her.'

'Just like,' Elkland says.

November 25, 1999

MY MOTHER DECIDES that it's time for her to move back home. Whether it is the approaching trial that fuels this decision, or the fact that she's sick of sleeping in our guest room, I don't know. I help her pack up her things in the little suitcase that she has had since I was a young girl.

On the bed I fold her nightgown into thirds, and thirds again. She is in the bathroom, gathering together the creams and pastes and powders that make up a smell I will always associate with her. It reminds me of the night Ian and I spent at her house. I would have thought that this scent, so familiar from childhood, would make me rear away from the thought of making love with Ian in my mother's house, but I was wrong. It was the smell of security, of comfort, oddly seductive to both Ian and myself.

'I haven't thanked you,' I say, as my mother comes out of the bathroom carrying a toiletry kit.

'For what?' She waves a hand at me. 'This was nothing.'

'I didn't mean you staying here. I meant . . . well, for making me go.'

My mother's head comes up. 'Ah. I was wondering when we were going to get around to that.'

I can feel my cheeks going red. After all these years, I still cannot speak of boys to my mother without feeling as if I'm eleven again. 'It was a nice gesture,' I say diplomatically.

'Good lord, Mariah, call a spade a spade, will you? It was a rendezvous. An assignation. A trysting spot. A love—'

'Let's just leave it at that, okay?' I grin. 'You *are* my mother.'

She cups my cheek. It tingles, as if she were holding my childhood right there in her palm. 'But somewhere along the way, I also became your friend.'

It is a silly thing, to put it in such terms, but it is true. The women in my life, my two best friends, are my mother and my daughter. A few weeks ago, I almost lost one. A few days from now, I might lose the other.

'You need me, no question about that. But you needed him, too. And I figured I was the best one to make that happen.'

My mother methodically matches shoes and lays them into her suitcase. She is beautiful, softened at the edges and tempered with a spine of steel. I want to grow old and be like her. 'The best one,' I say softly. 'You are.'

December 2, 1999

JOAN HAS DINNER with us the night before the hearing. Afterward, while my mother and Faith are clearing the table, we go down to my workshop for privacy. We rehearse my testimony once again, until Joan is sure that I am not going to falter on the stand. Then she hooks her heels over the rung of a stool and stares at me. 'You know, this isn't going to be a picnic for you.'

I laugh. 'Well, I figured as much. I can think of a thousand other places I'd rather be.'

'I don't mean that, Mariah. I mean what people are going to say. Colin will be downright nasty. And Metz has a parade of other witnesses he's coached to say things that make you look like a sorry excuse for a parent.'

Not Ian, I think, and I wonder if I am convincing myself.

'That's not even counting what he's going to do to you on the stand. He's going to try to trip you up and get you confused, so that you look like the basket case he's been setting you up as in his direct examinations of witnesses.' She leans forward. 'Don't let him get to you. When you go home at the end of each day during this trial, know that Malcolm

Metz doesn't really know you from Adam. You're not a person to him; you're a means to an end.'

I look up at Joan and try to spread a smile across my face. 'Don't you worry about me. I've grown thicker skin lately.' But all the same, I'm hugging myself as if I'm suddenly chilled; as if I'm suddenly wary of falling apart.

The doorbell rings at ten-thirty. When I open it, braced for the quick flash of cameras, I find Colin standing there looking just as shocked to see me as I am to see him.

'Can we talk?' he asks after a moment.

For all that I want to turn him away, or tell him to contact my lawyer, I nod. We have a history between us, and in some ways I think that is thicker than anger, thicker than blood. 'All right. But Faith's asleep. Be quiet.'

As he follows me through the hallway, I wonder what he is thinking: *What did she do with that photograph of the Andes? Has the tile always been this dark?* What is it like to come back to your own house and not quite recognize it?

He pulls out a kitchen chair and straddles it. I imagine Joan, shouting at the top of her lungs that I shouldn't be here without an attorney present. But I smile halfheartedly and duck my head. 'So talk.'

The air leaves Colin in a great whoosh, like a hurricane. 'This is killing me.'

What? The chair? The fact that he's back in our house? Jessica? Me?

'Do you know why I fell in love with you, Rye?'

The countertop is just behind me. I work very hard at digging my fingernails into it. 'Did your attorney tell you to come here?'

The shock on Colin's face is geniune. 'God, no. Is that what you think?'

I stare at him. 'I don't really know what to think anymore, Colin.'

He stands and walks toward the spice rack, running his finger over each bottle. Anise, basil, coriander. Celery salt, crushed red pepper, and dill. 'You were sitting on the steps of the library at school,' he says. 'And I came up with a bunch of the guys from the team. Gorgeous spring day, but you were studying. You were always studying. I said we were going to get subs, and did you want to come?' He looks down at the floor and shakes his head. 'And you did. You just left your books sitting there in this pile like you didn't give a shit who took them or whatever, and you followed me.'

I smile. I never did get that economics text back, but I got Colin, and at the time I believed it was more than a fair trade. I take the small vial of bay leaves Colin's set on the counter and put it back in its place. 'I should have kept on studying.'

Colin touches my arm. 'Do you really believe that?'

I am afraid to look at him. I stare down at his hand until he removes it. 'You didn't want someone who'd follow you, Colin. You wanted someone you had to chase.'

'I loved you,' he says fiercely.

I do not blink. 'For how long?'

He takes a step away. 'You're different,' he accuses. 'You're not like you used to be.'

'You mean I'm not huddled in the corner, crying into a dish towel. Sorry to disappoint.'

At that, I know I've pushed too far. 'How long this time, Rye?' Colin presses. 'How long until you start looking in the medicine cabinet for escape routes? Or stare at a razor blade for the six hours that Faith's in school? How long until you check out on her?'

'And you didn't?'

'I won't,' Colin says. 'Not now. Look, I made a mistake, Rye. But that was between you and me. I've never been less than one hundred percent there for Faith. So what if you pat Faith's head every morning now, if you tell her how much you love her? Up until that minute in August, you *weren't* the sure thing—*I* was. Do you think she's forgotten how it was when she was little, how her mom spent afternoons lying down with a headache, or sleeping off Haldol, or talking to a fucking shrink instead of taking her to preschool?' He points a shaking finger. 'You are not any better than me.'

'The difference between us is that I never said I *was*.'

Colin looks at me so angrily that I wonder if I am in danger. 'You won't take her away from me.'

I hope he cannot tell how hard I am shaking. 'You won't take her away from *me*.'

We have worked ourselves into such a fury that neither one of us notices Faith standing nearby until she draws a shaky breath.

'Honey. We woke you up?'

'Sweetheart.' Colin's face dissolves into a smile. 'Hi.'

Something in her eyes stops me just seconds before I touch her shoulder. Faith is stiff, her eyes wide with fear, her hands fisted at her sides, and her face drained of color. 'Mommy?' she says, her lower lip trembling. 'Daddy?'

But before either of us can explain ourselves or our behavior, we see the blood that wells between the seams of her fingers.

Within seconds Faith is writhing on the floor and crying out words I do not understand. 'Eli! Eli!' she calls out, and although I have no idea who this is, I tell her he is coming. I try not to notice that this time she is bleeding from her side, too. I hold her shoulders down so that she will not hurt herself, and all the while her palms leave smears of blood on the tile.

I hear Colin's voice, high and panicked, speaking into the portable phone. 'Eighty-six Westvale Hill, first driveway on the left.' Once he hangs up, he gets to the floor beside me. 'The ambulance is on its way.' He presses his cheek against Faith's, which actually calms her for a moment. 'Daddy's here. Daddy's going to take care of you.'

Faith shudders, then twists in pain. Her voice sounds like a river, syllables and grunts that escalate into sobs.

Colin's mouth drops open. Then he mobilizes to action, taking off his jacket and wrapping it around Faith, swaddling her in his arms the way he used to when she was a baby. He sings a lullaby I have not heard in years, and to my surprise Faith goes limp and docile.

The paramedics burst into the house. Colin steps back and lets them work on Faith. I watch these people lay hands on my daughter and say what I already suspect: that her blood pressure is fine, that the pupils are responsive, that the bleeding will not stop. After all, I have played out this scene once before. I feel Colin's hand slip over mine like a glove. 'We can ride in the ambulance,' he says.

'Colin—'

'Look,' he announces in a tone that brooks no argument, 'I don't care what the hell is going on in court. We're both her parents. We're both going.'

I want to talk to Dr Blumberg alone, yet I want Colin to hear him say the things he has already said to me. I want to yank my hand out of Colin's and stand completely on my own. I want, badly, to speak to Ian. But Colin has always had a pull on me, like the moon with the tide, and I find my feet following him out of habit, into the belly of the ambulance, where I sit with Colin's shoulder bumping mine and my eyes adjusting to darkness, watching the shifting snakes of IVs that feed into my child.

Colin and I sit side by side on the ugly tubular couches that make up the waiting room of the ER. By now Faith's bleeding has been stabilized, and she's been carted off to X-ray. The emergency physician, referring to her chart, has summoned Dr Blumberg.

Colin has been busy for the past half hour. He answered the questions of the paramedics and the doctors, he paced incessantly, he smoked three cigarettes just outside the glass doors of the ER, his profile gilded with moonlight. Finally he comes back inside and crouches down beside my seat, where I am resting my head in my hands. 'Do you think,' he whispers, as if giving voice to the thought will make it take wing, 'that she's doing it for attention?'

'Doing what?'

'Hurting herself.'

At that, I raise my eyes. 'You'd believe that of Faith?'

'I don't know, Mariah. I don't know what to believe.'

We are saved from an argument by the arrival of Dr Blumberg. 'Mrs White. What happened?'

Colin extends his hand. 'I'm Colin White. Faith's father.'

'Hello.'

'I understand this isn't the first time you've examined Faith,' Colin says. 'I'd appreciate being brought up to date on her history.'

Dr Blumberg slants a glance at me. 'I'm sure that Mrs White—'

'Mrs White and I are estranged,' Colin says bluntly. 'I'd like to hear it from you.'

'Okay.' He sits across from us and settles his hands on his knees. 'I've already done a variety of tests on Faith, but have found no medical explanation why she spontaneously bleeds.'

'It's definitely blood?'

'Oh, yes. It's been laboratory tested.'

'Is it self-inflicted?'

'Not that I can see,' Dr Blumberg says.

'Then it might be someone else?' Colin asks.

'Pardon me?'

'Did someone hurt Faith?'

Blumberg shakes his head. 'I don't believe so, Mr White. Not the way you mean.'

'How do you know?' Colin shouts. There are tears in his eyes. 'How the hell could you know? Look—I watched her fall into some fit and start bleeding for no reason. I have insurance. Don't you tell me you've got no medical explanation for this. Order a frigging CT scan or do bloodwork or something. You're a doctor. You're supposed to figure it out, and I want my daughter here until you do. Because if you release her again and she has another episode, I'm going to sue you for malpractice.'

I think of a piece of research Dr Blumberg told me about—of doctors at the turn of the century who hospitalized a stigmatic and welded an iron boot over his bleeding foot to make sure that the man was not producing the wound himself. I wonder how Colin can accuse *me* of ruining Faith's life.

Dr Blumberg hesitates. 'I can't run tests without her mother's consent.'

'You have her father's,' Colin says coldly.

'I'll admit her,' the doctor concedes. 'But I don't expect to find anything new.'

Satisfied, Colin stands. 'Can we see her now?'

'Faith will be up on the pedi ward in a few minutes. She'll be groggy; I gave her a sedative.' He looks from me to Colin. 'I'll check on her again in the morning. Hospital policy says that one of you can remain overnight in her room.' With a nod, he walks off.

I straighten my shoulders, gearing for a fight, but to my surprise Colin announces that he'll leave. 'Faith will expect you. You stay.'

We walk in silence to the elevator and take it to the pediatric floor. The desk nurse tells us which room is Faith's, although she hasn't yet returned from radiology. Colin and I enter the room, where he takes the only chair and I stand by the window with a view of the hospital's helicopter landing pad.

After a few minutes a nurse wheels Faith inside and helps her stumble into the bed. Her hands are wound in white bandages. 'Mommy?'

'I'm here.' I sit on the edge of the bed and touch Faith's cheek. 'How are you feeling?'

She turns away. 'I want to go home.'

I brush her bangs back from her face. 'The doctor wants you to sleep here overnight.'

Colin leans down on the other side of the bed. 'Hi, cookie.'

'Daddy.'

He gently takes her bandaged hand and strokes the skin above the gauze. 'How did this happen, honey?' he asks. 'You can tell me, and I won't get mad. Did you hurt yourself? Did someone else hurt you? Grandma, maybe? Or that priest who visits?'

'Oh, for God's sake—' I interject.

Colin narrows his eyes. 'You're not there every minute. You never know, Mariah.'

'Next you're going to be saying that *I* did it to her,' I spit out.

Colin simply raises his brows.

• • •

After Faith falls asleep, Colin gets to his feet. 'Look, I'm sorry. It's just eating me up inside to see her like this and not know how to fix it.'

'You know, apologies don't count when you qualify them.'

Colin looks at me for a long moment. 'Do we have to do it like this?'

'No,' I whisper. 'We don't.'

And then I am in Colin's arms, my face pressed against his neck. He touches his forehead to my brow in a gesture that brings a stream of memories. This man I was supposed to spend my life with, I will instead be meeting in a courtroom tomorrow. 'I'll be back in the morning. I'm sure the judge can give us a continuance.'

'I'm sure,' I repeat against his chest.

'For what it's worth,' he says, so quietly that I may be dreaming it, 'I know it's not you.'

With that assurance, Colin leaves me once again.

Kenzie microwaves a box of Pizza Bites and pours a big glass of red wine before she sits down to finish writing her recommendation to Judge Rothbottam. She imagines eating the entire box of hors d'oeuvres and maybe another and then methodically working her way through the refrigerator and freezer, stuffing herself until she cannot move. Cannot lift a finger. Cannot write this report of a guardian ad litem.

Judge Rothbottam is expecting this report on his desk tomorrow morning, before the custody hearing is in session. Kenzie—the objective observer, the eye in the storm—is supposed to lay a foundation upon which he can balance the arguments of the plaintiff and the defendant.

Kenzie takes a long, slow sip of wine. The White case is so filled with shades of gray that sometimes Kenzie doubts her ability to see clearly.

On the one hand, she has Colin and Jessica White, a new family anchored by a father who clearly loves Faith. But Kenzie can barely stomach giving custody to a man who was so grievously unfaithful. On the other hand, there's Mariah White, carting her emotional baggage from the past and even now—Kenzie's sure of it!—lying, either to herself, or to Faith, or to Kenzie herself. If she leaves Faith in her mother's custody, she does so without knowing the whole story. Yet she cannot help but notice that Mariah White, self-professed poster child for insecurity, has truly begun to turn her life around. It's clear, too, that Faith feels very attached to her mother. But is it a healthy connection, or does Faith simply feel the need to take care of a mother who isn't strong enough to take care of *her*?

Kenzie sets down her wine and waits for the cursor on the computer screen to focus at the top of the document. Then she turns it off, wishing for a miracle.

A pair of grieving relatives stand around the bed of Mamie Richardson, age eighty-two. After last week's stroke, she's been comatose. The doctors have explained the extent of the massive brain damage. The family has come together to pull the plug.

Mamie's daughter sits on one side of the bed in the ICU; Mamie's husband of sixty years sits on the other. He strokes her leopard-spotted hand as if it were a good-luck charm, oblivious to the tears that have made a small wet spot in the waffle-weave blanket that covers Mamie's thin legs.

The daughter looks to the resident beside the heart-lung machine, then at her father. 'All right, Daddy?' The elderly man just bows his head.

She nods to the doctor and is suddenly stopped by the strident sound of her mother's voice. 'Isabelle Louise!' Mamie shouts, sitting up in bed. 'What in the name of the good Lord do you think you're doing?'

'Mother?' the woman breathes.

'Mamie!' her husband yells. 'Oh, God. God! Mamie!'

The old woman yanks the breathing tube out of her nose. 'What kind of contraption have you got me hooked up to, Albert?'

'Lie down, Mother. You had a stroke.' The daughter looks at the doctor, who first steps away in shock and then falls to checking Mamie.

'Get a nurse,' the doctor orders Albert. But it takes a moment, because Albert cannot tear his eyes away from the woman who has defined him for half a century, the woman whose passing would have made a major part of him die, too. Then he rushes into the corridor with the energy of a man half his age, waving his arms and shouting for medical personnel to come quickly, to converge on the ICU room that happens to be one floor directly above that of Faith White's.

In the middle of the night Faith's arm shifts and strikes me across the face. The pediatric ICU offers a cot for the parent who's sleeping in, but I preferred to crawl into the narrow bed with Faith. This way, I could protect her, be there if she was in pain.

Faith tosses and turns, and I press my lips to her forehead. Immediately, I draw back—she is burning up, hotter than I can ever remember her being. I lunge toward the headboard and push the call button.

'Yes?'

'My daughter's got a fever.'

'We'll be right in.'

When the nurses come, poking and prodding with thermometers and sponges of alcohol, Faith doesn't even stir. There is a strange soundtrack accompanying their movements; it takes me a moment to recognize it as a rhythmic, tiny moan coming from deep inside Faith.

'Can't you page Dr Blumberg?'

'Mrs White,' says one nurse, 'just let us do our job, all right?'

But I am her mother, I want to say. Won't you let me do *mine*?

'She's a hundred and five point five,' I hear one nurse murmur.

A hundred and five? I start thinking of infections of the blood, spinal meningitis, spreading cancers. If it was serious, wouldn't the tests this evening have picked it up—a high white-blood-cell count? But if it *wasn't* serious, why would she have such a high fever?

I do not want to leave her, but I know I have an obligation. Stepping into the hallway, I ask to borrow the phone at the nurses' station. There are too many people crowded into Faith's room to let me use the one beside the bed. I rummage in my purse and unfold a small green sheet of paper with a phone number on it. 'Jessica, this is Mariah White,' I manage to say. 'Can you tell Colin that Faith's taken a turn for the worse?'

When Malcolm Metz gets to the office, called by an extremely apologetic Elkland—who was pulling an all-nighter when Colin White stormed into the lobby like an unconfined tiger—his head is still wet from his shower and his eyes are bloodshot. It pisses him off, particularly because he likes to look his best on days he litigates, yet he's due in court in less than five hours, and he's going to look as if he's been out carousing the whole night before. He draws up short at the sight of his client—hair standing in tufts around his head, jacket looking slept in . . . and is that blood on the sleeve?

'Christ,' Metz says. 'You look worse than *I* do.'

'Okay,' Colin begins, not even bothering to look at his attorney. 'This is the thing. She's in pain. She's in the goddamned hospital. And I don't care what you say, people listen to TV, and it's going to sway what the judge thinks. Look at that nanny trial in Boston! I'm paying you a shitload of money to get a winning verdict. And I'm telling you, it's happening to her in the house, Malcolm. I saw it with my own eyes. Someone or something in there is making her sick.'

'Hang on,' Metz says. 'Who's sick? Who's in the hospital?'

Colin looks at him as if he is crazy. 'Faith.'

Metz's eyes widen. 'Faith's in the hospital?'

'She started bleeding last night. It happened right in front of me. She was just standing there and all of a sudden . . .' He shakes his head. 'Christ, I've got to believe they can do more than give her drugs to take the edge off. I mean . . . something has to happen to make you bleed.'

Metz holds up a hand. 'Your daughter is is the hospital,' he clarifies.

'Yeah.'

'She's under observation.'

'That's right.'

A smile breaks across Metz's face. 'Oh, God, how perfect.'

At Colin's glare he hastens to explain himself. 'We've been working up an angle for your case, Colin, and strangely enough, this corroborates it.' As Elkland outlines Munchausen Syndrome by Proxy for Colin, Metz thinks back to his original ex parte motion, lobbed at the judge for the hell of it, but clearly now an unconscious stroke of genius. 'Picture this: We walk into chambers this morning and file an emergency motion, begging Rothbottam to separate Faith from her mother because her life is in serious jeopardy. The first time we did it, he thought we were bluffing, and he let her stay with her mother. But thanks to his faulty judgment, the kid's now in the hospital. I explain Munchausen's and tell him that our expert will prove why we need this emergency provision. Then I ask for a court order keeping Mariah away from Faith. The judge will feel so guilty about throwing out the first motion that this time he'll jump right through my hoop.'

Colin stares at him, scowling. 'I've never heard of this Munchausen thing.'

Metz grins. 'Me neither. But by the time the hearing's over, we'll be pros.'

He shakes his head. 'I don't know, Malcolm. Mariah . . . well, she may be a little preoccupied with herself sometimes, but she'd never intentionally hurt Faith.'

Elkland bites her lip. 'Mr White, from what I've read, that's part of the psychological disorder—looking like the ideal, concerned parent while you lie about what you've done.'

'I stood two feet away from Faith last night and watched her just start to bleed,' Colin says slowly. 'She didn't prick herself on anything; she didn't touch anything at all, in fact . . . and Mariah was even farther away than I was. But you're saying that you think . . . you think—'

Metz shakes his head. 'The question isn't what *I* think, or what *you* think, Colin,' he says, 'but rather, what do you want the judge to think?'

Kenzie is asleep beside her laptop when the phone rings. 'Ms van der Hoven,' says a silky voice when she lifts the receiver.

It would be impossible, even in her state of muzzy confusion, to not recognize Malcolm Metz. 'You're up early.'

'Five A.M. is the best part of the day.'

'I wouldn't know.'

Metz chuckles. 'I guess you've already sent in your report.'

With a sinking sensation, Kenzie looks at the computer screen, blank as a wall.

'I assume you faxed it to His Honor last night so the judge could read it before today's trial. But I felt honor-bound to let you know something before court began.'

'Which is what, Mr Metz?'

'Faith White was hospitalized last night.'

At that, Kenzie snaps upright. 'She *what?*'

'As I understand from my client, she started bleeding from her hands again, and that escalated into a more serious condition.'

'Oh, my God. Who's with her now?'

'Her mother, I assume.' There is a hesitation on the line. 'But I wanted you to know that I plan to amend that. I'm asking the judge for a restraining order to keep Mariah away from the child. I have reason to believe that Mariah's the one who's harming Faith.'

'You have evidence?' she asks.

'I've come to the conclusion that Mrs White suffers from a certain psychological disorder. I have an expert who's reviewed the case, and who agrees with me.'

'I see.'

'Well, you will anyway. I just thought you might like to know in advance,' Metz says, and then he hangs up.

Kenzie turns on her computer and waits for the screen to spring to life. It makes her wince—too much energy all at once. She begins to type furiously, hoping that she will have a chance to visit Faith before court is in session, hoping that if there is indeed a heavenly being watching over Faith, it can follow her into an ambulance, a hospital, a new and safer home.

'*I recommend that custody of Faith White*,' she types, '*be awarded to her father.*'

fourteen

He saved others; himself he cannot save.

—Matthew 27:42

December 3, 1999—Morning

THERE HAD BEEN TIMES, when Faith was an infant and Mariah was still slightly amazed to find a baby sleeping beside her or nursing at her own breast, that she'd be overwhelmed with terror. Years stretched out in front of her like red roads on a map, filled with hazards and errors. Faith's life, at that point, was unmarked and unscarred. It was up to Mariah to keep it that way.

It became clear to her quickly that this was a job she could never adequately fill, not without feeling deficient. How could she even be considered remotely qualified to be a mother, knowing that she was every bit as fallible as this baby was perfect? In the stitch of a moment, anything could go wrong—an earthquake, a viral flu, a pacifier dropped into the gutter. She would look into her daughter's face and see accidents waiting to happen. And then her vision would clear and she would see only love, a well so deep that you could try and try and never know its bottom, but only suck in your breath at its frightening depth.

Faith stirs in her sleep, and immediately Mariah turns. Of its own volition, Faith's bandaged hand twitches across the covers of the hospital bed and burrows beneath Mariah's. At the contact, Faith stops moving and relaxes again.

Suddenly Mariah wonders if moments like this are what qualify you as a good parent: realizing that no matter how you try, you will not be able to protect a child from the tragedies or the missteps or the nightmares. Maybe the job of a mother is not to shelter but to bear witness as a child hits full force . . . and then to cushion the fall when it's over.

Mariah's hands are pressed tight against her mouth. She has to keep them that way, because if she doesn't she will surely break into loud, hoarse sobs or shout at one of the well-meaning nurses to get away from her daughter.

'I don't understand,' Millie says quietly, standing with Mariah a few feet from Faith's bed. 'She's never been sick like this before. Maybe it's a bug, something she caught on top of the bleeding.'

'It's not a bug,' Mariah whispers. 'She's dying.'

Millie looks up, startled. 'What on earth makes you say that?'

'*Look* at her.'

Faith is pale against the hospital sheets. Her hands, still oozing blood, are matted with bandages that have not yet been changed. Her fever has fluctuated from 104 to 106 degrees, no matter how many tepid baths and alcohol washes and grams of Tylenol and Advil she's been given intravenously. Watching her makes Mariah nervous. She finds herself staring at the slight flare of Faith's nostrils, counting the subtle rhythms of her chest.

Millie purses her mouth and walks from Faith's room to the comparative quiet of the front desk. 'Has Colin White called?' she asks, knowing that the phones in Faith's room have been diverted to allow her to sleep.

'No, Mrs Epstein,' the nurse says. 'I'll come in the minute he does.'

Instead of returning to Faith, Millie moves down the corridor. There, she leans against the wall and covers her face with her hands.

'Mrs Epstein?'

She quickly wipes away tears to find Dr Blumberg standing before her. 'Don't mind me,' she sniffs.

They fall into step, slowing as they approach the door to Faith's room. 'Has there been any change since last night?'

'Not that I can tell,' Millie says, pausing at the threshold. 'I'm worried about Mariah. Maybe you could say something.'

Dr Blumberg nods and enters the room. Mariah lifts her eyes just enough to see the nurses scatter. The physician pulls up a chair. 'How are you doing?'

'I'd rather talk about Faith,' Mariah answers.

'Well, I'm not sure what to do for her just yet. You, though . . . you want something to help you sleep?'

'I want Faith to wake up and come home with me,' she says firmly, staring at the shell of Faith's ear. There were times when Faith was a baby that Mariah would watch the blood coursing through the thin membrane of skin, thinking that surely she could see the platelets and the cells, the energy going to this tiny body.

Dr Blumberg clasps his hands between his knees. 'I don't know what's the matter with her, Mariah. I'll run more lab tests this morning. And I'll do whatever I can to keep her comfortable; you have my word on that.'

Mariah stares at the doctor. 'You want to know what's the matter with her? She's dying. How come I can see that, even without a medical degree?'

'She's not dying. If that were the case, I'd tell you.'

Mariah focuses on Faith's face with a passion, gazing at the blue smudges beneath her eyes, the tiny slope of her nose. She leans close, so close that only Faith will be able to hear her words. 'Don't you give up on me,' she whispers. 'Don't you dare. You didn't for years and years. Don't you do it now.'

'Mariah, honey, we've got to go to court.' Millie taps her wristwatch. 'Ten o'clock.'

'I'm not going.'

'You don't have a choice.'

Mariah turns so quickly her mother takes a step back. 'I'm

not going. I'm *not* leaving her.' She touches Faith's cheek. 'I do have a choice.'

The only concession that Joan Standish has made to the fact that she'll be facing the infamous Malcolm Metz in a courtroom is the addition of fifteen minutes of butt exercises to her daily routine. They come in between brushing her teeth and drinking coffee, a brutal procession of squats and lunges and lifts that leave her clenched and sweating. She likes to picture Metz while she does them, imagines him gaping at her fanny after she wins the case and sashays away down the hall of the superior court.

So on the morning of the custody hearing, she does her exercises, showers, and then pulls a red wool suit from her closet. It's conservative, but it's bright, and she's willing to use any trick she can to draw attention away from Malcolm Metz.

Sometime during her bowl of Frosted Mini-Wheats she remembers that she needs gas in her car. Joan gives herself a mental pat on the back for attention to detail; maybe even at this very moment Metz is running ten minutes late because he forgot to fill up. She washes her hands carefully so as not to splatter her suit and gathers up the briefcase she's packed the night before.

She leaves twenty minutes ahead of schedule, thinking it's good to be a little early, never knowing that the phone in her house rings just moments after she is gone.

Joan can feel the perfect cone of calm she's erected around her professional self crack the moment Millie Epstein comes running toward her, clearly agitated. 'Tell me Mariah's in the bathroom,' Joan says warily.

'The hospital. I tried to call you.'

'*What?*'

'It's not what you think,' she explains. 'It's Faith. She's incredibly sick, and Mariah refuses to leave her.'

'Goddamn it,' Joan mutters as Malcolm Metz and Colin and a young female associate approach the plaintiff's table of the courtroom.

'Joan,' Metz says pleasantly, 'I've got one for you: What's the difference between a lawyer and a catfish?'

'Not now.' Joan is vaguely aware that the gallery of the court, usually deserted for custody hearings, is now packed to the point of discomfort with media representatives.

'One's a scum-sucking bottom feeder,' Metz says, laughing, 'and the other one's a fish. Get it?'

'Speak for yourself, Malcolm,' Joan says, extracting files.

'All rise for the Honorable Judge A. Warren Rothbottam!'

Joan stands, lifting her gaze at the last possible moment. Judge Rothbottam flips briefly through the file in front of him, then glances from the plaintiff to the defendant. 'Ms Standish. Are you missing something?'

'My client, Your Honor. May I approach?'

Rothbottam sighs. 'I just knew this one couldn't go easy. Come on up.'

Metz falls into place beside Joan, looking like the cat that has swallowed the canary. 'Your Honor,' Joan says, 'there's been a terrible emergency. My client's daughter was hospitalized last night, and she won't leave her bedside in order to be present in court. I request a continuance until the girl is released from the hospital.'

'Hospitalized?' Rothbottam looks for confirmation to Metz, who shrugs. 'Is she dying?'

'I don't believe so,' Joan answers. 'It's my understanding that Faith is suffering from medically inexplicable bleeding.'

'So-called stigmata,' Metz interjects.

'The doctors have not come to that conclusion yet,' Joan snaps.

'Oh, that's right. It could be something worse.'

Rothbottam scowls at him. 'If I feel that I need an interpreter, Mr Metz, you'll be the first one I call.' Turning to Joan, he says, 'I assume the girl is in critical condition?'

'I . . . I think so, Your Honor.'

'I see. However, the child's father managed to make it to the courtroom; I expect the mother to do the same. And don't think I can't see through some "angel of mercy" device. My docket is a nightmare until Christmas. I'm denying the request for a continuance. You've got twenty minutes to figure out how to get your client to come to court, or I'm sending a sheriff out there to bring her in locked up. We'll resume at ten-thirty.'

'Before she goes to find the defendant, Your Honor,' Metz interjects, 'I need a court order.'

'Do you,' the judge says dryly.

'Your Honor, time is of the essence here, and I need a ruling this morning on an issue that might make the difference between life and death for the girl.'

'What the hell is this?' Joan says. 'An emergency hearing? Now?'

Metz bares his teeth at her. 'That's why they call it an emergency, Joan.'

'That's it,' Rothbottam announces. 'I want you two in chambers. Now.'

Joan walks to the defense table to collect her notepad. Seeing the judge leave, she runs down the aisle to the door and beckons Millie. As a sequestered witness, she's not in the courtroom—but isn't allowed to stray too far. 'Do whatever it takes to get her here,' Joan hisses. 'She'd better be in court by the time I get out of chambers, or she'll be dragged in by the police.'

When Joan enters the judge's chambers, Metz has already taken the comfortable chair. Rothbottam waits for Joan to sit, too. 'Malcolm, what are you doing? This isn't Manchester. This isn't New York City. This isn't the three-ring circus you like to run your dog-and-pony show in. This is New Canaan, boy. Grandstanding isn't going to get you jackshit.'

'Your Honor, this isn't just a ploy for positioning. I need a restraining order against Mariah White, preventing her from visiting her daughter.'

Joan laughs. 'Get over yourself, Malcolm.'

'Your Honor, I won't dignify that outburst. I was concerned enough when the physical damage to the child just involved Faith's hands, but the situation's gotten worse—the child is in critical condition at Connecticut Valley Medical Center. We've taken the liberty of contacting an expert, who's on his way here from the West Coast as we speak, and who will explain why Mariah White exhibits the classic characteristics of a person suffering from Munchausen Syndrome by Proxy—a mental illness that would cause her to harm her own daughter.'

Joan narrows her eyes, smelling a rat. She's savvy enough to know that Metz wouldn't pull this strategy out of a hat overnight. It's something he's had lined up for a while, certainly long enough for her to depose his expert. This surprise witness is no surprise at all—at least not to Metz.

But he is the picture of innocence and righteous fervor. 'It's a complicated disorder. The mother actually makes a child physically or psychologically ill to attract attention to herself. If the child is left in the mother's care, well, God only knows what might eventually happen. Paralysis, coma, even death. Clearly, this issue will weigh upon who gets custody of the child in the long run, but for now, Your Honor, I beg you to protect Faith by issuing a restraining order against Mrs White for the length of the trial.'

Joan waits for him to stop speaking, and then bursts out laughing. 'Are you going to let him get away with this, Your Honor?'

Metz doesn't even spare her a glance. 'Just listen to the evidence, Your Honor. Isolating the child from the mother is the way Munchausen by Proxy is usually detected by mental-health professionals. If the mother can't get to the child, the child suddenly isn't sick all the time.' He leans forward. 'What have you got to lose, Judge? This is a win-win situation. If Mariah White isn't suffering from Munchausen by Proxy . . . well, Faith's in the hospital anyway, and in good hands. If Mrs White *is* suffering from it, then you've saved the kid's life. How can it possibly hurt to have a temporary order enforced until you've listened to the testimony of my expert and drawn a conclusion of your own?'

Judge Rothbottam turns to Joan. 'You have anything to say, Standish?'

She looks at Metz, then at the judge. 'This is bullshit, Your Honor. In the first place, unlike Mr Metz's client, who clearly is putting his own interests first, the reason *my* client isn't here is because she needs to be at her daughter's bedside. That merits a commendation, not a restraining order. In the second place, Mr Metz is trying to divert attention from my client's devotion to her child with this new disease-of-the-week ploy. I don't know what this syndrome is; I don't even know how to spell the damn thing. This trial is starting in less than a half hour, and I'm ready to go, but out of nowhere Metz waltzes in with this obscure clinical diagnosis—not that I remember him getting a degree in psychology, come to think of it—and I'm going to need time to research it and make a rebuttal.'

'M-U-N—' Metz says slowly.

'Go jump in a lake.'

He raises his hands in mock affront. 'Just trying to help you "spell the damn thing."'

'I'm not done yet, Metz.' She turns toward the judge. 'He can't pull in a witness from thin air the day—no, correction—the minute the trial starts. That's totally unfair.'

Judge Rothbottam turns to Metz. 'If you cut out all the soliloquies I'm sure you've budgeted into your directs, how long will it take to run through your other witnesses?'

'I don't know. Possibly into tomorrow.'

Rothbottam considers for a moment. 'All right. I'll grant the restraining order for now. Let's play it by ear. We'll start the trial, and, Mr Metz, you'll put your Munchausen expert on last. When it comes to that, we'll adjourn to chambers and see if Ms Standish needs more time to prepare her cross.'

'I think it would be beneficial if everyone could hear testimony on the disorder first—'

'You're lucky I'm letting you put the guy on the stand, period. This is what we're doing. I like it—the child is safe, Joan gets at least a day to prepare, and frankly, Metz, I don't care what you think at all.' The judge cracks his knuckles and gestures toward the door. 'Shall we?'

Early that morning Father MacReady walks into Faith's room. He stops for a moment at the threshold, taken by the sight of Faith, intubated and deathly still, of Mariah holding her daughter's forearm and dozing. Perhaps this wasn't the time to bother them; he'd just heard from one of the parishioners that the girl had been taken off in an ambulance the night before, and he wanted to pay a call. He backs up toward the door quietly, but the sound of his boots on the linoleum makes Mariah startle awake.

'Oh,' she says huskily, then clears her throat. When she realizes who the visitor is, she becomes visibly upset. 'Why are *you* here?'

Father MacReady puts two and two together, realizes that for some reason Mariah thinks he's been summoned for last rites. It would never happen, since Faith is not a Catholic child, and yet that hasn't stopped his interference in her life before. He sits down beside Mariah on a chair. 'I'm here as a friend, not as a priest,' he says.

He gazes at Faith's small, pinched face—so tiny to have caused so much controversy. 'It was her hands again?'

Mariah nods. 'Now it's her fever, too. And her dehydration. And the screaming and the fits.' She rubs her hands over her face. 'It was worse than the first time, much worse.'

'Fits?'

She shudders. 'Colin and I—we could barely hold her down. The first time this happened, she was unconscious. But this time . . . this time she hurt.'

Father MacReady gently strokes his palm along Faith's cheek. '*"Eli, Eli, lama sabachthani,"*' he murmurs.

The words make Mariah go still. 'What did you say?'

Surprised, he turns. 'It's Hebrew, actually.'

Mariah thinks back to the previous night, when Faith called out for Eli. She cannot be sure of the other unfamiliar syllables, but they could have been what Faith was moaning, as well. She tells this to the priest.

'It's a biblical verse,' he says. 'Matthew twenty-seven: forty-six.'

'Faith doesn't speak Hebrew.'

'But Jesus did. That was his language. The words translate to "My God, My God, why hast thou forsaken me?" Saint Matthew tells us that Christ didn't go gently into that good night. At the last moment, he wanted to know why God was making him go through this.' He hesitates, then looks at Mariah. 'The bleeding, the pain, that phrase—it sounds like Faith was in ecstasy.'

'Agony is more like it.'

'It's not the word as you know it. Most accredited stigmatics experience periods of religious ecstasy. Without it, it's just bleeding from the hands.' At that moment Faith shifts in her sleep, and the blanket falls away to reveal the wound on her side. Father MacReady draws in a breath. 'This, too?' When Mariah nods, he knows that he is fairly glowing, that his response is inappropriate for the severity of the occasion. But the wound on Faith's right side falls almost exactly where Jesus was supposedly nailed to the cross. It makes him dizzy, just to think of it.

Sobering, he calls upon his resources as a pastoral counselor. 'Mariah, Faith isn't feeling pain of her own. From everything you've told me, she was simply reliving Jesus' pain, acting out his sufferings on the cross.'

'Why her?'

'Why Him?' Father MacReady says quietly. 'We don't know why God gave us His only son, to die for our own sins. And we don't know why God lets some people experience the Passion of Christ when others can't even understand it.'

'Passion,' Mariah spits out. 'Ecstasy. Whoever came up with these names didn't go through it.'

'Passion comes from the Latin *passio*. "To suffer."'

Mariah turns away from Father MacReady's earnest convictions. Passion. She repeats the word softly to herself, and thinks of Ian, of Colin, of Faith, wondering if all love—earthly or divine—is certain to hurt.

When the nurses come to take Faith for x-rays again, Mariah says good-bye to the priest. She does not particularly care what happens to Father MacReady. She does not care if Faith is experiencing Christ's suffering or her own. She only wants it to go away.

Faith is sitting in a wheelchair, nodding in and out of sleep. Mariah's hand rests on her shoulder as the nurse wheels her into the elevator. They get out on the third floor and wait in the hallway while the nurse finds out which room they are headed to.

While they stay there, a man is rushed by on a stretcher,

surrounded by a knot of doctors all working frantically en route to the ER. Mariah hears them yelling out things about defibrillation and operating room number three and she shudders, thinking of her mother's heart. The man's hand dangles off the stretcher, brushes Faith's knee as he is wheeled by.

But Faith, moaning softly, doesn't even seem to notice.

'*Mariah*.'

When she doesn't answer, Millie grabs her shoulders and gives her a shake. 'Have you heard anything I've been saying?'

'You go, Ma. I'll try to come later.'

'You don't understand. If you don't get up and walk out this door, the police will physically carry you out.' Millie leans over her. 'If you don't come to the hearing, *Colin will get Faith*.'

That one sentence spikes through Mariah's confusion. 'He can't,' she says, slowly getting to her feet. 'He just can't.'

Millie tugs her upright, sensing that she's started to make some progress. She folds Mariah into her coat with the easy motions of a mother. 'Then stop him,' she says.

'Call it.' Dr Urquhart sighs. In OR Three the cardiac surgeon strips off his gloves and balls them inside out, trapping the blood from his patient's chest within. He hears a nurse say 'nine fifty-eight,' and the faint scratch of her pen on the patient's chart. Urquhart's fingers are throbbing. Ten minutes of manual stimulation had not been enough to save the man, but then again, having cracked open the fellow's chest, Urquhart knows that another few rashers of bacon would have finished him off, too. At 80 and 75 percent blockage, respectively, it's a wonder that Mr Eversly made it this long.

He hears one of the surgical residents readying to prepare the patient so that he'll be fit for a final viewing by family. With a groan, Urquhart realizes the worst is yet to come. There's nothing worse than telling a relative a patient's died under the knife, right before Christmas.

He takes the patient's chart to sign off on the death, goes so far as to click his ballpoint pen, and then he's stopped by the voice of the resident. 'Dr Urquhart. Look at this.'

He follows her eyes to the monitor—no longer a flatline—and then to the open chest cavity of the patient, inside which a heart—healthy, unclogged—is furiously beating.

'All rise! The Honorable A. Warren Rothbottam presiding!'

The courtroom swells with the sound of feet hitting the ground and pocket change jingling as everyone stands. The judge stalks to his seat, one eye on the group of onlookers packing the gallery. Rothbottam has heard that so many people were trying to get in, the bailiffs had to hold a lottery for the open seats.

He glances at the defendant's table and sees Mariah White, thank the good Lord, just where she ought to be. Her hands are folded, her eyes trained on them as if they might at any moment fly up and betray her.

Rothbottam levels his gaze on the gallery. 'Let's get this straight right now. I'm neither foolish nor naïve enough to assume that the congestion of bodies in this courtroom has anything to do with my prowess as a judge or a sudden media interest in routine custody hearings. I know exactly who you all are and what you think you're doing here. Well, this is not your news station. This is my courtroom. And in it, *I'm* God.' He braces his hands on the bench. 'If I see a camera come in with one of you, if I hear you cough too loud, if anyone applauds or boos a witness—at the first sign of any crap, you're all out of here. And you can quote me on that.'

The reporters roll their eyes at each other. 'Counselors,' Rothbottam says to the attorneys. 'I'm going to assume no other emergency motions have cropped up in the past half hour?'

'No, Your Honor,' Metz says. Joan shakes her head.

'Terrific.' He nods at Metz. 'You may begin.'

Malcolm gets to his feet, squeezes Colin's shoulder, and adjusts the button on the jacket of his suit. Then he walks over to the podium beside the stenographer and angles it slightly, pointing it in the direction of the gallery.

'Mr Metz,' the judge says. 'What are you doing?'

'I know it goes against the norm of a custody hearing, but I've prepared a short opening statement, Your Honor.'

'Do you see a jury, Counselor? Because I don't. And I already know everything about this case that you do.'

Metz stares at him evenly. 'I have a right to give an opening statement, and I'm going to object on the record, Your Honor, if you don't let me.'

The judge thinks, briefly, of what he could be doing if he'd retired five years early, as his wife wanted: watching the waves roll in on a Florida beach, driving a motor home into a national park, listening to Betty Buckley sing again on Broadway. Instead, he's stuck watching Malcolm Metz play to an audience, because the last thing he wants is for Metz to have grounds for appeal. 'Ms Standish,' the judge says, resigned, 'do you have a problem with this?'

'No, Your Honor. I'd actually like to see it.'

Rothbottam inclines his head. 'Make it brief, Counselor.'

Malcolm Metz stands silently behind the podium for a moment, pretending to gather words that have been memorized cold for the past week. 'You know,' he says, 'when I was seven years old, I used to go fishing with my dad. He taught me how to pick the best worm from the overturned earth . . . how to thread it on the hook just so . . . how to reel in a striper that was the most beautiful thing on earth. And after we went fishing, just the two of us, we'd go to the diner down the road from the pond and he'd buy me a root beer and we'd sit and count the cars that passed by on the highway.

'Then my dad and I would go home, and Mom would have a big lunch waiting. Sometimes it was soup, sometimes a ham sandwich . . . and while she set the table, I'd go outside and look under the porch for spiders, or lie on my back and stare at the clouds. Do you know what Faith White is doing at the age of seven? She's lying on a hospital bed, hooked up to intravenous tubes, getting blood drawn from a dozen different places on her body. She's in excruciating pain, both mental and physical. She has a battalion of nurses and doctors watching her around the clock, and people gathered outside the hospital doors waiting to hear about her welfare. I ask you: Is this any way to spend a childhood?' He shakes his head sadly. 'I think not. In fact, this child has not been able to be a child for some time. Which is why her father—my client—has made a place for his daughter, ready to take her with open arms and protect her from the unsavory influences that brought her to the point where she is now . . . that continue to endanger her very life.'

'All right,' Rothbottam bellows. 'Approach!'

Metz and Joan walk to the bench. The judge covers his microphone. 'Mr Metz, let me give you a tip: I'm not going to make a ruling based on what you say to the media reps here today. I highly recommend you wrap this up now, because you've started to piss me off.'

Metz returns to his podium and clears his throat. 'In conclusion, we're going to prove that—without a doubt—custody should go to Colin White. Thank you.' He nods, and goes to sit behind Colin.

'Ms Standish,' the judge says, 'do you want to make an opening argument, too?'

Joan gets to her feet and fans herself with her hand. 'Can you give me a minute, Your Honor? I'm still feeling a little emotional from that speech—the fishing and all.' She takes a cleansing breath and then smiles prettily at the judge. 'Ah. I'm better now. Actually, I don't think I have anything to say at this moment that could possibly top that. Tell you what, though: If I feel the need to pontificate, maybe I could do it at the beginning of my case?'

'Fine. Mr Metz, you can call your first witness.'

With an encouraging look at his client, Metz calls Colin White to the stand. Colin rises, managing to look sheepish and polished all at once. He steps into the witness box and turns toward the clerk of the court, who is holding out a Bible. 'Do you swear to tell the truth, the whole truth, and nothing but the truth?'

'I do.'

Malcolm approaches the stand and has Colin state his name and address. 'Mr White,' he begins, 'what's your relationship to Faith?'

'I'm her father.'

'Just for background, can you tell us about the circumstances of this past summer?'

'I was having trouble with my marriage,' Colin admits. 'I didn't know who to talk to about it.'

Metz frowns. 'Why not your wife?'

'Well, she has a history of being emotionally fragile, and I was a little scared of what she might do if I told her I felt that the marriage was in trouble.'

'What do you mean?'

'She was institutionalized seven years ago for depression, after she tried to kill herself.'

'If you didn't confront her, then what happened to initiate the divorce proceedings?'

'Well,' Colin says, reddening, 'I sought the solace of another woman.'

Beside her, Mariah hears Joan murmur, 'Oh, for God's sake . . .' She feels herself root more firmly in the seat, afraid to breathe or move a muscle, because in spite of Colin's embarrassed admission, she wants only to sink through the floor.

'Then what happened?' Metz prods gently.

'One day this woman was at my house, and my wife found out about us.'

'That must have been very uncomfortable for you, Colin.'

'It was,' he admits. 'God, I felt terrible about it.'

'What action did you take at that time?'

'I was selfish. I just knew that I needed to get my life together. I guess I thought that Faith would be all right with Mariah while I did . . . but in the back of my mind I understood that at some point I was going to want my daughter to come live with me.'

'Did you ask her to live with you?'

'Not then,' Colin says, grimacing. 'I didn't think it was right to uproot her when her family had just broken apart.'

'So what did you do?'

'I filed for divorce. I tried to visit Faith whenever I could. And I made it implicitly clear to my ex-wife—at least I thought I did—that I still wanted Faith to be a part of my life. After I . . . left, I tried to go back and see her. One time I practically got shoved out the door. But Faith wanted to see me then; I know she did.'

'Colin, maybe you can share with us some special moments you had with Faith.'

'Oh, we used to be very close. There are little things that stay with me . . . like brushing out her hair after her bath, or pulling up the covers when she was asleep. Having her bury my feet in the sand.'

'What is your current marital status?'

Colin smiles toward the gallery, where Jessica gives him a tiny wave. 'I've been happily married for the past two months, and in fact we're going to have a baby. Faith's going to love having a baby brother or sister.'

'Don't you think people might wonder why, in two scant months, you've changed your mind about who should have custody of your daughter?'

Colin nods. 'I'm not saying I've been perfect. I haven't. I've made mistakes that I wish I could take back. But I never changed my mind about Faith. I just wasn't willing to take her out of a familiar environment when the rest of her world had been turned upside down.' He looks at Jessica. 'I love my new wife, and I love the life we're making for ourselves. I can't be a father to this new child without being one to Faith. I need her. And from what I've seen, she needs me just as badly.'

Metz crosses in front of the judge. 'Colin, why are you here now?'

He swallows hard. 'Well, not too long ago I turned on the news one night and my daughter was the feature story. She was hospitalized, and there was this insane story about her being a religious visionary and her hands bleeding, for God's sake. All I could think was that Mariah cut open her wrists once, and here she was alone with my daughter, and all of a sudden Faith was bleeding. I always knew my wife was crazy, but—'

'Objection!'

The judge frowns. 'I'm not going to listen to what you just said, Mr White. Please answer the questions as they are asked.'

Metz turns back to his client. 'What made you file for a change of custody?'

'I realized several weeks ago that Faith wasn't nearly as safe as I'd thought.'

'Did you ever have any previous reason to believe that Mariah wasn't a fit caretaker?'

'Not since years ago, when she'd just been released from Greenhaven. She was pretty fragile back then, and taking care of herself was hard enough, not to mention a newborn. But then things got better, much better—or so I believed,' Colin says.

'Do you feel you can provide a safer home for Faith?'

'God, yes. We live in a wonderful neighborhood, with a terrific backyard for her to play in—and I wouldn't let the reporters get to her. I'd nip the whole issue in the bud, just so that she could have her childhood back.'

'As a father, how do you feel about Faith's situation?'

Colin's eyes meet Mariah's. His are wide and honest and bright. 'I'm worried about her,' he says. 'I think her life is in danger. And I think her mother is to blame.'

Mariah tugs on Joan's sleeve before she stands to do the cross-examination. 'They think I hurt Faith,' she whispers, stunned. 'They think I'm doing this to her?'

Joan squeezes her client's hand. She's coached Mariah to expect the worst, but—like Mariah—she figured that would mean some calculated barbs about her hospitalization, not posing her as an abusive parent. Mariah's late arrival at court prevented Joan from warning her about Metz's strategy, and she is not about to break the news to her client now, in the middle of testimony, that the judge has instructed Mariah to have no contact with Faith for the duration of the trial. 'Relax. Just let me do my job.' Joan stands, staring at Colin long and hard, so that he knows just how reprehensible she truly thinks he is. 'Mr White,' she says coolly, 'you say your marriage was in trouble.'

'Yes.'

'Yet you didn't talk about this with your wife, because she was emotionally fragile.'

'That's correct.'

'Can you define "emotionally fragile" for me?'

'Objection,' Metz says. 'My client isn't a professional in the field of psychology.'

'Then he shouldn't have used the term in the first place,' Joan counters.

'I'll allow the question,' the judge says.

Colin shifts in his chair, uncomfortable. 'She was in a mental institution seven years ago, because she had suicidal tendencies.'

'Ah, that's right. You said she tried to kill herself.'

Colin glances at Mariah. 'Yes.'

'She just tried to kill herself out of the blue?'

'No, she was very depressed at the time.'

'I see. Was there any reason that she was depressed?'

Colin nods shortly.

'I'm sorry, Mr White. You're going to have to speak up for the court stenographer.'

'Yes.'

Joan moves beside Mariah, so that the judge's eye—not to mention the voracious gaze of the press in the gallery—must fall on her as well. 'Maybe you could help us out by telling us the reason she was depressed.' Seeing the mutinous set of Colin's jaw, she crosses her arms. 'I can ask you, Mr White, or you can tell me.'

'I was having an affair, and she found out.'

'You were having an affair seven years ago, and it made your wife depressed. And four months ago, when you were having yet another affair, you were worried that the discovery might make her depressed again?'

'Correct.'

'Was the only mistake you made in your marriage these liaisons with other women?'

'I think so.'

'Would it be correct to say that these two incidents—four months ago and seven years ago—were the only times in your marriage that you—how did you put it?—that you felt a need to *seek solace*.'

'Yes.'

'I guess, then, that the names Cynthia Snow-Harding and Helen Xavier don't ring a bell.'

As Colin turns white as his shirt, Mariah digs her nails into her thighs. Joan had warned her this was coming, and yet she still feels like running out of the room, or maybe up to the witness stand to scratch his eyes out. How could Joan have so quickly discovered something Mariah had not known for years?

Because, Mariah thinks, *she wanted* to know. I didn't.

'Isn't it true, Mr White, that Cynthia Snow-Harding and Helen Xavier are two additional women with whom you had affairs?'

Colin glances toward Metz, fuming behind the plaintiff's table. 'I wouldn't say they were affairs,' he quickly responds. 'They were very brief . . . connections.'

Joan snorts. 'Why don't we move along?' she suggests. 'When your wife, Mariah, became severely depressed seven years ago after finding out that you were having an affair with another woman, you say she was institutionalized.'

'Yes. At the Greenhaven Institute.'

'Did the people from Greenhaven just show up at your door to get her?'

'No,' Colin says. 'I arranged to have her sent there.'

'Really?' Joan feigns shock. 'Did you try psychiatric counseling for Mariah first?'

'Well, briefly. It didn't seem to be working.'

'Did you ask the psychiatrist to have Mariah put on medication?'

'I was more worried about what she—'

'Just answer the question, Mr White,' Joan interrupts.

'No, I did not ask the psychiatrist that.'

'Did you try to support her through this crisis?'

'I did support her through it,' Colin says tightly. 'I know it's easy to make me look like the bad guy, the one who locked up his wife so he could conveniently keep having an affair. But I did what I felt was best for Mariah. I loved my wife, but she was . . . like a different person, and I couldn't make the old Mariah come back. You don't know until you've lived with someone who's suicidal—how you keep obsessing over the fact that you didn't see this coming, how you blame yourself for the really bad days, how you panic about keeping them safe. I could barely forgive myself every time I looked at her, because—somehow—I'd turned her into that. I wouldn't have been able to handle it if she'd tried to kill herself again.' He looks into his lap. 'It was already my fault. I only wanted to do something right for a change.'

Mariah feels something turn over in her chest. It is the first time she's truly considered that being sent to Greenhaven might have hurt Colin as well as herself.

'Did you take time off work to be home with Mariah, so that you could keep watch over her for safety's sake?' Joan asks.

'Briefly—but it scared the hell out of me. I was afraid that if I turned my back for a second, I'd lose her.'

'Did you ask her mother, living in Arizona at the time, to come stay with Mariah?'

'No,' Colin admits. 'I knew Millie would think the worst. I didn't want her to believe that Mariah wasn't improving.'

'So instead you got a court order, and you had Mariah institutionalized against her will?'

'She didn't know what she wanted at the time. She couldn't drag herself out of bed to go to the bathroom, much less tell me how to help her. I did what I did for her own safety. I listened to the doctors when they said that round-the-clock supervision was best.' His troubled gaze meets Mariah's. 'I am guilty of many things, including stupidity and naïveté. But not of malicious behavior.' He shakes his head. 'I just didn't know what else to do.'

'Hmm,' Joan says. 'Let's come back to the present now. Seven years have passed, and your wife catches you in the act again.'

'Objection!'

'Sustained.'

'After Mariah discovered you were having another affair,' Joan says smoothly, 'you were worried that she might become depressed again. So rather than taking the time to talk it over, you just ran off?'

'It wasn't like that. I'm not proud of what I did, but I really needed to get myself together before I took on anyone else's responsibilties.'

'You weren't worried that Mariah might be a little upset finding you in bed with another woman, just like seven years ago?'

'Of course I was.'

'Did you make an effort to get Mariah psychiatric help?'

'No.'

'Even though the last time this happened, she became severely depressed?'

'I told you, I just wasn't thinking past myself at that point.'

'Yet you left your daughter with her,' Joan says.

'I honestly didn't think Mariah was going to hurt her. I mean, for God's sake—she's her *mother*. I assumed she'd be okay.'

'You assumed Mariah would be emotionally stable in spite of your behavior.'

'Yes.'

'And you assumed Faith would be fine in your wife's custody.'

'Yes.'

'You asked no one to come to the house to double-check; you called no doctor, no social services, not even a neighbor.'

'No. It was a mistake that I deeply regret, and I'm ready to atone for my wrongs.'

Joan briskly moves past the witness stand. 'We're all glad, I'm sure, that you're ready. Now, let me see if I get this straight. By your own admission, you assumed incorrectly that Faith would be better off with your ex-wife. Just like you *assumed* incorrectly that you needed to get yourself settled before you could even think about your daughter's welfare. Just like you *assumed* incorrectly that your wife would be better off in a mental institution than with a different form of treatment for depression. Just like you *assume* incorrectly today that you're the better parent here.'

Before Colin can answer, Joan turns her back on him. 'Nothing further,' she says.

Dr Newton Orlitz loves the feel of a witness stand. Something about the smooth wood beneath his hands and the smell of furniture polish that always lingers in a courtroom makes him blissfully happy with his longtime job as a forensic psychiatrist. He knows that most of the time his opinion as a doctor appointed by the court is repudiated by a private psychiatrist being paid a hell of a lot of money to say something contradictory, but it doesn't take away from his pleasure. He not only believes in the justice system, he is humbled to know he has a place in it.

He likes to play games with himself on the stand, too. Sometimes he watches the attorneys and diagnoses them in his mind. As he sees Malcolm Metz approach him for his testimony, he thinks: megalomania, clearly. Maybe even a God complex. He imagines Metz dressed in a white robe, sporting a long, ethereal beard, and he chuckles to himself.

'Glad you're happy to be here, Dr Orlitz,' Metz says. 'Did you interview Colin White?'

'Yes,' Orlitz says, consulting his small salt-and-pepper notebook, in which he's recorded his observations for this particular case. 'I found him emotionally stable and perfectly capable of providing a good, solid home for a young child.'

Metz smiles broadly, as well he should. Orlitz knows not all attorneys get to hear what they want when the court psychiatrist gives his evaluation. 'Did you also have the opportunity to interview Mariah White?'

'I did.'

'Could you tell us a little bit about her psychiatric history?'

Orlitz thumbs through his notes. 'She was institutionalized at Greenhaven for four months, for suicidal depression. While there, she received psychotherapy and antidepressant medication. As I'm sure you know, though, Mr Metz,' he says, smiling blandly, 'her behaviors were a response to an extremely stressful situation. This is how her mind happened to cope with it. She thought she'd lost her husband, and her marriage.'

'In your expert opinion, Doctor, do you think Mariah White might go through that sort of psychological crisis again?'

Orlitz shrugs. 'It's possible. She's vulnerable to that type of reaction.'

'I see. Is Mariah taking medication now, Doctor?'

Orlitz runs his finger down the side of a page. 'Yes,' he

says, when he finds the notation. 'She's been taking twenty milligrams of Prozac daily, for the past four months.'

Metz raises his brows. 'When was this prescribed?'

'August eleventh, initially. By a Dr Johansen.'

'August eleventh. Do you happen to know what day Colin White left?'

'I understand that it was August tenth.'

'In your opinion, Dr Orlitz, did Mariah White obtain this medication because she could not handle the stress of the current situation without it?'

'Most likely, but you should ask her private psychiatrist.'

Metz gives him a dirty look. 'Doctor, did you have an opportunity to interview Faith?'

'I did.'

'Did she appear to be a normal little girl?'

'Normal,' the doctor says, laughing, 'is a very relative term. Especially when you're defining a child who's suffered through a traumatic divorce.'

'Does Faith seem to seek the approval of her mother?'

'Yes, but that's a very common response after a divorce. A child is so afraid the remaining parent might leave, too, that she will do anything necessary to keep her interest.'

'Perhaps even imitate behavior?'

'Absolutely,' Orlitz says. 'A parent might be consciously or unconsciously enforcing the behavior, playing the child off the other parent by pushing her to act a certain way—so that the child, in effect, becomes a pawn. Some experts refer to this post-divorce pattern as "parental alienation syndrome."'

'Enforcing the child's behavior,' Metz repeats. 'Interesting. I have nothing further.'

Joan stands and buttons the front of her suit jacket. She knows Metz well enough to realize that he's laid the foundation for a future witness. 'Why don't we start with this issue of enforced behavior?' she says. 'Did Faith's interview suggest to you that her, shall we say, more extraordinary behavior of late was directly motivated by her mother?'

'No.'

'Thank you. Now, Doctor, you had a chance to interview

both of Faith's parents. And you said that you found Colin White to be emotionally stable and capable of providing a good home for a child. Did you find Mariah White to be emotionally stable?'

'Yes, she's functioning well right now.'

'Did you find her to currently be a good parent?'

'Yes. Faith is very attached to her.'

'Let's shift gears again, Doctor. How many people in America, would you say, are on prescription antidepressant medication?'

'I believe,' Dr Orlitz says, 'close to seventeen million.'

'In what percentage of the cases do the drugs work?'

'Well, if the patients stay on them for a certain period of time and are in therapy, they're effective in approximately eighty percent of the cases.'

'Does Prozac affect normal day-to-day functioning?'

'No.'

'Would it interfere with parenting capabilities?'

'No.'

'Dr Orlitz, did you speak to Faith about the afternoon her father left?'

'Yes, I did.'

'Did it affect her in any way?'

'She didn't understand the dynamics of the adult relationships—which is a blessing, actually—but because of that, she felt her father's subsequent absence might have been her fault. She's going to need therapy regarding that issue.'

'How unfortunate,' Joan says. 'So even though, in your opinion, Colin White is a capable parent *now*, he did do something *once* that hurt Faith.'

'Yes.'

'Did you find proof of anything Mariah has ever done that in some way has hurt Faith?'

'No. She's been a stable, continuous thread for Faith to cling to during a crisis.'

'Thank you,' Joan says, and turns to sit down beside her client.

• • •

Judge Rothbottam announces there will be a short break, and the reporters run out of the courtroom to call their affiliates with updates. Metz shepherds Colin out, and they disappear in a crush of bodies. Mariah does not move from her seat, but instead rests her head in her hands.

Joan touches her on the shoulder. 'The reason we're called the defense,' she says, 'is because we fight when they're finished. It doesn't matter what they say, Mariah, truly. We're going to give it back in spades.'

'I know,' Mariah says, rubbing her temples. 'How long do we have?'

Joan smiles gently. 'About long enough for a bathroom break.'

Mariah is out of her chair in a heartbeat; anything to get away. She walks out of the courtroom and sees a sea of faces. Her gaze slides to Ian, who sits in the lobby awaiting his turn as a witness, pretending he does not know her.

It has to be like this; they have discussed it. But right now, with her mother at Faith's bedside, Mariah could have used a strong and solid ally.

She forces her eyes to move past Ian. It takes all her self-control to walk past him without glancing back, just to see if he's watching her go.

Dr DeSantis is a small, compact woman with a cloud of black hair that bounces when she speaks. She recites her impressive background to the court, and then smiles at Malcolm Metz. 'Dr DeSantis,' he says, 'did you have a chance to interview Colin White?'

'I certainly did. Mr White is a wonderful, caring, perfectly stable man who very much wants his daughter to be in his life.'

'Did you interview Mariah White?'

'No,' the psychiatrist says. 'She declined the opportunity.'

'I see. Did you have a chance to review Dr Johansen's findings on Mariah White?'

'Yes.'

'What can you tell us about her psychological health?'

'This woman has a history of severe depression. Such a

history places her at high risk for future major episodes of instability, and nobody can predict what will trigger another one.'

'Thank you, Doctor.' Metz nods at Joan. 'Your witness.'

Joan stands up, but doesn't bother to move forward. 'Dr DeSantis, are you Colin White's therapist?'

Beneath the cloud of hair, the psychiatrist pinkens with indignation. 'I was called in to consult on his case.'

'Isn't it true, Dr DeSantis, that the first and last time you met with Colin White was October twenty-ninth, just two days after the initial hearing on his motion to change custody?'

'I suppose so.'

'Ah. Doctor, how many trials have you testified in?'

'Over fifty,' the psychiatrist says proudly.

'How many of those fifty trials has attorney Metz asked you to testify in?'

'Twenty-seven.'

Joan nods thoughtfully. 'In any of those twenty-seven trials, Doctor, have you ever found his client to be mentally deficient?'

'No,' Dr DeSantis says.

'So, just to recap, then: Mr Metz has hired you yet again, and—correct me if I'm wrong, Dr DeSantis—in your *expert* opinion, you found his client to be perfectly stable, and my client to be an emotional basket case.'

'I wouldn't use those terms—'

'Yes or no, Doctor?'

'I found Mr Metz's client to be more stable than yours, yes.'

'Well,' Joan says dryly. 'What a surprise.'

The hospital chapel is a sad little room that used to be a broom closet. There are six pews, three on each side of a small podium with a cross hanging overhead. The chapel is non-denominational, but somehow this symbol of Christian culture escaped notice. Father MacReady is on his knees, his lips moving silently in a paternoster while his heart sinks lower and lower in his chest.

He tries to ignore the sound of the door opening, but the creaking is phenomenally loud, and as a man of the cloth, he feels duty-bound to offer support to a grieving soul, if need be. He gets to his feet, wipes off the knees of his jeans, and turns around.

To his surprise, Rabbi Solomon is staring at the cross as if it were a rattlesnake poised to strike. 'Interfaith, my foot.'

'Rabbi,' Father MacReady says.

They size each other up, never having met but aware through the grapevine that they are both here in support of Faith White.

Rabbi Solomon nods.

'Have you heard anything?'

'I went up to Pediatrics. They wouldn't let me into the room. Something's going on.'

'Something good?'

The rabbi shakes his head. 'I don't think so.'

The two men stand in silence. 'Don't Jews need a minimum number of people to pray?' MacReady asks after a moment.

Solomon grins. 'It's not a minimum, really. It's a *minyan*, ten men. It's the smallest group you can have if you want to say some particular prayers.'

'Strength in numbers, eh?'

'Exactly,' the rabbi says. And without saying another word, the rabbi and priest sit down side by side in the pew, and silently begin to pray together.

'This is the situation,' a smooth-faced young doctor says to Millie. 'Her renal system's gone into failure. If we don't put her on dialysis, she's likely to poison her whole bloodstream.'

Millie stares at this man for a moment, uncomprehending. How can this boy, younger than Mariah even, be telling her what they have to do? For the past half hour Faith's room has been buzzing with nurses and doctors and aides ferrying in equipment that gleams bright and unfamiliar, setting hooks and tubes and masks on her granddaughter until she resembles nothing more than an astronaut preparing to journey to an unknown world.

Not for the first time, Millie wishes that it were her mind, and not her heart, that had been cleared and resurrected. She stares at Faith, willing her to open her eyes, to smile, to tell them it wasn't as serious as they all thought. *Where,* she wonders, *is your God now?*

Just an hour ago, Mariah had called from the courthouse, and Millie had been able to say that everything was just the way it had been when she left. How could so much have gone wrong so quickly? 'I'm not the one you should be asking,' Millie hedges. 'Her mother . . .'

'Is not here. If you don't sign the consent form, this little girl will die.'

Millie swipes her hand over her eyes, then picks up the pen that he extends like a peace pipe, and gives her permission.

Ian steps into the witness box, and there is a moment of levity when the clerk of the court approaches with the customary Bible. He laughs, then good-naturedly looks up at the ceiling. 'Okay, y'all. Get ready for lightning to strike.'

Metz swaggers toward his witness. 'Please state your name and address for the record.'

'Ian Fletcher, Brentwood, California.'

'What do you do for a living, Mr Fletcher?'

'As I do sincerely hope everyone knows, I'm a professional atheist. I currently coproduce and star in a television show that features my views. In addition, I'm the author of three *New York Times* nonfiction bestsellers. Come to think of it, I had a cameo in a film once, too.'

'Can you explain to the court what your television show is like, for those who may not be familiar with it?'

'Well, my show's been described as the anti-Billy Graham. I have a TV pulpit, but I use it to prove God doesn't exist, through theory and scientific inquiry.'

'Do you believe in God, Mr Fletcher?'

'Kind of hard to when you're an atheist.' There are snickers from the gallery.

'For the past two months, what alleged religious miracles have you been examining?'

Ian crosses one leg over the other. 'A bleeding statue over

in Massachusetts, a tree in Maine—and most lately, Faith White.'

'Why were you following that particular case?'

Ian shrugs. 'She supposedly was seeing God and performing miracles and exhibiting stigmata. I intended to prove she was a hoax.'

Metz moves in for his kill. 'Mr Fletcher, can you tell us what you found?'

For a moment Ian looks at the attorney, replaying in his mind the testimony he'd practiced with Metz as recently as yesterday. A long, slow smile transforms his face. 'To tell you the truth, Mr Metz,' he says, 'not a hell of a lot.'

Metz, ready to throw his next question like a dart, falters in his steps. 'Pardon me?'

Ian leans closer to the microphone. 'I said, "not a hell of a lot."' He nods at the stenographer. 'Is that about right?'

The gallery begins buzzing and humming, picking up on the disconnection between the plaintiff's attorney and the famous witness.

'What you're saying,' Metz paraphrases, 'is that you haven't seen a lot of these so-called miracles.'

'Objection,' Joan calls out. 'Leading.'

'Sustained.'

'Actually, Mr Metz,' Ian answers, 'what I'm saying is that I've found nothing to support the theory that Faith White is a charlatan.'

Metz starts shaking; he wonders if it is visible to the judge or to Joan Standish. He remembers his first meeting with Fletcher, when Fletcher had expressly said there was something big about Faith White that he was keeping under wraps. He recalls Fletcher's deposition—how the man had pleaded the fifth for every question. At the time Metz had found it amusing, for all it rattled Joan Standish. But now he sees that Ian pleaded the fifth because he knew, all along, that he wasn't willing to perjure himself by refusing to give testimony sworn in a deposition. Whatever he promised Metz he'd say in the confines of the law office was a lie—and there is nothing at all Metz can do about it. Fletcher could get up here and sing 'The Star-Spangled Banner' if he wanted, and as long as his deposition couldn't be called into question, it would not reflect badly on himself, but only on Metz, who had underestimated his own witness.

Although it made him uneasy, Metz had been willing to let Fletcher keep his big revelation about Faith White to himself, just so long as he was planning to offer up a few lesser ones for the court. But this flat refusal to cooperate—it just doesn't make any sense. 'Surely you've dug up *something*.'

'Counselor, you wouldn't be asking me to lie, now would you?'

Metz feels the vein in his temple throb. He tries some different questions, questions they've rehearsed, to see if Fletcher will fall back into line. 'Did you ever see Faith White perform a miracle?'

Ian hesitates for a fraction of a second. 'Not precisely,' he says.

'Where were you on the evening of October thirteenth?'

'Parked on the White property.'

'What happened that night, at about ten P.M.?'

'I ran into Faith. Literally. She was in the woods, after dark.'

'Did her mother know she was outside?'

'No,' Ian admits.

'What happened?'

'She was bleeding. She . . . passed out, and I carried her to the house. To her mother.'

'Let me get this straight. The child was running around in the dark, bleeding and nearly unconscious, and her mother was unaware?'

Ian frowns. 'Once I brought Faith to Mrs White, she was extremely responsive. She took Faith to the hospital for immediate medical attention.'

'Is it possible that Faith White was running away because her own mother had hurt her?'

'Objection!'

'Overruled,' Judge Rothbottam says.

Ian shrugs. 'I didn't see her mother do that.'

'But it is possible?'

'I didn't see you hurt Faith that night either, Mr Metz, but I guess it's possible that you did.'

Metz hesitates. He cannot figure out Fletcher's game. They are on the same side—both of them needing to show that the child is a fake—even if they desire that proof for very different reasons. 'Can you give us other examples of Mrs White being an unfit parent?'

Ian furrows his brow, as if in deep concentration. Then his expression clears, and he smiles at Metz. 'Nope. Matter of fact, I've only seen evidence to the contrary. In all the time I've been trying to discredit Faith, Miz White has looked like she's doing a pretty good job.'

Ian's gaze floats over the gallery, coming to rest on Mariah. *You see?* Then Ian turns his attention back to Metz, to the calculating gleam in the attorney's eyes.

'You say you spent two months investigating Faith, and her mother?'

'That's about right.'

'Can you tell us about some of these investigations?'

Ian steeples his hands together. 'At the moment, nothing specific comes to mind.'

'How interesting,' Metz says, 'since you were both on the passenger list of a plane en route to Kansas City about a month ago.' He enters into evidence a piece of paper, an airline's logo emblazoned on top.

Ian tries not to let his body betray him; there has always been the very real possibility of Metz's private investigators turning up a paper trail. However, knowing the fact that a trip is taken was a far cry from knowing why. The real question here is how much Metz has uncovered.

'Maybe you can tell us what you learned on that trip about Faith and Mariah White?'

Metz stares at Ian, willing him to tip his hand, to admit that he'd tracked them to Kansas City for investigation—and then to admit what he found out.

'Huh,' Ian says, feigning surprise. 'I didn't know they were on the flight. I was in first class . . . never even went into the back of the plane.' He grins at Metz ingenuously. 'Talk about coincidence.'

'If you weren't on that flight specifically to investigate Faith White, yet you were, by your own admission, in the middle of an ongoing investigation of her miraculous claims, then what *were* you doing on that plane, Mr Fletcher?'

Ian's face is schooled into a blank mask. 'Visiting friends.'

Metz is so close now that his words rain against Ian. 'What friends?'

'Objection, Your Honor,' Joan says. 'I have no idea why, but Mr Metz is badgering his own witness.'

'Yes, Mr Metz,' the judge agrees. 'Mr Fletcher's answered your question.'

Metz cannot glance at Fletcher again; he's not sure he can trust himself to keep from strangling the son of a bitch. 'Nothing further,' he grinds out, sitting down beside Colin White.

'What the fuck was *that*?' Colin whispers.

Metz watches Joan whisper furiously to her client. 'That,' he says, 'was a sting.'

'What the fuck was *that*?' Joan whispers.

Mariah says nothing, just pleats and unpleats the fabric of her skirt. For a moment, when Ian walked up to the witness stand, she could not breathe; she wondered if, in spite of what Ian had said to her these past few weeks, he'd been lying, if he were going to play her for a fool.

'You knew,' the attorney breathes. 'Jesus Christ.'

'He wants to help me,' Mariah says quietly. 'He didn't think you should know beforehand.'

Joan stares at her for a beat. 'Then tell me now: How far is he willing to go?'

When Ian looks at Joan, a current passes between them, a bond forged of common purpose. 'You say you spent some time investigating Mariah?' she asks.

'Yes.'

'You've seen Mariah being a good mother.'

'Yes.'

'Can you tell me about that?'

Ian leans forward in the witness stand. 'I have never seen

a woman so protective of a child, ma'am. Miz White has done her best to shelter Faith from the media, from the religious zealots on the property, and even from me. As Mr Metz just pointed out, she attempted to take her daughter away from the whole affair by apparently running off to Kansas City. When I accompanied her to the hospital with her daughter, the time Faith's hands started bleeding, she didn't leave that girl's side for a moment. I have to confess that when I came to New Canaan I was expecting to see some kind of harridan—a woman who was trying to get attention by setting her own kid up as some kind of religious miracle worker. But the facts just didn't add up. Miz White's a good woman, a good mother.'

'Objection!' Metz shouts.

'Grounds?' the judge asks.

'Well . . . he's my witness!'

'Overruled.' Rothbottam nods at Ian. 'Please continue, Mr Fletcher.'

'I was just going to add that when I was growing up in Georgia, I was told never to come between a mama bear and her cub, because the mama would tear through anything—including you—to get to her baby. Course, even back then I didn't listen to what I was supposed to believe. Sure enough, when I was about eight years old I got 'tween a mama bear and her little one, and spent three hours in a tree until she lost interest in punishing me. But I've never forgotten the look in that animal's eyes—there was just something in them that made me realize I was a fool to cross her. And thirty years later, I've seen the same kind of conviction written all over the face of Mariah White.'

Joan tries not to smile. First and foremost, Ian Fletcher is an actor. He knows how to sell a line. 'Thank you, Mr Fletcher.' Then she grins. 'And thank *you*, Mr Metz. Nothing further.'

At one thirty-five, Faith opens her eyes for the first time in twelve hours. The nurse's back is to her, so it takes a moment for the monitors to make her realize the girl is conscious. 'Don't fight it, honey,' she says, as Faith begins gulping for air.

'You've got a tube down your throat.' She pages Dr Blumberg and the pediatric surgeon on call. 'Just breathe,' she instructs.

But Faith continues to round her mouth and flatten it, in what looks like a gasp for breath, but what is actually the word 'Mom.'

'Mr Metz,' the judge continues. 'Your next witness?'

Metz lifts his head. 'Your Honor, may I approach?' Joan walks beside him, gearing up for the fight she knows is about to happen—the battle over the expert Metz mentioned that morning. 'I need to call a witness who isn't on the list.'

'I've already stated my objection to this witness, Your Honor,' Joan says immediately. 'I had no knowledge of this alleged expert of Mr Metz's, and I need time to research this ridiculous psychological syndrome he's found buried in the Encyclopaedia Britannica.'

'I'm not talking about the Munchausen expert,' Metz answers impatiently. 'This is someone else. And as a matter of fact, he's not sequestered. He happens to be in the courtroom.'

Joan's mouth drops open. 'Why did you even bother giving me a witness list?'

'Look, Ian Fletcher was an unexpectedly hostile witness, and I didn't cover what I was supposed to during his testimony.'

The judge turns to Joan. 'How do you feel about this?'

'No way, Your Honor.'

Metz smiles at her, silently mouthing, 'Appeal issue.'

Joan sets her jaw and shrugs. 'Fine, then. Go ahead.'

Metz walks away, satisfied. This next witness will paint Fletcher as a liar—putting into question his entire testimony and his inexplicable championing of Mariah. At the very least, after this, Metz will have negated whatever unexpected damage Fletcher's done to his case.

'The plaintiff would like to call Allen McManus to the stand.'

There is a flurry of confusion in the gallery as the reporters shift to let one of their own move from his seat to the witness stand. McManus hesitantly walks toward the clerk of the court, clearly surprised, as he lets himself be led through the swearing-in.

Metz silently blesses Lacey Rodriguez for once again turning up more information than he'd expected to use—information that most people weren't even aware existed, such as long-distance service provider's logs of incoming and outgoing phone calls at office buildings.

'Could you state your name and address for the record?'

'Allen McManus,' the witness says. 'Two-four-seven-eight Massachusetts Avenue, Boston.'

'Where do you work, Mr McManus?'

'I'm an obituary editor for the *Globe*.'

Metz clasps his hands behind his back. 'How did you first hear about Faith White?'

'I, uh, was assigned to cover a psychiatric symposium in Boston. And a lady psychiatrist was talking about one of her cases, a little girl who was talking to God. At that time, though, I didn't know the little girl was Faith White.'

'How did you find out?'

'I was at the office, and I got this fax about a dead woman who'd come back to life after her granddaughter had worked a miracle. Turns out it happened in the same town where this lady psychiatrist practices. And then the phone rings, and it's this anonymous call telling me to think about who would benefit by having the kid be considered some kind of healer.'

'What did you do after that call?'

McManus lifts his chin. 'I've tucked a lot of years of investigative reporting under my belt, so I figured I'd dig into it. I did a little research on the kid's mother.' He smiles widely. 'I was the one who broke the story that Mariah White was institutionalized for four months.'

'Was it unusual for you to receive that anonymous phone call?'

Allen tugs at the collar of his shirt. 'Well, working obits, I don't get Deep Throat calls very often. At the *Globe* we have Caller ID, so I copied it down, just in case I needed to get back in touch.'

'What was the number, Mr McManus?'

'I can't reveal a source, sir.'

The judge frowns, as the press corps in the gallery murmur their respect. 'You can and you will, Mr McManus, or I'll hold you in contempt of court.'

Allen is quiet for a moment, considering his options. Then he digs into his pocket for a small notebook and flips through several pages. 'Three-one-zero, two-eight-eight, three-three-six-six.'

'Did you ever have it traced?'

'Yes.'

Malcolm Metz walks in front of the defendant's bench and turns toward Mariah. 'Mr McManus, whose number was it?'

The judge clears his throat, a warning, but there is no need. By now McManus is staring at one man, his eyes narrowed as he remembers a past indignity. 'It's a personal cell phone,' he says. 'Registered to Ian Fletcher.'

The minute Allen McManus takes the stand, Ian feels himself rooted to his seat, unable to move and equally sure that staying is the worst possible thing he can do. How could he have underestimated Metz? Now Ian sits two rows behind Mariah, watching her shoulders stiffen as she discovers that Ian was responsible for the slanderous story published about her. *I should have told her*, he thinks. *If I had told her, she would have forgiven me*.

He wishes she would turn to him. He wishes he could see her face.

Just moments ago, when he was excused from the witness stand, he walked past her and winked. Her entire face was glowing, as luminous as the moon. Now it is pale, her eyes standing out like bruises, deliberately fixed away from him.

He finds himself staring at Mariah the way one cannot help but watch a building collapse or a fire burn out, committed to the tragedy. He does not blink when she covers her face with her hands, when the cries come.

Joan spends thirty seconds trying to console her client, something that has never been her forte. Then she stands, vibrating with anger. If this were a jury trial, it would be totally different. She could do her cross of McManus and somehow plant doubt that Ian was holding his phone at the time the call was placed. It could have been an intern, it could have been stolen—who the hell knows what the possibilities are? A judge, though, will have already weighed the possibility of whether or not Ian Fletcher was actually using his own phone to call Allen McManus. And—like everyone else—will have concluded that Ian is guilty of several counts of betrayal.

'You work at the *Globe*?' she barks out.

'Yes.'

'How long have you worked there?'

'Six years.'

'What's your training?'

'I went to the Columbia School of Journalism and worked at *The Miami Herald* as a stringer before coming to the *Globe*.'

'Who assigned you to this particular case?'

'The special-events editor, Uwe Terenbaum. He sometimes asks me to cover symposiums and conferences if obits aren't too busy.'

Joan moves back and forth in front of him, like the shuttle of a loom. McManus's eyes follow her, dizzy. She does not know what she can get out of this worm, but she has a hunch that his ego is an Achilles' heel. And the stupider she makes him look, the better. 'Do you think you're a good reporter, Mr McManus?'

For a moment, Allen preens. 'I like to think so.'

'Do you have a good reputation among your colleagues?'

'Sure.'

'Were you assigned to this case because you're one of the *Globe*'s best reporters?'

'Probably,' he says, seemingly growing taller in the chair.

'You must have felt pretty good when you traced that number back to Ian Fletcher.'

'Well, yeah,' Allen admits. 'I mean, he's certainly a household name.'

Joan drums her fingertips on the railing of the stand. 'Did you talk to Mr Fletcher after you found out that it was his number?'

'I tried, but—'

'Yes or no?'

'No,' he says.

'You simply took his tip and ran with it.'

'Yes.'

'You went to Greenhaven?'

'Yeah,' Allen says.

'Where you were able to get Mariah White's file?'

'No. I got a doctor to confirm that she had been in the hospital.'

'I see. Was he Mariah's doctor?'

'Well, no—'

'Did he treat Mariah at all when she was at Greenhaven?'

'No.'

'Did he know particulars about her case?'

'He knew the essentials.'

'That wasn't my question, Mr McManus.' Joan's brows draw together. 'Did you find out during your thorough investigations that Mariah was placed in Greenhaven involuntarily by her husband?'

'Um, no . . .'

'Did you find out that she was not given the opportunity to pursue other treatment alternatives for depression before being institutionalized?'

'No.'

'Did you find out that because her husband was running around screwing other women, Mariah White had what's colloquially called a nervous breakdown?'

'No,' the reporter murmurs.

'Did you find out that *that* was the reason she was suicidal?' Joan regards McManus steadily. 'You didn't find out the basic facts, Mr McManus. You didn't find out anything at all. So what makes you think you're such a great investigative reporter?'

'Objection!'

'Withdrawn,' Joan says, but by then she does not care.

When it becomes clear that Mariah cannot stop crying, the judge suggests an hourlong recess. Before the press has even managed to get out of their seats, Joan whisks Mariah out of the courtroom and down the hall that leads to the bathroom. Once they are inside, Joan holds the door shut so that no one will intrude. 'Mariah, Fletcher's testimony wasn't that damaging. Not even the newspaper article. Really. By the time we get onto the stand, no one's going to remember.' When Mariah does not answer, Joan suddenly understands. 'It's not what he said,' she murmurs. 'It's that he said it at all. That's how you knew he was going to cross Metz on the stand. Jesus, you're in love with him.'

'It's not as simple as that—'

'It hardly ever is!'

Mariah waves her away. 'Right now, I just think I need to be by myself.'

The attorney eyes her carefully. 'I don't know if that's such a good idea.'

'Afraid I might have a razor blade up my sleeve?' Mariah says bitterly. 'Is the testimony of the morning getting to you?'

'I didn't mean that. I—'

'It's all right, Joan. Please.'

The attorney nods and exits the bathroom. Mariah stands in front of the sinks and gazes into the mirror. Her eyes are puffy and red; her nose is running. Beside her, in the reflection of the towel dispenser, is a distorted view of this mirror, so that her ravaged face is repeated over and over.

She should have known better. Maybe what Metz has been suggesting is the truth: that once you have experienced pain, it knows your address. It comes to prey upon you in the middle of the night, sneaking up when you least expect it and leveling you before you have a chance to fight.

Ian must have laughed at her, at finding such an easy target. How could she have believed that his interest in her was anything more than a ploy to get closer to Faith?

Those remarkable nights with him, those words that had cast a spell and turned her into someone she has always wanted to be—to Ian, they were just words, just nights. All in the line of duty.

With tremendous resolve she forces herself to look in the mirror again. She will get a grip on herself and she will march back into that courtroom. She will say everything that she and Joan rehearsed. She simply must keep custody of her daughter.

She doesn't have anything else.

When she exits the bathroom, she is expecting a crowd of reporters and photographers, waiting to glimpse some sign of her distress in an area of the courthouse where their cameras are sanctioned. But the only person standing there is Ian.

'Mariah,' he begins, coming toward her.

She pushes past him. The contact of her shoulder with his upper arm almost brings her to tears again.

'I didn't know back then. I didn't know what you were like.'

Mariah stops, turns, and fixes her gaze on his face. 'That makes two of us,' she says.

Joan is about to enter the courtroom again when she feels a hand grab her shoulder and draw her to the side. 'Don't say anything,' Ian warns when she immediately opens her mouth.

'Ah, if it isn't James Bond. If you'd told me you were going to play double agent, we might have been able to avoid this McManus crap.'

'My apologies.'

Joan crosses her arms. 'I'm not the one who's crying her heart out.'

'I tried to make her understand that the *Globe* story came before we . . . well, before. She won't listen to me.'

'Can't say I blame her.' She glances toward the courtroom, beginning to fill. 'Look, I'll talk to Mariah later. I can't help you right now—'

'Actually,' Ian interrupts, 'you can.'

Joan and Metz approach the bench. 'Your Honor,' he says, 'I've gone through all my witnesses except for the psychiatrist I mentioned at this morning's emergency hearing.'

'Judge,' Joan adds, 'as I mentioned earlier today, I don't know Munchausen Syndrome from tennis elbow. I need time to prepare a rebuttal to Mr Metz's ridiculous theory about my client. Moreover, this is the second witness Mr Metz has pulled out of a hat; Allen McManus's name, astoundingly, didn't manage to make it to the witness list either.' She glances at the other attorney. 'If Mr Metz wants to put his psychiatrist on the stand, I want to recall Ian Fletcher.'

'No way. The whole point of putting Allen McManus on was to illustrate how Ian Fletcher was lying during my direct, Your Honor. Having him questioned by the defense again is only going to be confusing,' Metz says.

'I think I'll be able to keep it straight in my head,' the judge says dryly. He addresses the gallery. 'Mr Fletcher, would you mind taking the stand again?'

Ian climbs onto the witness stand in silence. Joan watches him carefully, hoping this is going to work the way Ian thinks it is. She is not doing it, really, to further the case. She is doing it as a gift for her client. And as Ian pointed out correctly, since Mariah has not yet testified, getting her back together again is clearly in the best interests of the case.

Joan walks toward Mariah and squeezes her arm. 'Sit up and listen,' she whispers, then approaches the witness stand. 'Mr Fletcher, when did you call Mr McManus?'

'In early October.'

'Why did you call him?' Her questions are clipped, tight. To observers, she appears angry with Ian . . . and rightfully so.

'I wanted to disprove Faith White's claims. It would have meant a huge ratings coup for my show. I didn't know Faith, or her mother, from Adam.' He spreads his hands. 'I've given anonymous tips before. It looks better when other people create the rift at first, and I step in to peel back the layers and expose the fraud. McManus seemed to be a halfway decent reporter, and I thought he might be able to help.'

'It sounds very underhanded.'

'It's part of being a journalist,' Ian says, 'and my job involves that from time to time. On occasion I get anonymous tips; on occasion I hand them out. Reporters often do this for each other.' He glances at McManus. 'Sometimes we even serve as those sources that other journalists refuse to reveal. I meant no harm to Miz White, because I wasn't thinking of her then. I was only thinking of exposing her daughter, no matter what it took.'

'What's different now?' Joan asks.

'Now I know her,' Ian says softly.

Joan glances from her client to Ian, holding her breath. 'Nothing further.'

Metz is already on his feet to redirect. 'You couldn't find anything? Not one measly bit of dirt on Faith White?'

'I postponed my digging,' Ian answers, his eyes steely.

'Are you implying that Faith White's visions are real?'

He thinks carefully about his answer. 'I'm implying that Faith White is one extraordinary little girl, and that I don't think she's deliberately lying.'

'But, Mr Fletcher, you've said repeatedly that you're an atheist. Does this mean you now believe in God?'

Ian freezes. He realizes what Metz has done to him: He cannot get into Mariah's good graces again unless he ruins himself completely. If he admits that Faith is a miracle worker, the attorney will press for proof, and Ian doesn't care to divulge information about the private joy of his twin brother's few lucid moments. He glances at Mariah, who is staring at him, waiting for his answer.

I'm sorry, he thinks.

'Mr Fletcher? Do you believe in God?'

Ian raises his brows and adopts the charming mask of his television persona. 'The jury's still out on that one,' he says, playing into the hands of his audience, watching their grinning faces, instead of the one that matters most.

Joan asks for a short recess. Mariah is remarkably controlled, if incredibly quiet, and for some reason this scares Joan even more than an out-and-out tantrum. 'I can try for a continuance. I can tell the judge you're sick.'

'I only want an hour. I have to see Faith,' she explains. 'It's been all day.'

Until that moment, Joan has forgotten the restraining order signed that morning. In the confusion of the testimonies, she still hasn't had a chance to tell Mariah about it. 'You can't.'

'But if you ask the judge . . .'

'You can't go now, and you can't go later. Judge Rothbottam signed a restraining order to keep you away from Faith for the duration of the trial.'

It starts like a slow-motion avalanche, the gradual disintegration of Mariah's calm. 'Why?'

'If she gets better when you're kept away, Metz will use it as evidence.'

'Because I'm not there? Because I left when she needed me the most?'

'No, Mariah. He's got an expert testifying, who'll say that when you were separated by force, you weren't able to make Faith hallucinate or bleed.'

She covers her mouth with her hand and turns away. 'What do they think of me?'

Joan frowns, not liking the direction of her own thoughts. Mariah had kept silent about Ian Fletcher's testimony for Metz; what else might she be hiding? 'They think,' she says, 'that eventually you'll kill her.'

fifteen

Children are the anchors
that hold a mother to life.

—Sophocles, *Phaedra*

IT TAKES SEVERAL long seconds before Joan's words sink in. 'Are you *kidding*?' I finally manage. It is laughable, really, except that the whole thing makes me want to cry. 'They think I'm going to kill my own daughter?'

'Malcolm Metz is painting you as an emotionally unstable woman in a crisis. Supposedly he's got some expert who's going to testify about other mothers who have done the same thing. There's a name for it—Munchausen Syndrome by Proxy.'

A crisis. How much, after all, am I supposed to bear? My daughter is hospitalized. The man I've fallen in love with has been lying to me. The man I used to love thinks I'm capable of killing our child.

'It's not true,' I say firmly. 'Can't you make them see that?'

'I'm gonna try. But Metz is allowed to say anything he wants to. If it strikes his fancy, he can build a case around the idea that you're programming Faith's behavior with voodoo dolls. Whether or not it's the truth doesn't matter. The important thing is that we can get up when he's done and make the judge realize what a load of bullshit he's been handed.' She sighs. 'Look. You've got a weak spot. You were in a mental hospital. If I were in Metz's position, I'd probably be running with that particular play, too.'

'Joan,' I say shakily, 'I've got to be able to see my daughter.'

The pity in her eyes almost sends me over the edge.

'I'll call the hospital for you and find out how she's doing.'

I know she is trying to give me hope, but it slips through my grasp like sand.

'We're going to get Faith back home with you.'

For her sake, I nod and manage a smile. But I do not say what I truly think: that a custody battle means nothing at all if the child is dead.

When Joan walks back into the courtroom, she feels as if she's just finished climbing Mount Washington. There's nothing like reducing your client to emotional Jell-O before you need her to be coherent on the stand. She glares at Metz with all the horrible thoughts that are on her mind, praying for a brief moment of psychic connection. He's leaning over the gallery railing, speaking to a smaller, slighter, carbon copy of himself who could only be another underling from his office.

He turns as the judge enters and summons counsel to the bench. 'Well, Mr Metz, as I recall, we agreed to rendezvous about now. I assume that you're ready to put on your expert witness?'

Before he can answer, Joan interrupts. 'Excuse me, Your Honor, but I have to raise an objection once again. My client was just told that she can't see her daughter for the duration of the trial, and, frankly, she's a basket case. It's three o'clock in the afternoon, and since I don't have the same army of human resources available to me that Mr Metz does at his big-city firm, I still have not had a chance to research Munchausen Syndrome by Proxy. I don't know this expert, I don't know his credentials, and I certainly don't know about this esoteric disorder. Out of fairness, if you're going to allow Mr Metz to put on his witness, I feel that I ought to have at least the weekend to prepare my cross.'

Metz nods. 'I agree. In fact, I recommend that we break for the day, if it pleases Your Honor, so that Ms Standish has the rest of the afternoon to begin her research.'

'You do?' Joan says, surprised.

Judge Rothbottam frowns. 'Hang on a second. You were

too fired up this morning for an about-face. What's the problem, Mr Metz?'

'My witness has apparently tried several times to interview Faith White today, which of course would be germane to his testimony, but she is too incapacitated to speak to him.' He smiles, conciliatory, at Joan. 'It turns out that I'm going to need a little more time, too.'

'Too damn bad,' the judge says. 'You jumped in the water, you're going to swim. As you pointed out, it's three. I have supreme faith that you'll be able to keep your expert on the stand for an hour reciting credentials. We'll get through whatever you can, and pick up on Monday. Your doctor will have a chance to talk to the girl this weekend.' He turns to Joan. 'And by then, I assume, you'll have a cross-examination prepared.'

'Yes, Your Honor.'

'Marvelous.' He looks at Metz. 'Call your witness.'

Metz's expert psychologist, Dr Celestine Birch, clearly resembles the tree that shares his surname. Tall and cadaverously thin, pale as the silver bark, he sits on the stand stiffly with the air of supreme confidence that comes when you know you are outstanding in your field.

'Where did you go to school, Doctor?'

'I attended Harvard University, then Yale Medical School. I did my residency at UCLA Medical Center and practiced for ten years at Mount Sinai in New York City before setting up my own private practice back in California. I've been practicing there for eleven years.'

'What is your major field of practice?'

'I deal mostly with children.'

Metz nods. 'Are you familiar, Doctor, with a psychiatric disorder called Factitious Disorder by Proxy?'

'Yes, in fact I'm considered one of the top three specialists in the nation on the disorder.'

'Could you describe it for us?'

'Certainly,' Birch says. 'According to the American Psychiatric Association's DSM-IV, Factitious Disorder by Proxy is a rare disorder in which a person deliberately produces physical or psychological symptoms in another person under his or her care.' The psychiatrist begins to warm to his subject. 'Basically, it involves one person making another look or feel sick. It's often called Munchausen Syndrome by Proxy—or MSP—after Baron von Munchausen, an eighteenth-century mercenary who became famous for his exaggerated tales.

'The majority of victims of Munchausen by Proxy are children. Most often, a mother artificially creates or exaggerates symptoms in a child, and then presents the child for medical care claiming to have no knowledge about the etiology of the problem. The theory of mental-health professionals is that these women do not want to inflict pain on a child, but to indirectly assume the role of the sick person—by getting sympathy from doctors whom they encounter when they bring in the ailing child.'

'Whoa,' Metz says. 'Let's take this a little more slowly. You're saying that the mother makes her own kid sick, just to get attention?'

'That's exactly what it boils down to, Mr Metz. And making a child sick would be the simpler end of the spectrum. Some mothers contaminate urine samples with blood, create leaks in an IV, or suffocate newborns. Munchausen Syndrome by Proxy is considered a form of child abuse, and there's a nine-percent mortality rate.'

'These mothers kill their children?'

'Sometimes,' Dr Birch says. 'Unless they can be stopped.'

'What are some of the ailments produced by these mothers?'

'Bleeding presents in forty-four percent of MSP cases. Then seizures, forty-two percent. Followed by central-nervous-system depression, apnea, and gastrointestinal disorders. Not to mention psychological symptoms.'

'Can you tell us what might trigger this behavior in a mother?'

The doctor shifts in his chair. 'Remember, this isn't going to happen to ninety-nine percent of mothers—it's not like a flu virus you come down with. These women are disturbed. Often it's triggered by life stressors—marital conflict, divorce.

Perpetrators may have a history of being abused themselves, and they often have some exposure to medical communities, so they know the ins and outs and the lingo. They need—no, they *crave* support and attention. To them, being sick is a way of being loved and cared for.'

'You said psychological symptoms can be produced in a child, too? Can you explain?'

'By symptoms, I mean hallucinations or delusions; memory loss or amnesia; or conversion symptoms, like pseudoblindness. It's harder to understand how a mother can "fake" them in a child, but basically it involves the mother selectively reinforcing maladaptive behavior. For example, she may provide tremendous nurturing when the child reports a vivid dream and ignore or harm a child when the child is acting perfectly normal. Eventually, the child will learn to give her mother what she wants, so to speak.'

'Would it make a difference if that child had only one parent living with her?'

'Absolutely,' Birch says. 'In fact, it makes parental approval that much more integral.'

'So an alleged vision is something that might be reinforced in MSP?'

'Yes, although you'd be more likely to find delusions and hallucinations reinforced in a child if the mother has had some personal experience with either delusions or hallucinations.'

'Such as a mother who spent time in a mental institution?'

Dr Birch nods. 'Entirely consistent.'

'Doctor, what happens if the mother is confronted with her behavior?'

'Well, they lie and say they're not doing it. In rare cases, the mother may honestly be unaware of her behavior, because she's unconsciously harming the child during a dissociation that occurs as a result of earlier trauma.'

'You mean that you could ask these women flat-out if they're hurting their children, and they'll tell you no?'

'They'll all tell you no,' Birch says. 'It's part of the symptomatology for this disorder.'

'So a woman who seems shocked, confused, even righteously angry when confronted with this behavior—a woman with no memory of harming her child—might still have done it?'

'That's correct.'

'I see,' Metz says slowly. 'How do you diagnose MSP, Doctor?'

Dr Birch sighs. 'Carefully, Mr Metz, and not often enough. Remember, the ones with the presenting symptoms are the children—and they're not going to tell you what's happening, because it's what buys the mother's love. Parents are the primary informants for doctors, who assume their honest report of a child's illness. But most physicians don't make the mental leap and move from trying to diagnose the child to diagnosing the parent.

'Moreover, these mothers don't exactly have scarlet letters on their chests. They deny harming the child and ironically look rather attentive to the child. One way a health-care provider can be tipped off to MSP is to see a long, complicated medical history. Or a description of symptoms that's almost too textbook. Or, in the case of psychological symptoms, to discover that administering drugs doesn't help a whit . . . since these children of course are not truly psychotic.' Birch leans back. 'But the only conclusive way to diagnose MSP is to catch the mother in the act—with video cameras rigged in hospital rooms—or to remove the child from the mother's care. Presumably, if it's Munchausen Syndrome by Proxy, the acute illness will remit once the child is taken away.'

'Doctor, have you seen Faith White?'

'No, but not for want of trying. I tried to get access to her hospital room three times today but was told she was too ill to speak to me.'

'Have you interviewed Mariah White?'

'No, I've reviewed information on her institutionalization and her current mental health.'

'Does Mariah White fit the profile of a perpetrator of MSP?'

'In many ways. The behaviors in her child ensued after a period of great personal stress. Mrs White has seemed a concerned parent, taking her daughter for psychiatric treatment—which, note, did not respond to drug therapy—and to the emergency room. And perhaps what is most telling, in this case, is the choice of stigmata as a presenting ailment. Bleeding is easy to produce in a victim, yet stigmata are fairly brilliant. It *has* to be a symptom with a textbook description, because there aren't any chronicled cases. What physician can say that the child's not a stigmatic, when he's never seen one in his life?'

'Is that all, Doctor?'

'No. Mrs White also has a history of mental-health problems. As a result of marital stress, she attempted to commit suicide—and suddenly a hundred doctors and nurses were there for her support. On some level she equates being loved and taken care of with attention from health-care personnel. Which could explain why, when a similar marital stress occurred, she began to make her child sick. Every time she brings Faith in to be treated, Mrs White herself, by proxy, receives the attention she got seven years ago from doctors and psychiatrists.'

'Could she be hurting her daughter and not know it?' Metz asks.

The doctor shrugs. 'Not having examined her, it's difficult to say. But it's possible. Mrs White suffered from severe depression before, and the shock of finding her husband involved in another extramarital affair might be enough to cause a dissociative break. Rather than face the pain all over again, she absents herself mentally. It's during these episodes that she feels most neglected, and therefore it's during these episodes that she harms her daughter.'

'What do you imagine would happen if you confronted Mrs White with this behavior?'

'She'd flatly deny it. She'd be very upset that I would accuse her of something so heinous. She'd tell me that she loves her daughter and only wants her to be healthy.'

Metz stops at the defense table. 'Dr Birch, as you know, Faith is in the hospital. If her mother were allowed no contact with her for a period of time, what would you expect to happen?'

The psychiatrist sighs. 'I wouldn't be at all surprised to see Faith White bounce back to health.'

December 3, 1999—Late Afternoon

AFTER THE COURT EMPTIES, Joan and I are left sitting alone. 'What are you going to do now?' she asks.

'I'm *not* going to go to the hospital, if that's what you mean.'

'It wasn't. I just . . . well, I didn't know if you had other plans.'

I smile at her. 'I was thinking of going home, taking a hot bath, and then sticking my head in a gas oven.'

'Not funny.' She touches my arm. 'Do you want me to call Dr Johansen for you? I'm sure, given the circumstances, he could squeeze you in for an appointment, just to talk.'

'No. Thanks.'

'Then let's go out for a drink.'

'Joan,' I say, 'I appreciate this. But I don't feel like having company right now.'

'Well, I'm going to go to the hospital to check on Faith. I'll fill your mother in on the court order and ask her to call you at home.'

I thank Joan and tell her I'm going to sit for another moment, and then I listen to her heels click down the long aisle of the courtroom. Resting my head on the table, I close my eyes. I try very hard to picture Faith. If I do, maybe she will know that I'm here, thinking of her.

When the custodian comes in with the machine that buffs the floor, I leave, surprised to find a bustle of activity in the hallways and lobby of the courthouse. Just because our hearing is finished for the day does not mean anyone else's is. Leaning against a wall is a weeping woman, an elderly man with his arm ratcheted over her shoulders. Three toddlers weave through a bank of plastic chairs. A teenager hunches like a question mark over the receiver of the pay phone, whispering furiously.

Although I don't want to see Ian, it is still a disappointment not to find him waiting.

It has started to snow, the first snow of the winter. The flakes are thick and fat; they melt against the pavement as if I have only been dreaming them. I am so caught up in the beauty of it that I do not notice Ian standing beside my car until I am only a few feet away.

'I have to talk to you,' he says.

'No, you don't.'

He grasps my arm. 'Aren't you going to speak to me?'

'Do you really want me to, Ian? Do you want me to thank you for calling that idiot reporter from the *Globe* and getting him to dig up Greenhaven, so that Malcolm Metz could twist it into some sick psychological disorder I have that makes me mutilate my own child?'

'If I hadn't called, Metz would have dug it up by himself.'

'Don't you *dare* make excuses,' I say, my voice low.

I get into the car and try to close the door, but Ian holds it fast. 'I think I'm in love with you,' he says.

'And why is that? Because I had the good fortune to give birth to an extraordinary child you could use to boost your show's ratings?'

'What did you want me to say? I didn't know you when I called McManus. Afterward, I didn't want to tell you, because I thought you'd hate me for it. And as for what I said about Faith—well, Christ, I had to be vague. I thought the last thing you wanted was for me to tell the world that I believe Faith can heal.'

'Somehow, Ian, I have a hard time believing you had Faith in mind up there on the stand. I have a hard time believing you were thinking of anything but your show-biz reputation.'

A muscle jumps along Ian's jaw. 'All right, maybe I was. But I was also thinking of Faith. And you. What do I have to do to convince you? I'll give the money Metz paid me to Faith's college fund . . . or to the frigging Jesuits. I'll go public saying whatever you want. I made a mistake, and I'm sorry. Why can't you just believe me?'

Because, I want to say. Because of what's happened to Faith. *She* believed, and look at where it's gotten her.

'Mariah,' Ian begs hoarsely, 'let me come home with you.'

With a tremendous yank, I manage to pull the door out of his grasp. 'You can't always get what you want,' I say. 'Not even you.'

Let me tell you what you feel like when you know you are ready to die.

You sleep a lot, and when you wake up the very first thought in your head is that you wish you could go back to bed.

You go entire days without eating, because food is a commodity that keeps you here.

You read the same page a hundred times.

You rewind your life like a videocassette and see things that make you weep, things that make you pause, but nothing that makes you want to play it forward.

You forget to comb your hair, to shower, to dress.

And then one day, when you make the decision that you have enough energy left in you to do this one, last, monumental thing, there comes a peace. Suddenly you are counting moments as you haven't for months. Suddenly you have a secret that makes you smile, that makes people say you look wonderful, although you feel like a shell—brittle and capable of cracking into a thousand pieces.

I was looking forward to dying. I remember holding the razor blade and hoping to make the cleanest, deepest cut. I remember calculating how long it would be until I heard the voices of angels. I wanted nothing more than to be rid of myself, of this body and this person who had nothing coming to her but pain.

In short, I have been there. I, of all people, should understand wanting to give up, when the ache is too great. But instead I feel myself fighting furiously, grasping at straws to keep Faith from succeeding where I once failed.

'Her temp's at one-oh-six. Something's got to give.'

As if the doctor's words have prompted it, Faith's limbs stiffen, and she begins to thrash from side to side. 'She's going into seizures,' the doctor calls out. A nurse gently pulls Millie away from the bedside. 'Ma'am, I'm going to have to get in here.'

The doctor holds down one of Faith's wrists. The nurse holds the other one. Faith's body continues to buck and heave, with the jerky rhythm of an amusement-park ride. 'She's bleeding again,' the nurse murmurs.

'I want pressure and elevation,' the doctor calls, and the bed levitates with the push of a button as two nurses begin to press against her palms.

High-pitched beeps suddenly break the flurry of activity and make Millie jerk her head toward the monitors behind Faith's bed. 'She's coding. Get a cart!' The doctor moves to the side of the bed and starts to perform manual CPR.

Within minutes, the room is filled with nurses and doctors.

'Ressler, bag her and intubate her. Chest compressions at fifteen per minute.' The doctor checks the rhythm of Faith's heartbeat and continues shouting orders. 'Wyatt, put in a central line and pour in lactated Ringer's as fast as it'll go, for one liter. And Abby, I want a CBC, platelets, and a clot sent to the blood bank for type and cross.'

'Ma'am, why don't you come with me, so we can help her?' The nurse tugs Millie out to the hall, where she stands with her face pressed to the glass of the pediatric ICU. Millie watches someone rip open Faith's hospital johnny and set defibrillator paddles on her small chest. She does not realize that her hand has crept up to cover her own strong heart.

A Half Hour Later

JOAN SITS BESIDE Millie in the patient lounge. She's never liked hospitals; this one is no different . . . but there's something she can't put her finger on that seems even more unnerving than usual. She smiles gently at Mariah's mother, encouraging her to continue.

'The doctor,' Millie tearfully relates, 'says that she has an excellent prognosis because she spent less than a minute in cardiac arrest. Her airway's clear, and her rhythm's been steady.'

Joan glances at the girl, limp on the hospital bed. 'She doesn't look good.'

'But they've got her heart under control, and her fever is down. The only thing they can't stop is the bleeding.' Millie takes a deep breath. 'So how long before Mariah gets here?'

'Actually, that's why I needed to speak to you. Mariah can't come to the hospital.'

'Did something happen? Is she all right?'

'She's fine. She's just under a restraining order, courtesy of the judge and Malcolm Metz. They think she's causing Faith's symptoms.'

'That's . . . that's ridiculous!' Millie sputters.

'You and I know that, but you don't mess with a restraining order. I'm going to need you to stay with Faith and call Mariah with updates.'

'She can't even *call*?'

Joan shakes her head.

'This must be killing her.' Millie rubs her temples, clearly torn between keeping watch over her granddaughter and going to her own child to provide emotional support.

Joan glances down the hallway. It suddenly hits her: The strange thing about this pediatric ICU ward is that Faith is the only patient in it. With the exception of the doctors and nurses called in for Faith, there's no one around. 'When you call—'

'I won't make it sound this bad,' Millie says. 'I'm not a fool.'

Colin walks into the darkened ICU room and stands at the foot of his daughter's bed.

Her arms are spread wide, loosely tied with restraints to the bedrails to keep the wounds in her palms from reopening. Her feet are anchored by the blanket. His eyes touch upon the wires taped to her chest, the tube in her throat, the gauze pads cupped in her hands.

He does not know what to believe. He listens to the doctors when they speak to him. He listened to that psychiatrist, Birch. And he listens to Mariah when she swears she'd never hurt Faith. Colin sits gently on the bed next to Faith.

'"Hush little baby, don't say a word. Daddy's gonna buy you a mockingbird."' He presses his wet cheek against Faith's, hears the steady beep of the monitor attached to her chest. '"If that mockingbird don't sing, Daddy's gonna buy you a diamond ring."'

The doctors told him that Faith's heart gave out. That with all the stress put on it by the other failing systems of her body, it simply stopped.

He knows what that feels like. He would drop the custody case this minute if it meant Faith would walk out of the hospital as healthy and hale as any seven-year-old.

He leans down and awkwardly wraps her in his arms. 'Hug me back,' he whispers, and then more forcefully, 'Come *on*.' Just one slight twitch and he'll be happy. He shakes her a little, urging her to consciousness, but then a nurse is beside him and pulling him from the bed. 'You need to let her rest, Mr White.'

'I want her to hold me. I just want her to do that one thing.'

'She can't,' the nurse says. 'Her hands are tied.' And while Colin is still turning that phrase over in his mind, she ushers him out of the room.

'You're telling me everything?' I ask, hanging on to the receiver of the portable phone so tightly I must be leaving nail marks.

'Would I lie to you?' my mother answers. 'She's in there sleeping.'

'So she hasn't gotten better, but she hasn't gotten worse.' Stability I can handle. It is having to sit idly while Faith is in trouble that sends me over the edge.

'Kenzie van der Hoven's here,' my mother says. 'She's been at the hospital for an hour.'

'Did that idiot psychiatrist show up?'

'The one who kept coming all day? No.'

She hesitates; I can hear it in her voice. 'What, Ma?'

'Nothing.'

'It's something,' I press. 'What?'

'Nothing. It's just that Colin came, too.'

'Oh,' I answer, in a very small voice. 'Did Faith wake up?'

'No. She didn't even know he was here.'

I'm sure my mother says this to make me feel better, but it doesn't. I hang up the phone, realizing moments later that I never said good-bye.

Ian has walked the streets of New Canaan for the past three hours. The town is tiny and dark, and every store is closed, with the exception of the Donut King, and he can't go back inside there yet again without looking like a jerk. The problem is, there's nowhere else to go.

He sits on the curb. He doesn't want to head back to the Winnebago and face the people who work for him, people sure to be confounded by his testimony today. He doesn't want to go anywhere near the hospital, where he's certain to be accosted by the press.

He does want to be with Mariah, but she won't let him.

Ian doesn't know when, exactly, he went from thinking that Mariah was some kind of 'Mommie Dearest' putting her kid up to this kind of attention, to thinking that Mariah was the victim in this whole mess. Most likely it was in Kansas City. He'd done such a thorough job of pretending to want to help Mariah that at some point it became an honest emotion.

But, just maybe, Mariah wasn't the one who needed help. Maybe that distinction belongs to Ian himself.

He's never really asked himself why he's an atheist, but the answer's there for the taking. Knocked down as a child by fate, he couldn't buy into the concept of a loving God. After all the people close to him were taken away, he couldn't buy into the concept of love, period, so he re-created himself into someone who wouldn't have to. And, like the Wizard of Oz, he's learned if you hide long enough behind a curtain of bluff and principle, people stop trying to find out who you are in the first place.

Maybe there is more to a person than a body and a mind. Maybe something else figures into the mix—not a soul, exactly, but a spirit that hints you might one day be greater, stronger than you are now. A promise; a potential.

Mariah has fallen apart and pulled herself back together. She may weave in the wind, but she stands there, scars and all. And, unlike Ian, she's stood up to the same bolt of lightning that knocked her down before, willing to risk it again. For all intents and purposes, she, too, should shy away from love. But she doesn't—and no one knows that better than Ian himself.

Mariah might have tried to kill herself once; she may be the one whose credibility and mental stability are being debated in a court of law; but in Ian's eyes, she is one of the strongest people he's ever met.

Ian stands, dusts off his bottom, and starts walking down the street.

The last person I expect to find when I open the door is Colin. 'Can I . . .?' he gestures inside. I nod, step back, so that he can enter the house he used to own.

I close the door behind him and hold my hand to my throat, needing to physically keep all the horrible things I want to say from springing to my lips. 'You shouldn't be here. Neither of our attorneys would allow it.'

'I don't really give a flying fuck what Metz thinks right now.' Colin crosses to the stairs and sits down, burying his face in his hands. 'I just saw Faith.'

'I know. My mother said you were there.'

Colin glances up. 'She's—God, Rye. She's so, so sick.'

After the initial shock of fear that runs through my system, I force myself to relax. After all, Colin was not around the first time her hands bled. He wouldn't know what to expect.

'They say that her heart's going to be all right . . .'

'Her heart?' I say, my voice dry as ash. 'What about her heart?'

Colin seems honestly surprised that I do not know. 'It stopped. This afternoon.'

'It *stopped*? She went into cardiac arrest and nobody *told* me? I'm going there.'

Colin is on his feet in one smooth motion, grabbing my arm. 'You can't. You can't, and I'm so sorry about that.'

I stare down at his hand on my arm, his skin on my skin, and then suddenly he is holding me and I am crying against his chest. 'Colin, tell me.'

'She's been intubated, to help her breathe. And they used defibrillator paddles—you know, those things—to get her heartbeat steady again. Her hands started bleeding again after she had a seizure.' I hear the tears in his throat, and stroke his back. 'Did we do this to her?'

I look at him, wondering if he is accusing me. But he seems too upset for that; I think he is truly just shaken. 'I don't know.'

Suddenly I remember the night that Faith was born. It was only a month after I'd left Greenhaven, and still buffeted by the drugs I'd been given, I found that there was very little that seemed real. Not Colin, not my home, not my life. It wasn't until the pain of a contraction sliced down my middle that I realized I'd come back.

I remember the lights that were set up at the foot of the birthing bed, like some Hollywood production. I remember the plastic mask the doctor wore, and the smell of latex when she snapped on her gloves. I remember the sound of Colin's head striking the edge of the nightstand when he fainted, and the fuss that was made over him while I splayed my hands over my belly and waited my turn. I remember thinking of my heart, balanced just above the baby's feet, like the ball on a trained seal's nose. And then there was the remarkable drive that came when I realized the only way to stop the pain was to get it out of me, to push and push until I was certain I'd turn myself inside out, even as I felt her head widening and changing me and the small knob of her nose and chin and shoulders as they slipped in succession, streaming between my legs in a shuddering rush of breath and blood and beauty.

But what I remember the most was the nurse who held Faith up before her umbilical cord had been cut. 'What a beautiful daughter!' She brought her closer, so that I could see the swollen face, the pumping legs. And the baby, purely by chance, kicked the umbilical cord. I felt it all the way up inside me, an odd tug and a trembling that continued straight along to the belly of my daughter, so that Faith's eyes startled open, too. And I thought for the first time, *We are connected.*

Colin buries a sob against my hair. 'It's all right,' I say, although it isn't, not by a long shot. I turn in his arms and realize I am glad he is here; I am glad we can do this for each other. 'Sssh,' I soothe, as I might have soothed Faith if I'd been by her side.

December 4, 1999

FIRST THING SATURDAY MORNING Joan gets a cup of very strong, very black coffee at the Donut King and enough jelly rolls to last through an extended day, and then continues fifty yards down the street to her law office. She starts to set the key in the door and finds it already unlocked. Thinking of vandals, robbers, and, actually, Malcolm Metz, she pushes the door so that it swings open.

Ian Fletcher is hunched over her secretary's computer. He looks over his shoulder. 'It's about time. I've printed out everything I could find on the Web about Munchausen by Proxy. I think your best bet's going to be pointing out the specificity of the disorder. There were only two hundred cases nationwide last year. What's the chance of Mariah being one of them? Plus, she doesn't have the background for it. She wasn't abused as a child, and if Millie's on the stand—'

'Wait. What are you doing here?'

Ian shrugs. 'What does it look like I'm doing? I'm your legal assistant.'

'The hell you are! Mariah doesn't want you within state limits anymore, much less helping out on the case. For all I know, you might be playing double agent again, trying to bring us down before we even get to present our side.'

'Please,' Ian says seriously. 'This is what I do for a living. I dig things up. I unearth. I disprove. If Mariah won't let me help *her,* at least let me help *you.*'

Realistically, Joan has a marginal shot at finding out enough to bring down Dr Birch—that is, if she's working alone. She doesn't have the time or the resources Metz does at his high-end law office; plus, she doesn't even know where to start.

Sensing her weakening, Ian holds up a sheaf of papers. 'You need a defense against Munchausen by Proxy. So I've been talking on-line to a doctor out at UCLA who's a specialist in psychosomatic illnesses that present in children of divorce.' He raises a brow. 'Dr Fitzgerald says there have even been cases of psychologically based bleeding.'

Joan hands him the box of jelly rolls. 'You're hired,' she says.

When my mother calls first thing that morning, I let her have it. I yell at her so long and so loud for lying to me about Faith's condition that I bring her to tears. She hangs up the phone, and immediately I feel awful; I can't even call her back to apologize.

Colin stayed until 4:00 A.M. It crossed my mind that his new wife was probably trying to find him. Then again, maybe she wasn't. Maybe that's why she was his new wife.

Before he left, he kissed me good-bye. Not with passion, but with an apology that slipped between my lips like licorice, and tasted just as bitter.

The house is quiet. I sit in Faith's bedroom, staring at her dollhouse and her art set and her Barbies, trying to get up the nerve to touch them. I sit so rigidly that my jaw hurts, just from keeping it clenched.

I ought to be with her now, the way my mother used to stay with me when I was sick, holding the cup of juice to my lips, circling the Vicks VapoRub over my chest, sitting there when I woke up, as if she hadn't moved a muscle all night.

It's what mothers do. They keep vigils; they put their children first.

It is exactly what I have not done.

My first act of motherhood was to blame my unborn child for her father's infidelity. My second act of motherhood was to swallow a rainbow of pills, although the doctors did not know what the consequences would be to a fetus. They told me that it was more important to cure my depression than to worry about the risks to the baby. And I—fool—believed them.

I spent months hoping Faith would be born healthy, so I'd be off the hook. Then, when she was, I kept waiting for the other shoe to drop. But now I see it was a waste of time. Motherhood isn't a test, but a religion: a covenant entered into, a promise to be kept. It comes one-size-fits-all, and it camouflages flaws like nothing else. How could it have taken this to make me see that Faith is the one thing in my life I got right on the very first try?

I look down at my hands. Without realizing it, I have wandered into the bathroom, picked up the razor I use to shave my legs, and snapped open its harmless plastic holder, so that I'm now holding the lethal edge of a blade.

With care, I throw it into the trash.

'What do you mean we can't speak to her?' Malcolm Metz yells. 'Do you have any idea what we had to do to get upstairs? It's a fucking zoo in the lobby.'

A nurse turns toward Dr Blumberg. 'What's up?'

'A bunch of AIDS patients. Their T-cell counts are suddenly in normal range.'

'No kidding?' the nurse says.

'I don't care if the bodies in the goddamned morgue are now eating lunch in the cafeteria,' Metz growls. 'I want Dr Birch to be granted permission to speak to Faith White.'

'Oh, he has my permission,' Blumberg says. 'Just don't expect him to get too far.'

At the sound of raised voices, Kenzie comes out of Faith's room. She's been reading to her for the past three hours, even though Faith is unconscious. 'What's going on?'

'This is the fifth time Dr Birch has tried to interview Faith,' Metz says. 'My case will be seriously hampered if we don't walk into court on Monday with this information.'

'I'm sorry Faith can't accommodate you,' Kenzie says tightly. 'She's comatose.'

At that, Metz looks surprised. 'She *is*? I thought Standish was exaggerating to win sympathy. Christ, I'm sorry.' He turns to Birch. 'Maybe you could speak to her doctors.'

'I'd be happy to talk to you,' Dr Blumberg says.

But before he and Dr Birch can leave, Millie suddenly sways on her feet. Malcolm Metz catches her in his arms before she hits the floor.

'Millie?' Kenzie asks. 'When was the last time you got some rest?'

'I don't know. I guess it's been a while.'

'Go lie down. There are enough free beds around here. I'm not going to let anything happen to Faith.'

'I know. I just don't want to miss it when she comes around. Maybe if I close my eyes for ten minutes . . .'

'Take your time,' Kenzie answers, but she does not say what she's thinking: that Faith may never wake up.

That night I dream I am talking to Faith's God.

She is, quite definitely, a She. She comes to sit at the foot of my bed, and I stare at the bright edges of Her hair, at the glow at the seams of Her fingers, like a child cupping a flashlight. Her mouth is turned down at the corners, as if She, too, is missing Faith.

A peace settles over the bed like an extra blanket, but I feel myself stirring and sweating. 'You,' I say, anger clawing its way up my chest.

'She isn't in pain.'

'Do you think that makes it all right?' I shout.

'Believe in what I'm doing.'

I cannot trust myself to answer right away. I think of Ian, of what he has said about God. 'How can I believe in You,' I whisper, 'when You would do this to a little girl?'

'I'm not doing it to her; I'm doing it for *her.'*

'Semantics don't make much difference when you're about to die.'

For a while God just sits on the edge of my bed smoothing Her hand over the covers and leaving behind a silver patina, like the gilding of great ages gone by. *'Did you ever consider,'* She says softly, finally, *'that I know what it's like to lose a child?'*

• • •

December 5, 1999—2:00 A.M.

FAITH GOES INTO cardiac arrest again an hour later. This time Kenzie stands outside the glass windows with Millie, watching the doctors fight to stabilize the little girl. After several minutes of confusion and brutal intervention on Faith's body, Dr Blumberg approaches them. He knows of the court order, and disapproves. He invites Millie to step aside so they can speak privately, but she waves away the suggestion and tells him to speak in front of Kenzie.

'She's hanging on, but her heart stopped beating for a while, and she lost oxygen. We won't know if there's brain damage until she wakes up.'

'What . . .' Kenzie tries to ask a question, but it lodges in the pit of her stomach.

'I can't say for sure. Kids can tolerate a lot more than adults. But in Faith's case, things are happening that don't follow logic.' The doctor hesitates. 'There's no apparent medical cause for Faith's cardiac distress, but her body is failing. She's comatose. We're keeping her alive on machines. And I don't know how long that's going to last.'

Millie tries to steady her voice. 'Are you telling me—'

Blumberg inclines his head. 'I'm telling you that friends and family should think about saying their good-byes,' he says gently. Then he turns to Kenzie. 'And I'm telling you to think about whether a piece of paper signed by a judge is as important as that.'

As he walks away, Kenzie finds herself frozen in place. It is early Sunday morning. Only twenty-four hours till they all return to the courtroom. If that's even necessary.

At the sound of a muffled sob, she turns. Millie's face is stoic; even now, she is trying to be the strong one.

Kenzie embraces her. They both know what has to be done. 'Don't call Colin,' Millie blurts out. 'He's the one who's keeping Mariah away. He doesn't deserve to be here.'

She watches the older woman clutch on to her anger like a lifeline. 'Millie,' she says softly, 'I'll be right back.' Then Kenzie walks down the hall to the nearest pay phone. Digging into her pocket, she pulls out a piece of paper, and dials the phone number on it.

The telephone rings in the middle of the night. 'Mariah,' Kenzie van der Hoven says, 'I want you to listen carefully.'

Now, nearly twenty minutes later, I feel foolish walking through the entrance of the hospital wearing my mother's spare pair of reading glasses and an old wig Faith used to use for dress-up. I act as if I know where I am going, and, true to her word, Kenzie is waiting at the elevator banks. Once the doors of the elevator close behind us, I put my arms around Kenzie in gratitude. She told me, on the phone, that Faith was not getting better. That her heart had stopped again. That she might even die. 'At this point I don't care about the judge,' Kenzie said. 'You ought to be here.'

She did not point out the obvious—that keeping me from Faith had done no apparent good, that, in fact, since I've been away from her, she's been failing faster.

I move through the halls of the hospital quietly behind Kenzie, terrified that at any moment someone is going to jump out and point a finger, tag me, cart me off to jail. I concentrate instead on keeping a center of calm, like a hard little nut in my chest, so that when I see Faith—no matter how bad it is—I do not fall apart.

At the elevator it strikes me that something is odd. There is virtually nobody in this hospital. Even at two in the morning, there should be red-eyed doctors, tired relatives, women having babies. As if Kenzie can read my thoughts, she turns to me. 'The rumor mill says Faith's healed a bunch of patients,' she explains simply. 'Just by being here.'

For only a moment, I wonder if it's true. Then I think: at what cost? After bringing my mother back to life, Faith's strength had been sapped. How many patients have come in contact with her in the past two days? And suddenly I understand why Faith is so much sicker this time.

Healing others has been killing her.

Just before the elevator doors open, I say what has been on my mind since Kenzie telephoned. 'You have to call Colin.'

'I already did. He told me to call you.'

'But—'

'He didn't care about the court order either. He said you ought to be here, too.'

Then we are on the pediatric ICU floor. I follow Kenzie to Faith's room—she's been moved since I last saw her. At the glass window, I stop. My mother is sitting on a chair beside Faith's bed, and I'm struck by how old she suddenly looks. Faith . . . well, I would not have recognized her at all. Full of tubes and pads and wires, she looks so small on the narrow bed.

A nurse moves like a shadow as I enter. My mother stands, embraces me. Without speaking, I sit down in the spot she's vacated.

Right now I understand those mothers who can lift automobiles off children who are pinned, women who step heroically in front of bullets. I would give anything to be the body that is lying so still. I would give anything to take her place.

I lean over, my words falling on her face. 'I never told you that I'm sorry,' I whisper. 'For a long time I was so busy with myself that there was no time for you. But I knew you would still be waiting for me, when I was ready.' I touch my hand to her cheek. 'It's your turn, now. Take your time. When you look over your shoulder—days from now, months from now—well, I'm not going anywhere without you.' I close my eyes, listening to the fleeting, occasional whir of the machines feeding into Faith. One piece of equipment picks up its pace, beeping with quick regularity. The nurse looks up, frowns. 'Something's going on,' she says, reading the printout from the electrocardiogram. 'I'd better page Dr Blumberg.'

She's barely left the room when Faith's eyes fly open. They focus on Kenzie first, then my mother, and finally come to rest on me. Faith opens and closes her mouth, trying to speak.

The doctor flies into the room, pulling his stethoscope from around his neck. He checks Faith's vital signs, murmuring quietly to her as his hands move over her body. 'Don't talk yet, kiddo.' He nods to a nurse, and she braces Faith's shoulders while he extracts the endotracheal tube. Faith coughs and gags, and then her voice comes in a sandpaper snap. 'Mommy,' she rasps, smiling, her bandaged hands coming up to frame my face.

sixteen

So lonely 'twas that God himself
Scarce seemed there to be.

—Samuel Taylor Coleridge,
'The Rhyme of the Ancient Mariner'

December 6, 1999

BECAUSE IT IS BITTERLY COLD, the snow does not stick to the pavement. It swirls beneath the undercarriage of Mariah's car; it lies down in her path before twisting out of reach of the wheels.

Mariah keeps her eyes on the road. She concentrates on where she is going, on when she will arrive.

'Dr Birch,' Malcolm Metz says, 'did you interview Faith White this weekend?'

'I went to the hospital, and I did get to see her, but we didn't speak.'

'Why was that, Doctor?'

'She couldn't conduct a conversation. She was comatose.'

'Were you able to speak to anyone affiliated with her case?'

'Yes. I spent some time with a doctor in charge of Faith's medical care, who outlined her symptoms and test results for me.'

'Can you tell us what you learned?'

'She was admitted for observation due to unexplained

bleeding from the hands. Once hospitalized, she developed a high fever, along with febrile convulsions, renal-system failure, and she went into cardiac arrest. This wasn't caused by pulmonary problems, nor does it seem to be a myocardial infarction, myocarditis, or a cardiomyopathy. In short, the doctors are treating the symptoms without necessarily knowing the cause.'

'Could any of these symptoms have been caused by her mother?'

'I suppose so, under the right circumstances,' Birch says. 'Of course, in this case, since Mrs White has not been present at her daughter's bedside since Friday, I'd have to say that the bleeding and the fever are the symptoms most likely produced by her hand. I would have to reserve final judgment until interviewing Faith.'

Metz pauses in front of the witness stand. 'In your expert opinion, Dr Birch, how would you summarize the case of Faith White?'

'Again, this is hypothetical without a chance to talk to the child herself. But if the interview corroborates my gut feelings, I'd have to say that she's a victim of Munchausen by Proxy. The child is obviously failing, and requires immediate long-term separation from her mother to ensure her mental and physical health. Her father is the obvious alternative—he can provide a supportive, loving, and mentally healthy environment for the girl. Of course, this is all dependent on whether the physicians can patch up the damage that's already been done. But if Faith *is* a victim of MSP, if she comes out of the coma and is separated from her mother and given constructive psychotherapy, I think her prognosis would be excellent.'

'Thank you, Doctor.' Metz glances at Joan. 'Your witness.'

Joan braces her hands on the defense table. She is wearing her kick-ass pink suit, as she likes to call it, and feeling confident. 'Dr Birch, are you here at the request of Mr Metz?'

'Yes.'

'Has he paid you to be here?'

'Objection,' Metz says. 'Asked and answered.'

'Withdrawn. How many years have you been practicing?'

'Twenty-three.'

'In those twenty-three years, how many patients have you treated?'

'Oh . . . five hundred? Six?'

Joan nods. 'I see. Out of those five or six hundred patients, how many have you personally diagnosed with Munchausen Syndrome by Proxy?'

'Sixty-eight.'

'In each of these sixty-eight cases, did you have a psychiatric interview with the mother?'

'Yes.'

'In each of these sixty-eight cases, did you have a psychiatric interview with the child?'

'Yes.'

'Have you had a psychiatric interview with Mariah White?'

'No.'

'Have you had a psychiatric interview with Faith White?'

'No. She's in a coma, for God's sake.'

'So you're basing your diagnosis of this case—of this incredibly rare disease—on newspaper articles you've read, and doctors' reports, and seven-year-old records from a psychiatric institution . . . oh, and on hearsay?'

'No—'

'You can't truly diagnose this illness without interviewing Faith and Mariah, can you?'

The psychiatrist's cheeks flag with color. 'I can make a contingent diagnosis. I'm just one step removed.'

Joan arches a brow. 'I see. So, you've . . . contingently diagnosed Mariah White with Munchausen Syndrome by Proxy. Are there any other diagnoses this case might support?'

'Well, there's always something, Ms Standish. But having studied this syndrome for years, I'd say it's a likely diagnosis.'

Joan looks at a pad. 'Have you ever heard of somatization disorder?'

'Of course.'

'Could you define it for us?'

'It's when a child manifests symptoms that are psychologically induced—in other words, he's sick, but it's his mind that's making him sick. Imagine a child who breaks out in hives every time his father has visitation rights; the child is expressing some internal psychological disturbance with physical symptoms. Often it's an unconscious means of getting attention.'

'Have you ever seen clients with somatization disorders?'

'Many times.'

'It's far less rare than Munchausen by Proxy, then.'

'That's correct.'

'Is it true, doctor, that often the victim of a somatization disorder looks a lot like a victim of MSP?'

'Yes. In both disorders, the presenting symptoms have no organic etiology—in MSP because they're faked, in somatization disorder because they're psychologically driven.'

'I see. How do you go about diagnosing somatization disorder, Doctor?'

'You'd interview the parents and the child. And you'd order many medical tests.'

'The same strategy you'd use to diagnose Munchausen Syndrome by Proxy, then.'

'Yes. However, in MSP separation from the parent results in a disappearance of ailments. If the child suffers from somatization disorder, they'll continue.'

Joan smiles. 'May I approach the bench?' Judge Rothbottam beckons the attorneys. 'Your Honor, can I have a little leeway here? I'd like to bring in a live exhibit.'

Metz frowns at her. 'What the hell have you got? A chicken?'

'You'll see in a second. Your Honor, there's really no other way to make my point.'

'Mr Metz?' the judge asks.

'Why not? I'm feeling charitable today.'

After Rothbottam agrees, Joan nods to Kenzie van der Hoven, who walks to the doors at the rear of the courtroom. She summons a bailiff, who enters with Faith in tow.

Faith is wearing a pink dress a shade lighter than Joan's suit. Her hair is bright and silver, her smile infectious. She waves at Mariah as she approaches, and doesn't seem to see the press snapping shut its collective jaw. With the exception of her pallor and tiny bandages at her throat and palms, there is no evidence that hours ago the girl was hovering on the edge of death.

Malcolm Metz does a double take. He turns to Colin, who is suddenly very interested in his lap. 'Did you know about this? Did you?'

But before Colin can answer, Joan speaks. 'Dr Birch, do you know this child?'

'I think . . . I *assume* . . . that it's Faith White,' he says.

'When was the last time you saw her?'

'Late Saturday night. She didn't look like she'd live through the weekend.' His eyes are wide with wonder, riveted to Faith.

'How does she look to you now?'

Birch grins, triumphant. 'Absolutely fine.'

'What's your explanation for this?'

The psychiatrist looks proudly at Malcolm Metz, then at Joan. 'Clearly, my hunch was right. Mariah White is suffering from Munchausen by Proxy. When sequestered from the mother by court order, Faith's illness—very obviously—abated.' He gestures toward Faith, sitting primly beside the guardian ad litem. 'I only hope that the court continues to keep her mother at a distance.'

Joan smiles broadly. 'Doctor,' she says, 'I can't thank you enough.'

Somewhat flustered, Malcolm Metz announces that the plaintiff rests. He doesn't trust Joan Standish as far as he can throw her, but he certainly isn't about to question her if she wants to make his case for him. He touches his client on the shoulder after the judge orders a short recess. 'Let's go get some coffee,' he says to Colin. 'It's looking good, don't you think?'

'Joan,' Mariah says, as soon as they are alone in a small room the size of a janitorial closet, 'what are you *doing*?'

'Trust me,' the attorney says.

'You're making it look like I hurt her! Why didn't you tell Birch I saw her Sunday?'

'Well, because you'd get slapped into jail right now, for one.'

Mariah narrows her eyes. 'Faith isn't making herself sick either, you know,' she says.

Joan sighs. 'Mariah, there are three branches to your defense: to prove that you're a fit mother, to prove that Faith isn't psychotic, and to show the judge there might be a different disorder, other than Munchausen by Proxy, to explain what's going on. It's a loophole defense—we just need to come up with an alternative to the plaintiff's story. And if our story is better than theirs, we win. It's that simple.' She stares directly at Mariah. 'I'm not trying to place the blame on Faith instead of you. I'm just trying to arrange things so you get to keep your daughter.'

Mariah looks up. 'All right,' she says, resigned. 'You do what you have to.'

Judge Rothbottam peers at Joan over his half-glasses. 'Ms Standish,' he says, 'I believe you're entitled to make an opening statement, if you're so inclined.'

'You know, Your Honor, I wasn't planning on making one—'

'Ah,' the judge mutters. 'Maybe God *does* have a hand in this case.'

'—but after all that's been happening, I think I actually would like to say a few things.' She gets to her feet and walks in front of the defense table. 'This is a confusing case,' she says flatly. 'It's confusing because it's a custody case, but there's a side issue going on, too. And we can't help but notice that issue—namely, that there's a reason this little girl has been in the news. If you listen to all the reports, well . . . Faith White says she's seen God. Pretty wild, don't you think?' Joan smiles, shakes her head. 'Mr Metz says that all this is her mother's fault. That somehow Mariah White is managing to get Faith to hallucinate and see God, and is physically harming her daughter to boot. And, actually, I think *that's* pretty wild, too.'

Joan turns toward the window, looking at the rapidly falling snow. 'You know, I just read the other day that Eskimos have over twenty words for snow. There's crusty snow, there's sleety snow, there's powder. I might look out this window and see something beautiful. Mr Metz might look out and think it's going to make the commute a mess. And, Judge, you might look out here and see a day on the slopes.

'There are many ways to look at the same thing. You've seen Mr Metz's case. I'm going to show you the same facts, but I view them a little differently. In the first place, unlike Mr Metz, I don't think this is a case about Mariah White. I think it's about Faith. So I'm going to prove that, number one, Faith is a happy little girl. She's not sick, she's not psychotic, and she's certainly not comatose. I'm not going to prove whether or not she's seeing God, because that's not my job. My job is to show you that she's psychologically happy, she's physically okay, and she's going to act the same way no matter which parent she is living with. The question is: Which parent should that be?'

Joan takes a deep breath. 'The answer is Mariah White. And that's the second thing I'm going to prove. Regardless of what happened seven years ago—right now, the best parent for Faith is her mother.' She trails her fingers on the edge of the defense table. 'Mr Metz has given you his interpretation of the circumstances surrounding Faith White. He's shown you what *he* wants to see. Don't rely on his eyes.'

Dr Mary Margaret Keller seems nervous on the stand. Her eyes dart about the courtroom as if they were following a mouse no one else can see. She crosses and uncrosses her legs. And when Joan first asks her to list her credentials, her voice shakes.

'How long have you been a child psychologist, Dr Keller?'

'Seven years.'

'What are your specialties, Doctor?'

'I do a lot of work with younger children who've suffered family trauma.'

'Why were you chosen to be Faith's psychiatrist?'

'I was referred to Mrs White by her own psychiatrist, Dr Johansen. He called me up and asked me, as a favor, to take this case.'

'How many times did you see Faith?'

Dr Keller folds her hands in her lap. 'Fourteen,' she says.

'What sorts of things did you do?'

'Basically, I watched her play. It's an excellent way to pick up on disturbing behaviors.'

'What were some of the behaviors you noticed?'

'Well, there was a very strong defense mechanism she'd developed—an imaginary friend who could keep her safe. Faith referred to her by a certain name—her guard, I thought she was saying. It made wonderful psychological sense: A little girl who's been dealt several difficult blows found someone to protect her. I thought it was very healthy.'

'Then what happened?'

'Mrs White became concerned because Faith began to exhibit behaviors not consistent with her upbringing. She was quoting Bible verses, although she'd never seen a Bible in her life. And there were a couple of instances where Faith came in contact with an ill person, and managed to make them better.'

'What did that lead you to believe, Doctor?'

Dr Keller smiles ruefully. 'I didn't jump to any conclusions at first. But I started to wonder if instead of calling her imaginary friend her "guard," Faith was actually saying "God."' She removes her glasses and wipes them on the hem of her skirt. 'Seeing God is usually a sign of psychosis,' she explains. 'It didn't sit well with me, because Faith was able to function normally in every aspect of her life, with the exception of these hallucinations. But I recommended to Mrs White that Faith go on a trial run of Risperdal.'

'What happened when she was taking the medicine?'

'She became groggy and tired, but the visions didn't abate. We tried a different antipsychotic medicine, and she still exhibited this behavior.'

'Finally, Dr Keller, what did you decide to do?'

'I called in a colleague, a specialist in childhood psychosis. He observed Faith and agreed that she didn't seem psychotic. I felt validated. There are a great deal of things I don't understand in this world, but I do know what a psychotic child looks like, and Faith isn't it.'

Metz stands up for his cross-examination and walks toward the psychologist. 'Dr Keller,' he says, 'do you know what you're suggesting here?'

She blushes. 'Yes.'

'Isn't it true you went to parochial school for twelve years?'

'Yes.'

'And didn't you have a very strong Catholic upbringing?'

'Yes, I did.'

'At a symposium, Doctor, didn't you go so far as to admit that once you personally felt God beside you when you were praying?'

Dr Keller looks into her lap. 'I was only a child, but I've never forgotten it.'

'Don't you think that you might be predisposed to believing Faith is also seeing God?'

At that, the psychiatrist glances up with a cool, professional demeanor. 'Regardless of my personal beliefs, Mr Metz, I conducted a variety of clinical tests—'

'Yes or no, Dr Keller?'

'No,' she says militantly.

Metz rolls his eyes. 'Aw, come on, Doctor. Don't you believe in God?'

'Yes.'

'Don't you go to Mass every week?'

'I do.'

'And the conclusion you've drawn is that Faith's seeing God. Do you think your conclusion might be different from someone who's . . . say . . . an atheist?' Metz turns around, his eyes skimming over Ian, sitting in the gallery.

'If I was an atheist,' she says, 'I'd still be a very thorough psychiatrist. And I'd still say this child is not psychotic.'

Metz narrows his eyes. This is not going the way he planned. The little wren of a woman should have folded five questions ago. 'Dr Keller, didn't you present Faith's case at a psychiatric symposium?'

'Yes, I did.'

Metz advances on her. 'Isn't it true that you brought up

the case at the symposium because you wanted to make yourself look good, Doctor?'

'No. In fact, I was putting my reputation on the line.' She smiles sadly. 'How many psychiatrists honestly want to go on record as saying that a child is seeing God?'

'But you did get attention for yourself, at the expense of the client's confidentiality,' he repeats. 'Isn't that somewhat unethical?'

Surprising him yet again, Dr Keller withdraws a piece of paper from the notebook on her lap. 'I have a signed release right here from Mariah White, authorizing me to take her daughter's case to the symposium as long as Faith's name was not mentioned.'

'Really!' Metz says. 'So we have evidence of Mrs White trying to prostitute her daughter to gain an audience.'

'Mrs White and I discussed this in depth,' Dr Keller says. 'It was our hope that we could involve a specialist with more experience than I have, who might help us get to the root of Faith's visions. As you know, twenty degrees working together on a case is considerably better than just one. We weren't looking for an audience, Mr Metz. We were looking for a cure.'

'Did you ever interview Mrs White in the role of a therapist?' Metz asks.

'No, I was her daughter's psychiatrist.'

'Then can you say with absolute certainty that somewhere in this mother's twisted mind she wasn't trying to make you put her daughter on display?'

Dr Keller looks at Mariah, then at Faith sitting several rows behind her. 'No,' she says, her word soft as it falls into Metz's outstretched hand.

'She was brought into the emergency room, bleeding from both palms,' Dr Blumberg says in response to Joan's question. 'Traditional emergency-medical procedures failed to stop the bleeding, and I was called in for a consultation.'

'What did you do, Doctor?'

He leans back in the chair. 'I x-rayed her hands.'

'What did you find?'

'No sign of trauma. Literally, a hole went straight through. No tearing of tissue, no mangled bones, nothing to indicate that this was a puncture wound of any kind, in spite of the slow and steady flow of blood.'

'Had you ever seen anything like this before, Dr Blumberg?'

'Absolutely not. It stumped me. I called in experts and colleagues, pediatric and surgical and orthopedic specialists, and we ruled out the medical possibilities one by one. Eventually I just treated the symptoms and sent the girl home, then went back to my office and started reading medical journals.'

'What did you discover?'

'That, as many people know, this had happened in the past. And I mean in the way, way past. I was wary of believing it myself, but apparently several Catholic saints have exhibited stigmata, or spontaneous bleeding from the palms, side, and/or feet that is medically inexplicable, but also medically verifiable. And there is no physical cause for it.'

'When was the last documented case?' Joan asks.

'Objection—Dr Blumberg hasn't been ordained.'

'I'll allow it,' the judge says. 'Doctor?'

'There was a man named Padre Pio, who died in 1968. But the most famous stigmatic would probably be Saint Francis of Assisi, who lived in the twelfth century. According to the reports I read, the wounds are quite real, quite painful.'

'What are the main characteristics you found in journals about stigmata?'

'They can't be cured by ordinary remedies used to control bleeding or induce clotting. They last for months or years at a time, but unlike long-term natural wounds, don't fester.'

'How does that correspond to Faith's wounds?'

'Very closely,' the doctor says.

'Did you officially diagnose Faith with stigmata?'

Blumberg grimaces. 'No. I was too skeptical. On her record I wrote that after weighing all medical possibilities, the conclusion I'd reached was that it was *possible* that Faith suffered from stigmata. But frankly, I'm still not comfortable with that diagnosis.'

'This past weekend, what was Faith's medical status?'

'She was critically ill. She had been put on dialysis and had gone into cardiac arrest twice, her hands and side were bleeding again, and she'd slipped into a comatose state. My professional opinion was that she wasn't going to recover.'

'What is Faith's medical status now?'

Blumberg grins. 'Shockingly healthy. Kids tend to bounce back quickly, but this is truly remarkable. Nearly all her bodily systems are functioning at a hundred percent, or are well on the way to doing so.'

'In your opinion, Doctor, was Faith's heart and kidney failure intentionally caused by someone?'

'No. There are too many medical personnel around in an ICU for that to happen. Not to mention that traces of medicine which might, for example, cause the heart to arrest were not found in Faith's bloodwork.'

'Were her hand and side wounds caused by someone?'

He shakes his head. 'As I've said, there was no indicative trauma. Just a tiny tunnel . . . right through the skin and muscle and bone and sinew.' He holds up his palm. 'There are more bones in the hand than anywhere else in the body, Ms Standish. It's virtually impossible to puncture it without causing some trauma. Yet that's what I saw. Faith was just . . . bleeding.'

'Doctor, are you required by law to file reports of possible child abuse?'

'Yes, any physician must.'

'Did you file this report after seeing Faith White a month and a half ago?'

'No, I did not.'

'Did you file this report after admitting Faith White on Thursday night?'

'No.'

'Was there any reason for you to file that report?'

'Absolutely none.'

'Thank you,' Joan says. 'Nothing further.'

'Dr Blumberg,' Metz asks, 'how many cases of stigmata have you treated?'

The doctor smiles. 'Just this one.'

'But you feel qualified to give us an expert opinion here? Isn't it true that because you couldn't diagnose Faith's wounds, you made an educated guess?'

'First let me tell you what I ruled out, Mr Metz. I considered both direct and indirect trauma to the appendage. I examined the possibility of skin secretions, or nerves adjacent to the skin producing some substance, but the emissions were laboratory-tested, and they were indeed blood. Stigmata was the only diagnosis I could find that even came close to matching the clinical observations I made.'

'Can you say without a doubt that this is stigmata?'

'Of course not, it wouldn't be my job. It's the pope's, I guess. All I can tell you is, Faith White was bleeding. And there was no medical explanation for it.'

'Is there a psychological explanation for it?'

Blumberg shrugs. 'In journals I read, there were attempts to replicate stigmata in patients under hypnosis. In a couple of very rare cases, psychiatrists managed to induce a kind of colored sweat . . . but no blood. There's no scientific proof that the imagination can produce stigmata apart from a religious idea.'

'Could the wounds have been produced during a sleepwalking episode?'

'I doubt it. As I said, they looked nothing like puncture wounds.'

'Can you say conclusively that Faith's injuries were not caused by Faith herself, or by another person?'

'It wasn't apparent,' Blumberg says carefully. 'I certainly couldn't come down with an absolute, but this clearly was not a case of child abuse. Mrs White refused to leave her daughter's side, was extremely concerned about Faith's prognosis, and became very agitated when I hypothetically suggested a diagnosis of stigmata.'

'Have you ever seen cases of child abuse, Dr Blumberg?'

'Unfortunately, yes.'

'In any of those cases did the parent harm the child in front of you?'

'No.'

'In any of those cases did the parent seem concerned about the child's prognosis?'

'Yes,' the doctor admits.

'In any of those cases did the abusive parent herself bring the child in to be treated?'

Blumberg clears his throat. 'Yes.'

Metz turns on his heel. 'Nothing further.'

Faith leans to the right. 'Kenzie,' she whispers, 'I've got to pee.'

'Now?' the guardian ad litem asks.

'Yeah. Like *right* now.'

Kenzie grabs the girl's hand and makes their excuses down the row of seated people. Outside the courtroom, she turns left toward the ladies' room. She waits for Faith to finish in a stall and come out and wash her hands. Then she smooths the girl's hair. 'How you doing?'

'It's boring in there,' Faith whines. 'Can we get a Coke?'

'It's important that we stay inside. It won't be too much longer.'

'Just a Coke? Five minutes?'

Kenzie stretches out the kink in her back. 'All right. Five minutes.' She leads Faith to the machines just inside the main lobby of the courthouse. People mill about: sequestered witnesses awaiting their limelight, attorneys on cell phones, uniformed men laying new mud mats on the floor. Kenzie deposits seventy-five cents and lets Faith push the buttons so that the can hurtles out of the chute.

'Mmm. That's good,' Faith says after taking a sip. She pirouettes, testing out her legs after sitting so long, and stops abruptly when she looks through the glass doors of the courthouse. On the steps, on the snow-covered lawn, are hundreds of people. Some of them hold up placards with Faith's face posted; some of them wave rosaries in the air. Their shout of support swells like a tsunami as they catch a glimpse of her.

She had not seen them coming in; Kenzie had taken her through a rear entrance simply so that she would avoid this. 'Hold my drink, please,' Faith says, handing Kenzie the Coke can.

'Faith, don't—' she calls, but she's too late. Faith has already pushed open the doors to stand on the stone steps that lead into the courthouse. After a rousing cheer from her supporters, she raises her hands, and they cry out even louder. Stupefied, Kenzie finds herself unable to move. 'Hello,' Faith says, waving. She smiles as their prayers fall over her, accepting her due like a queen.

'I've been treating Mariah White for seven years,' Dr Johansen says. 'Ever since she left Greenhaven.'

'What was your opinion about her institutionalization?'

'It never should have happened in the first place,' the doctor says. 'There were a variety of other treatments for depression that would have been just as effective.'

'Was there any way Mariah could have prevented herself from being hospitalized?'

'No. Her husband believed it was the best option. Her mother was in Arizona at the time, unaware of the proceedings. Mariah was heavily medicated, and so removed from reality that she couldn't stick up for herself.'

'What was your opinion of Mariah White's mental state upon release from Greenhaven?'

Dr Johansen frowns. 'I found her to be emotionally fragile, but receptive to learning coping skills. And, of course, she was very preoccupied with her pregnancy.'

'Did she exhibit signs of psychosis at that time?'

'No.'

'No delusions, no hallucinations?'

'Never. Even when Mariah was hospitalized, it was for depression.'

'Dr Johansen, what is your opinion of Mariah's mental state today?'

The psychiatrist stares at his client as if divining her thoughts. 'I think she's getting stronger and stronger,' he says solemnly. 'As evidence of that, you need only consider that she's waived doctor/patient confidentiality here in court, in an effort to retain custody. And look back to August: When presented with virtually the same trigger situation that once made her suicidal, she reacted this time in a much healthier manner. She pulled herself together, took care of her daughter, and went on with her life.'

'Doctor, in your mind is there any possibility that this woman would harm her daughter?'

'No.'

'In your therapy over the past seven years, has there ever been an admission, inclination, or thought of Mariah harming her daughter?'

'Absolutely not.'

'Has Mariah spoken to you about the current circumstances surrounding Faith?'

'You mean the visions and the media? Yes.'

'Does Mariah believe that her daughter is, indeed, a visionary?'

Dr Johansen is silent for so long that Joan starts to repeat the question. 'Mariah believes her daughter is telling the truth,' he says. 'For whatever that's worth.'

'How do you go about getting someone committed to a mental institution?' Metz begins.

'It's a court process,' Johansen says. 'A psychiatrist evaluates the person, and the judge reviews the files.'

'So several people are involved in the decision.'

'Yes.'

'Does the system work?'

'Most of the time,' the psychiatrist says. 'In the cases where you can't trust a person's own judgment on the matter.' He stares pointedly at Metz. 'However, in this particular case the system didn't work. Mariah White was severely depressed and overmedicated, and her own wishes were not respected.'

'If the judge had believed that Mrs White didn't need institutionalization, would the court order have been passed?'

'No.'

'If the psychiatrist had believed that Mrs White didn't need institutionalization, would the court order have been passed?'

'No.'

'If the next of kin, Colin White, had believed that Mrs

White didn't need institutionalization, would the court order have been passed?'

'No.'

'I see. So you're suggesting that these various people should have set aside their observations and taken the opinion of a woman who cut open her wrists a week earlier?'

'That's not—'

'Yes or no, Doctor?'

The psychiatrist nods firmly. 'Yes, that is what I'm saying.'

'Let's move on. What did you prescribe for Mariah White when she first left Greenhaven?'

Dr Johansen looks down at his notes. 'Prozac.'

'Was this a continuous prescription?'

'For a while. But after a year she went off it, and she functioned beautifully.'

'You considered her emotionally stable?'

'No question in my mind,' Johansen answers.

'Has Mariah White asked for a refill of that prescription?'

'Yes.'

'When?'

'Three months ago,' the psychiatrist says. 'August.'

'Right after her husband left? Then she wasn't as stable as you thought—right, Doctor?'

Dr Johansen straightens. 'The same exact thing that threw her for a loop seven years ago happened again, Mr Metz. This time, instead of attempting suicide, she called me up and said, "I need help." Any psychiatrist in the country is going to view that as a mark of mental stability.'

'Are there side effects to Prozac?'

'Occasionally.'

'Such as?'

'Sometimes fluoxetine may cause headaches, chills, nervousness, insomnia, drowsiness, anxiety, dizziness. Also hypertension, rashes, nausea, diarrhea, weight loss, chest pain, and tinnitus.'

'What about hallucinations?'

'Yes,' Dr Johansen admits. 'But quite rarely.'

'And suicidal ideation?'

'On occasion. However, you must remember that I've seen

this particular patient on this particular drug at a dosage of twenty milligrams P.O. for over a year. I know how her body reacts to it. Were this a new prescription, Mr Metz, you might be right. But not in the case of Mrs White.'

'Was she off the drug, Doctor, for a period of several years?'

'Yes.'

'Aren't there adverse effects associated with its discontinuation?'

'Yes.'

'Such as suicide attempts, psychosis, delusions, and hallucinations?'

'Again,' Johansen cautions, 'you're talking about a minute percentage of people.'

'But *might* she have had some adverse effects to discontinuation?'

'None that she reported, Mr Metz.'

The lawyer turns. 'Dr Johansen, what's the likelihood of someone who undergoes successful treatment of depression having a recurrence of the illness?'

'I don't have statistics.'

'But it happens fairly often, doesn't it?'

'Yes. But usually the well-adjusted ones know to return to a psychiatric professional, at that point, for help.'

'I see. So basically you're telling us that someone who's crazy once has a good shot at going crazy again.'

'Objection!'

'Withdrawn,' Metz says. 'Nothing further, Doctor.'

Joan is out of her seat before the words leave his mouth. 'I'd like to redirect,' she snaps. 'I'd like to qualify the terms "mental disorder" and "depression." Are they one and the same?'

'Of course not.'

'What was Mariah's diagnosis?'

'Suicidal depression,' Johansen says.

'Have you ever heard of Munchausen Syndrome by Proxy?'

'Yes.'

'Does it stand to reason that a person diagnosed and

treated for suicidal depression would seven years later develop Munchausen Syndrome by Proxy? Is that a direct relationship?'

Dr Johansen bursts out laughing. 'No more than saying that because you eat breakfast in the morning, you're likely to be wearing underwear.'

'Thank you, Doctor,' Joan says. 'I'm through here.'

What Millie decides as she sweeps up to the witness stand is that she's held her tongue long enough. As long as Joan intends to make her a character witness for Mariah, she wants to get her two cents in. She settles in the chair and nods at the attorney, ready to begin.

'Mrs Epstein, how often do you see Faith?'

'At least every other day.'

'How often do you see Faith interacting with Mariah?'

'Again, just as frequently.'

'In your opinion, is Mariah a good mother?'

Looking every inch the proud parent, Millie beams. 'She's a wonderful mother. She works twice as hard as any other parent because she's so intent on doing the best possible job.'

'How has Mariah dealt with the media surrounding Faith these days?'

'How would *you*?' Millie says. 'She's pulled Faith out of school; she keeps her hidden from their cameras. She does whatever she can to give her a normal life.' There. That's her obligation to Joan, the material they've rehearsed ad nauseam. But she continues to speak, causing Joan to stop in her tracks and glance up, surprised at the change in script. 'You all think that Mariah's the one who has to measure up. But whose fault is this, really?' With a trembling finger, she points to Colin. 'He's the one who did this to my daughter before. He had her committed. Well, *he* should be the one committed, for not being able to keep his pants zipped—'

'Mrs Epstein,' Joan says firmly. 'If you could just please stick to the questions?' She clears her throat and gives Millie a very pointed look.

'No, I think now that I'm up here, I'd like to talk. Who wouldn't be depressed if your husband starts sleeping around behind your back? I don't know why—'

'Ma'am,' Judge Rothbottam warns, 'I must ask you to control yourself.'

Joan walks toward the witness stand during this digression, smiling tightly. 'Cut it,' she says through clenched teeth, and turns away, muttering something about loose cannons. 'Mrs Epstein, there are a variety of reasons to legally support a change of custody. To your knowledge, has Mariah ever sexually abused Faith?'

'God, no.'

'Has she ever hit her daughter?'

'She doesn't even smack Faith on the bottom when she's being wise.'

'Has Mariah ever emotionally abused Faith?'

'Absolutely not!' Millie says. 'She's completely supportive.'

'Does Mariah work outside the home, or in any other way spend most of the day away from her daughter?'

'She's with her every minute.' Millie looks sourly toward the judge. 'When she's allowed to be.'

'Thanks,' Joan says, and then sits down before Millie has a chance to say anything else.

Metz eyes Millie Epstein with calculation. He knows damn well why Joan wrapped up so quickly—the old bat's loopy. Like Joan, he plans to steer clear of questions involving reincarnation and second leases on life, questions that would only make him the butt of jokes in the legal community. He smiles, catching Millie off guard. From what Joan's told her, he's sure that he's been built up as a piranha. 'Mrs Epstein, you really love Mariah, don't you?'

Millie's face softens. 'Oh, yes.'

'She grew up very close to you, I bet.'

'Yes.'

Metz leans against the witness stand. 'You watched her graduate from high school?'

'Class valedictorian,' Millie says proudly.

'And college? Magna cum laude?'

'Summa.'

'That's amazing. I barely made it through Freshman

English,' Metz jokes. 'And you, of course, were there when she got married.'

Millie's mouth turns down at the corners. 'Yes.'

'I bet you taught her everything she knows about being a good mother.'

'Well,' Millie says, flushing modestly, 'you never know.'

'I bet you taught her how to help Faith through these difficult times. Am I right?'

Millie's chin comes up. 'I told her over and over: When you're a mother, you stick up for your child. And that's that.'

'Is that what Mariah's been doing all along for Faith?'

'Yes!'

Metz pins her with his gaze. 'And is that what you're doing now for Mariah?'

Millie glances at the judge. 'So? Is that it?'

Judge Rothbottam taps his fingers on the desk. 'You know, Mrs Epstein, actually *I* have a couple of questions.' He glances at each of the attorneys in turn. 'Apparently our esteemed counsel is running a bit shy.'

Millie preens under his regard. 'Go right ahead, Your Honor.'

'I've, um, read in some of the papers that you were . . . resurrected?'

'Oh, yes. In fact,' Millie rummages in her large purse, 'I've got my death certificate somewhere in here.'

'I don't need to see it.' He smiles at her. 'Can you tell me about it, though?'

'The death certificate?'

'Well, no. The resurrection. For example, how long were you clinically dead?'

Millie shrugs. 'About an hour. Signed, sealed, and delivered.'

'What happened?'

'I got into a shouting match with Ian Fletcher. The next thing I know, I'm lying on the floor and I can't breathe. After that, I don't remember.' Pausing dramatically, she leans toward the bench. 'Then I'm all of a sudden in a hospital room with Faith leaning over me.'

The judge shakes his head, amazed. 'Any medical explanations for what happened?'

'As far as I know, Judge, the doctors can't explain it.'

'Mrs Epstein, what do *you* think happened?'

She looks at him seriously. 'I think my granddaughter brought me back to life.'

'What do you make of Faith's visions?'

'I believe her. Goodness, if I didn't believe her now, I'd be an idiot, wouldn't I?' She smiles. 'Or worse—I'd be *dead*.'

'Thank you, Mrs Epstein. Mr Metz, do you have any more questions?' The attorney shakes his head. 'Well,' Rothbottam says. 'I think *I* need a recess.'

Mariah watches her daughter leave the courtroom with Kenzie. She's still not allowed to go near Faith, and to her surprise it's harder to keep her distance now, knowing that Faith is no longer ill. She cranes her neck, watching Faith disappear into the hallway.

She hopes Kenzie is taking care of her.

From the corner of her eye she sees Ian. Immediately she turns away.

'Mariah.' Joan draws her attention. 'You're on after Dr Fitzgerald.'

'That soon?'

'Yeah. Are you going to be all right?'

She presses a fist to her stomach. 'I don't know. It's not you I'm worried about; it's Metz.'

'Listen to me,' Joan answers. 'When you're up there, no matter what he says to you, you look right here.' She points behind her, to the row where Faith has been sitting. 'She's going to get you through this.'

Dr Alvin Fitzgerald has no sooner taken the stand than Metz stands up. 'Approach!' The attorneys walk up to the bench. 'I want to know if this guy interviewed Faith.'

Joan barely spares him a glance. 'No, because I knew you'd complain if he did. If there needs to be an interview at a later date, both of our experts can have a chance. However, I can show what I need to show without Dr Fitzgerald interviewing Faith.'

At this, some of the wind goes out of Metz's sails. 'All right,' he says tightly.

'Dr Fitzgerald,' Joan begins, 'can you state your credentials for the record?'

'I graduated from the University of Chicago's medical school, did a residency and fellowship in child psychology at UCSF, and I was the principal investigator on a large grant studying CFS and somatoform disorders.'

'We've heard an awful lot about Munchausen Syndrome by Proxy. Can you tell us if this particular case fits the criteria for that disorder?'

The psychiatrist shrugs. 'Well, there's a lot that matches the basic DSM-Four criteria.'

Joan watches Metz's mouth drop open in surprise as the psychiatrist repeats the highlights of Dr Birch's testimony. Then she asks, 'Are there elements in this case that *don't* seem to fit MSP?'

'Yes. For one, Faith's symptoms are real, and bizarre. It's a lot easier to fake nausea than to fake stigmata. As for the hallucinations, I disagree with Dr Birch. Just because Mariah White was at an institution with psychotics doesn't mean she could make Faith convincingly fake a hallucination—that's like saying that riding on the Bulls' team bus will make you play like Michael Jordan.' He grins. 'Another discrepancy is that Munchausen by Proxy is chronic. These parents go from emergency room to emergency room so that doctors don't pick up on what they're doing. Yet Mrs White has taken Faith to the same health-care provider, Dr Blumberg, repeatedly. She's gone so far as to request him to examine Faith numerous times.'

'Is that all, Doctor?'

'Oh, I'm just getting warmed up. The perpetrators of Munchausen by Proxy traditionally have an emotionally distant childhood, which Mariah White did not have. But the biggest problem I have with a diagnosis of MSP is simply that there are alternative diagnoses that explain this case equally as well.'

Joan acts surprised. 'Really? Like what?'

'Somatoform disorder, for one. Basically, it's when a patient experiences emotional distress in a physical way. Imagine a child who develops severe stomach cramps every time she has to take a test, because she's so anxious about school. She's truly hurting, but she can't articulate why. Remember Freud's hysterical patients? They were the great-grandmas of today's somatoform-disorder patients.'

He holds up his hands, demonstrating a sort of scale. 'It's helpful to consider these disorders by imagining a range,' the psychiatrist says. 'On one end is malingering, which we've all done: You pretend you have the flu to get out of jury duty, for example—symptoms are intentionally faked to achieve an intended goal. On the other end is somatoform disorder, where a patient unintentionally produces a symptom that looks and feels like the real thing—and doesn't know that she's doing it, much less why. Somewhere in between these is Munchausen Syndrome by Proxy, where symptoms can be intentionally feigned . . . but for unintentional reasons.'

'So the difference, Doctor, is in the intent.'

'Exactly. Otherwise, these two disorders look similar. Just as in Munchausen by Proxy, a doctor will examine a child with somatoform disorder and not be able to find any organic etiology for the symptom. She may undergo CT scans and MRIs and dozens of tests, to no avail, because the presenting problem doesn't fit with the physiology. However, in a somatoform disorder, the symptom is set off by stress. In MSP, the symptom is set off by Mom. In somatoform disorders, the symptom is real. In MSP, it's faked. Often deciding which is which comes down to a judgment call requiring the knowledge of the context of the illness, the players involved, and what gains have been made by them.'

'Then part of the diagnosis involves who's trying to get attention—the mother or the child.'

'Exactly.'

'How do Faith's symptoms fit a somatoform disorder, Doctor?'

'First, the presenting problem isn't organic. She's bleeding from her hands, but there's no tissue mutilation inside—kind of hard to fake a wound like that. She may be hallucinating, but she's not psychotic. And there's an argument to be made that the illness was brought on by stress, that she unconsciously believes that by being sick, the stressor will go away.'

'Would a divorce qualify as a stressor?'

Fitzgerald grins. 'You catch on fast, Ms Standish. In a child's mind is the unconscious thought, "If I get sick, my parents will stay together to take care of me." Without even knowing she's doing it, the child makes herself ill and draws attention to herself. Not having actually met Faith, of course, I can only hypothesize that her mind is making her body sick, in the hopes that her family will remain intact. And look—it's working. Her parents are both here today, aren't they?'

'If that were true, would Mrs White be in any way involved in her daughter's illnesses?'

'Oh, no. It's all being done psychogenically, by Faith's mind.'

Joan pauses. 'How would you go about determining whether Faith's illnesses were caused by her mother's hand or by her own mind?'

'By default. I'd remove Mrs White from her child to see if the symptoms abated.'

'What if I told you that a comatose child whose bodily systems were in acute distress was restored in a period of an hour to perfectly normal levels of functioning once she was reunited with her mother after an extended separation?'

'Well,' Dr Fitzgerald says, 'it would certainly rule out Munchausen by Proxy.'

'You're not a hundred-percent sure, are you?' asks Metz. 'That it's somatoform disorder plaguing Faith . . . or that it's Munchausen by Proxy plaguing her mother.'

'Well—'

'Do children always develop somatoform disorders after messy divorces?'

'No,' Dr Fitzgerald says. 'A variety of maladaptive behaviors might occur.'

'Can you list them for us, Doctor?'

'Sometimes kids act out behaviorally, or sexually. Grades drop in school. Appetites rise or wane. There's a whole range, Mr Metz.'

'I see. Are only a small percentage of Munchausen by Proxy cases reported?'

'Yes.'

'So, although it is a rare disorder, it may be more prevalent than one might think?'

'That's right.'

'Is it true that most patients diagnosed with MSP are female, with a median age of thirty-three?'

'Yes.'

'How old is Mariah White, and what sex is she?'

'She's a thirty-three-year-old female.'

'Is it true that the perpetrators of MSP are usually mothers?'

'Yes.'

'Is Mariah White Faith White's mother?'

'Yes.'

'Have most people who suffer from MSP undergone a significantly stressful life event, such as a divorce?'

'Yes.'

'Did Mariah White just go through a divorce?'

'Yes.'

'Most of the perpetrators of MSP have some experience in the health field, as either patients or professionals, correct?'

'Yes.'

'Did Mariah White spend several months in a mental institution?'

'Yes.'

'Is it true that in MSP, the parents seem very interested in the child's treatment?'

'Yes,' Dr Fitzgerald says dryly. 'But most parents with a sick child—whether they have MSP or not—tend to be interested in the child's treatment.'

Metz shrugs off the response. 'Has Mariah White been very interested in her child's treatment?'

'That's what I hear.'

'Is it true that most symptoms presented in cases of MSP do not often respond to conventional medical treatment?'

'Yes.'

'Have Faith White's hand wounds resisted responding to traditional clotting medicines?'

'Yes.'

'Have Faith White's hallucinations persisted in spite of antipsychotic drugs?'

'Yes.'

'Is it true that patients with MSP are unconsciously looking for attention?'

'Yes.'

'Is there an incredible amount of attention focused on the case of Faith White?'

'Yes.' The doctor sighs.

'Is it true that the perpetrators of MSP deny what they're doing, either because they're pathological liars or because they've dissociated from the behavior?'

'Yes.'

'Has Mariah White admitted to harming Faith?'

'Not to my knowledge.'

'Does that fit the MSP profile?'

'Yes, it does.' Fitzgerald raises a brow. 'Of course, it also fits the profile of a mother who *hasn't* hurt her child.'

'All the same, Doctor, you've just given me about ten specific reasons that this case looks like Munchausen by Proxy. If it looks like a skunk and smells like a skunk and acts like a skunk . . . well, you can't say honestly that this is clearly somatoform disorder, can you?'

Dr Fitzgerald's mouth flattens into a line. 'That's completely specious logic.'

Metz shakes his head. 'Yes or no.'

'No.'

'And what does that leave us?'

The psychiatrist meets the attorney's gaze. 'If it's not somatoform disorder,' he says, smiling slowly, 'I guess it could always be a seven-year-old seeing God.'

seventeen

Woman's at best a contradiction still.

—Alexander Pope

December 6, 1999

'THAT,' I SING, 'was incredible!' Inside me, it feels as if small bubbles are rising, which at any moment may burst into laughter. I embrace Joan tightly. 'Where did you find Dr Fitzgerald?'

'On the Internet,' she says, looking at me carefully.

Well, she could have found him under a rock for all I care. Not only has the psychiatrist laid the groundwork for an alternative explanation of Faith's symptoms, he's also stood toe-to-toe with Malcolm Metz and won. 'Thank you. You made such an issue about getting thrown this surprise on Friday—I didn't think you'd be able to pull together such a good defense strategy this quickly.'

'I didn't, so don't thank me.'

I smile hesitantly. 'What do you mean?'

'I don't have the manpower or resources that Metz does, Mariah. Under ordinary circumstances, I couldn't have pulled it off. I would have walked in here this morning and flown by the seat of my pants. But Ian Fletcher spent the entire weekend in my office, finding Dr Fitzgerald and corresponding with him on-line and ruminating over this particular defense.'

'Ian?'

'He did this for you,' Joan answers matter-of-factly. 'He'd do anything for you.'

A witness stand is a tight spot. You are gated in on all sides. You are broadcast by microphone. You sit on a chair that is so uncomfortable you can't help but straighten your spine and look the gallery in the eye. My heart begins to batter in my chest like a lightning bug trapped in a jar, and suddenly I understand why this is called a *trial*.

Joan's heels click on the wooden floor. 'Can you state your name for the record?'

I draw the swan neck of the microphone toward my lips. 'Mariah White.'

'What is your relationship to Faith White?'

'I'm her mother.' The word is a balm; it slides from my lips to my throat to my belly.

'Can you tell us how you're feeling today, Mariah?'

At that, I smile. 'Actually, I feel terrific.'

'How come?'

'My daughter's out of the hospital.'

'I understand she was very ill over the weekend?' Joan asks.

Of course Joan knows that Faith was sick; she saw her several times. This formality, this rigamarole, seems ridiculous. Why wade through the theories and hypotheses when I could just high-step to the gallery, sweep Faith into my arms, and be done with this?

'Yes,' I answer instead. 'She went into cardiac arrest twice, and she was comatose.'

'But she's already out of the hospital?'

'She was discharged on Sunday afternoon, and she's doing very well.' I glance at Faith, and even though it is against the rules, I wink.

'Mr Metz is alleging that you are a perpetrator of Munchausen Syndrome by Proxy. Do you understand what that means?'

I swallow hard. 'That I'm hurting her. Making her sick.'

'Are you aware, Mariah, that two experts now have stated

in this court that the best way to determine Munchausen Syndrome by Proxy is to keep the mother away from the child and look for improvement?'

'Yes.'

'Were you able to see Faith this weekend?'

'No,' I admit. 'I was restrained by court order. I wasn't allowed any contact with her.'

'What happened to Faith between Thursday and Sunday?'

'She got worse and worse. Around midnight on Saturday, the doctors said they didn't know if she was going to live.'

Joan frowns. 'How do you know, if you weren't there?'

'People called me. My mother. And Kenzie van der Hoven. They were both with Faith for long periods of time.'

'So from Thursday night through Sunday morning, Faith's condition declined, to the point where she was comatose and near death. Yet she's healthy and present today. Mariah, where were you from two A.M. Sunday morning to four P.M. that same day?'

I look right at Joan, the way we've practiced. 'I was at the hospital, with Faith.'

'Objection!' Metz stands and points at me. 'She's in contempt of court!'

'Approach.'

I should not be able to hear their conversation, but they are angry enough to be shouting. 'She's in direct violation of a court order!' Metz says. 'I want a hearing on this today!'

'Jesus, Malcolm. Her child was *dying*.' Joan turns to the judge. 'But then Mariah showed up, and she didn't die, did she? Your Honor, this testimony proves my theory.'

The judge looks at me. 'I want to hear where this is going,' he says quietly. 'Ms Standish, you may proceed, and we'll deal with the violation of the court order later.'

Joan addresses me. 'What happened when you got to the hospital?'

I think of the moment I first saw Faith, hooked up to machines and tubes. 'I sat down next to her and I started to talk. The machine that was hooked up to her heart started to beep, and a nurse said she needed to page the doctor. When she left the room, Faith opened her eyes.' I envision the red flush of her cheeks while the tube was being drawn out of her throat, her voice like brittle leaves as she called for me. 'The doctors started to run tests. Everything—her heart, her kidneys, even her hands—were all back to normal. It was . . . well, it was amazing.'

'Was there a clinical explanation for this?'

'Objection,' Metz says. 'When did she get her medical degree?'

'Overruled.'

'The doctors said sometimes the presence of a family member acts as a catalyst for comatose patients,' I answer. 'But they also said they've only seen as dramatic a recovery as this once before.'

'When was that?'

'When my mother came back to life.'

Joan smiles. 'Must run in the family. Did anyone else witness this remarkable recovery?'

'Yes. There were two doctors, six nurses. Also my mother and the guardian ad litem.'

'All of whom are on my witness list, Your Honor, should Mr Metz feel the need to speak with them.' But Joan has explained to me why he won't. It won't do his case any good to have eight people announce that a miracle happened.

'Mariah, there have been some things said about you in this courtroom, some things the judge might want to hear your explanation for as well. Let's start with your hospitalization seven years ago. Can you tell us about that?'

Joan has coached me. We rehearsed these questions until the sun came up. I know what I am supposed to say, what she is trying to get across to the judge. In short, I am prepared for everything that is about to happen—except how I feel, telling my story in front of these people.

'I was very much in love with my husband,' I start, just as we've practiced. 'And I caught him in bed with another woman. It broke my heart, but Colin decided that it was my head that needed fixing.'

I turn in the seat, so that I am looking at him. 'It was clear that Colin didn't want me. I became very depressed, and I believed that I couldn't live without him. That I didn't *want* to.' I draw a deep breath. 'When you're depressed, you don't pay a lot of attention to the world around you. You don't want to see anyone. There are things you want to say—real things, honest things—but they're buried so deep inside it's an effort to drag them to the surface.' My face softens. 'I don't think Colin was a tyrant for having me committed. He was probably terrified. But I just wish he'd talked to me first. Maybe I still wouldn't have been able to tell him what I wanted, but it would have been nice to know he was trying to listen.

'Then all of a sudden I was at Greenhaven, and I was pregnant. I hadn't told Colin yet, and it became my secret.' I look at the judge. 'You probably don't know what it's like to be in a place where you belong to everybody else. People tell you what to eat and drink, when to get up and go to bed, they poke at you with needles and sit you in therapy sessions. They owned my body and my mind—but, for a little while, I owned this baby. Of course, eventually the pregnancy showed up on the blood tests, and the doctors told me that I still had to go on medication. They said a baby wouldn't be much good if I killed myself before giving birth. So I let them pump me full of drugs, until I didn't care about the risk to the baby. Until I didn't care about anything at all.

'After I left Greenhaven, I began to panic about what I'd done to this baby just by trying to save myself. I made this little deal: It was all right if I wasn't a perfect wife, just as long as I became a perfect mother.'

Joan catches my gaze. '*Have* you been a perfect mother?'

I know what I am supposed to say: Yes, the best that I could be. It made us laugh, because it sounded like an old Army slogan, but neither Joan nor I could come up with a better response. However, now that I am here, I find that the words will not come. I reach down, and the only thing that leaps to hand is the truth.

'No,' I whisper.

'*What?*'

I try to look away from Joan's angry expression. 'I said no. After I had Faith, I used to go to playgrounds to watch other mothers. They could juggle the bottles and the stroller and the baby without breaking a sweat. But me, I'd forget her lunch when she went to school. Or I'd throw away a piece of paper with scribbles on it that was supposed to be a Valentine. Things every mother's probably done, but that still made me feel like I'd screwed up.'

Joan interrupts me with a quiet question. 'Why is it so important to you to be perfect?'

They say that there are moments that open up your life like a walnut cracked, that change your point of view so that you never look at things the same way again. As the answer forms in my mouth, I realize that this is something I've always known, but never before understood. 'Because I know what it's like not to be good enough,' I say softly. 'That's why I lost Colin, and I don't ever want to go through it again.' I twist my fingers together in my lap. 'You see, if I'm the very best mother, Faith won't wish she had someone else instead.'

Sensing that this is a place I need to get away from, and fast, Joan throws me a lifeline. 'Can you tell us what happened on the afternoon of August tenth?'

'I was at my mother's home with Faith,' I recite, grateful to be bogged down in the details. 'She was going to ballet practice, but realized she'd forgotten her leotard. So we detoured home and found Colin's car in the driveway. He'd been on a business trip, so we went in to say hello. Faith ran upstairs first, and found Colin in the bedroom, getting ready to take a shower. I came in to tell Faith to get her leotard quickly, and then the bathroom door opened and . . . Jessica stepped out in a towel.'

'What did Colin say?'

'He ran after Faith. Later he told me he'd been seeing Jessica for a few months.'

'Then what happened?'

'He left. I called my mother. I was miserable, I was sinking fast, but this time I wasn't alone. I knew she'd take care of Faith for me, while I tried to get sorted out.'

'So although you were upset, you were functioning well enough to provide for Faith?'

'Yes.' I smile fleetingly.

'What else did you do after Colin left?'

'Well, I talked to Dr Johansen. About getting a refill of Prozac.'

'I see,' Joan says. 'Has your medication continued to keep you in control of your emotions?'

'Yes, absolutely. It certainly helped me cope.'

'How did Faith cope with this whole upheaval?

'She was very distant. She wouldn't talk. And then all of a sudden she developed an imaginary friend. I started to take her to Dr Keller.'

'Did the imaginary friend concern you?'

'Yes. It wasn't just some playmate. Faith was suddenly saying things that made no sense. She was quoting Bible verses. She referred to a secret from my childhood that I've never spoken about. And then—crazy as it sounds—she brought her grandmother back to life.'

At the plaintiff's table, Malcolm Metz coughs.

'And then?'

'A few local newspaper articles appeared,' I say. 'Ian Fletcher showed up, along with a cult, and about ten network-affiliate TV reporters. After Faith healed an AIDS baby, more press arrived, and more people who wanted to touch Faith, or pray with her.'

'How did you feel about this?'

'Awful,' I say immediately. 'Faith's seven. She couldn't go out to play without being harassed. She was being teased at school, so I pulled her out and began doing lessons at home.'

'Mariah, did you in any way encourage Faith to have hallucinations about God?'

'Me? Colin and I were a mixed-faith marriage. I don't even own a Bible. I couldn't have planted this idea in her mind; I don't know half the things she's come out with.'

'Did you ever harm your daughter in a way that would cause her to bleed from her hands and her side?'

'No. I never would.'

'What do you think would happen to Faith if she went to live with Colin?'

'Well,' I say slowly, 'he loves her. He hasn't always had her interests at heart, but he loves her. It isn't Colin I'm worried about . . . it's Faith. She'd have to deal with a new sibling, and a mother that isn't really hers, and right now I don't think it's fair to ask her to change her world again.' Glancing at Colin, I frown. 'Faith's performing miracles. Taking her away from me won't change that. And it won't change the fact that wherever she goes, people are going to follow her, or want a piece of her.'

I can feel my daughter's eyes on me, like the sun that touches the crown of your head when you step outside. 'I can't tell you why Faith's like this,' I say softly. 'But she is. And I can't tell you why I deserve to have her. But I do.'

Metz likes to call it his 'snake in the jungle' approach. With a witness like Mariah White, he has two choices: He can go in there and batter away, preying on her confusion, or he can appear nice and question gently and then, when she least expects it, strike her fatally. The most important thing is to make Mariah doubt herself. By her own admission, it's her Achilles' Heel. 'You must be tired of talking about this depression from seven years ago.'

Mariah gives him a small, polite smile. 'I guess.'

'Was that the first time in your life that you were so ill?'

'Yes.'

His voice is rich with pity. 'You've had recurrent depression many times since then, haven't you?'

'No.'

'But you have been on medication,' Metz chides, as if she's given the wrong answer.

She looks puzzled for a moment, and inside, he smiles. 'Well, yes. But that's what's kept me from getting depressed again.'

'What medication are you on?'

'Prozac.'

'Was that specifically prescribed to alleviate the wild mood swings?'

'I don't have wild mood swings. I suffer from depression.'

'Do you remember the night you tried to kill yourself, Mrs White?'

'Not really. I was told at Greenhaven that I'd probably block it out of my mind.'

'Are you depressed right now?'

'No.'

'If you weren't taking medication, you'd probably be very depressed.'

'I don't know,' Mariah hedges.

'You know, I've read about these cases where people on Prozac have flipped out. Gone crazy, tried to kill themselves. Don't you worry it might happen to you?'

'No,' Mariah says, looking toward Joan a little nervously.

'Do you have any recollection of going crazy while on Prozac?'

'No.'

'How about harming someone while on Prozac?'

'No.'

'How about just having some violent reactions?'

'No.'

Metz raises his brows. 'No? You consider yourself an emotionally stable person, then?'

Mariah nods firmly. 'Yes.'

Metz walks toward the plaintiff's table and picks up a small videocasette. 'I'd like to introduce the following tape into evidence.'

Joan is out of her seat in an instant, approaching the bench. 'You can't let him do this, Your Honor. He's springing this evidence on me. I have a right to discovery.'

'Your Honor,' Metz counters, 'Ms Standish was the one who opened up the line of questioning during her direct examination, with regard to how stable Mrs White is under the influence of Prozac.'

Judge Rothbottam takes the tape from Metz's hand. 'I'll look at it in chambers and make my decision. Let's take a short recess.'

The attorneys head back to their seats. On the witness stand, unsure of what is happening, Mariah remains frozen, until Joan realizes her predicament and quietly approaches to help her step down.

'What's on the tape, Mariah?' Joan asks as soon as we are sitting at the defense table.

'I don't know. Honestly.' Although it is cold in the courtroom by anyone's standards, sweat trickles between my breasts and down my back.

The judge enters from a side door, settles into his chair, and asks me to return to the witness stand. From the corner of my eye I see a bailiff wheeling in a TV/VCR combination. 'Shit,' Joan mutters.

'I'm going to allow the tape to be entered into evidence,' Rothbottam says. Metz goes through the legal process, then says, 'Mrs White, I'm going to play the following tape for you.'

As he hits the play button, I bite my lip. The small screen fills with an image of me lunging toward the camera so that my features spread and blur. I'm shouting so loud that the words don't register, and after a moment my hand comes up, clearly aiming to strike whoever has been filming.

Then the camera swings wildly, panning in an arc of color to touch briefly upon Faith, cowered in a corner; on my mother in a hospital johnny; on Ian and his producer.

The tape from the stress test, the footage Ian said he would not use.

He's lied to me again. I turn toward the gallery, my eyes scanning until I find him—sitting just as still and white-faced as I must be.

The only way this tape could have come into Metz's hands is, somehow, via Ian. And yet to look at him, one would believe that he is as surprised to see it surface in court as I am.

Before I can consider this, Metz begins to speak. 'Mrs White, do you remember this incident?'

'Yes.'

'Can you tell us about the day the video was taken?'

'My mother was having a stress test done after her resuscitation. Mr Fletcher was being allowed to film it.'

'What happened?'

'He promised not to turn the camera on my daughter. When he did turn it on her, I just . . . reacted.'

'You just . . . reacted. Hmm. Is that something you do often?'

'I was trying to protect Faith and—'

'A simple yes or no will do, Mrs White.

'No.' I swallow hard. 'If anything, I usually think things through to death before I act on them.'

Metz crosses the courtroom. 'Would you say this tape shows you being "an emotionally stable person"?'

I hesitate, choosing my words carefully. 'It is not one of my finer moments, Mr Metz. But on the whole I am emotionally stable.'

'On the whole? What about during those other odd incidents of fury? Is that when you physically harm your daughter?'

'I do not harm Faith. I've never harmed Faith.'

'Mrs White, you yourself said you're an emotionally stable woman, and yet this videotape clearly disproves your claim. So you've lied to us under oath, haven't you?'

'No—'

'Come on, now, Mrs White . . .'

'Objection!' Joan calls out.

'Sustained. You've made your point, Counselor.'

Metz smiles at me. 'You say you'd never harm your daughter physically?'

'Absolutely not.'

'You'd never harm her psychologically either, right?'

'Right.'

'And you're an intelligent woman. You've followed the testimony in this courtroom.'

'Yes, I have.'

'So if you had Munchausen Syndrome by Proxy, and I accused you of harming your daughter, what would you probably say?'

I stare at him, bile burning the back of my throat. 'That I didn't do it.'

'And you'd be lying—just like you lied about being emotionally stable. Just like you've lied about protecting Faith.'

'I don't lie, Mr Metz,' I say, fighting for control. 'I don't. And I have protected Faith. That's what you saw me doing on the video—primitively, maybe, but protecting her all the same. It's why I took her out of school when other children began to tease her. It's why I took her away, in secret, before this hearing started.'

'Ah, yes. Going into hiding. Let's talk about that. You disappeared the night after your husband informed you that he'd be filing for a change of custody, correct?'

'Yes, but—'

'Then you had the misfortune of discovering that your great escape wasn't that great, after all. Ian Fletcher had managed to follow you. We've already proven Mr Fletcher to have been less than honest up on the witness stand, and now we've seen evidence of your own falsehoods. Maybe you'd like to tell us—truthfully, for a change—what happened in Kansas City?'

What happened in Kansas City?

This, Ian knows, is the moment that Mariah will be able to exact revenge. First the McManus incident, then the video—regardless of the fact that he personally had nothing to do with the latter, it's not going to soften Mariah's heart toward him just now. Plus, the simplest way for her to regain her credibility is to offer up as proof the evidence that Faith is truly a healer. The evidence that's all tangled up in the story of Ian's own brother.

An eye for an eye. At that, Ian almost laughs. It is downright ironic for him to be brought down by biblical justice. But just as he exploited Mariah's privacy, she now has the opportunity to uncover his own.

Ian braces his hands on the wooden seat and prepares himself for Judgment Day.

What happened in Kansas City?

Malcolm Metz is standing right in front of me. To his right, I know that Joan is desperately trying to catch my attention so I will not say anything stupid. But the only person I can see is Ian, buried in the middle of the courtroom gallery.

I think of Dr Fitzgerald and his testimony. Of Joan walking into her office to find Ian waiting for her, ready to play paralegal. Of the look on Ian's face when Allen McManus walked up to the witness stand, when that horrible videocassette began to play.

He isn't perfect. But then again, neither am I.

I look at Ian, wondering if he can tell what I am thinking. Then I turn to Malcolm Metz. 'Absolutely nothing,' I say.

The bitch is lying. It's written on her face. Metz would bet his life savings that, somehow, Fletcher's arrival in Kansas City led to direct proof that all the mumbo jumbo surrounding Faith is just that, and that, consequently, the miraculous hallucinations and physical trauma are actually being caused by Mariah. Fletcher's been closemouthed because he doesn't want to give away his big story; Mariah's keeping quiet because it only ruins her credibility. But short of accusing her of fabricating testimony again, there's very little he can do.

He takes a moment to compose himself. 'You love your daughter, don't you?'

'Yes.'

'You'd do anything for your daughter?'

'Yes.'

'Would you give up your life for her?'

He can practically see her imagining Faith in that pitiful hospital bed. 'I would.'

'Would you give up custody of her?'

Mariah falters. 'I don't understand.'

'What I mean is this, Mrs White: If it was proven to you by a series of experts that Colin was the better parent for Faith, would you want her to go?'

Mariah frowns, then looks at Colin. After a moment she faces the attorney again. 'Yes.'

'Nothing further.'

Furious, Joan asks to redirect. 'Mariah,' she says, 'first I want to address that clip of videotape. Can you tell us what happened prior to the outburst on that tape?'

'Ian Fletcher had sworn that he wouldn't exploit Faith. It was the only way I agreed to allow him in to film my mother's stress test. When I turned away for a minute, he had his cameraman pan over to Faith, and I jumped between her and the lens.'

'What was going through your mind at that moment?'

'That he not film Faith. The last thing I wanted was more

media interest in her. She's just a little girl; she ought to be allowed to live like one.'

'Do you think that you were emotionally unstable at that moment?'

'No. I was steady as a rock. I was completely focused on keeping Faith safe.'

'Thank you,' Joan says. 'Now I want you to consider Mr Metz's final question. Under this scenario of his, Faith would be moved to a new environment. She'd be living with the woman she caught in a compromising position with her father. She's got a new sibling coming. She's not in familiar surroundings. Not to mention the fact that her groupies from the front lawn will probably drive across town to take up residence at her new home. Does this sound like an accurate representation?'

'Yes,' Mariah says.

'Good. Now, during this trial, did Colin convince you that he was the better parent for Faith?'

'No,' Mariah answers, confused.

'Did Dr Orlitz, the state-appointed psychiatrist, convince you that Colin was the better parent for Faith?'

'No,' she says, her voice a little stronger.

'Did Dr DeSantis, the private psychiatrist for the plaintiff, convince you that Colin was the better parent for Faith?'

'No.'

'How about Allen McManus?'

'No.'

'Mr Fletcher?'

'No.

'What about Dr Birch? Did he convince you that Colin is the better parent for Faith?'

Mariah smiles at Joan and pulls the microphone a little closer. Her voice is strong and steady. 'No. He did not.'

After the defense rests, the judge calls a recess. I go to wait in the tiny conference room Joan and I have been using, and after a few minutes the door opens and Ian enters. 'Joan told me I'd find you here,' he says quietly.

'I asked her to.'

He doesn't seem to know how to respond.

'Thank you for finding Dr Fitzgerald.'

Ian shrugs. 'I sort of owed it to you.'

'You didn't owe me anything.'

Pushing away from the table, I stand and walk toward him. His hands are deeply set in his pockets, as if he is afraid to touch me. 'Maybe I should thank you, too,' he murmurs. 'For what you didn't say.'

I shake my head. Sometimes there aren't words. The silence between us is flung wide as an ocean, but I manage to reach across it, to wrap my arms around him.

His hands close over my back; his breath stirs the hair at the nape of my neck. He will be with me. Right now, that's enough. 'Mariah,' he whispers, 'you may be my religion.'

The judge calls the guardian ad litem to the stand. 'The attorneys and I have all read your report. Do you have anything you'd like to add at this point?'

Kenzie nods briskly. 'I do. I think the court needs to know that I am the one who let Mariah White into the Medical Center at two A.M. on Sunday.'

At the plaintiff's table, Metz's jaw drops. Joan looks into her lap. The judge asks Kenzie to explain herself.

'Your Honor, I know that you can hold me in contempt of court and send me to jail. But before you do, I'd like you to hear me out, because I've become very attached to the child in this particular case, and I don't want a mistake to be made.'

The judge eyes her warily. 'Continue.'

'As you know, I've filed a report. I met with many people, and I originally concluded that if the child's life was at all endangered, moving her out of that situation would be best. So in the paper you're holding in your hand, I recommend that custody be granted to the father.'

Metz claps his client on the shoulder and grins.

'However,' Kenzie says, 'I made a decision late Saturday night, after a doctor told Mrs Epstein that Faith might be dying. I didn't think that the U.S. justice system had the right to keep a mother from saying good-bye. So I called Mrs White and told her to come to the hospital. I thought, Your Honor, that I was simply being kind . . . and I would have expected my report to stand on its own.

'But then something happened.' Kenzie shakes her head. 'I wish I could explain it, really. All I know is that I saw, with my own eyes, a child who was comatose and failing come back from the edge once her mother was at her side.' She hesitates. 'The courtroom is no place for personal observation, Your Honor, but I want to share a story with you because it has relevance to my decision. My great-grandmother and great-grandfather were married for sixty-two years. When my great-grandfather died of a stroke, my great-grandma—who was in perfect health—passed away two days later. In my family we've always said that Nana died of a broken heart. It may not be medically accurate . . . but then again, doctors concentrate on people's bodies, not their emotions. And if it *is* possible to die of grief, Judge Rothbottam, then why on earth can't someone be healed by happiness?'

Kenzie leans forward. 'Your Honor, I switched from being a lawyer to being a guardian ad litem ten years ago, and I have a fairly legal mind. I've tried to come at this from a rational viewpoint, and it just doesn't work. I had people telling me about visions and crying statues and the passion agony of Christ. I had other people telling me about religious hoaxes. I heard about people who were very sick, then completely healthy after brushing Faith in the hospital elevator.

'I've witnessed a lot of inexplicable things lately, but none of them point to the fact that Mariah White is hurting Faith. In fact, I think she saved her life. And it's not going to help this little girl one whit to be moved away from her mother's influence.' She clears her throat. 'So I'm sorry, Judge. But I'd like you to completely disregard my report.'

The courtroom erupts in confusion. Malcolm Metz furiously whispers to Colin. The judge rubs his hand over his face.

'Your Honor,' Metz says, getting to his feet, 'I'd like to give a closing argument.'

'You know, Mr Metz, I bet you would.' Rothbottam sighs. 'But you're not the one I want to hear from. I've listened to you and Ms Standish, and to Ms van der Hoven, and I don't know what the heck to believe. I need a little lunch break—and I'd like to spend it with Faith.'

Mariah turns toward her daughter. Faith's eyes are wide, confused.

'What do you say?' Judge Rothbottam asks. He comes out from behind the bench and walks toward the gallery. 'Would you like to have lunch with me, Faith?'

Faith glances at her mother, who nods imperceptibly. The judge holds out his hand. Faith slides hers into it, and walks out of the courtroom beside him.

She likes his chair. It goes around and around, faster than the one at her father's office. And she likes the music he plays. Faith glances at the collection of compact discs on one shelf. 'Do you have Disney stuff?'

Judge Rothbottam plucks out a CD, slides it into the player, and the strains of the Broadway-cast recording of *The Lion King* fill the room. As he shrugs out of his robes, Faith gasps.

'What is it?' he asks.

She looks down, feeling her cheeks heat the way they do when she's caught stealing a brownie before dinner. 'I didn't know you had clothes on under there.'

At that, the judge laughs. 'Last time I checked.' He sits down across from her. 'I'm glad you're feeling better.'

She nods over the turkey sandwich he's placed on the massive desk for her. 'Me, too.'

He draws a chair closer. 'Faith, who do you want to live with?'

'I want them together,' she says. 'But I can't have that, right?'

'No.' Judge Rothbottam looks at her. 'Does God talk to you, Faith?'

'Uh-huh.'

'Do you know that a lot of people are interested in you because of that?'

'Yes.'

The judge hesitates. 'How do I know if you're telling the truth?'

Faith lifts her face to his. 'When you're in court, how do you tell?'

'Well, people swear it. On a Bible.'

'If I'm *not* telling the truth . . . then wouldn't they just be saying words over some book?'

He grins. So much for God not belonging in a courtroom; He's already there.

But Faith's God, according to the media, is a She. 'People have pictured God as a man for many years,' he points out.

'My teacher in first grade said that long ago people used to believe all kinds of things, because they didn't know any better. Like you shouldn't take a bath, because it could make you sick. And then someone saw germs under a microscope and started to think different. You can believe something really hard,' Faith says, 'and still be wrong.'

Rothbottam stares at Faith, and wonders if maybe this girl isn't a prophet after all.

Judge Rothbottam slides his half-glasses down his nose and glances out at the plaintiff, the defendant, and the tightly packed gallery of reporters. 'I stood up several days ago and told you that in a trial, there's only one God, and that's the judge. A very wise young woman reminded me that's not necessarily the case.' He holds up the Bible. 'As Mr Fletcher pointed out so eloquently during his swearing-in, we do still rely on convention in a court, regardless of one's religious tendencies.

'Now, I'm not here to talk about religious tendencies. I'm here to talk about Faith White. The two subjects are related, but not mutually exclusive. As I see it, we've raised two questions here: Is God talking to Faith White? And is Mariah White harming her child?'

He leans back in his chair, folds his hands over his stomach. 'I'm going to start with the second question first. I can see why Faith's father is concerned. I would be, too. I've heard astounding things from Mr Metz and his succession of experts, and from Ms Standish and her experts, and even from the guardian ad litem assigned to this case. But I don't believe that Mariah White is capable of intentionally or unintentionally harming her daughter.'

There is a gasp to the right of the gallery, and the judge clears his throat. 'Now . . . for that first question. Everyone came into this courtroom—myself included—wondering if this kid was really some kind of miracle worker. But the job of this court isn't to ask whether Faith's visions and hand wounds are of divine origin. We shouldn't ask if she's Jewish or Christian or Muslim, if she's the Messiah or the Antichrist. We shouldn't ask whether God's got something important to say to a seven-year-old girl. What this court must ask, and answer, is this: Who listened, when *this particular* seven-year-old girl had something important to say?'

Judge Rothbottam closes the legal file spread out in front of him. 'Based on all the testimony I've heard, I think Mariah White's ears are wide open.'

eighteen

For where your treasure is,
There will your heart be also.

—Matthew 6:21

December 6, 1999, Early Evening

'WHO THE HELL am *I*,' says Ian, 'to tell you all what you should and should not think?'

His voice rings as high as the rafters in the Town Hall, unsettling the old bird's nest that's been there for as long as anyone can remember. In front of the makeshift podium, two cameramen weave back and forth. A confection of spotlights and reflectors decorates the sides of the stage where the voting booths are usually set up in November. And in a shoving, jostling knot are the representatives of over two hundred networks and newspapers.

The Town Hall's auditorium is the only place large enough in New Canaan to accommodate Ian's no-holds-barred press conference. Announced with two hours' lead time in the lobby of the courthouse, it is packed. The media want to hear what Ian Fletcher will have to say, now that custody has officially been retained by Mariah.

Ian smiles. 'Why are you guys even here? Why does it matter what I have to say?'

A reporter in the rear yells out, 'Because of the free coffee?'

Laughter ripples through the press, as well as Ian. 'Maybe.' He sweeps the crowd with his gaze. 'For years I've made a name for myself condemning God, and the people who believe in God. Trying to win people over to my side. I know y'all are waiting to hear what I have to say about Faith White, and you're going to be disappointed. I told the truth to Mr Metz on the witness stand—nothing happened in Kansas City. I'm not going to say whether that girl's got God in her back pocket. I'm going to say that it isn't my business, and it isn't your business.'

He rocks back on his heels. 'Quite a kick, isn't it? That after building a whole bankable empire on atheism, I'd tell you religious beliefs are a private affair? And I can see it right now, you shakin' your heads, saying that reporters can damn well make anything their business—but it's not so. There's a difference between a fact and an opinion; any newsman knows that. And religion, for all that it's provocative, isn't about only *what* people believe in—it's also about the simple act of believing. Just like I have a right to walk out here and say that God is a farce, Faith White has a right to shout out her bedroom window that God's alive and well. My opinion, versus her opinion. But nowhere in that tangle is there a pure, hard fact.

'So who's right? The answer is . . . I don't know. And I shouldn't care. My mama used to tell me you can't change the way someone thinks about God or their politics, although I've certainly given both a run for my money. But, you know, I might wind up living next door to the pope one day. Or down the road from Faith. Or in the hotel room beside the Dalai Lama's. And going from door to door trying to convince them I'm the one who's right is going to be a waste of time. No, correction: It *has* been a waste of time. We don't have to accept each other's beliefs . . . but we do have to accept each other's right to believe them.'

He nods toward the rear of the auditorium. 'Now, I said this was open season on me, and I don't go back on my promises. Anyone got a question?'

'Yeah, Ian,' calls a reporter from *Time*. 'That's a nice,

politically correct speech, but what kind of proof did you get on the kid's miracles?'

Ian crosses his arms. 'My guess is, Stuart, that you really want to ask me if Faith's a healer.' The reporter nods. 'Well, I saw things I've never seen before, and that I doubt I'll see again. But you might say the same thing about surviving a world war, or watching the northern lights, or assisting at the birth of Siamese twins. None of which are, by definition, miraculous.'

'So is she seeing God?'

Ian shakes his head. 'I think you're all going to have to decide that for yourself. For some people, Faith's the genuine article. For others, she doesn't come close.' He shrugs, effectively ending his comment.

'Sounds like a cop-out to me,' says a reporter in the front row.

Ian glances down at her. 'Too damn bad. I'm up here speaking my mind. Maybe you just don't want to hear what's on it.'

'Will Pagan Productions be dissolved?' calls out a voice.

'I certainly hope not,' Ian says. 'Though we may have to rewrite our corporate goals.'

'Are you involved with Mariah White?'

'Now, Ellen,' Ian chides the *Washington Post* reporter, 'if I'm up here going out on a limb to tell you God is nobody's business but your own, what do you think I'm going to say about a personal relationship?' He glances back over the crowd, finally pointing to a young man wearing a CBS News baseball cap. 'Yes?'

'Mr Fletcher, if you're not going to tell people God's a crock, what *will* you do?'

He grins. 'I don't really know. Are y'all hiring?'

'Let me take you out to dinner,' I say impulsively, but Joan shakes her head.

'I think you've got your own party to attend.'

By unspoken agreement, she lets me walk her to her car while my mother takes Faith to the bathroom. 'You deserve to be there, too.'

Joan smiles. 'My idea of a victory dance is a lot of bubbles in a tub and a very large glass of wine.'

'I'll send over some Calgon, then.'

She laughs. 'You do that.'

We have reached her car. Joan sticks her briefcase in the back and then turns, arms crossed. 'You know, it's not over. Not by a long shot.'

'You think Colin will appeal?'

She shakes her head, thinking of the thousands of people who have heard about Faith, who will still want a piece of her. 'I'm not talking about Colin,' she says.

In Vatican City, Cardinal Sciorro has spent the morning organizing his desk at the Sacred Congregation for the Preservation of the Faith. He sets decrees in formal files, he passes along deposition information, he stacks and he sorts. Several cases, he tosses into the trash can.

Faith White's he sets in an 'active' pile, under a large stack of other issues the office is considering, and has been for years.

I have just entered the courthouse to find Faith and my mother when I am waylaid by Colin. 'Rye!' He catches me by the shoulders before I plow into him in my haste. 'Hey.'

Immediately, I feel a rush of triumph, and on its heels, guilt. 'Colin,' I say evenly.

'I, uh, wanted to say good-bye to Faith. If that's all right with you.'

He is staring at his shoes, and I can only imagine how difficult this must be for him. I wonder where Jessica is. I wonder, uncharitably, if he'll go home and stroke his new wife's belly and think about replacing Faith. 'It's fine. I just have to find her.'

But before I have a chance, she tears around the corner, her dress hiked up on her bottom. I tug it down and smile, tuck her hair behind her ear. 'Daddy wants to say good-bye.'

Her face crumples. 'Forever?'

'No,' Colin says, kneeling down. 'You heard the judge. I get to see you on weekends. Every other one.'

'So, like, not this one but maybe the one after that.'

He tips his forehead against hers. 'Exactly.'

This could have been me. Colin could be taking Faith home and I could be the one begging for a minute of her attention. I could be bent on one knee, trying hard not to cry.

I have never understood how children know you better than you know yourself, how they can touch you when you need it most or offer a distraction when the last thing you want is to focus on your problems. Faith strokes her father's cheek. 'I'll still be with you,' she says, and she slides her hand into his shirt pocket. 'Right here.'

She leans forward, flutters her eyes closed, and kisses a promise onto his lips.

Malcolm Metz sits in the parking lot of his law office in Manchester and considers if he should just go home for the day. He knows that by now people will have heard. By now he might even have been subtly demoted, doomed to negotiating real-estate transactions or probate controversies. 'Well, shit,' he says to his reflection in the rearview mirror. 'Gotta go back inside sooner or later.'

He walks up the curiously quiet steps into the curiously quiet lobby. Usually when he returns—hell, *every* time—there's a throng of reporters waiting for him to throw off a witty comment about how easy it was to win. He doesn't even get a grunt from the security guard standing beside the elevator, and he takes this as a harbinger of what is yet to come.

'Mr Metz,' the receptionist says as he comes through the double glass doors. 'You've had messages from *Newsweek*, *The New York Times*, and Barbara Walters.' At this, he almost stops. Do they always talk to the losers, too?

'Thanks.' He nods at the associates he passes, trying to cultivate an aura of absorption. He completely ignores his own secretary and goes into his corner office like a wounded lion seeking refuge in his den. He locks his door, something he never does. Then he closes his eyes and lays his head on his desk.

Ma nish-tah-naw ha-lie-law ha-zeh me-call ha-lay-los.

Why is this night different from all other nights of the year?

Metz blinks. They are words from the Passover Seder. Words he spoke when he was Faith White's age, the youngest Jewish boy in his family. Words that, until now, he did not remember.

With slow, shaky movements, he rises, unlocks the office door, and props it open.

My mother is the one who notices first. 'Why did I think they'd all have disappeared?'

I stop the car just in front of the driveway. Faith is back, she is healthy, it is a new start. But the groupies and the press and the cult members remain, thicker than ever. The police are absent; there's no one to help to clear a path so that we can enter safely. As I inch down the gravel, people reach for the car, smoothing palms over Faith's window with light, tapping noises.

'Stop,' Faith says quietly from the backseat.

'What? Are you hurt?'

As the car comes to a standstill, people jump on the hood. They pound on the windshield. They scrape at the paint, trying to get inside. Faith says, 'I'll walk.'

At that, my mother puts her foot down. 'I don't think so, young lady. Those *meshuggenahs* will probably trample you before they know what they're doing.' But before my mother and I can stop her, Faith pulls open the back door and vanishes into the swarm of the crowd.

Immediately, I panic. I rip off my seat belt and get out of the car, pushing aside people in an effort to save Faith. I'm more worried for her now than when she was hospitalized, because these people do not want to make her better. They only want to make her theirs.

'Faith!' I yell, my voice lost in the roar. 'Faith!'

Then the crowd falls back on either side, cleaved in two to form a narrow lane that leads to our front door. Faith stands halfway down it. 'You see?' she says, waving.

• • •

His body is lined with the light of the moon, and the stars fall into place around him. 'Wow,' I say, as Ian steps into the house. 'You actually used the front door.'

'I actually walked up the front steps. And actually shoved about ten people out of my way.' Coming into the parlor, he locks his arms around my waist so that our legs and foreheads are pressed together. 'You must be happy.'

'Very.'

'Is she asleep?'

'Yes.'

I slide my hand down his arm and pull him to the stairs. 'I saw your press conference on the news. You *are* being evasive.'

Ian laughs. 'God. You just can't win with some people.'

I lace my fingers with his. 'You . . . hinted that we had something going on.'

'We clearly must. After all, you *did* let me in that front door.'

'Really, Ian,' I say softly. 'What are you going to do?'

He leans over, and I smell the night, still on his skin. He kisses my cheek. 'Be with you.'

I can feel myself blushing. 'That wasn't what I meant.'

Ian's mouth traces the line of my neck, the edge of my ear. Then he pulls away, and stares at me until we are both perfectly still. 'Why wasn't it?' he says, and smiles.

Her mother thinks she is asleep. She knows because she can hear the house settling like a fat lady arranging her skirts, twitching and creaking and sighing all around her. Faith sits up in bed and turns on the tiny lamp on the nightstand. She pulls up her pajama top, examining critically the thin ladder of her ribs, the rainbow bruises on her skin where tubes and needles were connected. Then she holds one palm beneath the lamp and feels for the small flap of skin where the hole was. It's gone now, nothing but the smooth pink bowl of her hand.

'God,' she whispers aloud.

Nothing.

She glances from the windowsill to the nightlight to the dresser. 'God?'

Faith tosses back the covers and gets onto her hands and knees. She checks under the bed, and then gathers all her courage and throws open the door of the dark, dark closet. She hears only the rhythm of her own breathing, and the fan from the bathroom down the hall. The round sounds of her mother and Ian, talking downstairs. 'God?' she tries again.

But with the same casual confidence she has that the sun is going to come up in a matter of hours, Faith knows that she is alone inside these white walls.

Suddenly she is very cold, and a little scared. She dives beneath the covers, thudding hard enough as she sprints across the floor for her mother to come investigate. She hears her footsteps on the stairs, the creaky one at the count of seven, the muffle of her shoes once she hits carpet. She guesses how long it is before her mother is within spitting distance of the bedroom.

'They asked a lot of questions,' Faith says just loud enough for her words to carry, her eyes on the slice of light from the nearly closed door. 'But then again, they've never seen You.' She holds her breath. From the corner of her eye she sees the knife edge of her mother's tired smile.

With her heart pounding and her fists clutching the comforter, Faith continues to talk to no one at all, until she hears her mother's voice again downstairs, until she is certain that nobody is listening.